King Arthur Stories

KING ARTHUR STORIES

Three Books in One
by
Rosemary Sutcliff

RED FOX

A Red Fox Book

Published by Random House Children's Books
61-63 Uxbridge Road, London, W5 5SA

A division of The Random House Group Ltd
London Melbourne Sydney Auckland
Johannesburg and agencies throughout the world

5 7 9 10 8 6

The Light Beyond the Forest, The Sword and the Circle and
The Road to Camlann
first published in Great Britain by
The Bodley Head Children's Books 1979, 1981 and 1981

This Red Fox edition 1999

Phototypeset by Intype London Ltd
Printed and bound in Great Britain by
Bookmarque Ltd, Croydon, Surrey

Papers used by Random House Group Ltd are natural,
recyclable products made from wood grown in sustainable forests.
The manufacturing processes conform to the
environmental regulations of the country of origin.

The RANDOM HOUSE Group Limited Reg. No. 954009

www.kidsatrandomhouse.co.uk

ISBN 0 09 940164 9

CONTENTS

AUTHOR'S NOTE

Some time early in the fifth century AD – history books used to say AD 410, but now the experts think that probably there were a few auxiliary troops left in Britain a good deal later than that – the last Roman legions were withdrawn from Britain to defend Rome itself, and the British were left to hold off the invading Saxons as best they could. In the end they failed, but they put up such a fight that it took the Saxons around two hundred and fifty years to complete their occupation; and they never did take over all of the Western country. But none the less, the withdrawal of Rome was the beginning of what we call 'the Dark Ages' chiefly because so little record of them has survived.

It is to some time early in these Dark Ages that King Arthur belongs.

Many people believe, as I do, that behind the legends of King Arthur as we know them today, there stands a real man. No king in shining armour, no Round Table, no fairy-tale palace at Camelot, but a Roman-British war leader, who when the dark tide of the barbarians came flooding in, did all that a great leader could do to hold them back and save something of civilisation.

But if the hero-tale had never grown up, and gathered to itself the mass of Celtic myth and folklore and the medieval splendours that we know now as the legends of King Arthur, we should have lost something beautiful and mysterious and magical out of our heritage. All down the ages, the stories have been told and told again, most splendidly of all by Sir Thomas Malory in *Morte d'Arthur*.

In *The Sword and the Circle* I have followed Malory in the main, but I have not followed him slavishly – no minstrel ever follows exactly the songs that have come down to him from the time before. Always he adds and leaves out and embroiders and puts something of himself into each retelling. And some of the stories in this retelling of mine are not to be found in Malory at all.

So – I have based the first story, of Vortigern and Merlin, Utha and Igraine and the dragon-light in the sky, upon Geoffrey of Monmouth's *British History*.

Sir Gawain and the Green Knight comes from a Middle English poem.

For *Tristan and Iseult* I have turned back to a much earlier version, which Malory doesn't seem to have known, by Godfrey of Strasburg. But this story is in outline the same as the still older Irish tragedies of *Deirdre and the Sons of Usna* and *Diarmid and Grania*.

Geraint and Enid is from the ancient Welsh book, *The Mabinogion*.

Sir Gawain and the Loathely Lady is based on a Middle English ballad.

The early part of Sir Percival's adventures are loosely based on another Early English poem with a few incidents from the *Conte de Graal*, but the end is largely my own invention — and why not, when the story of *Beaumains, the Kitchen Knight* seems to have come entirely out of Malory's own head?

The story of how the Knights of the Round Table went questing for the Holy Grail, as we have known it for the past eight hundred years or so, stands out on its own from among all the rest of the Arthurian legends, because above them all, it is a Christian story and carries within it the things of the Spirit that seemed especially important to the people of the Middle Ages. At one level it is the story of King Arthur's knights searching for the cup of the Last Supper; on a deeper level, like *The Pilgrim's Progress*, it is an account of Man's search for God. But the medieval Christian story is shot through with shadows and half-light and haunting echoes of much older things; scraps of the mystery religions which the legions carried from end to end of the Roman Empire; above all, a mass of Celtic myth and folklore. For, despite its medieval French and German and English tellings and re-tellings, the Grail Quest, like all the other Arthurian legends, is Celtic in its beginnings. The Celts also had their quest stories, their unexplained happenings and shifting forests and beckoning lights. They had their cup (only for them it was a cauldron) and spear and sword and stone, which were the four treasures of Anwn, that strange realm which was both the World of the Dead and the World of Faery.

In reading *The Light Beyond the Forest* try to remember, as I have done all the time I was writing it, the shadows and the half-lights and the echoes behind.

Two things I think I should explain. One is that in medieval times dinner was at about ten o'clock in the morning and supper at about six in the evening. The other is that a tilt or joust was a trial of strength and skill between two knights at a time; a form of sport, though a dangerous one; but a tournament was a kind of sham battle between any number, which frequently got out of hand and ended in a lot of people being killed.

THE SWORD AND THE CIRCLE

King Arthur and the Knights of the Round Table

1

THE COMING OF ARTHUR

In the dark years after Rome was gone from Britain, Vortigern of the narrow eyes and the thin red beard came down from the mountains of Wales, and by treachery slew Constantine of the old royal house and seized the High Kingship of Britain in his place.

But his blood-smirched kingship was little joy to him, for his realm was beset by the wild hordes of Picts and Scots pouring down from the North, and the Saxons, the Sea Wolves, harrying the eastern and southern shores. And he was not a strong man, as Constantine had been, to hold them back.

At last, not knowing what else to do, he sent for two Saxon warchiefs, Hengest and Horsa, and gave them land and gold to bring over their fighting men and drive back the Picts and the Scots and their own sea-raiding brothers. And that was the worst of all things in the world that he could have done. For Hengest and Horsa saw that the land was rich; and at home in Denmark and Germany there were many younger sons, and not enough land nor rich enough harvests to feed them all; and after that Britain was never free of the Saxon-kind again.

They pushed further and further in from the

coasts, sacking the towns and laying waste the country through which they passed, harrying the people as wolves harry the sheep in a famine winter; and many a farmer died on his own threshold and many a priest before his altar, and ever the wind carried the smell of burning where the Saxons went by.

Then, seeing what he had done, Vortigern drew back into the dark fastnesses of Wales and summoned his wise men, his seers and wonder-workers and begged them tell him what he should do.

'Build yourself a mighty tower and lie close in it. There is nothing else left to you,' said the foremost of the seers.

So Vortigern sent out men skilled in such matters to find the best place for building such a stronghold, and when he had listened to their reports, his choice fell upon Eriri, the Place of the Eagles, high in the mountains of Gwynedd. And there he gathered together workmen from the North and the South and the East and the West, and bade them build him a tower stronger than any tower that ever had stood in Britain before then. The men set to work, cutting great blocks of stone from quarries in the hillsides; and the straining teams of men and horses dragged them up to the chosen place. And there, on the cloudy crest of Eriri, they began to set the mighty foundations that should carry such a stronghold as had never been seen in Britain until that time.

But then came a strange thing. Every morning when they went to start work, they found the stones that they had raised and set in place the day before cast down and scattered all abroad. And day by day it was the same, so that the stronghold on the Place of the Eagles never grew beyond its first day's building.

Then Vortigern sent again for his seers and magicians and demanded to know the cause of the thing, and what they should do about it.

And the seers and magicians looked into the stars by night and the Seeing-Bowl of black oak-water by day, and said, 'Lord King, there is need of a sacrifice.'

'Then bring a black goat,' said Vortigern.

'A black goat will not serve.'

'A white stallion, then.'

'Nor a white stallion.'

'A man?'

'Not even a man who is as other men.'

'What, then, in the Devil's name?' shouted the High King, and flung down the wine-cup that was in his hand, so that the wine spattered like blood into the moorland heather.

And the chief of the wise men looked at the stain of it, and smiled. 'Let you seek out a youth who never had a mortal father, and cause him to be slain in the old way, the sacred way, and his blood sprinkled upon the stones, and so you shall have a sure foundation for your stronghold.'

So Vortigern sent out his messengers to seek for such a youth. And after long searching they came to the city of Caermerddyn; and in that city they found a youth whose mother was a princess of Demetia, but whose father no man knew. The princess had long since entered a nunnery, but before that, when she was young, she had been visited, as though in a dream, by one of those who the Christian folk call fallen angels, fair and fiery, and lost between Heaven and Earth. And of his coming to her, she had borne a son and called him Merlin.

All this she told freely to the High King's messengers when they asked her, thinking no harm. But when they had heard all that she told, they seized the boy Merlin and brought him to Vortigern in the fine timber hall that he had caused to be set up in the safety of the mountains hard by Eriri. And Vortigern sat in his great seat spread with finely dressed wolf-skins and cloth of crimson and purple, and pulled at his meagre beard and looked at the boy through the smoke tendrils of the hearth fire. And the boy stood before him, lean and whippy as a hazel wand, with dark hair like the ruffled feathers of a hawk, and stared back at him out of eyes that were yellow as a hawk, also, and demanded, as a man demanding of an equal, to know why he had been brought there.

The High King was not used to being spoken to in that tone, and in his surprise he told Merlin what he asked, instead of merely ordering him to be killed at once.

And the boy listened; and when it was told, he said, 'And so my blood is to be shed that your tower may stand. It is a fine story that your magicians have told you, my Lord King, but there is no truth in it.'

'As to that,' said Vortigern, 'the matter is easily put to the proof.'

16

'By scattering my blood upon the stones of your stronghold? Nay now, do you send for your magicians, and bid them stand before me, and easily enough I will prove them liars.'

Vortigern tugged at his beard and his narrow eyes grew narrower yet. But in the end he sent for his wise men, and they came and stood before the boy Merlin.

And Merlin looked them over from one to another, and said, 'The Sight and the Power have grown weak in you and your like in the long years since the passing of the true Druid kind. Therefore, because you are darkened to the truth, you have told the King that my blood shed upon these stones shall make his tower stand. But I tell you that it is not the need for my blood that causes his stones to fall, but some strange happening beneath the ground which every night engulfs the work of the day. Let you tell me then in your wisdom, what thing that is!'

The magicians were silent, for their powers had indeed grown dim.

Then Merlin turned from them to Vortigern. 'My Lord the High King, let your men dig beneath the foundations until they come to the deep pool that they will find there.'

So the King gave his orders and the men set to work, and in a while they broke in through the roof of a vast cave; and all the floor of the cave was one deep, dark pool, from the depth of which slow bubbles rose to the surface as though some great creature lay asleep and breathing deeply far below.

Then Merlin turned to Vortigern who had come from his hall to look on, and to his magicians behind him, and said, 'Tell me, oh workers of wonders and walkers in secret ways, what lies at the bottom of this pool?'

And again they could not answer.

And Merlin said to the King, 'My Lord Vortigern, now let you give orders that this pool be drained, for at the bottom of it you shall find two dragons lying asleep.'

And when the pool was drained, there, far down among the rocks, lay the two dragons, sleeping; and one of them was white as frost and the other was red as fire. And the King and all those who stood about the pool were struck with amazement. But the magicians had slipped away.

'By day,' said the boy Merlin, 'these creatures sleep as you see them now; but every night they wake and fight together, and their battle lasts until the sunrise gives them sleep again; and their battling shakes the mountain crest, and the earth gapes and closes and the waters of the pool are lashed to tempest; and it is so that the tower that you would build above them does not stand.'

Now the end of the day had come, and the dusk was deepening fast, and even as he spoke the sleeping dragons began to rouse. Fire-red and frost-white coils rippled and stirred and the great heads reared up, and the jaws gaped and began to breathe out thin jets of fire that grew and strengthened to rolling clouds of flame; and with a waking roar that made the very ground thrum beneath the watchers' feet, the two monsters sprang together.

. All night long, by the levin-light of their own breath that filled the great chasm and played like summer lightning upon the whipped-up shallows remaining of the pool, the two fought. And first the white dragon had the advantage and drove the red to the far end of the pool; and then the red dragon rallied and turned the fight again; and the water boiled about their lashing coils, and all the crest of the mountain shuddered with the tumult of their battle. And slowly the red dragon drove the white back until he in his turn was at the end of the pool. And then when it seemed that all was over, the white dragon gathered himself and hurled himself yet once more upon the red . . .

But the first light of day was waking in the sky, and the fire of the dragons sank and their movements grew slower, and little by little the great coils relaxed, and they sank to sleep.

Then Vortigern demanded of the boy Merlin the meaning of what he had seen; and Merlin told him that the red dragon was Britain and the white dragon was the Saxon kind, and that every night they fought out the conflict between the two.

'Then surely the red dragon had the victory,' Vortigern said, 'and I and my realm have nothing to fear.'

'But the white dragon was gathering his fighting power again when this new day laid sleep once more upon them both,' said Merlin. And he looked as though into a great distance; but a distance that was within himself. Three strains of power ran deep within Merlin; from his mother who was of the Demetii he had the herb-skills and the ancient half-lost wisdoms of the Old People, the Little Dark People; and from the old Druid, almost the last of his kind, who had taken and reared and trained him after his mother entered her nunnery, he had star-knowledge and the skills of shape-shifting and art-magic; and both these he could use at will. But from his father he had the power to look into the future as other men look into the past; and this came not at his own will but at the will of the power itself, that was like a great wind that snatched him up into some place where past and future were one. So now he began to shake like a young aspen tree in the wind. And he began to prophesy in a high clear voice many things concerning the red dragon and the white.

And when at last the high wind of prophecy forsook him and he ceased to shake, and looked again out of his own golden eyes and spoke again in his own voice, he said, 'But all these things will be after your time, my Lord the King.'

And a pang of fear shot through Vortigern, and he said, 'Then how can they concern me? Tell me now of *my* time!'

'Your time?' said Merlin. 'Your time is short, and ends in fire at the hands of the sons of the dead High King Constantine, Ambrosius and Utha. They have gathered many fighting men in Less Britain, which some call Brittany, that gave them shelter when you slew their sire; and already their ships are fitted out, already they spread their sails to the wind that shall carry them across the Narrow Seas. They will drive back the Saxon hordes; but you they will burn shut up in your strongest tower, in vengeance for their father's murder. Then Ambrosius shall be crowned High King; and he shall do great things for this realm of Greater Britain; but he shall die at the Saxons' hands; and after him Utha shall take the crown; but his days, too, shall be cut short, by poison. Yet after him, to Britain in her need, shall come another, greater than they.'

Then between fear and rage, Vortigern cried out to his guards, 'Seize him! Stop his mouth with your swords!'

But the rim of the sun was lifting above the rim of the mountains eastward, and the first rays shone level into the eyes of King and court and guards, making them blink; and when the dazzle cleared from their sight, the dark gape of the dragon-pool had closed over, and only the mountain grasses shivered in the dawn wind where it had been. And of the boy Merlin nothing remained but a kind of shimmer in the air that was gone almost before they saw it; and a voice that lingered after the rest was gone, 'There shall come another . . . another . . . greater than they . . .' and was lost in the soughing of the wind through the grasses.

Within three days Ambrosius and Utha his brother landed on the coast of Britain with a great war host behind them. They marched upon the stronghold to which Vortigern had fled, and sought to beat down the walls; and when the walls proved too strong for them they piled timber and brushwood all round the place and kindled it, and shot fire arrows into the thatch of the tall roof; and the flames leapt up day and night until the stones cracked and flew apart, and the great timbers roared up and crumbled into ash, and the whole tower was eaten by the flames as by a dragon, and Vortigern with it; and so their father Constantine was avenged.

Then Ambrosius was crowned High King, and with Utha his brother he turned upon the Saxons, and by long and desperate fighting drove them back from the lands that they had over-run.

But the time came when Utha, leading his troops up through Wales to meet a Scottish thrust from the north-west, saw a great star blazing in the night sky above his camp fires. And from the star shone a beam of light which became a dragon all of misty fire as though the star-trace that men call the Milky Way had gathered itself into the shape of a great winged beast. And from the dragon's mouth shone two more rays that bestrode the whole of Greater and Less Britain. Then Utha sent for Merlin, who had been with one brother or the other from the time they landed, and asked him the meaning of the strange lights in the sky. And Merlin said, 'Grief upon me! Grief upon us all! For Ambrosius your brother is dead! Yet the light foretells also great things to come, for in the battle that lies before you the victory shall be yours, and you shall be High King of Britain, for

22

the star and the dragon beneath it are yourself, and the two rays from the dragon's mouth foretell that you shall have a son greater than his sire whose power shall reach over all the lands that the rays bestride.'

So Utha grieved for his brother, and rode on against the men of the North and West. And when he was crowned High King of Britain in Ambrosius's place, he took the name of Utha Pendragon, which in the British tongue means Utha Dragon's-Head.

And in battle after battle he fought and defeated the Saxons and the Picts and the men from over the Irish Sea, until all the southern part of Britain was free of fire and sword; and then he drew a breath of quiet and set his mind to keep Easter in London, and make a great thanksgiving feast. And he bade all his lesser kings and nobles with their wives to come and join him there. Now among those who gathered to him in London that Eastertide were Gorloise, Duke of Cornwall, and his wife, the Duchess Igraine. And Igraine was the fairest of all the ladies about the court, and as soon as he saw her, the King's whole heart fixed itself upon her as it had never done upon any woman before, for all his life since he came to manhood had been too full of fighting to have room for love. He sent gifts to her chamber, gold cups and jewels for her neck; and whenever she sat at table or walked abroad she had but to look up to find his hungry gaze upon her.

Then the Duchess Igraine went to her husband and said, 'The King sends me overmany gifts and his eyes are always upon me. Therefore let us leave here quickly and go back to our own place.'

So the Duke gave his orders, and with the Lady Igraine and all their following, left the King's court before he knew it and set the horses' heads towards Cornwall.

And when the King found them gone, he was fiercely angry, and sent after them demanding that they should return. And when they did not return, he gathered his fighting men and marched after them and made war on the Duke of Cornwall.

Duke Gorloise set his lady in Tintagel Castle, which was the strongest hold in all Cornwall, being set on a headland above the pounding sea, with but one causeway leading to it from the mainland, and that so narrow that it could be held by three men against an army. And he pitched his war camp in another strong place inland of the castle and barring the way to the King. Then Utha Pendragon came up, and made his own camp opposite to where Duke Gorloise was. So the fighting began between them and lasted many days. And all the while his hot and hungry love for Igraine tore at the King, giving him no peace, whether in the red heart of the battle by day or in his lonely tent at night. At last, when a week had gone by, he called to him Merlin, who was with the camp. And Merlin came and stood like a tall shadow in the entrance to the tent, with the flicker of the camp fires behind him, not asking why he had been sent for, for he had been watching the great star hanging in the green twilight sky over Tintagel, and he already knew.

'I am sick with my heart's longing for Igraine,' said the King, 'and no nearer to her than I was seven nights ago. You who have the wisdom of the Old Ones, tell me what I must do to come to her.'

Merlin never moved. He knew that the time was come for the beginning of Utha's son, who should be greater than ever his father was. And he said, 'If you will give yourself up to my skills, I can give you the outer-seeming of Duke Gorloise for one night, and take upon myself the outer-seeming of Brastius, one of his household, that I may accompany you. And so you may go to Igraine in Tintagel Castle this night, none stopping you. But there is a price to pay.'

'Anything!' said Utha Pendragon. 'Anything under the sky.'

'Swear,' said Merlin.

'On the cross of my sword, I swear.'

Then Merlin came in and stood beside the brazier, looking at him across the little licking flames. 'If you go to the Lady Igraine tonight, your son will be born at Christmas; the son I told you of, when we saw the great lights in the sky on the night that Ambrosius died. And within the hour of his birth you shall give him into my keeping, that I may take and rear him for his destiny.'

Silence came down between them; and in the silence Utha said, 'It will be from Duke Gorloise that you must claim that.'

And back across the small licking birch flames in

the brazier he looked at Merlin, with a frown-line deepening like a sword-cut between his brows. He had not thought until that moment that any child of his begun as this one was to be, would seem ever after, in the eyes of all men, even in the eyes of the Lady Igraine, to be Duke Gorloise's and not the High King's.

'No,' said Merlin, seeing the thought. 'It will be from you that I must claim it.'

And the King believed him. But he asked, 'Why do you ask this price?'

'Because you may have other sons. That could mean danger to this one, this chosen one, with a cloud lying over his birth, and because your way of life is not a safe one, and if you die before he is of an age to take the crown, in the struggle for power among your nobles he will be trampled underfoot.'

And Utha saw the truth of this; and he was bound by his blindly taken oath; but more than either of these things, he was driven by his love for Igraine. And he agreed the price.

So Merlin went away, and in a short while returned to the King's tent with many things hidden under his cloak; and he cast a powder on to the brazier that filled the tent with a strange-smelling smoke; and he called up figures in the smoke, and made a magic that was older than the Druid kind. And at moonrise, two who to all outward seeming were Duke Gorloise and Sir Brastius of his household knights slipped out of the camp, and away, skirting the Duke's camp, by secret ways to the gates of Tintagel high on its rocks above the crooning sea.

The gate-guard passed them through, thinking only that the Lord of Cornwall had snatched a few hours to come home to his wife; and they crossed the narrow courts of the castle and climbed the outside stair to the Duchess's chambers. And down below in the walled shelter of the castle garden, a whitethroat was singing as though it were already dawn.

And the Duchess's ladies gave him entrance, thinking only as the men of the gate-guard had done, and as the Lady Igraine thought also when he stood within her chamber, that her lord was come home.

And that night, in the great chamber high above the crooning of the western tide, with the whitethroat singing in the castle garden and Merlin standing with a drawn sword before the door, Arthur of Britain was conceived.

But meanwhile Duke Gorloise had made a night attack on the royal camp, and in the desperate fighting had met his death before ever the King came to the door of Igraine's chamber.

Before dawn the High King took his leave of Igraine, saying that he must return to his men by daybreak; and so, with Merlin, slipped away.

And when soon after, news was brought to her of the night attack and her husband's death, Igraine was struck with grief, and also with a great wonder as to who and what it was that had come to her in his likeness that night. But she kept the matter in her own heart, and did not speak of it even to the nearest of her ladies.

By and by King Utha Pendragon came into Tintagel in his own seeming and as a conqueror, but a gentle conqueror, for truly he was grieved at the death of Duke Gorloise, though glad that now Igraine was free. And when enough time was passed, he began to pay court to her; and though for a while she fought her own heart, it seemed to her that there was something about him that she remembered, and the something was sweet. And so after six months they were married with great rejoicing.

Later, when it was not far short of the time for the Queen's child to be born, Utha asked her one night when they were alone in their chamber to tell him the truth of the strange story he had heard concerning the father of the babe she carried. And at first she was afraid, but then she gathered her courage and told him. 'Truly I do not know, for the night that my lord died, at the very hour of his death, as his knights told it to me, one came to my chamber who seemed to be my lord, and in the dawn he went away again. And in the night that he was with me, the child was begun. There was a whitethroat singing in the castle garden. I noticed it because we so seldom have any birds but gulls and ravens here.'

'I remember the whitethroat,' said the King.

'You?' said the Queen.

And in his turn he told her all the truth.

Then she wept afresh for Gorloise her first lord. But it was on Utha's shoulder that she wept.

At Christmas time the Queen bore her child; a fine manchild. But within an hour of his birth a message was brought to the King that a poor man stood at the postern gate and sent word to him to remember the vow taken on the cross of his sword.

And the King gave orders to two knights and two ladies to take the babe and wrap him in cloth-of-gold and then in warm skins for a winter journey, and to give him to the poor man they would find waiting at the postern gate.

So all was done as he ordered, and the child handed over to Merlin in his beggar's guise. And Merlin took him to a certain good knight called Sir Ector, who lived far away from the court, to be brought up along with his own son in all the ways of knightly valour and courtesy. And when Ector would have known whose son it was that he was to foster with his own, Merlin told him, 'His name is Arthur, and whose son he is, you shall know when the time comes for knowing.' And Sir Ector asked no more.

And Utha, with his own heart sore within him, was left to comfort the Queen in her grieving.

2

THE SWORD IN THE STONE

Now Igraine had borne three daughters to Gorloise her first lord, before ever she became Utha's Queen, and two of them being above twelve years old were already married. Margawse the eldest to King Lot of Orkney, and Elaine the next to King Nantres of Garlot; but the youngest, Morgan La Fay, was still a child and at school in a nunnery. And in all three of the Cornish princesses the blood of the Old People, the Little Dark People, was strong, and with it the old wisdom and the old skills, so that all of them had something of magic power; but in Morgan La Fay it ran strongest of all, and she was a witch and of dark kinship with the Faery Kind before ever she left her nunnery to become wife to King Uriens of Gore.

But after Arthur, Utha and Igraine had no more children. And in two years the Saxon wars broke out again, and though the High King flung them back as strongly as he had done before, the Saxons and the men of the North sent spies into his war camp, who poisoned his wine-cup so that on the very night of his victory over them, he died.

Then Britain fell upon dark days indeed, for with no stronghanded heir to take up the High King's

30

sword when he laid it down, the lesser kings and the great lords fought among themselves as to who should be High King after him; and the Saxon kind, seeing the realm without a leader, came thrusting in again, deeper and deeper, until the greater part of all that Ambrosius and Utha Pendragon had won back from the barbarians was lost once more. And from his retreat in the mountains of Gwynedd, Merlin watched with a sorry heart the sorrows of Britain, but knew that the time was not yet come for the strong hand that should save the realm.

And in the castle of Sir Ector, in the dark country bordering Wales that men called the Wild Forest, Arthur grew from a child to a boy, along with Kay, Sir Ector's son and his foster brother, learning those lessons of honour and courage and gentleness and self-discipline, and the weapon-skill and the patience with hawk and hound and horse that would fit him one day to be a knight – and fit him also to be a king. But this he did not know, any more than he knew that the wandering harper or travelling smith or wounded soldier making his way home from the wars who would appear at the castle from time to time were all Merlin in one guise or another, come to see how it went with the future High King of Britain.

So the dark years went by, until at last Merlin judged that the time and the new High King were both ready. And then he betook him to the City of London, which was still in British hands, and spoke with Dubricius the Archbishop. Merlin held by an older faith than the Archbishop's, and followed the patterns laid down by other gods. But Dubricius was a wise man, wise enough to allow for other wisdoms and other patterns beside his own. And he listened to what Merlin had to say; and he called a great gathering of knights and nobles and lesser kings for Christmas Day, promising that Jesus Christ who was born upon that day would show them by some miracle who was the rightful High King, and so put an end to all their struggling among themselves.

Christmas came, and with it a great gathering who thronged the abbey church, while those for whom there was no room inside crowded the churchyard to watch the distant glimmer of candles and hear the singing and share in the Mass as best they could through the great West door which stood open wide. And when Mass was done, and they turned to go, and those within the church began to come out, suddenly there began a murmur of wonder which spread out and out through the throng like the ripples spreading when a trout leaps in a pool.

For there in the midst of the churchyard, none having seen it come, was a great block of marble, and rooted in the block, an anvil; and standing with its point bedded in the anvil and through into the marble beneath, a naked sword. And round the block was written in letters of gold, clear in the winter sunshine, *'Who so pulleth out this sword from this stone and anvil is trueborn King of all Britain.'*

Then one after another the lesser kings and the lords and at last even the simple knights of their followings began to try to draw the sword from the stone. But none succeeded; and far on towards evening when the last had tried, there stood the sword, as firmly set as it had been at the first moment of its appearing; and the crowd stood around, weary and baffled, with their breath smoking in the cold air.

'He is not here, who shall draw this blade,' said the Archbishop, 'but God shall send him in good time. Hear now my counsel: let messengers be sent out the length and breadth of the land, telling of this wonder, and bidding all who would seek to win the sword and with it the kingdom come to a great tournament to be held here in London upon Candlemas Day. And meanwhile let a silken pavilion be set up to shelter the wonder, and let ten knights be chosen to stand guard over it night and day. And so maybe God shall send us our King that day.'

So the messengers rode out on the fastest horses that could be found, carrying the word far and wide through the land, as though it had been a flaming torch. And at last it came to the castle of Sir Ector in the Wild Forest on the fringes of Wales.

Now Sir Ector was a quiet man, and growing old; but his son Kay had been made a knight at the feast of Hallowmas only a few months before, and felt his knighthood bright and untried upon him, and longed like every other young knight in the kingdom to try his fortune at drawing the wonderful sword.

His father laughed at him, but kindly. 'Do you think, then, that you are the rightful High King of all Britain?'

Kay, who could not bear to be laughed at, flushed scarlet. 'I am not such a fool as that, Father; but this will be the greatest and most splendid tournament that has ever been seen, and it would be a fine thing to prove myself there.'

'It would so,' said Sir Ector. 'Well, I remember when my knighthood was three months old I would have felt the same.'

Now Arthur, who was but just turned fifteen, was standing by and listening to the talk of his foster kin; a tall big-boned lad with a brown skin and mouse-fair hair and eyes that would be kind and quiet when he was older but just now were full of eager lights at the thought of the great tournament and the magic sword. And Kay turned on him impatiently: 'You heard! We're going to London for the tournament! Oh, don't just stand there like a shock of wet barley! You're my squire – go and get my armour ready or we'll never be in London by Candlemas!'

Arthur looked at him for a moment as though he would have liked to hit him. But then he thought, It is only because his knighthood is so new upon him. When he has had time to grow used to it, he will be different. He was used to making excuses to himself for Kay. And he went to see to his foster brother's armour, although he knew that Candlemas was as yet a long way off and there was plenty of time.

They reached London on a snowy Candlemas Eve, and found the city buzzing like a hive of bees about to swarm, so full of nobles and knights and their squires and trains of servants that at first it did not seem that they would be able to find lodgings for the night. But they found a corner in an inn at last; and next morning set out through the crowded streets to the tournament ground. All the world seemed going the same way, and it was as though they were carried along by a river in spate. The snow had been swept from the tournament field outside the city walls, so that it was like a green lake in the white-bound countryside; and all round the margin of the lake were the painted stands for the onlookers and the pavilions of those who were to take part; blue and emerald and vermilion, chequered and striped; and the crowds were gathering thicker every moment, and all among them horses were being walked up and down, their breath steaming on the cold air. And it all seemed to Arthur, fresh from his forest country, to be as beautiful and confusing as some kind of dream.

But just as they reached the tournament ground, Kay discovered that, with too much eagerness and too much anxiety, he had left his sword behind him at the inn.

'That is my blame,' Arthur said quickly. 'I am your squire, I should have seen that you were properly armed.'

And Kay, who had been going to say that same thing himself, could only say, 'It's over late to be worrying as to whose blame it is. Ride back quickly and fetch it and come on after us.'

So Arthur turned his cob and began to ride back the way they had come. But now he was going against the flow of the people, and when at last he managed to reach the inn, it was fast locked and shuttered, and all the people of the house were gone to watch the jousting.

Now what am I to do? thought Arthur. There will be jests and laughter if Kay comes to the tournament without a sword — and yet how am I to get one for him in this strange city and with so little time to spare?

And as if in answer, there came clearly into his mind the picture of a sword that he had seen earlier that morning, standing upright in a stone in the garth of the great abbey church close by. I wonder what it is there for, and if it lifts out of the stone? he thought, and found that he was already urging his cob that way.

For the strange thing was that in the moment that he thought of the sword in the stone, he forgot its meaning and why the tournament had been called. Maybe that had something to do with the passing beggarman whose strange golden eyes had met his for an instant as he turned his cob from the locked door of the inn; for assuredly if he had not forgotten, he would never have thought of trying to get it out of the stone, even for Kay his foster brother . . .

When he reached the garth of the abbey church he dismounted and hitched his cob to the gate and went in. The fresh snow lay among the tombstones, and in the midst of the tall black sentinel towers of the yew trees the pavilion glowed crimson as a rose at Midsummer; and the sword stood lonely in its anvil on the great stone, for even the ten knights were gone to the jousting.

Then Arthur took the sword two-handed by its quillions. There was golden writing on the stone, but he did not stop to read it. The sword seemed to thrill under his touch as a harp thrills in response to its master's hand. He felt strange, as though he were on the point of learning some truth that he had forgotten before he was born. The thin winter sunlight was so piercing-bright that he seemed to hear it; a high white music in his blood.

He drew the sword from the anvil in one familiar-seeming movement as though from a well-oiled sheath. And he ran back to the gate where his cob waited, and made all haste back towards the tournament field. The crowds in the streets were thinning now, and in only a short while he reached the place where Sir Kay had turned aside, sitting his horse in a fret, to wait for him.

'This is not my sword,' Kay said, as Arthur thrust it into his hand.

'I could not get in, the place was locked up – I came on this one by chance, in the abbey garth, sticking in a great stone – '

Kay looked at the sword again. He was suddenly very white. Then he wheeled his horse and began thrusting through the crowd towards Sir Ector, who had ridden on ahead. Arthur followed hard behind.

'Sir,' said Kay, when he reached his father, 'here is the sword out of the stone; here in my hand. It must be that I am the true High King of Britain.'

But Sir Ector looked at his son steadily and kindly, and from him to Arthur and back again, and said, 'Let us go back to the church.'

And when the three of them had dismounted and gone into the great echoing church, all glimmering with tapers for Candlemas, he made Kay put his hand on the Bible, and said, 'Now tell me in all truth, how you came by this sword.'

And Kay turned from white to red, and said, 'My brother Arthur brought it to me.'

Sir Ector turned to his foster son, and asked, 'How came you by this sword?'

Arthur, troubled because he could not think what Kay had meant when he said that he must be High King of Britain, but still not remembering, said, 'Kay sent me to fetch his sword, but the lodging was empty and locked up, and I could not think what to do — and then I thought me of this sword in the church garth, and it was serving no useful purpose there, while Kay needed a sword, so I pulled it out and brought it to him.'

'Were there any knights standing by, who saw you do the thing?' asked Sir Ector.

Arthur shook his head. 'No one.'

'Then,' said Sir Ector, 'put the sword back in its place.'

And when Arthur had done so, Sir Ector tried to draw it out again, and could not shift it. And then at his order Kay tried, but with no better success. 'Now do you draw it forth again, Fosterling,' he said. And Arthur, greatly wondering what all the to-do was about, drew the sword again, as easily as he had done the first time.

Then Sir Ector knelt down before him, and bowed his head, and Kay also, though more slowly; and Arthur, beginning to remember and trying not to, and suddenly more afraid than ever he had been in his life before, cried out, 'Father – Kay – why do you kneel to me?'

'Because you have drawn the sword from the stone, and it is ordained by God himself that none shall do that save he who is rightfully High King of Britain.'

'Not me!' Arthur said. 'Oh, not me!'

'I never knew whose son you were when Merlin brought you to me for fostering,' said Sir Ector. 'But I know now that you were of higher blood than I thought you.'

'Get up!' said Arthur. 'Oh sir, get up! I cannot bear that you should kneel to me, you who have been my father all these years!' And when Sir Ector would not, he dropped on to his knees also, to be on a level with the old man again.

'I kneel to my liege lord,' said Sir Ector. 'I will serve you in all things and keep true faith with you. Only be a gentle lord to me, and to Kay your foster brother.'

'Kay shall be Seneschal of all my lands, if I be King indeed,' said Arthur. 'And how could I be any but a gentle lord to you whom I love. And for the rest – I will serve God and the realm of Britain with the best that is in me. Only get up now, for indeed I cannot bear it!' And he covered his face with his hands and wept as though his heart would break.

Then Sir Ector and Sir Kay got up, and Arthur himself last of all; and they went to the Archbishop and told him of what had happened, and as the word spread, knights and nobles came pouring up from the tournament ground, demanding that they should also try for the sword, as was their right; and Arthur set it back into the stone, and one after another, they tried without avail.

Yet they would not accept that a boy not yet come to his knighthood, and with no proof of his fathering, should be king over them. And so the Archbishop ordained another gathering at Easter, and then yet another at Pentecost, and to each of these the great lords swarmed in to try again; but none could draw the sword save Arthur. And at last the people cried that they were weary of this striving, and would have Arthur for their king.

Then Arthur took his sword across both hands and offered it before the altar in the abbey church, and received his knighthood of the Archbishop. And that same day the Archbishop set the crown upon his head.

The royal circlet pressed down upon his forehead with all the weight of the fear and bewilderment that had been with him ever since he had first drawn the sword from the stone; so that it was all he could do to hold his head high as he turned to confront the knights and nobles who crowded the body of the great church. And then he became aware that as the Archbishop Dubricius stood beside him on his right, somebody else was with him on his left – a tall man in a dark mantle, with hair on his head like black ruffled feathers. Arthur did not know who he was; but it was clear that the Archbishop knew, and Sir Ector his foster father standing close by, and many others in the church, and that even those who did not know felt the power that flowed from him like light from a torch or the spreading quiver in the air from a lightly tapped drum.

There was faint stirring and shifting among the crowd, and a whisper began to go round, 'Merlin! It is Merlin!' 'He was with Utha and Ambrosius; often I saw him!' 'It is Merlin, the magician!'

And one of the great lords, leader of many fighting men, who had had high hopes of his own claim to the crown, shouted, 'It is Merlin and not God who has chosen for us this beardless boy to be our new king!'

And another joined him, as hound bays after hound, 'Aye, it is nought but Merlin's dream-weaving, this magic of a sword in a stone!'

Standing so still that save for his back-falling sleeve, not a fold of his dark mantle stirred, Merlin raised his arm, and silence flowed out from him the length and breadth of the church. Only a faint murmur seemed to hang between the pillars and in the emptiness under the high arched roof like the echo of the sea in a shell. And into the silence, Merlin lifted up his voice and spoke.

'Listen now, oh people of Britain, and you shall

know the truth. Truth that has been hidden from you many years until the time should come for you to hear it. Here stands your High King, true and rightful son of Utha Pendragon and his Queen Igraine; born to be the greatest king that Britain has ever known, born to drive back the enemies of the realm further even than the Pendragon drove them in his day. Born to bring that brightness between the Dark and the Dark that men shall remember beyond the mists of time and call the Kingdom of Logres. He was God's choice, not mine, but it was given to me to know him, before he was born, before even his king-star hung in the sky, and to do what must be done to bring him safely to this day!'

And standing still with his hand raised, he told the whole story of the dragon in the sky, and of Arthur's birth, and how he had taken the child and given him to Sir Ector's fosterage to be brought up in safety from the troubles that followed his father's death, until the time came for him to take the crown and the sword.

When he had done, he lowered his hand, and, as though it was a signal, the uproar broke out again, but now it swelled into a roar of acclamation; and men were shouting, 'Utha's son! Utha's son!'

And in the midst of the shouting the tall man in the dark cloak turned his head and looked at the boy beside him; and Arthur found himself looking back, into strange golden eyes that were not like the eyes of any mortal man that he had met before. And yet as he looked into them he seemed to remember for a moment a beggar by the inn doorway that Candlemas morning that now seemed a lifetime ago, and a stray harper playing by the fire in the hall of his old home, and a travelling tinker, and a wounded soldier making his way home from the wars. The rags of memory were gone before he could lay hold of them. But with them, all the fear and bewilderment went from his mind. The sorrow for the loss of his old life remained, but it no longer mattered. Suddenly his head was clear and his heart strong within him; and he knew that whatever he had to do in this new life, he could do it.

'Speak to them,' said Merlin, beside him.

And Arthur spoke, lifting up his voice clear for all the knights and nobles in the great church, and the people thronging beyond the open door, and for all the people of Britain. 'I am your King! I will keep faith with you. Do you keep faith with me! When this feast of Pentecost is over let us gather our forces, and together we will drive back the Sea-wolves and the men of the North who ravage these lands! We will free the realm of the strife and the fire and the sword that have torn it apart in the years since my father's death. You and I together, let us make this a good land, where men do not rule only because they are strong, but where men are strong for the Right, none the less! Give me your love and your faithkeeping, oh people of Britain, and I will give you mine through all the days of my life!'

And there was no more shouting and acclamation; only a deep silence in the great church. But it was a good silence; and the tall man with the golden eyes smiled, as one that is well content.

3

THE SWORD FROM THE LAKE

From the day of his crowning, Merlin was always beside the new High King, as he had been with his father Utha before him. And with Merlin to advise and council him, Arthur Pendragon gathered his war hosts and thrust back the Saxons and the Picts and the men from over the Irish Sea. And he led his men also across the Narrow Seas to Less Britain to aid King Ban and King Bors of Benwick, who had sheltered Ambrosius and Utha after their father was slain, when they in their turn were beset by enemies on their borders.

And when all this was done, and it seemed as though there might be peace for a while, he made his capital at Camelot. And some people say the place where Camelot once stood is now the city of Winchester, and some that Cadbury Hill is what remains of it today; but no man knows for sure where the towers of Camelot once rose, just as no man knows for sure the last sleeping-place of Arthur the King.

But wherever his capital might be, neither Arthur nor his knights were left long to be at peace in it. For the dust of the fighting was scarcely sunk and the wounds were scarcely healed, when eleven lesser kings from the outland and mountain places along the fringes of Britain gathered each their war hosts and came against the new High King. King Lot of Orkney and King Nantres of Garlot, King Anguish of Ireland and King Idris of Far Cornwall and King Uriens of Gore and six more beside, they gathered to the great forest that furred all the mid-lands of Britain, and there laid siege to the great Castle of Bedegraine which was one of Arthur's chiefmost strongholds, meaning to make it their headquarters against him.

Then, by the advice of Merlin, Arthur sent word into Less Britain, to King Bors and King Ban of Benwick; and they in their turn came with their fighting men; and together they raised the siege of Bedegraine, and overthrew the eleven kings and drove them back into their own mountains and away over the Irish Seas, all save those who sued for peace and swore their fealty to the High King.

But no sooner was that done with, and Bors and Ban were away to their own lands once more, than word came from King Leodegraunce of Camelaird who was of Arthur's following, that Rience of North Wales made war upon him and pressed him sore. And again Arthur gathered his war hosts and marched to the aid of his vassal.

Six days they were on the march, and when he heard that they were coming, Rience laughed, and swirled about him his great war-cloak that was fur-bordered with the beards of kings and princelings that he had overcome; and he made ready to meet them upon the skirts of Snowdon and make an end of them.

But when they came together, it was the war host of Rience the tyrant which broke and scattered; and Arthur rode victorious into Camelaird town.

And when, in a few days, his men being rested, he rode south again, he carried with him not only another victory, but something that went deeper with him, though he did not know it, and was to remain with him all his days. For in the high-walled garden of the castle there, he saw Guenever, King Leodegraunce's daughter, for the first time. She was sitting with her ladies, and all of them weaving garlands of honeysuckle and columbine and the little loose-petalled Four-Seasons roses to braid into their hair. The Princess's hair was black with a shimmer of copper where the sun caught it, and her eyes, when she looked up from the flowers in her lap, were grey-green as willow leaves and full of cool shadows.

And Arthur saw all this; but she was scarcely more than a child, and though he was but eighteen himself, he was feeling very old, old and weary with his hard-won victories and the deaths of men. And though they gave each other one long grave look before her father swept him on his way, he thought no more of that first encounter after he rode south again, than that he had seen a girl making a flower-chain in the King's garden.

Yet something of him was changed from that moment. Something in him that had been asleep before, began to stir and to ache, longing for – he did not know what. Almost he forgot, as time went by, but never quite, until the time came for him to remember fully once again.

Arthur rode south to his great castle of Caerleon. And while he was there, Margawse his half-sister, she who was Queen to King Lot of Orkney, came to spy out for her husband the secrets and the strengths and weaknesses of his realm. She came, no man knowing who she was, as a noble lady on a journey, seeking a night's shelter for herself and her ladies and escorting men-at-arms. And Arthur, who had never seen her before, did not know her either, and gave her courteous welcome.

Merlin could have warned him, but for once Merlin was not at his side but had gone north on a visit to his old master who had reared and trained him. Cabal, Arthur's favourite hunting dog, growled and raised the hackles on his neck when she came near, but Arthur paid no heed, only thrust him back with his heel and ordered him from the Great Hall lest he frighten their guest.

That evening they made merry in the Great Hall in honour of the lady's coming, and when supper was over, the harpers made their music that was as sweet as the music of the Hollow Hills. But the night was heavy, full of thunder in the air, and the torches in their wall-sconces burned tall and unwavering; and by and by, the lady said, 'My Lord King, the night is overheavy within doors, and there is no air to breathe; is there a garden in this castle?'

'There is a garden behind the keep,' Arthur said, 'it will be cooler there.'

'Then by your leave, I and my maidens will walk alone there in the dusk.'

And so the lady and her maidens went out to the garden; and in the Great Hall the harpers played on, and the pages set out the boards for chess, and cleared the floor for the games that the young knights and the squires played after supper.

But in a while one of the pages came to Arthur and whispered, 'Sir, the lady asks that you go to her in the garden, for she bears a message for you which she says cannot be spoken here in the crowded Hall.'

So Arthur got up and went quietly from the Hall, and down the narrow stairway in the wall and through the postern door that gave on to the castle garden. The air was like warm milk, and the scent of honeysuckle and sweet briar hung heavy between the high walls, and the full moon was pale and blurred in the hazy sky. And in the entrance to the vine-trained arbour at the far end, the lady waited for him, quite alone, for all her maidens it seemed were gone.

Queen Margawse was twice as old as he was; she had borne four sons to the King of Orkney, and the eldest of them, Gawain, was not much younger than Arthur himself; but he neither knew nor cared for that. Something to do with another garden was stirring at the back of his heart, waking an old longing and loneliness in him. And she was very beautiful. He had seen how beautiful in the light of the Hall torches, and he saw it still more now in the blurred

lily-light of the moon; beautiful with a warm richness like ripe fruit, and the scent of musk and rose-oil
came from the folds of her gown and her unbraided
hair.

Her hands were held out to him; and Arthur took
them, and never remembered to ask her what was the
message she brought, that could not be told in
the crowded Hall.

Why she did it, there can never be any knowing; for
she knew, though he did not, what kin they were to
each other (but for herself, she had never cared for
any law save the law of her own will). Maybe she
thought to have a son to one day claim the High
Kingship of Britain. Maybe it was just revenge; the
revenge of the Dark People, the Old Ones, whose
blood ran strong in her, upon the Lords of Bronze
and Iron, and the People of Rome, who had dispos-
sessed them. Maybe it was because she had never
loved King Lot and dreaded growing old, and Arthur
was young and good to look upon. Maybe she
thought it might help her in her spying. Maybe it was
all these things mingled together . . .

Nine months later, far away in the North, Queen
Margawse bore a fifth son, and his father was not Lot
of Orkney, but Arthur the High King. And she sent
word to Arthur that she had borne him a son and
would name him Mordred, and that one day she
would send him south to be a knight of his father's
court.

And she told him who she was.

Then Arthur knew that he had done one of the forbidden things. He had done it all unknowing, but he had done it, and no tears or prayers or penance could undo it again. He had let loose his own doom, and in the end, as night gives place to day and day turns to night again, his doom would return upon him. He spent three wakeful nights wrestling with certain horrors within himself. Then, seeing that he had a life to lead and a kingdom to rule as best he might, meanwhile, he put the thing from him until the appointed time the web of things should bring it back again. And he called for horses and hounds, and rode hunting. And if, during the day's hunting, it seemed to the High King that he, and not the fleeing red deer, was the quarry, no one knew.

Only those who were closest to him knew that suddenly the last of his boyhood was gone from the High King.

But all that was still nine months in the future, and the lady had scarcely gone her way northward from Caerleon, when one day a young squire rode into the castle courtyard, leading a second horse, across whose back his knight lay newly slain. And dropping wearily from the saddle, he cried out, 'Vengeance, my Lord King! Christian burial for my master, as good a knight as ever set lance in rest, and vengeance upon his slayer!'

'The one you shall have without question,' said Arthur. 'The other if it be deserved. Who is the slayer?'

'King Pellinore,' said the squire. 'Not many leagues

from here he has set up his pavilion close to a well beside the high road; and there he challenges all comers to joust with him; and there he slew my master. Pray you let one of your knights ride out to take up the challenge and avenge my master's death!'

Now there was a squire at court called Gryflet, of about the same age as Arthur himself; and when he heard this he came and knelt before the King, and begged to be given his knighthood, that he might take the challenge upon himself.

And Arthur looked down at him, and knew that he had been a good squire, and would be a good knight also if he lived. But, 'You are over young to be taking up such a challenge,' he said, 'not yet come to your full strength, while King Pellinore of Wales is one of the strongest and most skilful fighters of any in this world.'

'Yet pray you give me my knighthood,' said the boy. 'It was I who spoke up first for the taking of this challenge.'

And Arthur sighed, and gave him the light blow between neck and shoulder that made him a knight. 'And now, Sir Gryflet, since I have given you what you ask for, I claim something of you in exchange.'

'Anything that is mine to give.'

'A promise,' said Arthur. 'Promise me that when you have ridden one course against King Pellinore, whether you be still in the saddle or unhorsed and on foot, you will let the thing rest there, and return to me without more ado.'

'That I promise,' said the young knight. And since

he had as yet no squire of his own, he fetched his horse and spear for himself; and hitched his shield on his shoulder and was away with one stirrup still flying.

He followed the summer-dry road in a cloud of his own dust, out of the sunlight into the forest shade, until he came to the well beside the way. And there he saw a rich pavilion and close by a fine horse ready saddled and bridled; and hanging from the lowest branch of an oak tree, a shield blazoned with many colours and beside it a great spear. Reining up and standing in his stirrups he hammered on the shield with the butt of his own spear as was the custom when taking up such a challenge, until the forest rang and the splendid shield came crashing to the ground.

Then King Pellinore, fully armed, came out from his pavilion, and asked, as was the proper custom also, 'Fair knight, why smote you down my shield?'

'For that I would joust with you,' said Sir Gryflet.

Then King Pellinore left the proper custom, and said, 'It were better you do not, for you are but young, and as I judge a newly made knight, and have not yet come to your full strength to match with mine.'

'For all that, I would still joust with you,' said Gryflet.

'It is by no wish of mine. But if you take up my challenge I cannot refuse. Yet if we are to fight, tell me first whose knight you are.'

'I am King Arthur's knight,' said the boy.

And King Pellinore took his spear and shield and

mounted his horse, and they drew apart the proper distance, and turning, set their spears in rest and rode full tilt upon each other.

Gryflet took King Pellinore in mid-shield, and shattered it to pieces; but Pellinore's point went clean through Gryflet's shield and deep into his left flank and there broke off short, the point lodging in his body, and horse and rider were brought crashing down.

Then Pellinore dismounted, and bending over the wounded knight unloosed his helm to give him air. 'This is a boy with a lion's heart,' he said, 'and if he lives, shall be among the best of knights.' And with the spearhead still in his flank, he helped him into the saddle, and turned the horse's head towards Caerleon, and set it to find its own way home.

Arthur was crossing the outer courtyard with a falcon on his fist when the horse and his sore-wounded rider returned. 'I rode but the one course as you bade me,' said Sir Gryflet, and fell out of the saddle at the King's feet.

Then the King was deeply angry, not only with King Pellinore, but with himself, that he had listened to the boy, and let him go upon a man's business (forgetting that he himself was no older) and when he had seen Gryflet carried away to be tended, he called for his squires to arm him and bring his best warhorse, and taking no companion, though many begged to ride with him, he set off along the track into the forest, to take up the challenge himself, and avenge the hurt to his youngest knight. And he rode with his vizor closed and the cover still upon his shield that no man might know him by the blood-red dragon upon it.

By and by he came to the rich pavilion beside the well. A new shield hung from the branch of the oak tree, and he beat upon it in a fury until all the forest rang with the clamour of it like a flawed bell; and out from the pavilion came the knight he knew must be King Pellinore.

'Fair knight,' said Pellinore, 'why do you beat upon my shield?'

'Sir Knight,' returned Arthur, 'why do you bide here, letting no man to pass this way unless he joust with you?'

'It is my custom,' said Pellinore. 'If any man would make me change it, let him try.'

'I am come to make you change it,' said Arthur.

'And I stand here to defend my custom,' said King Pellinore quiet in his helmet; and took up his new shield and his spear and mounted his horse which a squire had brought to him. And they rode apart the proper distance, then turned and spurred their mounts to full gallop, and so came thundering to meet each other. And each took the other in the centre of the shield, and their spears were splintered all to pieces.

Then Arthur made to draw his sword, but King Pellinore said, 'It is not yet time for swords. Let us try another course with spears.'

'I would be willing enough,' said Arthur, 'if I had another spear.'

King Pellinore flicked a finger at his squire, and the squire brought two more good spears and offered the first choice to Arthur; and when Arthur had chosen, King Pellinore took the other; and again they spurred their horses together; and again the spears shattered, and again Arthur would have drawn his sword.

'Nay,' said King Pellinore, 'let us ride one more course with the spears, for the love of the high order of knighthood, for you are such a jouster as my heart warms to.'

So the squire brought two more spears, and a third time they spurred against each other. But though Arthur's spear splintered yet again, this time King Pellinore's took him so hard on the right spot that both he and his horse were brought crashing to the ground.

Then Arthur sprang clear and drew his sword indeed, and Pellinore swung down from the saddle, drawing his own blade. And there began a great fight between them, and they hacked and hewed at each other until their armour was split and dinted and the blood ran down to slake the dust of the trackway like a crimson rain. At last their blades crashed together with such force that Arthur's sword flew to pieces, and he was left with the hilt and a jagged stump of the fine blue blade in his hand.

Then Pellinore let out a deep cry of triumph. 'Now you are mine to slay or spare as I will! Kneel to me and ask mercy as a beaten knight, and it may be that I will let you live!'

'There are two words as to that,' said Arthur. 'Death I will take when it comes, but I yield on my knees to no man!' And flinging aside his useless sword hilt, he leapt at Pellinore, diving low under his guard, and got him round the waist in a wrestler's grip and flung him down. So they wrestled upon the ground, a slow hard struggle in their armour; but King Pellinore was a big and powerful man, and Arthur, even as he had said to Sir Gryflet, was not yet come to his full strength; and in a while King Pellinore came uppermost, and tore off the young King's helmet and reached for his sword . . .

And in that moment something stirred among the tree-shadows around the well, as though one of the ancient thorns were moving; and out from among them stepped a tall dark man with golden eyes, and his black mantle powdered almost white about the hem with the dust of a long journey.

His shadow in the long evening light fell across the two figures, and Pellinore checked his hand and looked up.

'Nay, leave your sword where it lies,' Merlin said. 'If you slay this man you slay all hope for Britain.'

'Why, then, who is he?' asked Pellinore in a sudden quiet.

'He is Arthur, the High King.'

Then for the first time fear came upon Pellinore, for men who seek to slay a king, and fail, often themselves die ugly deaths; and again for an instant his hand moved towards his sword.

'Nay,' said Merlin, 'no need for that,' and he raised

his hand and pointed a long forefinger at Pellinore; and Pellinore gave a deep sigh and folded gently on to the grass, and lay still.

Then Merlin turned to Arthur, who could scarcely stand for his wounds, and helped him to remount his horse which stood nearby, and led him away.

But Arthur looked back at the still figure lying beside the well, and said, 'Merlin, what have you done? You have killed this good knight by your crafts; a strong and valiant knight, and I would give a year of my kingship that he should be whole and alive again!'

'Cease to trouble,' Merlin said, 'you are more like to die than he is, for you are sore wounded, while his hurts are less deep than yours, and he only sleeps, and will wake again in three hours. Aye, and you shall meet this King Pellinore many times in friendship, for he shall be a valiant knight of yours, and his son after him.'

So Merlin brought the King to a hermitage in the forest, where the hermit was a man of great skill with healing herbs, and within three days his wounds were so well knit together that he could ride again. And they set out for Caerleon once more.

But Arthur rode with his head on his breast. 'I am ashamed,' he said. 'I have no sword.'

'No need to be troubled as to that,' Merlin told him. 'Your old sword has served its purpose. It gave proof of your right to the High Kingship and it served you well through the battles that won back your kingdom, but now it is time for you to take your own sword; time for Excalibur, that shall go with you the rest of your days.'

So they went on deep and deeper into the forest, following ways that no man might know but only the light-foot deer; until at last the great hills rose about them and the trees fell back, and they came to the reedy margin of a lake. And though the light evening wind hushed through the branches of the trees behind them, no breath of moving air stirred the rushes, nor the surface of the water, nor the faint mist that scarfed its sky-reflecting brightness and hid the further shore. Almost, Arthur thought, it was as though there were no further shore, though he could see the hills that rose above it into the western sky. And there was no crying and calling of lake birds as there should have been; only a stillness such as, it seemed to him, he had never heard before. 'What place is this?' he asked at half breath as though he were afraid to break the silence.

'It is the Lake,' Merlin said, 'it is the Lake of the Lordly Ones, who have their palace in its midst, unseen by the eyes of men. Away over yonder – away to the West – there lies Ynys Witrin, the Glass Island; Avalon of the Apple Trees, that is the threshold between the world of men and the Land of the Living that is also the Land of the Dead . . .'

His voice seemed to come and go, so that Arthur was not sure whether he heard the words or if it was only the faint wind-song in the trees behind them.

'A strange place indeed,' he said.

'And not far off is Camlann,' said Merlin beside him, and his voice came back out of the faint wind-song and sounded heavy and old.

'Camlann?' Arthur said, feeling a sudden coldness between his shoulders, as men do when a grey goose flies over the place of their grave.

'Camlann, the place of the last battle . . . Nay, but that is another story, for another day as yet far off.' Merlin's voice lost its heaviness, 'See, there is your sword as I promised.'

And looking where he pointed, Arthur saw an arm rise from the midst of the lake, clad in a sleeve of white samite and holding in its hand a mighty sword. And even as he looked, he saw a maiden whose dark gown and hair seemed to float about her like the mists come walking towards him across the water, her feet leaving no ripple-track upon its brightness.

'Who is that?' whispered Arthur.

'That is the Lady among all the Ladies of the Lake. Speak to her courteously and she will give you the sword.'

So when the maiden came to the lake shore and stood before them swan-proud among the reeds, Arthur dismounted and saluted her in all courtesy and asked her, 'Damosel, pray you tell me what sword it is that yonder arm holds above the water.'

'It is a sword that I have guarded for a long time. Do you wish to take it?'

'Indeed I do,' said Arthur, looking out across the lake with longing eyes. 'For I have no sword of my own.'

'Then promise me never to foul the blade with an unjust cause, but keep it always as befits the Sword of Logres, and it is yours.'

'That I swear,' Arthur said.

'So,' said the Lady of the Lake, 'then step you into the barge that waits for you.'

And for the first time, Arthur saw a boat lying close by among the reeds.

He stepped aboard, and instantly the boat began to move, slipping through the water of its own accord and leaving no wake behind, until it checked like a well-gentled steed beside the arm where it rose from the lake depths.

Then Arthur reached out and said, 'By your leave,' and took the sword into his own hands, seeing how the milky waterlight played on the finely wrought gold and gems of the hilt and on the richly worked sheath. And as he did so, the arm in its white samite sleeve slipped quietly beneath the water.

And the boat returned as quietly to the nearby shore.

Of the Lady there was no sign, and it was as though she had never been; but Merlin stood where he had left him, holding the horse's bridle. And Arthur buckled on his sword, and mounted and they set forth once more towards Caerleon.

And as he rode, Arthur drew his new sword, and looked at it, letting the evening light play with the silken surface of the blade. 'Excalibur,' he said softly; and then, 'Excalibur,' again.

Merlin looked at him sideways, and asked, 'Which do you love better, the sword or the sheath?'

And Arthur laughed at the seeming foolishness of the question. 'It is a pretty sheath, fair to see, with all these gold threads on the crimson leather; but the sword is a sword, and I would rather a hundred times have that!'

'Nevertheless, have a care to that scabbard, and keep it always, for while it is safely buckled to your sword-belt, by the strength of the magic in it, however sore you may be wounded in battle, you shall lose not one drop of blood.'

'I will have a care,' said Arthur, sheathing his blade. 'But still I like the sword best.'

4

THE ROUND TABLE

It was not long before the High King had need of his new sword; for in the spring of the next year, word came to him that Rience of North Wales was once more gathering a war host; and wild-riding bands of his followers were already harrying the lands of Arthur's subject kings across his borders. And when Arthur sent word to him to cease his wolf-pack ways, all he received in reply was a message from King Rience that he had conquered more kings in his time than he could count on the fingers of both hands, and cut off their beards to make a border for his mantle, but that he would spare King Arthur if he sent his own beard to add to their number.

'This is the ugliest message that ever I received,' said Arthur to the messenger. 'Go now back to your lord, and tell him that it is unwise to send such messages to the High King of Britain. Tell him also that unless he ceases from his pillaging and comes in to swear fealty to me, as better men than he have done, I will come against him as I did before; but this time I shall do more than drive him back to his mountains. This time I shall take this kingly mantle of his, and not only his beard but his head to go with it!' And he felt the young man's down on his own chin, and added, with the laughter breaking through his wrath, 'Tell him also that in any case, I fear my beard would be of little use to him as yet.'

So the messenger returned to his lord. And Arthur gathered his war hosts yet again and marched into the mountains of North Wales. And there he found Rience and many rebel knights and war leaders waiting for him; and among them King Lot of Orkney, which grieved him, for he knew in his heart that it was Queen Margawse and not her husband who was truly his enemy, and that it was by her will rather than his own that he was there.

All one long summer's day they fought; and sometimes the battle swung this way and sometimes that; but as the day drew on, the tide of the fighting set more and more against the rebels, until, when the shadows of men and horses and spears grew long at evening, Rience and all his leaders lay dead, save for King Lot, who still fought on, stubborn as a boar at bay, with his bodyguard close about him.

Now King Pellinore of Wales was fated at times to ride questing after a strange beast which had the head of a serpent and the body of a leopard and the feet of a hart, and which made in its belly a noise as of thirty couple of hounds giving tongue. And it so happened that on that day the quest had led him into the hills among which the battle was being fought. And hearing the outcry and the ring of weapons, and seeing the red and golden standard of Britain above the dust of the struggle, he turned aside from the quest for a while to join his High King. He came just as Arthur was leading in another charge against the men of Orkney, and riding with him and his household knights, while all around them sounded the cry of thirty couple of hounds giving tongue on a hot scent, he drove deep into the enemy mass until he reached King Lot himself and in the close-locked struggle all around dealt him such a crashing blow that the sword blade bit through helm and bone, and King Lot pitched from the saddle and was dead before he hit the ground.

And the heart went out of the men of Orkney, and they fled away into the gathering dusk, that still seemed full of fading hound music.

So peace came to Britain for a while; and the men of the North and West were quiet again in their mountains and the Sea-wolves fled away overseas. There were stray war bands still loose in the land, and evil knights and wild men lurking in the forests, ripe for any ill-doing that came their way. And the men in the mountains told stories of ancient wrongs around the fires at night to keep their hate alive. Yet even so there was more of peace in Britain than there had been since long before the Romans left.

Now there was time for men to draw breath and think how they would choose to live their lives. And the best knights in the kingdom, many of whom had shared in the past fighting, gathered to Arthur in Camelot. Old knights such as Sir Ulpius and Sir Bleoberis the standard-bearer, who had served with King Utha Pendragon; young knights seeking glory and a shining cause to fight for, such as Sir Bedivere and Sir Lucan and Sir Gryflet le Fise de Dieu and Lamorack, who was the son of King Pellinore by his first love, before ever he wedded his queen; and unfledged squires eager for knighthood at the hands of the greatest king in Christendom. Even Gawain, the eldest son of King Lot and Queen Margawse, and with him Gaheris his younger brother (for all the sons of Margawse left home as soon as might be, until it came to the turn of Mordred, the last son of all. But that was another matter.)

Never, the harpers said, had such a court flowered about such a king.

Then, in a while, Arthur sent one evening for Merlin to come to him in the great chamber above the hall, and said to him, 'My lords and nobles are hounding me that I should take a wife. Give me your counsel, for always your council has been good for me to hear.'

'It is right that you should take a wife,' said Merlin. 'For now you are past twenty and the greatest king in all Christendom. Is there any maiden who comes close to your heart?'

And Arthur thought. And his thoughts touched in passing upon the fair faces of many maidens, and upon the dark ripe beauty of Queen Margawse, and flinched away from that memory to that which lay beyond. And so his thoughts came to rest upon a girl with smooth dark hair and shadowy grey-green eyes, making a garland of honeysuckle and columbine and Four-Seasons roses in a high-walled castle garden. And he said, 'Guenever, the daughter of Leodegraunce of Camelaird.'

Merlin was silent a moment, and then he said, 'You are sure of this?'

And Arthur was silent also. A big soft-winged moth hovered in through the window and began to flutter about and about the candles on the carved cloak-chest. Then he said, 'I am very sure. I love the Princess Guenever, though I did not know it until now; and my heart feels good and quiet and at rest when I think of her.'

Merlin, knowing what he knew of the future, could have said, 'Grief upon me! Look elsewhere! For if you marry the Princess Guenever, sorrow and darkness and war and death will come of it by and by, to you and her and your dearest friend and to all the kingdom.' But he knew that no man may escape what is written on his forehead, and he knew what was written upon Arthur's as surely as he knew what was written on his own. So he said, 'Sir, if you were not so sure, I could find you a score of maidens as beautiful and good as she, who could gladden your heart just as sweetly. But I know you, and I know that when your heart has gone out of your breast it will not lightly return to you again.'

'That is so,' said the King.

And the moth blundered into the sea-blue heart of a candle flame, and fell with singed wings.

Then Merlin set out next day for Camelaird, and stood before King Leodegraunce, and told him that the High King of Britain would have the Princess Guenever for his Queen.

When he heard this, Leodegraunce was overjoyed, and said, 'This is the best tidings that ever I heard. Assuredly the High King shall have my daughter to wife.' And then he thought, What shall I give him for her dowry, for of lands he has already all that he can wish for? And the answer came to him, and he said aloud, 'And her dowry shall be a thing that will mean more to him than lands or gold, for I will give him the great Round Table that belonged to Utha his father, and that Utha gave to me, and with it a hundred knights of my best and bravest!' he sighed. 'There's room at that table for a hundred and fifty; but after the wars of my lifetime I can spare no more.'

'The hundred will be enough, for Arthur has good knights of his own. He will be glad of your gift, and glad of the lady who you send to him to be his Queen,' said Merlin, with a small inward-turning smile, for he himself had fashioned the Round Table for Utha Pendragon, long years ago when he was young, and he knew its powers.

So the Round Table was taken apart for its journey, and loaded into great ox-carts. And the Princess also was made ready. No one had asked her wishes in the matter; but she remembered the young man with the tired face, and the long look that had passed between them in the castle garden, and how, after he had passed on, she had found that she had broken the garland in her lap; and though her heart made no singing within her, she was well content.

So, riding among her maidens, with Merlin beside her and the hundred knights following after, and last of all the great ox-carts lumbering along the summer-dusty tracks, Guenever set forth on her marriage journey; and three days before Pentecost, she came to Camelot, where Arthur waited for her. Across the three-arched bridge that spanned the river she went, and up through the steep streets of the town where the people crowded to see her pass, and the swallows swooped among the eaves and gables overhead. And in the outer courtyard of the palace Arthur stood to help her dismount and lead her into his Great Hall.

All things were made ready for their wedding in three days' time; and on the morning of that day – which was also the Feast of Pentecost – Gawain the son of King Lot and Lamorack the son of King Pellinore came to Arthur to beg the honour of knighthood; and both of them he knighted most gladly; and so when the High King went to his wedding in the tall church of Saint Stephen, they were among the knights who followed him.

Then came Guenever in robes of white and gold for her wedding and her coronation. And when two bishops had joined her hand and Arthur's, they took off the garland of white briar roses from her hair and set in its place the gold circlet of a queen. And hand in hand, under the golden canopy which four kings upheld on spear-points above their heads, they paced back through the crowded streets; and all the people shouted for joy that the High King had got him so fair a queen.

Guenever walked with her head held very high, for the crown was much heavier than the white rose garland had been. But she was proud that Arthur had chosen her to be his lady; and there was a great fondness for him growing within her, that she thought at that time was love.

In the Great Hall the Round Table had been set up; a table like the rim of a mighty wheel with all the space in the middle clear for the pages and serving squires to come and go. And about it were ranged tall-backed seats for a hundred and fifty knights, and on the back of each seat, written in fair gold, the name of the knight who should sit therein.

'Surely no king under Heaven ever had so fair a wedding gift as this!' said Arthur. And he and all his knights went to take their places, while the Queen and her ladies went apart to feast in another chamber, for such was still the custom of the British people at that time, that the men and women did not sit down to meat together upon state occasions.

And when they were all seated in their appointed places, the King turned to Merlin who stood beside his chair, and said, 'What of the four places I see about this wondrous table that are yet empty?'

'They shall be filled at the appointed time,' said Merlin. 'The first by King Pellinore, who rests a while from his questing to be with you this very day; see, his name is already upon his seat, there where the sunlight falls. The second waits for Sir Lancelot, son of King Ban of Benwick your old ally; and he shall be with you before next Pentecost morning. He shall be the best and nearest to you of all your knights, and of all your knights he shall bring you the most joy and the bitterest of sorrow. And the third seat is for Percival the son of King Pellinore, and he is not yet born; but when he comes it shall be as though he were a herald, for by his coming you shall know that in less than a year the Mystery of the Holy Grail shall come to its flowering, here in Camelot, and the knights shall leave the Round Table and ride out upon the greatest quest of all time; and it shall be as though all things draw to the golden glory of sunset, beyond which is the dark. But now it is yet morning.'

And for a moment it seemed that a stillness fell upon the Hall.

Then Arthur said, 'Yet one empty seat remains. Who shall sit there?'

'That is the Seat Perilous,' said Merlin. 'It is death for any man to sit there, until he who it was made for comes to claim it. He shall come at the appointed time – and he shall be the last comer of all.'

And even as he spoke, King Pellinore stood in the doorway.

When King Pellinore had been welcomed and brought to his waiting seat, and the feasting that began immediately after was drawing to a close, there broke out a great baying of hounds in the forecourt, so that for a moment all men thought that it was Pellinore's questing beast, but even as the latest comer half rose from the table to follow it as he must when-

71

ever it called him, a white hart came running into the Hall, fleet-footed and touched to silver by the light of the high windows; and hard behind it a milky white brachet, a small hunting-dog almost as fair and fleet; and after them thirty couple of great black hounds in full cry.

The hart fled round the huge table, and after it the brachet, and the black hounds, belling as they went. And as they came towards the door again the hart gave a great bound and swerved towards it, oversetting a knight called Sir Abelleus who was not of the Round Table but among those eating at a side-board. And Sir Abelleus seized the brachet, and springing up strode from the hall. They heard his horse's hooves outside as he rode away. And the hart also fled out through the palace gates, with the black hounds baying and belling after it. And almost in the same instant, while the blood-music of the pack still hung upon the air, a maiden rode into the hall upon a white palfrey, and cried to the King, 'Sir, let me not be so wronged, for the brachet is mine that yonder knight carried away!'

But before Arthur could answer her plea, another rider crashed into the hall, a knight, darkly armed and mounted upon a mighty war horse, who seized the palfrey by its bridle and wrenched it round and so dragged horse and maiden away, she crying and making shrill protest all the while.

For three heartbeats after she was gone, Arthur sat unmoving and stared down at the table before him; for she had made a great clamour, and no man wishes to be embroiled in quests and marvels upon his wedding day. But Merlin brought his strange golden gaze back from following the damosel, and said, 'That was not well done, that a maiden should be dragged from this hall crying for succour, and no men moving to her aid. Such an adventure must be followed to its end, for to leave it lying is to bring dishonour upon you and your knights.'

And Arthur knew that Merlin was in the right of it, and he said, 'I will do as you advise me.'

'Then,' said Merlin, 'send Sir Gawain to bring back the white hart, and Sir Lamorack to bring back Sir Abelleus and the brachet, for it is right that both of them should follow the first quest of their knighthood this day. And let King Pellinore ride after the damosel and bring her back, and bring back also, dead or living, the knight who carried her away.'

So King Pellinore and the two young knights were armed, and their horses brought from the stables, and they rode away.

Sir Gawain took his younger brother Gaheris with him to be his squire; and together they rode through the town and across the bridge and away through the forest, following the distant dwindling music of the hounds, until they came at last to a great castle. The hart fled across the causeway and in through the castle gate, followed by the few hounds that were still on the hunt; and after the hounds rode Sir Gawain, with Gaheris following hard behind. And in the castle courtyard the hounds overtook the hart and brought it to bay and killed it.

Then out from the armoury doorway came the lord of the castle, fully armed all save his helmet, for he had been at practice, his sword naked in his hand; and he began slashing at the hounds, slaying them one after another, and shouting in grief and fury, 'Die, you brutes that have slain my white hart! Alas, my white hart that my lady gave to me and that I have kept so ill!'

'Stop! Leave off from this butchery!' shouted Gawain, suddenly beside himself with fury at sight of the dead hounds. 'Spend your rage upon me, not upon good hounds who do but follow their nature and their training!'

'That will I!' roared the knight of the castle. 'I have killed the rest of the pack, now for the last of the whelps!'

Gawain swung down from his horse, and in the midst of the courtyard the two met, as though they had indeed been two hounds springing at each other's throats. Their blades hacked through the chain-mail again and again, and the red smell of battle came into the back of Gawain's nose and a red mist before his eyes, until at last, he did not know how it happened, the knight of the castle crashed down at his feet and lay crying his mercy.

Gawain knew that it was against all custom to slay a knight who cried his mercy, but the red mist was still before his eyes, and he swung up his sword for a mighty stroke that should sever the fallen knight's head from his shoulders; but in that instant, the lady of the castle, who had been watching from the window of her bower and come running, flung herself upon her lord's body to shield him; and Gawain could not check the down-sweep of the sword in time, and struck through her slender neck instead of his adversary's.

The red haze cleared from Gawain's eyes, and grief and horror came upon him for what he had done. 'Get up,' he said to the knight. 'I give you mercy.'

'I no longer ask for it,' said the lord of the castle, 'for you have slain my lady, my love, who was more to me than all the world, and it is not in me to care whether I live or die.'

'Grief is on me for that,' said Gawain, 'for I meant the blow for you, and had no thought to harm your lady. I cannot kill you now; therefore rise and go to King Arthur at Camelot, and tell him truly all that has happened. Say that the knight who followed the Quest of the White Hart sent you.'

The silent servants brought their master his horse; and silently he mounted and rode away. And looking after him Sir Gawain said hoarsely, 'I am but an ill knight after all, for I have slain a lady, and had I shown proper mercy to her lord, it would not have come to pass.'

'This is no place to stand grieving,' said Gaheris, 'for I am thinking that we have few friends here!'

And in the same instant four of the household knights came upon them with drawn swords. 'Stand and fight now, you who shame your knighthood!' cried one. And another, 'A knight without mercy is a knight without honour!' And the third, 'You have

slain a fair lady! Carry the shame to the world's end!'
And the fourth, 'You shall know what it is like to
need mercy, before you go from us!'

And all the while they were thrusting in upon
Gawain and young Gaheris who stood back to back
and fought them off as best they might. But the odds
were two to one, and in the end both were wounded
sore and taken captive; and the household knights
would have slain them on the spot, beside the dead
hounds and the dead lady, had not the ladies of the
household come and begged mercy for them, so that
they were flung living into a narrow chamber in the
bowels of the castle, and there left for the night.

And in the morning the oldest of the ladies, whose
hair was silver beneath her veil, came and hearing
them groan from the pain of their wounds, asked Sir
Gawain how it was with him.

'Not good!' said Sir Gawain.

'It is your own doing,' said the ancient lady, 'had
you not slain the lady of this place, you had been less
sorely hurt this morning. But tell me now, who you
are.'

'I am Gawain, son to King Lot of Orkney, a knight
of Arthur's court, and this is Gaheris my brother.'

Then the silver lady went and spoke with the
household knights, telling them that their captives
were near kinsmen of the High King's, and for
Arthur's sake they were set free and given leave to
return to Camelot. Only the penance was laid upon
them that Gawain should carry the body of the slain

lady across his saddlebow, and her head hung by its yellow hair about his neck.

And so those two rode sadly back the long way through the forest that they had come the day before.

Sir Lamorack, meanwhile, had ridden after Sir Abelleus and the brachet; and he had not gone far when suddenly a dwarf stood in his path, and struck his horse such a blow on the muzzle with the staff he carried that the poor beast shook his head and squealed, backing a full spear's length before Lamorack could get him under control again.

'Why did you strike my horse?' demanded Lamorack.

'For that you may not pass along this way until you have jousted with the knights in yonder pavilions,' said the dwarf.

And Sir Lamorack noticed for the first time that two pavilions stood back among the trees beside the way, and beside each pavilion a brightly coloured shield and spear, and a horse standing ready saddled.

'I have no time to spare for such a jousting,' said Lamorack, 'for I am on a quest that may not be left lying.'

'Nevertheless, you shall not pass,' said the dwarf, and raising the horn that hung from his shoulder on a silken baldric, he sounded an echoing blast.

Out from the first of the pavilions strode a fully armed knight, who leapt upon his waiting horse, and taking down his shield, set lance in rest and came spurring towards Sir Lamorack. And Sir Lamorack swung his horse to meet the attack and received him with a spear thrust that tipped him over the crupper of his steed. And before he could rise, another knight came from the second pavilion, and Sir Lamorack received him in the same manner. Then Sir Lamorack dismounted, and stood over the two fallen knights as they lay sprawled on the turf.

'Do you cry my mercy?'

'We cry mercy,' said they, with what wind was still left in them.

'Then mercy you shall have. What are your names?'

'I am Sir Felot of Landluck,' said one.

And the other, 'I am Sir Petipace of Winchelsea.'

'So then, Sir Felot and Sir Petipace, get up, and back on your horses, and ride you to the court of King Arthur, and tell him you were sent by the knight who follows the Quest of the White Brachet. Now God speed you and me.'

And when they were gone, swearing to do as he demanded, and Sir Lamorack was about to ride on, the dwarf, who had stood by watching all this while, came to him and said, 'Sir, pray you grant me a gift.'

'Ask it,' said Sir Lamorack.

'I ask only that you will take me into your service, for I would no longer serve such sorry knights as those. If I were your man, I could tell you where rode the knight with the white brachet.'

'Choose yourself a horse, then,' said Sir Lamorack glancing at the spare mounts that stood under the trees, 'and ride with me.'

So they rode together through the early summer forest.

Towards evening they came upon two more pavilions pitched beside the way; and beside the entrance to one pavilion leaned a shield that was as white as milk, and beside the other, one that was as red as a corn-poppy.

Then Sir Lamorack dismounted, and giving his bridle to the dwarf, went to the pavilion of the white shield and looked in. And there lay three maidens sleeping. He went to the pavilion of the red shield; and there lay a lady sleeping with the white brachet at her feet, which barked at sight of him so that the lady awoke, and her maidens also and came running. And Sir Lamorack caught up the brachet as it sprang towards him, and carried it out and gave it to the waiting dwarf, the lady and her maidens following after.

'Sir Knight,' cried the lady, 'why do you take my brachet from me?'

'Because Arthur the King sent me in quest of it for another lady who claims it for her own,' said Lamorack, 'and so I must bear it back to him.'

'She lies, that other lady! This is an ungentle thing you do, and you shall not go far without suffering for it!'

'Then I will abide what ill befall me as best I may,' said Sir Lamorack. 'But, lady, I must have the brachet,' and he mounted, and he and the dwarf rode on their way back to Camelot.

They had not ridden far when they heard the

furious drum of hooves coming hard behind, and Sir Abelleus ranged up beside them. 'Sir Knight, give back to me the brachet which you stole from my lady!'

'Nay, if you want it, you must joust for it!'

So they set their spears in rest, and fought together, first on horseback, and then when both were unhorsed, on foot, until Sir Lamorack had the victory and Sir Abelleus lay at his feet. 'Now yield and cry mercy!' demanded Lamorack.

But the other cried, 'Never while the life is in me!'

And in that moment, again there came the sound of flying hooves, and out from the trees burst a damosel on a grey palfrey, who cried to Sir Lamorack, 'Sweet knight, for King Arthur's love, grant me what I shall ask of you.'

'Ask,' said Sir Lamorack, still with his sword point at Sir Abelleus's throat. 'And if it may be, I will grant it to you.'

'Then give me Sir Abelleus's head, for he is the worst of living men, and a murderer most cruel!'

Then Lamorack was troubled. 'That was a rash promise, and I repent me of making it,' he said. 'May it not be that he can make amends for whatever wrong he has done you, and win your forgiveness?'

'Never!' cried the lady. 'For he slew my own brother before my eyes, though I kneeled in the mud an hour to plead his mercy; and for no more cause than that my brother had worsted him in a joust!'

Then Abelleus, hearing this where he lay on the ground, yielded him and cried his mercy.

'It is too late for that,' said Sir Lamorack. 'You could have had mercy, but you would not ask for it.' And he stooped to pull off the other's helmet. But Sir Abelleus squirmed over, and leapt to his feet and ran, and Sir Lamorack after him; and among the trees Sir Lamorack caught up with him and smote off his head.

When he came back, cleaning his sword with a handful of grass, to the place where he had left the dwarf and the horse, the lady on the grey palfrey was still there, and she spoke to him gently, 'Sir, my thanks are yours. And now — you must be weary; come therefore to my house, which is nearby, and eat and rest, and tomorrow return to Camelot.'

So Sir Lamorack went with her, and she and the gentle old knight her husband made him and his dwarf and his horses warmly welcome, and gave him many thanks for his avenging of the lady's brother; and bade him remember that a welcome awaited him always in their manor. And in the morning, fed and rested and with his wounds salved, Sir Lamorack set out once more for Camelot, the dwarf following him with the brachet across his saddlebow.

King Pellinore rode into the forest in yet a third direction, and he had not ridden far before, coming down into a gentle valley, he came upon a well bubbling out from beneath an archway of mossy stones, and beside the well a damosel sitting with a wounded knight in her arms. And seeing King Pellinore she cried out to him, 'Help me, Sir Knight! Help me for Christ's sweet sake!'

But King Pellinore was half deaf in his helmet, and too eager upon his quest to stop, and scarcely heard her even when she cried out after him, 'I pray God you may have as much need of help as I have, before your time comes to die!'

He rode on down the valley; and presently he heard the sound of fighting, and coming to an open space among the trees, he saw two knights, one black-harnessed and the other all in elfin green, locked in furious sword-combat, while a little to one side, the maiden he sought sat her white palfrey captive between two squires. He reined in beside her, and said, 'Lady, I have sought you all the forest ways. Now you must come with me, back to King Arthur's court.'

'That will I gladly, if only it may be,' said the lady, 'for it was by no wish of mine that yonder knight of the black armour dragged me from the King's Hall.'

But one of the squires cut in, 'Yonder two knights are fighting for this lady. Go you and part them and ask their leave, and if both give it to you, then may you take her with you back to Arthur's court.'

Then King Pellinore urged his horse between the two battling knights, forcing them to break off, and demanded, 'Why fight you for this lady?'

'I fight to save her from this foul knight who has carried her off by force, for she is the Lady Nimue, and distant kin to me,' returned the knight in green.

'I fight for what is mine!' swore he of the dark

armour. 'For I bore her off by my strength and courage this day from Arthur's court!'

'You lie!' said Pellinore. 'For you came in full harness when we were unarmed and at high feast, and carried her off before any man had time to take up arms against you! Therefore on the High King's order I ride in quest of her, and will take her or die in the attempt.'

Then he of the black armour turned his sword upon King Pellinore's horse and drove it through to the heart, and laughed. 'Fight for her then, but on foot as we do!'

Pellinore sprang clear as his horse crashed to the ground, and ripped his own sword from its sheath, and cried out in fury, 'That will I! And for my poor horse as well as for the lady!' And as the black knight made at him, he swung up his sword, and brought it whistling down, through helm and mail coif and bone, splitting the man's head to the chin, so that he fell dead upon the trampled ground.

Then Pellinore turned to the other knight, but he looked up from staunching his own wounds, and shook his head.

'What? Will you not fight for her?' said Pellinore.

'Nay, there is no need. She will come to no harm at your hands. Take her back to Arthur's court, as your quest bids you.'

'That will I do,' Pellinore said, 'and riding this dead knight's charger since he has slain mine.'

'Nay, come back and lodge with me this night, and I will give you a better horse in the morning.'

So King Pellinore and the maiden Nimue returned with the knight her kinsman to his dwelling-place, supped and slept, and in the morning a tall fine warhorse was brought for him, and he mounted, the lady on her white palfrey at his side.

'Tell me your name before you ride away with my kinswoman in your keeping,' said the knight in green.

'I am King Pellinore of Wales, a knight of the Round Table. Now, in fair exchange for my name, do you give me yours.'

'I am Sir Meliot of Logure.'

'If ever you come to Camelot, you shall find fair welcome,' said King Pellinore.

And he rode on his way.

But when he came again to the well where the lady had cried out to him for help, he found the wounded knight lying dead of his hurts, and beside him the lady, lying with her head upon his still breast, and her bright hair showered all about him, and the dagger which she had taken from his belt driven deep into her own heart.

And looking upon them, all the triumph of his accomplished quest drained out of him like wine out of a cracked cup.

'She cried to me for help,' he said, 'and I was in too much haste to stop and aid her.'

'And there is nought that you can do for her now, nor for the knight she loved, but see that they have fitting burial,' said the Lady Nimue. 'There is a hermitage not far from here. Take their bodies to the hermit and pray him see to all that must be done.'

And when King Pellinore had dismounted and carried them both to the hermitage, the dead knight slung across the back of his horse and the lady in his arms, and bidden the hermit see to all things and bury them together, and take the knight's harness for his pains, they rode on towards Camelot again. 'She was very light to carry,' said King Pellinore; and he rode with his chin sunk on his breast.

And on the way, they were joined by Sir Lamorack with the dwarf and the brachet; and then by Sir Gawain riding sadly, with the headless body of the lady he had slain across his saddlebow.

Towards evening of the day after his wedding and the coming of the white hart, Arthur and Merlin walked alone upon the ramparts of Camelot; and looked out over the roofs of the town to the water-meadows and the shining loops of the river, and the forest beyond that rolled away and away into the blue heat-haze of summer.

'Soon, very soon now, I shall leave you,' Merlin said.

And Arthur turned from the distant forest to look at him with startled eyes. 'Merlin, why?'

'Because it is the appointed time. I have told you often enough that the time would come.'

'But not yet! Oh, Merlin, what will I do without your guidance and counsel? What will I do without *you*?'

'If I have taught you well, and you have learned well, you will do without me.'

'But you are not old,' Arthur said, seeing the man beside him as tall and upright as ever, his eyes as brightly golden, the darkness of his hair only beginning to be streaked with ash colour.

'My kind do not grow old according to the passing years — not as you understand growing old. But I am tired and the life grows thin within me, and I shall be glad to rest. And there are things that I have to do first. For many years I have shared your fate and your father's before you. Now I go to follow my own.'

Arthur said, 'Tell me at least what it is.'

'The lady who rode into your hall yesterday after the white hart, and was herself dragged away by the knight in black armour — did you not know her?'

'Why should I?' Arthur said. 'Never did I see her before.'

'That was Nimue, the Lady of the Lake who gave you your sword.' Merlin saw the astonishment on Arthur's face, and smiled. 'She is of the Lordly People, and has powers of shape shifting beyond even my own, for I am half mortal. Yet even I have come to you often enough in the guise of an aged beggar or a child gathering blackberries and you have not known that it was I.'

'But what has she to do with you?'

'She has my love,' Merlin said simply, 'all of it that is not yours. She has had it a long time. Now I go with her a while, to give her my wisdom and my powers to add to her own, as a gift of love, and so that she may use them in your service, when I can do so no more. And when she has them all, she will lock me with one of my own spells into a magic sleep . . . A quiet, long sleep, in a cave beneath roots of a certain hawthorn tree . . .'

'Then she is wicked!' Arthur cried out. 'Wicked, even though it was she who gave me Excalibur! And with Excalibur I will kill her before she does this to you!'

'Nay, she is not wicked,' Merlin said, looking out over the forest into the dim blue distance. 'She is of the Lordly Ones, did I not say? The Lordly Ones are neither wicked nor good, just as the rain is neither wicked nor good, that can swell the barley or wash away the field. They simply *are*.'

'But even so — with your powers, surely there is something that you can do to escape this fate?' Arthur cried in desperate misery.

'Oh, yes; and so I would remain with you — with my powers beginning to fail. But to do so would be to turn aside from the road appointed for me. She is my fate; and in some sort she is yours also . . . She will be with Pellinore when he returns, and when she leaves the court again, I shall go with her.'

'So soon?' said Arthur.

'So soon,' said Merlin.

Arthur was silent a moment, watching the swallows darting sickle-winged about the battlements. Then he said, 'This sleep — will it be for ever?'

'Not for ever, no. We shall both come again, you and I, when the time and the need call for us.'

Arthur went on watching the swallows. He felt the warmth of the evening sunshine on his face, and Cabal's muzzle thrust lovingly into the palm of his hand, and thought of Guenever's face, and the faces of men who were his friends. 'What will they be like, the people we come back to? What will it all be like?' he whispered suddenly in anguish.

But before Merlin could answer, a little group of figures rode out from the woodshore towards the bridge; and he saw that they were Sir Gawain and Sir Lamorack and King Pellinore; and that Gawain carried something that looked like a woman's body across his saddlebow, and Sir Lamorack was followed by a mounted dwarf with a white brachet on a long leash, and beside King Pellinore rode a damosel on a palfrey as white as hawthorn blossom.

That evening in the Great Hall, before the knights sat down to supper, Arthur bade the three returned knights to give account of their quests. The Queen and her ladies had come in to listen, and when the three stories were told, Guenever said, 'Oh, King Pellinore, it is a sorry tale you tell, for though you succeeded in your quest, through you this wounded knight died of his wounds beside the well, and his lady also, who loved him too well to live without him; for both might have lived had you answered when she cried to you for help.'

'Indeed I was so set upon my quest that thought of all else forsook me,' said Pellinore. 'I shall grieve for that to my own dying day.'

'If that is so, then you will not again ride past any who need your aid,' said the King. 'Come therefore to your place at the Round Table – your son Lamorack also, for he has earned his place among my knights.' And then he turned to Gawain. 'And you? Think you that you also deserve to sit among them? You who come riding back from your quest with the severed head of a lady hanging round your neck, and her slain body across your saddlebow?'

Gawain, who had finished his story last, and stood by, ash white, flushed fiery red to the roots of his fiery red hair, and then grew white again. 'I do not know. I only know that I will swear to show more mercy in future days; and for the sake of the lady I slew, to fight for all women who seek my aid and be their knight, truly and in all honour.'

Arthur and he looked at each other straightly, for they were good friends and almost of an age. And then Arthur smiled. He was feeling the need of his friends even more than he usually did, after his talk with Merlin on the ramparts. 'Your name is still gold-written on the back of your seat. See? Come you and sit in it. And remember the oath that you have sworn.'

He looked to Merlin, as though to ask, with no word spoken, whether he had dealt rightly with his three knights, for he knew and accepted that this was the last time he would be able to ask Merlin anything.

And Merlin returned him the shadow of a smile.

Thus, then, was accomplished the Quest of the

White Hart and of the Brachet, and of the Maiden who was the Lake-Lady Nimue.

And that evening Arthur received the oaths of all his knights of the Round Table, that always they would defend the right, that they would be the true servants and protectors of all women, and deal justly in all things with all men, that they would strive always for the good of the kingdom of Britain and for the glory of the kingdom of Logres which was within Britain as the flame is within the lamp, and that they would keep faith with each other and with God.

And when the oath-taking was over, and before ever the feasting began, Merlin came and set his hand for a moment upon Arthur's shoulder; and when the young King looked up, feeling the farewell in the touch, he said, 'Remember the things that I have taught you.' And he turned away and walked down the Hall, out of the torchlight and into the dark. And the Lady Nimue rose from where she sat among the Queen's maidens, and walked with him. And the places in the Hall were empty where they had been.

5

THE SHIP, THE MANTLE AND THE HAWTHORN TREE

Then Merlin went on his last wandering, and the Lady Nimue with him, and ever, when he grew weary, she would make him to sleep with his head in her lap, and sing to him the songs of the Lordly People; so in a while when he awoke he would feel himself young again. And ever, as they went, for a gift of love he taught her his own magic arts to add to the magic of her own that she had already.

And so at last they came overseas to the kingdom of King Ban of Benwick; he who Arthur had aided when he was attacked by King Claudas, and who had afterwards fought beside Arthur at the Battle of Bedegraine. Now King Ban had a son, who was seventeen summers old and training for knighthood; and when he was a child and the kingdom sore beset by Claudas, the Lady Nimue had taken him from his mother and fostered him in her own palace of the Lordly Ones in the midst of the Lake, that he might be safe until the danger was past. And this she had done at Merlin's asking; for Merlin knew that the boy was to be the greatest of Arthur's knights, and the best knight in all Christendom.

But now, the boy remembered nothing of this, for mortals who have been inside the Hollow Hills bring back no memory of that time, lest their lives should be spent in hopeless longing and in seeking for the way back.

Therefore Merlin came to the palace of King Ban with Nimue beside him; and he spoke with the King and with Elaine the Queen, and then asked to see their son Lancelot.

'What would you with Lancelot?' said the Queen, who was always afraid of losing him, after that first time. 'He is as yet no more than a squire.'

'But he shall be more,' Merlin said. 'There are things I know of him that make me wish to see and speak with him this one time.'

'And these things?' asked the King.

'I know that he was christened Galahad,' said Merlin, 'before ever he was confirmed in the name of Lancelot. I know that there was a time when you feared him lost to you. But be easy, I have not come to take him from you again – or not in the way you fear.'

So then, still unwillingly, the King sent for his son.

Lancelot was schooling a young goshawk. All his life he was to have more joy from flying a bird he had trained himself than one that had been trained, no matter how well, by a falconer. When they had shared together the ordeal of the terrible three days and nights that man must carry bird where ever he went, allowing no sleep to either, something grew between them that was lacking if the bird had shared it with someone else. Lancelot had reached that stage with Starstrike and had just won through the second night when his father's summons reached him. He knew that if he set Starstrike down now, it would all be to do again, and the hawk might be marred for ever. So he went to his father's Hall still carrying the weary goshawk on his gloved fist, and stood respectfully before the strange dark man and the lady whom he found there.

And as he looked at them, especially as he looked at the lady, it seemed to him for a moment that he had seen them before. And for that moment there was a kind of mist in his head, like the mist that hangs over lake water, and in the mist some kind of vague half-memory that was gone again even before he knew that it was there.

And Merlin looked at Lancelot searchingly, knowing what he knew of future days. Lancelot was a very ugly young man; even when he was not so tired, he was ugly; with a face under his thick arched crest of dark hair that looked as though it had been put together by someone who had not troubled to make sure that the two sides matched. One side of his mouth was straight-set and solemn, while the other curled up with joy. One of his thick black brows was level as a falcon's wing, and the other flew wild as a mongrel's ragged ear. Presently it would be a fighter's face, and presently it would be a lover's face; and the hand that was not hidden in the great leather hawking glove was already a swordsman's hand. And though Merlin's heart bled for the joys and sorrows of his destiny that he would feel more deeply than most men, it warmed with pride because it was a great destiny and the boy was matched to it.

Then Merlin spoke to the Queen his mother, 'Aye, he is as I believed that he would be; and one day he will be the greatest knight in all Christendom.'

'Shall I live to see it?' said his mother.

'Surely, you shall live to see it, and for many summers and winters more. But though his fame shall be known in Benwick as in all other places, he shall not bide here with you.'

And to Lancelot he said, 'When you come to be eighteen, before the next Feast of Eastertide, let you leave this place and go to King Arthur at Camelot, and pray him to make you a knight of the Round Table.'

Lancelot held himself very still, that he might not disturb the goshawk on his fist. 'Often has the King my father told me of Arthur Pendragon and how they fought side by side at Bedegraine; and the harpers sing of him beside our fire on winter nights. There is nothing in the world that I would rather do than go to him and ask my knighthood at his hands and serve him. But why should he think me worthy? I am all untried.'

'Maybe he will do it for the sake of the fighting that he and I saw together,' said King Ban, who had sat quietly looking on.

But Merlin said, 'Tell him that Merlin sent you; and that it was the last thing he did before he went to find his long sleep under the hawthorn tree. He will give you your knighthood. And your place at the Round Table.'

And the joy flashed in Lancelot's ugly face like a bright blade drawn from a battered sheath.

Merlin rose to go, and the Lady Nimue with him. But before she went, she drew close to Lancelot – so close that he thought it strange, remembering afterwards, that the goshawk did not bate from his fist nor strike at her – and she looked deep into his eyes, her own eyes changeful and water-bright, and again for a moment the mist seemed to rise and swirl inside his head.

'You who were first Galahad and are now Lancelot,' she said in a voice that made him see lake water lapping among feathered reeds, 'when you come to Arthur's court and receive your knighthood, let you take your third name as a gift from me, and call yourself thereafter Sir Lancelot of the Lake.'

And when the mist cleared from his head, they were both gone.

Then again Merlin and the Lady Nimue with him wandered through this place and that, across water and among mountains and through valleys and forests, Merlin teaching her the last of his magic as they went. And so they came at last to Cornwall, where King Marc now ruled in place of Duke Gorloise of Tintagel. And at the appointed time they came to the hawthorn tree, all curdled with white blossom and the scent of it coming and going like breath upon the evening air.

And Merlin lay down under the tree with his head in the Lady's lap; and she let down her straight dark hair so that it hung like a curtain about them both; and she made a singing magic. And listening to it, it was to Merlin as though he heard the humming of wild honey bees among the heather of the hills of his boyhood; and he sank into a sleep that was deeper and quieter than any sleep known to mortal man.

And when she saw that he was deep sunk in his enchanted sleep, the Lady of the Lake arose, and made another magic; a dancing magic this time, woven with her footsteps about and about and about the hawthorn tree. Nine times she circled the tree, and as she circled, a cave opened among the roots, and the grass and the stones and the twisted roots rose up and twined together and roofed it in, and closed the last opening, so that Merlin lay within, and nothing remained but the hawthorn tree growing on a stony mound, to show where he lay.

'Bide there until your waking time,' said the Lady Nimue when she had done, and she went her way.

Now at about the same time, King Arthur rode hunting in the forest that stretched west of Camelot into the mountains, and with him for hunting companions were Sir Accalon of Gaul, and King Uriens the husband of Morgan La Fay – for despite Merlin's repeated warnings that she was a witch and would do him any harm she might, Arthur loved to have his half-sister often about his court. They hunted for three days, making further and further west; and on the third day they put up a mighty hart, and hunted it so far and fast that, grievously, they all three killed their horses under them; a thing which can be done too easily in the heat of a long chase, a horse's heart being willing beyond its strength.

The day was drawing on to dusk, and they knew that the forest was no place for unmounted men at night, and so pushed on, hoping to find a hermitage or a charcoal burner's hut. And so they came out from the trees on to the margin of a broad lake; and on the shore of the lake the hart that they had hunted also lay dead, the hounds all about it. They whipped off the hounds, and stood for a moment looking down at the dead beast; and then Arthur set his horn to his lips and sounded the long sad notes of the Morte for the death of the hart, sending the echoes flying through the shadowy forest. And as the echoes died, the hounds turned and went streaming back the way they had come, as though their huntsman was with them.

And in that same moment, out from behind a spit of the alder-grown shore glided a small ship, and came of its own accord to the bank where the three stood, like a well-trained dog when its master whistles.

'Sirs,' said Arthur, 'let us go aboard this ship, for it is a sorry thing to turn away from an adventure when it comes so sweetly to the hand.'

So they stepped on board, and found the ship fine and beautiful and richly hung with silks, but seemingly with no one on board save for themselves.

And as soon as they had come aboard it drew off from the bank, for all that there was no hand at the steering oar, nor any to man the sails. And as they went, the dusk deepened towards night about them; and suddenly there sprang up the flames of a hundred torches all along the vessel's sides so that it was lit from stem to stern with a golden glow. And up from below came twelve damosels, the fairest that any of them had ever seen; and they greeted Arthur and his companions and made them joyously welcome and brought them such delicious food and such rare and fragrant wines that Arthur thought he had never supped so magnificently before. They were very hungry, and merry also, and when they had eaten their fill the damosels led them below, each to a chamber that had been made ready for them; and they lay down upon beds that were so soft that they seemed to float upon them as upon thick-piled clouds; and faint music whispered all about them mingled with the lap of water along the vessel's sides. And so they fell asleep, and slept unstirring the night long.

And in the morning King Uriens woke to find himself in his own bed in Camelot, and wondered in great amazement how he came to be there. And when he looked at his wife Morgan beside him, she lay still sleeping, but with a little smile on her face as though she knew a secret that she would not tell.

And King Arthur awoke to find himself in a dark and dismal dungeon, and heard about him the groans and complaints of many other men.

'Who are you that make such grievous complaint?' asked Arthur when he had gathered his wits about him.

'We are twenty knights who have lain here captive, some of us as much as seven years,' one of them answered him.

'For what cause?' said Arthur.

And another answered, 'Sir Damas, the lord of this castle, is a cruel and unjust tyrant who refuses his younger brother Sir Ontzlake his share of the inheritance they had from their father. And often Sir Ontzlake has offered to fight his brother in single combat for the lands that are his; but Sir Damas knows himself no match for him with lance or sword, and so would have the matter fought out by champions instead. But no knight that he has asked will stand champion for him; so he has taken a hatred against all knights, and captured in these past seven years all who have come within his lands, and cast them into this foul dungeon. Many of us have died here, and we who are left are like to go the same way unless help come soon.'

And even as he spoke there came a damosel down the dark stair, carrying a lamp, for little light of day could come into that place. And she said to Arthur, 'Fair sir, how is it with you?'

'I hardly know,' said Arthur, 'nor do I know how I came to be in this place.'

'It matters not how you came here,' said the damosel, 'you shall go free of it if you will but fight as champion for my father against the champion his brother sends to meet him this day, the victor to become the lord of all these lands.'

Arthur was silent. He had never before fought in an unjust cause; but he was young and the blood hot and rising like spring sap within him, and he thought of life shut away in that dark place far from the light of the sun, and the faces of his friends and the feel of a horse under him; and he thought too of the twenty men around him in the gloom.

'I will fight for the lord your father,' he said at last, 'if I have his promise upon oath that whether I win or lose, the twenty knights here with me shall go free.'

'You shall have his promise,' said the damosel.

'Then I am ready – if I had but horse and armour.'

'Horse and armour you shall have, none better in all the land.'

It seemed to Arthur, looking at her face in the upward light of the lamp, that he had seen her somewhere before. 'Were you ever at Arthur's court?' he asked.

'Nay, I am Sir Damas's daughter and nothing more. I was never at court,' said the damosel; and in that she lied, for she was one of the maidens of Morgan La Fay.

But Arthur believed her, for he was a simple and trusting man; and the little warning whisper that had begun at the back of his mind died away.

And he followed her up the stairs towards the clear light of day beyond the stairhead door.

At the same time as King Arthur woke in his dungeon, Sir Accalon of Gaul woke to find himself beside a deep well in the courtyard of an old strong manor house; so close beside the well that if he had so much as turned in his sleep he must have crashed to the bottom and found his death there. When he saw and understood, Sir Accalon thought, Now God help the King, and King Uriens also, for it must be that the damosels in the ship were creatures of some foul enchantment, not mortal maidens, and have betrayed us all; and if I come out from this adventure with my life I shall slay such witches wherever I meet them!

And at that moment came a dwarf, very ugly, with a great mouth and a flat nose that spread all across his face, and saluted him. 'Sir, I come to you from your love, from Queen Morgan La Fay herself.'

Now Sir Accalon did indeed love Morgan La Fay, better than all else in the world, not knowing that she was even as the damosels of the ship, a witch and a worker of dark enchantments. And his heart leapt within him, and he said, 'What would my lady with me, here in this strange place?'

'She begs you to fight for her against a knight whom she has good cause to hate for an ancient wrong he did her; and that you may fight the better, she sends you King Arthur's own sword Excalibur; and she bids you, if you truly love her, to do battle to the uttermost and show no mercy.'

Then Sir Accalon reached out and took from the dwarf the sword which he held across his hands. It seemed to him strange that she should send him Arthur's sword instead of his own; but he thought that maybe she had done so for the power that was in it. And anyway, wherever Arthur was, it would not harm him to use his sword for this one time. And he felt the power in the sword as though it had been a live thing in his hands, and rejoiced in it. 'Go back to Queen Morgan,' he said to the dwarf, 'and tell her I will fight for her as truly as ever a knight fought for his lady.'

Then six squires came and led Sir Accalon into the Hall of the manor house, and set food and drink before him, and then armed him, and set him upon a fine warhorse, and led him to a fair level field that was midway between the manor house of Sir Ontzlake and the fine castle of his brother.

And at the same time, six squires were doing the same thing for King Arthur. But to King Arthur, in the last moment before he mounted his horse, came another maiden, saying, 'Sir, your sister Morgan La Fay has dreamed that you are to do battle this day, and sends you your sword.'

And Arthur saw that she held Excalibur across her hands, and he unbuckled from his side the borrowed sword that he had belted on, and took his own sword to belt in its place. Then he mounted his horse and rode out, the squires and the twenty freed captives following after. He wished that it had been Guenever and not his sister who had dreamed of his danger and sent him his sword. But he never doubted that it was indeed Excalibur that he carried at his side.

So then, the champions came to the field, and found it ringed about with folk who had come to watch. Their vizors were closed, and both carried maiden shields with no device upon them, so neither knew who the other was. They jousted against each other until both were dismounted, and then fell to with their swords. And great and many were the blows they gave each other, and often the sword in Sir Accalon's hand found the weak points in Arthur's harness and drew blood; but however strong and sure the blows that Arthur gave in return, it seemed that they drew scarcely any blood at all. Then the truth began to wake in Arthur's mind; the sword in his hand was not Excalibur. There was no potency, no battle-power in it, and no protection in the scabbard at his side; and seeing the ground growing red with blood, and none of it his adversary's, he began to be sure that the other knight wielded the true Excalibur. But there was nothing he could do save fight his best with the sword he held. So he struggled on, growing weaker from loss of blood. At last, far spent, he drew back a way, to fetch his breath and find fighting ground that was not yet blood-slippery under foot; and Sir Accalon leapt after him, shouting, 'Nay, Sir Knight, this is no time to be taking your rest!'

Then in a sudden fury of near despair, Arthur stumbled to meet him, and by chance rather than skill, for he was past skill, smote him a side-cut on the helmet that almost brought him to the ground; but with the force of the blow Arthur's blade flew into a score of flashing sherds; and for the second time in his life he was left holding only a useless hilt.

Then Sir Accalon pulled off, and said, 'You are unarmed and have lost much blood, and I am loath to kill you. Therefore yield now to my mercy.'

'Nay!' cried Arthur. 'That I may not, for I have vowed to do battle while the life is yet in me, and I had sooner die a hundred deaths with honour than live without it! If you slay me weaponless, to you is the shame!'

'I will accept the shame,' said Accalon, and dealt him another mighty stroke; but Arthur took it on his shield, and stumbling forward dashed the heavy sword-hilt into his opponent's vizor with such desperate force that it sent him lurching three steps back.

Now among the gaily coloured crowd that thronged the edge of the field stood a lady who had not appeared until the fighting was well started, and no one had seen her come. The Lady Nimue, she who had given Arthur his sword, she who had left Merlin sleeping under his hawthorn tree, was late upon the scene, for time means little to the Lordly Ones, but she had known that the young King was in sore danger from his witch-sister that day, and she had come before it was too late.

And as Sir Accalon steadied himself and raised his sword for another blow, she made the smallest of flicking movements with the blade of grass that she was turning between her fingers, and the true Excalibur seemed to twist from the hand that held it, and landed at Arthur's feet.

Arthur flung aside the useless hilt and swooped upon it, and sprang back out of touch, with his own sword in his hand once more. 'You have been away from me too long,' he said, 'and sore damage have you done me!' And then, seeing the scabbard still hanging at Sir Accalon's side, Arthur flung away his shield, and plunged forward under the other's guard, and grasping it, dragged it free, bursting straps and buckles, and hurled it far behind him.

Then he leapt upon Sir Accalon and dealt him such a blow on the head that he crashed to the ground, the red life-blood bursting from his mouth and nose and ears.

Arthur stood over him with sword upraised. 'Now it is for me to slay you, unless you cry my mercy.'

'Slay me then,' groaned Sir Accalon, 'I never fought with a better knight, and I see that God is with you. But I swore to do battle with you to the uttermost, and therefore I cannot cry your mercy.'

And it seemed to Arthur that he knew the voice, which he had not had time to do before. And he lowered his blade and said, 'You are a valiant knight. Of what name and country are you?'

'I am of King Arthur's court, a knight of the Round Table, and my name is Accalon of Gaul.'

Then grief and dismay rose in Arthur, and he remembered the magic of last night's ship and the morning's awakening, and asked, 'Ah, Sir Accalon, how did you come by Excalibur?'

'I had it from Morgan La Fay, whom I have loved above all else these many years. This morning she

sent it to me, bidding me fight to the death for her
sake against a knight who should this day come
against me.' He groaned again with the pain of his
desperate hurts. 'But tell me, who are you whom she
would have had me slay?'

'Oh, Accalon,' said Arthur, 'I am your King.'

Then Accalon cried out, for grief at what his lady
would have done more than for any other thing.
'Fair, sweet lord, now I cry your mercy, for we are
both betrayed, and I did not know you.'

'How should you?' said Arthur. 'Alas, all this is the
doing of my sister. Again and again Merlin warned
me against her, telling me what she was, and what
she would seek to do; but still I trusted her and
delighted to have her about my court. But never
again,' said Arthur in a weeping voice, 'never again.'

Then all the people gathered about the field came
and knelt to the High King, crying his mercy also;
and Arthur gave it to them, and summoned together
Sir Damas and Sir Ontzlake, and made judgement
between them, that Sir Damas should give over to his
brother all the manors and estates that were his by
inheritance, but that Sir Ontzlake should pay fee for
them with the yearly gift of a palfrey. 'For that,' said
Arthur in contempt, 'is a more fitting steed than a
warhorse for such as you, Sir Damas the Valiant!' And
he laid upon Sir Damas also that he should return to
the twenty knights their weapons and armour and let
them go free, and never again lay hand upon stray
knights who came by following their own
adventures.

And Sir Ontzlake he bade come to him presently at court.

Then, learning that there was an abbey of nuns nearby, he mounted, and with Sir Accalon drooping in the saddle beside him, he rode that way.

At the abbey they rested, and their wounds were tended. But from that last great blow dealt by Excalibur, Sir Accalon had lost so much blood that on the third day he died. Arthur recovered well and quickly, and in cold rage he had his friend's body laid on a horse-bier, and summoned six knights from Sir Damas's castle, and said, 'Now bear this to my sister, Queen Morgan La Fay, and tell her that I send it to her for a gift. And tell her also that I have my sword Excalibur again.'

Meanwhile, at Camelot, Morgan La Fay, knowing nothing of what had passed, thought that Arthur must by now be dead, and once she was wedded to Sir Accalon of Gaul they could seize the throne of Britain between them as she had always had it in her dark mind to do. And seeing King Uriens asleep on their bed, she decided that the time had come for the next thing that must be done. So she called to her softly one of her maidens, and said, 'Go, fetch me the King's sword.'

And the maiden looked into her face and saw the smile upon it and the darkly glittering eyes, and cried out in horror, 'Madam, no! No, I beg of you! If you slay your lord, you will never escape!'

'That is not a thing you need to trouble for,' said

the Queen. 'This is the day and the time I chose long since. Go now and fetch the sword.'

But the damosel fled to Sir Uwaine, the Queen's son, who was newly made a knight of the Round Table, and begged him, 'Come quickly to my lady your mother, for she is set upon slaying the King your father, and has sent me to fetch his sword that she may do it while he sleeps in his bed!'

'Go swiftly and do as she bids you,' said Sir Uwaine. 'I will see to the rest.'

So in a little while the damosel brought the sword and gave it with shaking hands into the steady hands her mistress held out for it. And Morgan La Fay took the sword and unsheathed it, never seeing that Uwaine had come in behind the damosel and remained hidden in the shadows of the hangings by the chamber door. And she stood for three breaths of time looking down at the sleeping man and deciding which would be the best place to strike. But as she swung up the heavy blade for the death blow, Uwaine sprang from his hiding place and seized her sword-hand and wrenched it aside; and as she whirled round to face him, he stood there panting, with a face like one that had taken his own death blow. 'Fiend!' he shouted. 'What would you do? If you were not my mother, and would God that you were not, I would plunge this sword now into your heart.'

'Nay, but the fiends of Hell tempted me!' cried his mother. 'It was their doing, not mine – and see, the madness has passed from me. Oh, sweet son of mine, have mercy, and I promise that never again will I listen to their evil whisperings in my ear.'

'Swear!' said Uwaine.

And shaking and shuddering under his merciless gaze, the Queen swore; and the young knight sheathed his father's sword and turned and walked away.

Towards the end of that day came the six knights with Sir Accalon's body and the High King's message.

Then Morgan La Fay's heart almost broke within her, for she had indeed loved Sir Accalon in her fashion, and it was more than her hopes of usurping the crown of Britain that lay dead upon his bier. But she hid her grief for her own safety; and knowing that if she were still at court when Arthur returned all the gold of the Hollow Hills would not buy her life, she contrived to learn from one of the knights where it was that her brother lay; and before full dawn next day she sent for her horse from the stables, and saying that she wanted none with her save certain of her ladies, she rode away.

She rode all that day and part of the night, and by noon of the next day came to the abbey where Arthur lay not yet fully mended from his wounds.

She asked of the Lady Abbess where the King might be, and was told that he was sleeping. 'Then do not wake him,' she said fondly. 'But I am his sister, and have ridden far to be with him, hearing of his wounds. Therefore I will sit with him a while, and maybe wake him myself later.'

And since she was his sister, neither the holy ladies

of the abbey nor the knight who kept watch before his chamber door thought to deny her. So she went in.

I cannot slay him, she thought, or only at the cost of my own life, with all these about him. But at least I can steal away Excalibur, and later maybe have him at my mercy. But when she crossed to the bed, she saw that though Arthur was indeed asleep, he lay with Excalibur gripped in his right hand. Only one hope of harming him remained to her. The blade in his hand was naked. She looked about and found the scabbard lying on a great carved chest at the foot of the bed. She knew the powers of the scabbard as well as Merlin had done; and she took it up and hid it in the folds of her mantle. It was less than she had hoped for, but it was better than nothing.

Then she sat beside the bed for a while, lest any should look in. And presently she rose and went out, saying to those in the outer chamber that the King slept so sweetly it would be a sorry thing to wake him. And so she mounted her horse and rode away, her ladies following.

Presently Arthur awoke and found his scabbard gone. He demanded in anger to know who had come beside him while he slept. And when they told him Morgan La Fay, he cried out on them, 'Falsely have you kept your watch over me!'

'Sir,' said the Lady Abbess, 'we dared not disobey your own sister's command.'

Then Arthur called for his armour and his horse, and for Sir Ontzlake to arm and come to him. And when Sir Ontzlake came in all haste, they rode out after Morgan La Fay.

Within a while Arthur caught sight of his sister far ahead, with her damosels all about her, and struck spurs to his horse to ride her down. But she, finding him hard behind her, spoke in her horse's ear, and sent it forward, fleet-footed as a Faery steed, and all her damosels streaming after her. But Arthur and Ontzlake were not to be easily shaken off, however fast she fled through the forest ways; and as she came at last skirting the margin of a dark lake among the trees, she cried out within herself, 'Whatever comes to me, at least my brother shall not have his scabbard to protect him again!' and flung the gleaming thing out into the centremost depths, where it sank at once, borne down by its weight of gold and jewels.

She knew now where she must go for refuge, and in a while, riding her desperate race with the hunt hard behind, she burst out from the trees into an open valley set about with many great stones standing in the grass. And there she made a swift and urgent magic. And when the magic was made, suddenly in the blink of an eye, there were seven more great stones in the valley than there had been before; and of Morgan La Fay and her ladies, no sign.

And the King, following on, saw what had happened and, when he could not even make out which of the stones were his sister and her ladies, thought that it was the vengeance of God, and despite his anger was even a little sorry for their fate. He hunted the valley for his lost scabbard, Sir Ontzlake helping him; but at last gave up the search and went heavily away, with none of the triumph in his heart that he felt he had a right to.

And when he had left the valley, Queen Morgan La Fay turned herself and her maidens back into their own likeness again, and said, 'Now, my damosels, we may go where we will.'

Arthur never found his scabbard again, and so had to have another made to sheathe Excalibur. It was as rich and beautiful as the old one had been, but it had no special virtue; and from that day forward, when he was wounded he bled as other men bleed.

Arthur, with Sir Ontzlake at his side, rode wearily back to Camelot, and there Queen Guenever and all the court were greatly rejoiced to see them.

But on the very first evening of the King's return, as they sat at meat in the Great Hall, there entered a damosel bearing a mantle of cloth of gold soft and heavy with furs and sparked with precious stones; the most splendid mantle that anyone there had ever seen. And she brought it to King Arthur and bowed before him. 'My Lord King, your sister Morgan La Fay sends me to beg your forgiveness for the evil that she has done, and to promise you truly that the evil spirits that tempted her have departed from her; and she will seek to harm you no more, and to show her sorrow for what she sought to do, she sends you this mantle, begging that you will wear it often, and find pleasure in it.'

Arthur looked at the mantle and saw how

beautiful it was, and he thought that maybe the evil had indeed gone out of his sister – always he was over-trusting. And he put out his hand to accept the gift. But before he could touch it, there was a swift movement among the ladies in the Hall, and he dropped his hand and looked around. And the Lady Nimue, who nobody had seen enter, was standing at his side. 'Sir,' she said, 'do not put on the mantle, nor touch it, nor let it come near any of your knights, until you have first seen it upon the shoulders of her who brings it to you.'

Arthur looked at her a moment, and saw through her shape-shifting – maybe she let him see – that she was that Lady of the Lake whom Merlin had loved, and who had given him his sword Excalibur. And he remembered Merlin saying, 'The Lordly Ones are not good or evil, any more than the rains that swells the barley or washes the field away, they simply *are*.' And then he seemed to be not remembering Merlin's voice, but hearing it afresh, speaking in his ear, 'Trust her. Whatever she is, *you* may always trust her. For a while, she is your fate as well as mine.'

The voice was silent, and Arthur saw that his knights were looking at him strangely, as though wondering why he stood listening while no one spoke.

Then he said, 'Lady, I accept your counsel.' And to his sister's messenger, 'Damosel, I would see this mantle first upon you.'

'Nay, sir,' she said quickly. 'It would ill become me to wear a king's mantle.'

'Nevertheless, you shall wear this one, before ever the King puts it about his shoulders,' said Arthur, and he made a sign to two squires standing nearby; and they seized the damosel and the mantle, and by force wrapped it close about her. And in that same moment, while she screamed and struggled, there was a bright flame of fire that leapt up between the squires' hands almost to lick the roof of the Great Hall, and of the damosel and the mantle nothing was left but a little smoking ash upon the ground.

From that time forward Morgan La Fay never dared to seek to do Arthur harm, but fled to her husband's kingdom of Gore, to a castle of her own that she had there, and fortified it strongly, and there she stayed. And so the kingdom was rid of one more of its enemies.

6

SIR LANCELOT OF THE LAKE

Just as the High King and his knights were about to sit down to supper on the eve of Easter, one of Arthur's squires came to him, saying that there was a stranger at the threshold who wished for speech with him but would not give his name. And Arthur looked away down the Hall and saw a young man standing in the doorway, and said, 'Bring him to me. It may be that he will tell *me* his name.'

So the young man came up the Hall and knelt wordlessly at the King's feet. He was a raw-boned and very ugly young man, with two sides to his face that did not match each other, so that one side of his mouth ran straight and sullen and the other lifted towards joy and laughter, and one of his black brows was level as a falcon's wing and one flew wild and ragged like the jaunty ear of a mongrel that has just come well out of a fight. But out from under those brows looked a pair of wide grey eyes that the King thought were the steadiest that he had ever seen.

'Who are you?' Arthur said. 'And for what purpose do you come to me?'

And the young man said, 'I am Lancelot, son of King Ban of Benwick, who fought beside you at

Bedegraine. And I come because I have wished to for as long as I can remember, and because Merlin bade me, to ask for knighthood at your hands. He bade me tell you that I was his last bequest to you before he went to find his long sleep under his hawthorn tree.'

'Knighthood you shall have, on tomorrow's morning, the fair morning of Eastertide,' Arthur said; and gave his hand to the ugly young man, who bent his head for a moment to touch his forehead upon it.

'I thank you, sir,' said Lancelot; and then he turned a little, and Arthur saw that a russet-haired young man had come quietly up behind him. 'Sir, here stands my cousin and good friend Lional, who came with me to be my squire; but he is at least as worthy of knighthood as I am myself.'

And the King looked at the russet-haired squire, and said, 'What says Lional as to that? Would you also be made knight upon Easter morning?'

'I would be made knight,' said Lional, 'but not on Easter morning; for then how could I play squire to my cousin Lancelot at the same time? I would not that some strange squire should see to his armour, and attend him through the ceremony.'

'That is well spoken,' said the King. 'You shall serve him as squire for three days, and if you are a good squire, you shall come to your knighthood on the fourth.'

For he liked the seeming of the young man, and beside Lancelot's own seat and the other three that waited, there were already empty places at the Round Table, whose knights had fallen during the past year; and those places must be filled. There would always be empty places, he realised suddenly, as though it were something he had not known before; and always they must be filled . . .

So all that night young Lancelot kept his vigil in the castle chapel, kneeling at the chancel steps with his sword and his armour laid before the altar in front of him. And all night long he prayed, and watched the moonlight through the high window move silverly across his harness, and prayed again, and thought long thoughts that he could not have shared with anyone.

Now Lancelot was as odd and ill-matching in his hidden inmost self as he was in his face for all to see. And maybe because of those strange lost years in his childhood, he always felt as though he was searching for something. He never felt he was quite like other boys; quite like other men. He had a great and terrible hope in him, more fitted to a monk than to a knight, that one day, if he proved himself worthy, God would let him perform a miracle. But for that to happen, he would have to be the best knight in all the world. So kneeling there in the moon-whitened chapel all night long, he prayed that he should become not just the strongest and bravest and most skilled knight, but the best. He prayed that he might never do anything to stain his honour or anybody else's; and he prayed for his miracle.

And the moon sank and the sun rose, and when the proper ceremonies of bath and arming were over, he received his knighthood from King Arthur in the Great Hall on Easter morning.

And after, two of the Queen's ladies buckled on his knightly spurs. But Queen Guenever herself buckled on his sword-belt; and this she did partly because he was a king's son, but mostly in kindness, because she had heard Sir Kay, the King's foster brother and Seneschal, sneering to another knight about the newcomer's ill looks and saying that he would not likely find a maiden's favour to wear on his crest at the jousts and tournaments.

The buckle was stiff, and though she was well used to fastening Arthur's sword-belt for him, the Queen found it hard to make the tang go into the right place. And Lancelot, seeing this, put his own hand to help her, and so their fingers touched – and instantly they looked up from the buckle into each other's eyes. And having looked, they did not know how to look away again. They both paled to curd white and the black pupils of their eyes grew enormous. For a long moment it seemed that nothing moved or sounded in the Hall, and even the fire on the hearth stopped crackling. Then they pulled their eyes away from each other, and Guenever finished securing the buckle. But her fingers were shaking.

During the next three days there was a certain muttering and complaining among some of the knights, led by Sir Kay, that a man so young and all untried as yet should have been knighted and given a place at the Round Table. And afterwards men thought this was the reason that Lancelot set off so soon on his first quest. They thought that he went to prove himself, and to quiet the muttering. And Lancelot let them think it; but he had another reason. On the first evening after his cousin Lional had been made a knight also, when supper was over in the Great Hall and the King and Sir Gawain were playing chess, he fell, without knowing it, to watching the Queen as she sat with the torchlight meshed in her dark hair, listening with her chin cupped in her hand to an old song that the King's harper was singing.

'Aye, is she not fair?' said Lional softly beside him. 'Surely she would be the fairest damosel in all this Court, if she were not the Queen.'

And Sir Lancelot said, 'Yes' and began instead to watch his own hands. And in a little, he said, 'I shall ask the King's leave to go on a quest.'

'Let me ride with you,' said his kinsman.

And as soon as the game of chess was over, Lancelot went and knelt before the King and asked leave to ride out next morning in quest of adventure, his cousin Lional with him.

The King looked at him a moment and then said, 'Pay no heed to them. Sir Kay was an unhappy boy and he's an unhappy man, and I fear me he always will be.'

'As to that,' said Lancelot, 'I do not care greatly whether Sir Kay thinks me worthy of my knighthood and my place at the Round Table, but I care whether I think myself worthy of them.'

So King Arthur gave him leave for the quest, and Lional also, and next morning after hearing Mass they rode out in search of whatever adventures awaited them.

And adventures they were like to find in plenty, for although the Sea-wolves and the men from the dark North and the western mountains had been over-come and driven back to their own places, the land was not quiet, for the long years of warfare had left behind them much unrest. There were many lords who had come to think that the strong arm was all that mattered, and right was the same thing as might. And as the months of spring and summer passed, Sir Lancelot and his cousin met and fought with many such, and overcame them. And when they were defeated and cried his mercy, Sir Lancelot would make them swear to be the High King's men thence-forth, and send them to swear fealty to Arthur. But sometimes the battle was to the death, as it was when he met with a certain Sir Carrados. Sir Carrados would not cry quarter, and Sir Lancelot slew him after a mighty battle, and freed the captives he was holding to ransom in his tower. And then he rode on his way, seeking the next thing.

But the time was to come when he would remember Sir Carrados.

Meanwhile, on a day of late summer when the air shimmered like a midge cloud with the heat, the two cousins came to a great old apple tree heavy with half-ripe fruit, that grew close beside a hedge. They were far over on the very borders of the land of Gore, though they did not know it. The shade lay deep and cool under the tree, and Lancelot, who was weary with riding and fighting and the aching heart that he carried within him for Guenever's sake, felt a great desire to lie down in that shade and sleep. So they dismounted, knee-hobbled the horses and turned them free to graze, then lay down themselves in the blissful coolth of the long grass under the apple boughs.

Almost at once Lancelot was asleep, his head on his helm for a pillow. But lying beside him, Lional could not sleep, and in a while he sat up again, and propped his back against the apple trunk, and sat there chewing grass stems and idly watching the horses graze.

Presently he heard the hoof-beats of other horses, hard ridden, and looking out over the open country before him, he saw three knights riding for their lives, and behind them a fourth in hot pursuit, who was the biggest and most powerful looking knight Lional had ever seen, and riding a warhorse that made the horses of the other three look no more than jennets. And even as Lional watched, he reached and overtook the first of the fleeing knights and struck him to the ground, then thundered on to serve the second and the third in the same way. Then he dismounted and, leading his own horse, returned on his tracks and flung each fallen knight across the back of his own mount, bound him there with his own reins, and then remounting, rode on, driving the three shamefully before him.

Sir Lional got up quietly and laced on his helm, taking care not to waken his cousin; for all that summer Lancelot had had most of the fighting, and he thought, Now this is surely my adventure; and if I can overcome this knight and free his captives, I shall win much honour. So he freed his horse's hobbles and, mounting, rode hard after the little group now almost lost in the late summer haze.

Riding hard, he overtook them at last, and shouted to the huge knight to halt.

The other turned without a word, and setting his lance in rest came charging back upon Sir Lional, and got in a blow to the shoulder-piece that hove him backwards clean over his horse's crupper; then he dismounted, bound Sir Lional and slung him over his own saddle, just as he had done with the others, and rode on, driving the four horses ahead of him. And when he reached his own manor, he had them stripped and beaten with thorn branches, and then flung into a stone chamber deep underground, where there were many doleful knights that he had taken captive at other times.

Now a short while before this, Ector of the Marsh, Lancelot's half-brother, had arrived at Camelot, craving knighthood; and finding Lancelot and Lional both away on quest, he asked leave to follow them, and rode out on his search. For a while he searched in vain, until one day he met with a forester, and knowing that wherever there was promise of adventure, there his kinsmen would be most likely found, he enquired, 'Good fellow, is there any place near here where adventure is to be had for the asking?'

'That there is, Sir Knight,' returned the forester.

'Not more than a mile from here there stands the strong fortified manor house of Sir Tarquine; and close by the house the river runs over a ford – a good place for horses to drink – and over the ford there leans a great willow tree, and from the branches of the tree there hang the shields of many knights who Sir Tarquine has overthrown and flung into a dungeon beneath his house. On this tree also hangs a basin of finest copper. Beat upon it with the butt of your spear, and Sir Tarquine himself will come out to fight with you. And may the good God be gentle with your soul.'

Sir Ector thanked the man, and rode on by the way that he had pointed out, until soon he came to the ford, and saw the ancient willow tree leaning over it; and hanging from the branches many shields, some of them rusted and weather-worn, others bright and new; and among them the shield of his cousin Lional. The anger rose in his throat, and seeing the copper basin, he beat upon it with the butt of his spear until all the forest rang and the wood pigeons clattered up from the trees. Then, since no one came, he rode knee-deep into the ford to let his horse drink. And while he was still in the water a great voice cried out to him from the bank, 'Sir Knight! Since you have summoned me, come up from the water and make ready to joust with me!'

Striking spurs to his horse, Sir Ector came plunging up from the ford, setting his spear in rest as he came, and charged the huge knight he saw waiting and ready for him on the bank with such dash and fury that he got in a blow which sent horse and rider plunging round in a full circle.

'That was well struck! A knightly blow!' said Sir Tarquine, and he laughed, and charged Sir Ector in his turn, and got him under the arm and lifted him clean out of the saddle and bore him away at a plunging gallop through his gates and across his courtyard and into his hall and flung him down all asprawl on the rush-strewn floor. 'Now you are at my mercy,' said the huge knight. 'Do you cry quarter?'

'Never!' said Sir Ector through his teeth.

'You shall have it, none the less; prisonment instead of death, for your boldness pleases me,' said Sir Tarquine; and he called his servants and men-at-arms and had Sir Ector stripped and beaten with thorn branches and flung into the dark stone place beneath the house. And there he found many knights before him, the owners of the shields he had seen hanging from the willow tree. And among them Sir Lional.

When they had greeted each other, sorrowfully enough, Sir Ector said, 'But tell me, where is Sir Lancelot my brother, for it was told me that you two rode together.'

'Alas!' said Sir Lional. 'I left him sleeping under an apple tree this very noon, when I rode off to follow the tyrant lord of this place. And for all I know, he sleeps there still.'

★

And under the apple tree meanwhile, Sir Lancelot lay sleeping until well into the afternoon. And while he slept, there came by four queens riding on white mules, and with four mounted knights in attendance on them, holding up a canopy of green silk upon the points of spears to shield their delicate complexions from the sun. And as they came near, Lancelot's horse caught the scent of the others and whinnied; and looking that way, they beheld a knee-hobbled warhorse, and hard by, a knight sleeping under an apple tree, fully armed save that his helm was off and serving him for a pillow. And one of them – it was Morgan La Fay – knew him by her magic powers. 'It is Sir Lancelot of the Lake,' she said, 'he that shall be the greatest of all my brother's knights.'

Then all four queens looked down at his sleeping face, seeing in its ugliness what most women saw in it all his life, and began to quarrel over which of them should have him for her lover.

'We need not bide here making war over him,' said Morgan La Fay at last. 'I will cast a web of sleep upon him, that he shall not wake for three hours, and we will carry him back to my castle; and when he wakes, he shall choose among us for himself.' For in her own dark heart she was sure that she had more beauty than the other three, and that if her beauty failed her she could win him to her by her spells.

So she dismounted, and kneeling beside him made the spell of sleeping, and laid it upon him with her two forefingers touching his closed eyes. And when she was mounted again, the knights laid Lancelot,

sleeping now as deeply as Merlin beneath his hawthorn tree, upon his own shield, and so bore him
between them, his own horse following aft, back to
the Queen's castle, that was called the Castle Chariot,
and laid him sleeping still upon a pallet bed in one of
the castle dungeons.

When Lancelot awoke and found himself in his
strange prison, he found also a young maiden
standing beside him with a platter of bread and meat
and a cup of wine.

'How is it with you, Sir Knight?' she asked, kindly
enough.

And Sir Lancelot looked about him in bewilderment and said, 'How did I come to be in this place,
when I fell asleep under an apple tree?'

'Nay, there is no time now for words,' said the
maiden. 'Make what cheer you may; and you shall
know more in the morning.' And her voice was soft,
for she was sorry for a young knight in the clutches
of her mistress and her mistress's fellow queens. And
she went away.

Lancelot did not touch his food, but lay hungry
and wakeful and afraid and raging through the night.

In the morning the door opened again and the
four queens came in, dressed each of them in her
fairest silks and sparkling with her brightest jewels.
And one of them, still beautiful but as old as his
mother at home in Benwick – he did not know that
she was Morgan La Fay – said to him, 'Ah, Sir Lancelot of the Lake, we know you, though you do not
know us; we know that you are a king's son, and

fated to be the greatest of all King Arthur's knights, and we know that there is one woman only in your heart, and she King Arthur's Queen. Yet now, you shall lose her and she shall lose you, for you shall never leave this place alive unless you choose one of us to be your love in her stead.' And she smiled and arched her neck, sleek and purring as a well-fed cat, sure of what his choice would be. 'Choose, then, sweet knight.'

'This is a hard choice that you set before me,' Sir Lancelot said, standing before them, 'to die or to choose one of you for my love. Yet I do not find it hard to make. If it must be so, I will die in this place, rather than take one of you to my heart, for you are all false enchantresses, and with death at least I shall not lose my honour. As for the Queen, my Lady Guenever – give me back my horse and harness and I will prove in combat with any champion you may bring against me, that she is the truest lady to her lord the King that ever lived!'

'So you refuse us?' said Morgan La Fay, and she narrowed her eyes like a cat's before it spits. 'You refuse *me*?'

And they turned and swept out, trailing the scent of musk and rose-oil behind them; and the prison door clanged shut once more.

Presently, when the light through the small high windows showed that the day was drawing towards evening, the young damosel returned with more meat and bread and wine, which she set down on the wooden stool beside the bed, and asked Sir Lancelot again, 'How is it with you?'

'I think that it was never so ill with me as it is now,' said Sir Lancelot, 'for I have gained the anger of the four queens who hold me here, and they will be quick to take some ugly revenge unless I can escape from them.'

The maiden looked at the food that she had just set down, and sighed a little. 'That is true, for I have heard them talking; and for refusing their love indeed they love you not!' And then, as though making up her mind all in a breath, she turned and looked into Lancelot's face. 'Indeed it grieves me to see you in the power of these queens, for they have been the downfall of many good knights. I have no love for them nor duty to them, and I will help you, if you in turn will help me.'

Lancelot returned her look searchingly, wondering if he could trust her, and thought he could. 'Help me to escape,' he said, 'and I will do whatever you ask of me, if it be not against my honour.'

'Then, sir, my father King Bagdemagus has cried a tournament for next Tuesday, between himself and the King of Northgalis, whose queen is one of the four who hold you here. A great tournament of many knights, and at the last such tournament three of those who are to fight on Tuesday overthrew my father. Fight on his side that day, and I will contrive your escape.'

'I have heard of your father as a good knight and a

just ruler,' said Sir Lancelot, 'and gladly I will fight in his ranks at this tournament.'

'Then tomorrow morning before light, I will come for you and lead you out of this place, and bring you your horse and armour.'

Next morning the maiden returned with a great bunch of keys in her hand. 'I have given drugged wine to the guards,' she said, 'but they will not sleep long. Therefore come quickly!'

And she led Sir Lancelot out by twelve locked doors; and the last door of all was a narrow postern in the curtain-wall of the castle, so that outside it was the scent of the forest in the early morning, and the scent of freedom. Then she brought him across the open ground to a hidden place among the elder and wayfaring trees of the forest verge where his horse and armour were waiting for him, and helped him to arm and mount.

'Twelve miles north of this place,' she said, 'there is an abbey of Dominican monks. Wait for me there and I will bring my father to you.'

'By the grace of God, I shall not fail you,' said Sir Lancelot, and he urged his horse forward into the forest ways.

Towards evening, he came to the abbey, and the brethren made him welcome and stabled his horse and gave him supper and a place to sleep. And there he remained two days, waiting for the coming of King Bagdemagus. And on the third day came the maiden with the King her father and a brave company of knights. And that was on the Sunday;

and on the Tuesday they rode together to the chosen tournament ground where the King of Northgalis and his knights waited for them, in a fair open meadow set about with pavilions striped and chequered in all the colours of a summer garden. And there, Sir Lancelot fought so nobly and so strongly among the knights of King Bagdemagus – none knowing who he was, for he carried the white shield, the Virgescue as men call it, such as knights carry who have as yet no device of their own – that he brought down three knights of the Round Table as well as many others, and King Bagdemagus was accounted the victor in that tournament.

And when Sir Lancelot had spared the lives of those knights he had brought down, he bade them go and swear fealty to King Arthur, saying that the Nameless Knight had sent them. And this he did because he would have no ill feeling between himself and his fellows of the Round Table.

And when the day was over, he returned to their own castle with King Bagdemagus and the maiden his young daughter, who could never of course return to her place as one of Morgan's handmaidens, after aiding Lancelot to escape. And there they made him warmly welcome and offered him many rich gifts. But these he would not accept, saying, 'Nay, the thing was a straight bargain between your daughter and me, and each of us has kept our side of it.'

And in the morning, he took his leave, for he had no thought now but to go in search of Sir Lional his cousin, who had disappeared from him while he slept under the apple tree. But at parting, he said to the King's daughter, 'If ever you should have need of my aid again, pray you let me know of it, and I will not fail you if I be yet living.'

And he rode away, never knowing that the King's daughter stood looking after him with the salt taste of her own tears on her lips.

For many days Sir Lancelot rode about the forest while the blackberries ripened on the bramble domes and the first gold kindled among the green fronds of the bracken, but could never come by any word of his cousin, until one day, following a narrow path among the trees, he came up with the forester whom Sir Ector had met, and asked him much the same question as Sir Ector had asked him, and received much the same reply. And so he came at last to the fortified manor house beside the ford, and the great willow tree leaning over the water, and the shields hanging like strange fruit from its drooping branches; and among them he saw the shields of his cousin Lional and his half-brother Ector.

Sir Lancelot rode in among the branches, and finding the copper basin, beat on it with the butt of his spear until the bottom fell out. But nobody came. He watered his horse at the ford, and then rode to and fro before the gates of the manor, working up a fret that made his horse fidget under him. At last he saw far off along the woodshore a huge knight in full armour and mounted on the tallest warhorse he had ever seen, and driving before him another horse with a knight lying bound across its saddle. And as they came nearer, Sir Lancelot recognised the device on the shield hanging from the saddlebow of the captive knight, and so knew him for Sir Gaheris, the younger brother of Sir Gawain.

So he turned from the manor gateway and rode to meet them. 'Fair sir!' shouted Sir Lancelot, 'set that wounded knight down off his horse and let him rest, while we two try our strength against each other, for you have caused shame and suffering enough to my brothers of the Round Table. Therefore defend yourself!'

'Willingly,' shouted back Sir Tarquine. 'The more so if you be of that fellowship. I defy you and all your brothers!'

'That is enough of words,' said Sir Lancelot, 'now is the time for fighting!'

And Sir Tarquine turned loose the horse with Sir Gaheris across its saddle, and he and Lancelot drew apart the length of the broad meadow before the manor house and, setting their spears in rest, pricked their horses to a gallop, and came thundering together, so that their spears, taking each other in the centre of the shield, brought each other crashing down, horses and riders both.

And when they had rolled clear of their horses' threshing hooves, they drew swords and came together again like a pair of stags in October, and so they battled, with great swinging strokes that cleaved each other's armour and drew blood wherever they found a joint, until the best part of two hours was gone by, and both were spent and weary, and drew off a space, leaning on their swords.

'You are the best and strongest knight that ever I fought with,' said Sir Tarquine, his breath coming and going heavy through the slits of his vizor. 'And ever I have loved a good fighter. I will strike hands with you, and free into your keeping all of the knights that lie captive in my hold – so that ye be any knight but one, in all the world.'

'And what knight is that?' asked Sir Lancelot.

'Sir Lancelot of the Lake; he who slew my brother Sir Carrados whom I have sworn to avenge.'

'Alas!' said Sir Lancelot. 'I am that one knight in all the world! I slew Sir Carrados in fair fight, but if you have sworn vengeance for him, then what must be must be.'

'That is sure,' said Sir Tarquine, 'and never we two shall part from each other or from this place until one of us be dead.'

So they fell again to their fighting, both blind and stumbling-weary as they were; and at last Sir Tarquine's guard wavered and went down; and Sir Lancelot, dropping his own shield, leapt in and seized him by the helmet-crest and got in a swinging blow to the neck that almost hacked his head from his shoulders. And Sir Tarquine fell with a clash and clatter of armour that echoed to the treetops of the forest.

Then Sir Lancelot went to Sir Gaheris and unbound him, and finding him not too sorely wounded, bade him go to the manor house and set free the knights held captive there. 'And I pray you greet them all from Sir Lancelot of the Lake, and bid them in all courtesy to ride to King Arthur's court before next Eastertide; and at Eastertide I will come and join them there.'

And while Sir Gaheris went up to the manor and threw down the doorkeeper who would have barred his way, and set the captives free, Sir Lional and Sir Ector and Sir Kay among many more, Sir Lancelot washed his hurts in the cold clear water of the ford, then whistled up his horse and rode on his way in search of more adventure.

Hither and yon he rode, while the forests flamed with autumn that chilled to the black and white of winter. And he rescued many damosels out of their distress, and overcame many evil knights, and met with adventures many and strange, while the year grew colder and he had no shelter from the winter rain and nowhere to lay his head at night.

One bitter cold evening when the year was drawing on towards Christmas, with the sun setting red behind the trees and frost already making his horse's hooves to ring upon the ground, he came to a fair manor house, and when he asked shelter for the night from the aged gentlewoman who was the mistress of the place, she welcomed him kindly and saw that his horse was fed and bestowed in a warm stable; and when she had given Sir Lancelot a fine filling supper – for she judged that she knew what boys' appetites were like, and he was little more – she took him to a warm dry garret over the gate, where a bed of last summer's hay, smelling still of clover and sweet fescue grass, was spread with sheets of clean rough linen and thick rugs. And when she was gone, Sir Lancelot took off his armour and clad in his shirt and breeches lay between the sheets and was soon asleep.

He had not slept long when he was awakened by the ring of hoof-beats on the iron-hard ground, a horse ridden at desperate speed, and then a beating on the gate. Sir Lancelot tumbled out of bed and peered down from the window. The world was white with moonlight, and the ground and the ledges of the gatehouse walls were all asparkle with frost, and by the light he saw a knight with his horse backed against the gate, desperately defending himself against three more.

'Three against one is no fair match,' said Lancelot to himself, 'no matter what the rights or wrongs of the case!' There would be no time to rouse the household. Everyone he had seen that evening was as old as its mistress, and like enough deaf. He whipped the sheets from the bed and, knotting them together, tied one end to the window transom and flung the rest out through the window; then snatched up his sword Joyeux from where it lay beside the bed. He flung his shield clanging down among the attacking knights, and climbing through the window, plunged after it by means of the makeshift rope. 'If you would fight three to one,' he roared, 'then fight with me!'

They had given back a little at his down-rush,

and dismounting from their startled horses, they did indeed turn upon Sir Lancelot, pressing in upon him and their original quarry from all sides. But Lancelot had snatched up his fallen shield, and used it with such skill that it was like another weapon and behind it he was almost as well covered as a man in armour; and he set his back to the stout timbers of the gate, and laughed, and drove them off. The fugitive knight would have shared the fight with him, but Sir Lancelot shouted him back, 'Nay, three to one they wanted, three to one let them have. Do you leave them alone to me!' And the other, seeming all too glad to obey, pulled his horse aside and took no more part in the fight.

And with six more strokes of Joyeux, that sliced through their helmet-crests and juddered the teeth in their heads but did them no more harm, Lancelot had felled all three.

Scrambling slowly and painfully back to their knees, while he stood leaning on his sword and breathing a little quickly, they all cried out, 'Sir, we yield to your mercy, as a man of matchless might!'

But Sir Lancelot had had time to glance at the fugitive's shield, and knew by the device on it that he was Sir Kay. And then he knew why he had fled so fast and stood aside so readily from the fight, for Sir Kay the Seneschal was in truth no great fighting man. And the laughter rose in Lancelot's throat, and he swallowed it, and said, 'Nay, but I do not choose that you should yield to me. Yield therefore to Sir Kay here instead.'

Then the three knights were crestfallen indeed. 'Sir,' said one of them, 'we chased Sir Kay here, and we would have overcome him easily had you not joined the tourney. Therefore why should we yield to him?'

'Because if you do not,' said Sir Lancelot simply, 'I shall take it that you refuse to yield to mercy, and I shall kill you.'

So they yielded to Sir Kay.

'Now,' said Lancelot, 'you shall betake you to Camelot, to the King's court at Eastertide, and you shall swear fealty to Queen Guenever, and put you all at her grace and mercy, saying that Sir Kay sent you. Now get you back to your horses and go!'

And when they were gone, he turned and beat upon the gate with the pommel of his sword, until the whole household with the aged mistress of the place among them came and opened to them.

'I had thought you were in your bed,' said the aged gentlewoman, surprised.

'So I was,' said Sir Lancelot, 'but I went out of the window to aid a friend and fellow of mine that needed it.'

And when they came into the light, Sir Kay knew him, and said stiffly, for thanks did not come easy to him, but warmly all the same, 'It seems I have to thank you for saving my life.'

'You are very welcome,' said Sir Lancelot, who was almost as ill-at-ease in being thanked as Kay was in thanking.

Then when Kay had been unarmed and food

brought for him, they went back to the garret over the gate, and lay down in the warm hay and pulled the rugs over them and slept.

But in the morning Lancelot woke early, while Kay was still snoring, and looking down at the King's foster brother in the sinking light of the night lamp, he remembered Arthur saying, 'He was an unhappy boy and he's an unhappy man, and I fear he always will be.' And he knew that many of the knights made fun of him and never missed a chance to take him down in his own esteem. And he laughed kindly within himself, and taking care not to wake him, he put on Kay's armour, which fitted him none so ill, for they were much of a size, though he had to slacken off the straps across the shoulders. He shall ride proud and unmolested for once, anyway, thought Sir Lancelot, and he took up Kay's shield, but his own sword, and went and bade farewell to the ancient gentlewoman; and then took Sir Kay's horse from the stable and rode away, leaving Sir Kay to find his horse and armour when he woke.

He was many miles away in the forest, when suddenly he wondered if Sir Kay would take the jest kindly, as it was meant, or if it was the cruellest and most conceited thing he had ever done in his life. But by then it was too late to turn back and do anything about it.

The very next day he came upon four knights of the Round Table gathered under an oak tree. And one was Sir Ector of the Marsh, his own half-brother, and one was Sir Segramour le Desirous, and one

Sir Uwaine the son of Morgan La Fay, and one Sir Gawain, who was captain of all the Round Table brotherhood. And when they saw Sir Kay as they thought, riding towards them, they laughed among themselves, and Sir Segramour rode out to give him a buffet, whereupon Sir Lancelot lifted him on his spear point clean out of the saddle and dropped him all arms and legs to the ground.

'Surely that man is broader across the shoulders than Sir Kay?' said Sir Ector. 'Well, we will see if his buffet can match mine!'

And Sir Lancelot tipped him out of the saddle to join Sir Segramour.

'By my faith,' said Sir Uwaine, 'that is not Sir Kay! Surely he has slain Sir Kay and stolen his armour!'

And he rode hard against Sir Lancelot — and knew nothing more for some while.

Then Sir Gawain fewtered his spear and came against Sir Lancelot full tilt. And Sir Lancelot, kindling his horse in the last instant before the strike-home, as few horsemen but he knew how to do, brought down Sir Gawain and his horse together.

Then Sir Lancelot rode quietly on; and he smiled to himself inside his helmet, and thought, Well, that is four bruising falls that I have saved Sir Kay, anyway. And he thought also, God give him joy who made this spear, for I never had a better in my hand!

And the four knights gathered their wits and aided each other and caught their horses. 'That was assuredly not Sir Kay,' said Sir Segramour.

And Sir Gawain said, 'I am thinking that it was Sir

Lancelot. He was but three days at court after his knighting, but I mind me how he did at the jousts on the second day, and I know him by his riding.'

And they continued on their way, for they were heading for Camelot to keep Christmas at Arthur's court.

And Sir Lancelot rode on through the wintry forest, seeking whatever adventure might befall him, while the winter wore on and the snow came and lay thick upon the ground and the straining branches of the trees, and the wind howled like a wolf pack in the long dark nights.

One day when the winter was nearly spent, he came upon the strangest of all the adventures that he met with in that year of lone riding; so strange that ever after when he looked back upon it, it was like looking back upon a dream.

And the beginning of the adventure was this; that as he rode along a forest track, he met with a damosel muffled close against the cold, who looked into his face — for he rode with his vizor open, as did most men except in time of fighting — and cried out, 'Ah, Sir Lancelot! Now Christ in his gentleness be praised that we are met!'

'How comes it that you know my name?' said Lancelot, who was growing accustomed to being mistaken for Sir Kay by the device on his shield.

'Last Easter I was at King Arthur's court, to watch my brother at the jousting on the day after you were made knight.' And in her desperate eagerness she twisted her hands in his bridle as though to draw him after her, so that his horse was startled and began to dance.

'Softly,' said Sir Lancelot, 'what is it that you would with me?'

'Ah, Sir Knight, I sorely need your help – and for that same brother. For this very day he fought with an evil knight, Sir Gilbert the Bastard. And Sir Gilbert he slew, but my brother was sore wounded, and the wound will not cease from bleeding so that now he lies upon death's threshold. And there dwells in the forest not far from here a sorceress called Allewes, and when in despair I went to her for help, she laughed at me, and said the blood-flow would not cease until I could find a knight valiant enough to go into the Chapel Perilous, where Sir Gilbert's body now lies, and bring out the sword that lies there and a piece of the cloth that covers the body. Then if the sword be touched to the wound, and the cloth bound about it after, the bleeding shall cease, and my brother be made whole again.'

'That is a marvellous thing,' said Sir Lancelot, 'but who is your brother?'

'Sir, he is Sir Meliot de Logure.'

At that, Lancelot was silent a moment, remembering the young knight who had been at Camelot only a short while when he himself came from Benwick, and who, it was whispered, was kin of some kind of Nimue the Lady of the Lake. And the hairs stirred a little on the nape of his neck, and the sense of being in a dream thickened about him.

141

But he said at last, 'Then he is my brother in the fellowship of the Round Table, and assuredly I will do all that is in my power to aid him.'

'Then, sir,' said the maiden, 'let you follow this track, for it will bring you to the Chapel Perilous. And I will wait here until you come again. And pray God that you *do* come again; for if you do not, then there is no knight living who may achieve this adventure.'

Then Sir Lancelot rode on, following the track where the ice was melting in the ruts, and the half-thawed snow falling from the branches of the trees. And in a while he came to a clearing in the forest beside the way; and in the midst of the clearing a grey and mournful chapel set among night-dark yew trees. Sir Lancelot dismounted and tied his horse to the narrow gate, and went into the churchyard. And then he saw, hanging from the twisted branches of the greatest and oldest tree that grew beside the chapel door, many shields, upside down in token of death. And he saw also, standing among the yew trees, more than thirty knights in black armour and with drawn swords in their hands; taller by a head than any mortal man; and their vizors were open and their faces bare, the faces of the long dead, and he saw that they grinned and gnashed their teeth at his coming, but no smoke of breath came from them upon the cold air. And fear rose like a cold fog in Lancelot, and again, and more strongly, the hair crawled on the back of his neck. But he drew his sword and readied his shield before him, and advanced steadily upon them like a man advancing into battle.

And at his coming, they gave back and scattered, their feet leaving no track upon the puddled snow; and Sir Lancelot passed through them and entered the chapel.

Within, the place was dimly lit by one lamp that hung from the vaulted roof; and beneath the lamp, a dead man lay upon his bier, covered by a pall of crimson silk. And it seemed to him that the cold of that place was ten times deeper than the raw winter's cold outside, for it ate into the very soul.

He drew his sword and, stooping beside the bier, cut a long strip from the crimson silk that covered the stark shape. And as he did so, the pavement tilted under him as though the earth had quaked beneath the chapel, and the lamp swung on its chain, casting weird shadows about the place so that for the moment it seemed full of dark wings, and almost it was as though Sir Gilbert's body stirred beneath the crimson pall. And Sir Lancelot's heart sprang racing into his throat.

But the earth steadied and the lamp hung quiet once more; the dark wings were gone, and the dead man lay still beneath his pall. And Sir Lancelot sheathed his blade, and as he did so, saw a splendid sword lying beside the bier. He took it up, and with the strip of crimson silk crumpled in his shield hand in the hollow of his shield, he stepped out into the grey light of the snowy churchyard.

The black knights still stood there, waiting among

the yew trees; and they spoke to him in one voice, and that a terrible one. 'Knight, Sir Lancelot, lay down that sword, or you shall die!'

'Whether I live or die,' said Lancelot, 'words shall not win this sword from me. Fight me for it, if you will.'

And as they had done at his first coming, they fell back before him, leaving no tracks in the snow; and so he came again to the gate where his horse was tied. But beside his horse, a strange damosel waited for him, nothing of her face showing in the shadow of her hood but the darkness of her two great eyes. And she said in a voice as soft and cold as the snow, 'Sir Lancelot, pray you leave that sword behind you; you will die for it else.'

'I leave it not, even for your pleading,' said Sir Lancelot.

And the damosel gave a little laugh with music in it like the chiming of icicles. 'How wise you are! For if you had left that sword at my pleading, you would never have come to Arthur's court nor seen Queen Guenever again. Now, in token that there is no ill-will between us, do you kiss me but once, and go your way.'

'Nay!' said Sir Lancelot, already reaching for his horse's bridle. 'God forbid!'

Then the damosel let forth a high wailing cry, and seemed to grow thin and shaken as though the wind blew through her very bones. 'Alas! I have had all my labours in vain. For many times I have seen you in my dreams, in running water by day and in the fire at night, and grown to love you; and it was I who raised the Chapel Perilous to entrap you and web you round with my spells as the spider webs the blundering crane-fly with her silk; and had you kissed me, you would have lain this moment dead in my arms, and been mine for all time, you who are the flower of all King Arthur's knights. But there is that in you which is too strong for me, and you have torn through all my spells. Have pity on me, now that I am torn and broken . . .'

Then Lancelot guessed that she must be the sorceress Allewes, of whom Sir Meliot's sister had told him; and he crossed himself strongly. 'Now God preserve me from your subtle crafts,' he said, and rounding from her to his horse, mounted and rode away.

He followed the track by which he had come, until at last he found Sir Meliot's sister standing where he had left her. And when she saw him she clasped her hands and wept for joy. Then she set her hand, lightly this time, on his horse's bridle, and led him to her brother's castle nearby, where Sir Meliot lay upon his bed with the physician and his squires standing helplessly about him, and the red life-tide still ebbing from the wound in his flank.

Sir Lancelot crossed to the bedside, and drawing the sword that he had brought from the Chapel Perilous, laid the blade against the streaming wound, then wiped and cleaned it with the strip of crimson silk, and at once the blood-flow ceased and the edges drew together, and Sir Meliot sighed, and sat up on the bed as well and whole as ever he had been.

And for one shaken heartbeat of time, Sir Lancelot wondered whether this was his miracle; the miracle that he had prayed so long and hard that one day God would allow him to perform. But then he knew that this was something of quite a different sort. This was magic and enchantment. And it came to him also, that if ever he were allowed to work his miracle he would know it by something in himself, some knowledge that the power of God had passed through him like flame and a high wind.

He had broken a spell, no more than that.

But still, he was glad that he had saved Sir Meliot, his fellow of the Round Table. And the three of them were joyful together, and he remained with them several days. But when the snow melted, he said to Sir Meliot, 'I must be on my way; for it ill befits one on a quest to sleep seven nights in a goose-feathered bed; and there are matters yet to be adventured before I return to Arthur's court at Eastertide. Come you back to court also at that time, that we may meet again.'

Far and wide through the forest country rode Sir Lancelot, and by marshways where the land was half water and flamed at sunset under the crying and calling of the geese as they began their northward flight, and up into the high moors and the mountains of the West, and back to the forest ways again, while the world woke from winter into spring around him, and the celandines starred the wayside banks and the wild cherry foamed into blossom, and the larks tore his heart with the sweetness of their singing high above the cultivated land. And he met with so many adventures that if a weaver of tales were to tell them all, the telling would never be done. And he made for himself a name on men's lips, though he was still but nineteen, a name like a banner, such as men weave into a harp-song for warriors and women to tell their children by the fire.

And in the last days before Easter, he rode back to Camelot.

When he came into the Great Hall, barcheaded but still in Sir Kay's armour, Sir Gawain and Sir Ector of the Marsh, Sir Uwaine and Sir Segramour saw indeed who it was who had felled them all with one spear, and there was a gale of laughter among them. And then Sir Kay, with his colour making two red spots on his cheekbones, told how Sir Lancelot had rescued him, and of the exchanging of their armour and how he had ridden home in peace, none daring to interfere with him in Sir Lancelot's harness. He could not find laughter, as the others could, in the story against himself, but he told it none the less; and Sir Lancelot felt as though he had been forgiven for something, and laid his arm for a moment across the Seneschal's shoulders.

And then came in King Bagdemagus, and Sir Meliot de Logure, and behind them the knights whom Lancelot had rescued from Sir Tarquine, and the knights whom he had overcome and bidden yield themselves to King Arthur or to the Queen, until there was scarce room for all of them in the Great Hall.

It should have been the proudest and most triumphant moment of Sir Lancelot's life, as he came forward and knelt to the High King. But the Queen had also come into the Hall to welcome him back and to receive the freed captives and vanquished knights who he had sent to her; and she sat beside the King in a gown of golden damask, her eyes brighter in the torch-light than the jewels about her neck.

'We have heard of your deeds these many months past,' said the King. 'You have indeed proved yourself, and no man now will question your right to receive knighthood so young.'

And the Queen leaned forward a little, and said, 'The time has seemed long while you were away, and we are glad that you are come home.'

And Lancelot moved to kneel before her with a suddenly pounding heart. It was for her that he had ridden away on his year-long quest, and now the year was over, and he had come back; and Guenever was still here, and nothing was changed.

7

SIR GAWAIN AND THE GREEN KNIGHT

Of all the knights who had their places at King Arthur's Round Table, Sir Gawain seemed always to be the one who had something strange about him. Gawain of the flaming red hair, and the temper that flamed to match it, as swift as fire to spring up and as dangerous, but as swift to sink again. He was of the Old People, the Dark People, but then so was Gaheris, and Agravane their younger brother who by now had also joined the court. So was his cousin Uwaine, and so was Arthur himself on his mother's side. It was more than that. Strange stories were told about Gawain; the country folk said that his strength waxed and waned with the sun. So it was fitting that one of the strangest adventures ever to befall the knights of the Round Table should come to him.

On the Christmas that Sir Lancelot was still away upon his own quest, Arthur held his court at Camelot, for the time had not yet come when he kept his Christmases at Carlisle. Yuletide went by with many festivities, and it came to New Year's Eve. Now Christmas was chiefly a matter for the Church, but New Year's Eve was for banqueting and merry-making, and so when dusk came, the whole court gathered to their feasting in the Great Hall; the knights of the Round Table each in their places; the lesser knights and the squires at the side boards. Even the Queen and her ladies had come to join the feast and look on from under their silken canopy at the upper end of the Hall, for there would be dancing after the banquet was done. Already the serving squires were bringing in the great chargers of goose and venison, and swans and ships and towering castles made of almonds and honey. The wine glowed red in crystal goblets and the Hall leapt with torchlight and lilted with the music of the harper who sat at the Queen's feet.

The boar's head was brought in, wreathed in scented bay leaves and heralded by trumpets and carried high on the shoulders of four pages. But just as it was set on the table, the great doors of the Hall flew open, and a gust of wind burst in, making the torches stream sideways and the flames of the huge log fires crouch down upon the hearths. And a little snow eddied in on the dark wings of the wind.

The harper fell silent between note and note. The voices of the revelling company fell away, as every face turned towards the door and the night beyond. And a great silence took the Hall, where the cheerful sounds of merrymaking had been.

And into the silence came the clang and bell-clash of horse's hooves upon the frostbound courtyard stones, and out of the darkness into the torchlight and firelight that steadied and leapt as though in greeting, rode a great man, almost a giant, upon a warhorse that was of a fitting size to carry him.

At sight of him a long gasp ran through the Hall, for he was the strangest sight that any man there had ever seen, mighty of limb and goodly of face and holding himself in the saddle like a king, wearing no armour but clad from head to heel in the fierce fine green that is the colour of the Lordly Ones and not of mortal men. His jerkin and hose under his thick-furred cloak were all of green, and green was the jewelled belt that circled his waist. His saddle was of fine green leather enriched with gold, so were his horse's trappings which chimed like little bells as the great beast moved. Spurs of greenish gold sparked the heels of his boots that were the colour of moss under ancient oak trees. Even his thick crest of hair and his curling beard were of the same hue, and the great horse beneath him green from proud crest to sweeping tail, its mane fantastically braided and knotted up with golden threads. In one hand he carried a huge axe of green steel inlaid with the same strange greeny-gold; and high in the other a young holly tree thick with berries that sparked like crimson jewels in the torchlight. But save for the holly berries of Christmas, all else, even the sparks that his horse's hooves struck from the stone pavement as he rode up the Hall, was green; blazing and fiery green; the living green of springtime itself.

When he came halfway up the Hall, he reined in, and flung down the holly tree upon the floor, and sat looking about him on all sides. And it seemed to everyone there, from the King himself to the youngest page, that the golden-green eyes, like the eyes of some proud and mighty forest beast, had looked for a moment directly and deeply into his own.

Then he cried out in a voice that boomed from wall to wall and hung under the roof and brought a startled spider down out of the rafters, 'Where is the lord of this Hall, for I would speak with him and with no other!'

After the thunder of his voice, for three heartbeats of time all men sat as though stunned, and there was no sound save the whispering of the flames upon the hearths. Then Arthur said, 'I am the lord of this Hall, and I bid you right welcome to it. Now pray you dismount, and while my stable squires tend to your horse, come and feast among us, this last night of the Old Year.'

'Nay, that I will not,' said the stranger. 'I have not come to feast with you; nor have I come in war. That, you may see by my lack of armour, and by the green branch that I bear. But word of the valour of your knights has reached me in my own place; and for a while and a while I have been minded to put it to the test.'

'Why, then,' said Arthur, 'I doubt not that you will find enough and to spare among my knights willing and eager to joust with you if that is your desire.'

'That is as may be,' said the Green Knight, 'but for the most part I see here only beardless bairns who I could fell with one flick of a bramble spray! Nay, it is a valour-test of another kind that I bring here for a

Yuletide sport. Let any man here stand forth as champion against me, and he may take from my hand this axe which has no equal in the world for weight and keenness, and with it strike me one blow. Only he must strike the blow in the place of my choosing. And he must swear to yield me the right to strike the return blow in the same place, if I am yet able, a year and a day from now.'

And again there was silence in the Hall; and the knights looked at each other and away again, and here one drew a quick breath, and there one licked his lower lip. But none dared to take up the challenge of the beautiful and terrible stranger.

Then the Green Knight laughed, long and loud and mocking. 'Not one of you? Is this indeed King Arthur's Hall? And you who feast here but dare not take up a simple challenge, are you indeed the knights of his Round Table? The flower of chivalry? Nay, let you go hang your heads in shame, I see I have had a bootless journey!'

Arthur sprang to his feet, though well he knew that it was not for the High King to take up such a challenge, and flung his shout of defiance in the stranger's face. 'Yes! One! Off your horse now, give me your axe and make ready for the blow!'

But almost in the same instant, Sir Gawain also was on his feet. 'My lord the King, noble uncle, I claim this adventure, for still I carry with me the shame of the lady's death whose head I cut off, and I have yet to prove my worthiness to sit at the Round Table!'

He seldom called Arthur 'uncle', for they were

almost the same age, and so when he did, it was as a jest between them. And now the familiar jest cut through the King's rage and reached him, and he knew that what Sir Gawain said was true. And so he drew a deep breath and unclenched his hands, and said, 'Dear my nephew, the adventure is yours.'

Then as Sir Gawain left his place and strode into the centre of the Hall, the Green Knight swung down from his horse, and so they came together. 'It is good that I have found a champion to meet me in Arthur's Hall,' said the Green Knight. 'By what name are you called?'

'I am Gawain, son of Lot King of Orkney, and nephew to my liege lord King Arthur. By what name do men call you?'

'Men call me the Knight of the Green Chapel, in my own North Country,' said the stranger. 'Swear now to the bargain between us; that you will strike the one blow in the place of my choosing, the one blow only. And that in a year and a day you will submit yourself to my blow, the one blow only, in return.'

'I swear by my knighthood,' said Gawain.

'Take the axe, and be ready to strike as I bid you.'

Gawain took the mighty and terrible axe in his hand, and stood swinging it a little, feeling its weight and balance; and the Green Knight knelt down on the floor, and stooping, drew his long flame-green hair forward over the top of his head to lay bare his neck.

For a moment all things in the Hall seemed to cease, and Gawain stood as though turned to stone.

'In the place of my choice,' said the Green Knight. 'Strike now.'

And life moved on again, and Gawain in a kind of fury swung up the great axe with a battle yell, and putting every last ounce of strength that he possessed into the blow, brought it crashing down.

The blade sheared through flesh and bone and set the sparks spurting from the pavement as though from an anvil; and the Green Knight's head sprang from his shoulders and went rolling along the floor almost to the Queen's feet.

There rose a horrified gasp, and while all men looked to see the huge body topple forward, the Green Knight shook his shoulders a little, and got to his feet, and walked after his head. He caught it up and, holding it by the hair, remounted his horse that stood quietly waiting for him. Holding his head high, he turned the face to Sir Gawain, and said, 'See that you keep your oath, and come to me a year and a day from now.'

'How shall I find you?' asked Gawain, white to the lips.

'Seek me through Wales and into the Forest of Wirrel; and if you bring your courage with you, you shall surely find me before noon of the appointed day.'

And he wheeled his horse and touched his spurred heel to its flank, and was away out into the darkness and the eddying snow, his head still swinging by its

155

long hair from his hand. And they heard the beat of his horse's hooves drumming away into the winter's night.

Behind him he left great silence in the Hall, and it was a while before the harper drew his hand across the bright strings again, and men returned to their laughter and feasting.

The snow melted and the buds began to swell along the wood shores. And at Eastertide Sir Lancelot returned from his questing, as has been told. The cuckoo came, the foxgloves stood proudly along the woodland ways and then were gone; and in farms and manors up and down the land the harvest was gathered in; and it was the time of blackberries and turning bracken once again. And at Michaelmas it was time for Sir Gawain to set forth upon his terrible quest.

King Arthur held his court at Caerleon that Michaelmas; and there gathered Sir Gaheris and Sir Agravane, and Lancelot and Lional and his brother Bors who was new-come from Less Britain to join him, Sir Uwaine and Sir Bedivere, King Bagdemagus and Sir Lamorack and Sir Gryflet le Fise de Dieu and many more. And their hearts were sore within them so that there was no joy nor savour to the feasting, for the sake of Sir Gawain, who was riding away from them and would surely never come riding back.

And Sir Gawain with his squire's help armed himself and belted on his sword, and mounted Gringolet his great roan horse, and set out.

For many days he rode through the ancient border country of Wales until he came to the wild dark mountain lands of North Wales; and he rode by steep valleys and roaring waters and mountain-clinging forests. And many times he was attacked by wild animals and wilder men and must fight for his life, knowing all the while that death must be waiting for him at the end of his quest. Autumn had turned to winter when he reached the end of the mountain country, and came down by Clwyd to the Holy Head near to Saint Winifred's Well on the shore of the broad and grey-shining Dee. He forded the river mouth at low tide, and barely winning clear of the sands and saltings before the tide came racing in again, he came to the black and ancient forest-fleece of the Wirrel.

And as he rode, whenever he came up with a forester or a wandering friar or an old woman gathering sticks, and whenever he found shelter at night in a swineherd's bothie or a charcoal-burner's hut (those were the nights he counted himself lucky; on other nights he slept huddled in his cloak under a pile of dead bracken or in the root-hollow of a tree brought down by the storms of some past winter), he asked for tidings of the Green Knight of the Green Chapel, but no one could tell him what he needed to know.

And the time was growing short . . .

On Christmas Eve, weary man on weary horse mired to the belly from the forest ways, he came out from among ancient trees that seemed to reach their twisted lichen-hung branches across his way as though to seize him and draw him into themselves, and saw before him open meadowland set about with fine tamed trees, a willow-fringed stream winding through; and beyond the stream, the land rising gently, crowned by a castle that was both strong and beautiful in the last light of the winter's day.

Now God be thanked, thought Sir Gawain, and he gently pulled Gringolet's twitching ear. There will be food and shelter to spare in this place and they will not refuse us welcome upon this night of all the year. And he forded the stream and rode up to the castle gate and beat upon the timbers with the pommel of his sword.

The gate opened almost at once, and the porter appeared in the entrance.

'Good fellow,' said Sir Gawain, 'pray you tell your master that a knight of King Arthur's court rides this way upon a quest; and begs shelter for himself and his horse.'

'My master, the lord of this castle, has a welcome for all comers, especially any who come on this night of all the year,' said the porter, standing aside, and Gawain rode through into the outer court of the castle. Squires came hurrying to take Gringolet to the stables, while others led Gawain himself through the inner court and then into the castle Hall, where the lord of the castle himself stood before a roaring fire with three great wolfhounds lying all about his feet, their bellies to the warmth.

He was a big man, broad across the shoulders and

running just a trace to fat; his face weather-beaten, kindly and open, his mane of hair as red as Gawain's own; and as his guest entered the room, he thrust the wolfhounds aside and came striding to meet him with hands outstretched.

'Welcome, knight-at-arms, my home is your home, and all that I have is yours for as long as it pleases you to bide here.'

'My thanks, noble sir,' Gawain said, his heart warming to the man in instant friendship. 'God be good to you, for the goodness of your hospitality.'

And they clapped each other upon the shoulders as though they were old friends indeed.

The squires led Gawain to the guest chamber high in the keep, where they helped him to unarm, and brought him a robe of thick russet wool lined with the softest dappled lynx fur; then they escorted him back to the Hall, where another chair had been set for him opposite the lord of the castle; and one of the hounds came with proudly swinging tail and laid its chin on his knee.

Meanwhile the squires and pages were setting up the table boards and spreading them with fine white linen; and bringing in the food and setting ready the wine jugs. And the soft warm hunger-water ran into Sir Gawain's mouth at the sight and smell of the dishes; and the warmth of the fire and the heavy furred robe seeped through his chilled and weary body, and he was very well content.

When supper was over, the lord of the castle said,

159

'Come, Sir Gawain, for you have not yet seen my lady, and she will be eager to greet you.'

And they went together, by the stairway behind the Hall, to the Private Chamber; a fair chamber whose walls were painted green and scattered with small golden stars; and the lady of the castle sat beside the fire with a little silky lapdog on her knee, and her maidens all about her. And Gawain thought when she smiled at him that she was the fairest lady he had ever seen; fairer even than Queen Guenever. She made him sweetly welcome, while her maidens brought a chessboard with men of silver and crystal, for her lord and his guest to play; and the evening passed as happily as any that Gawain had ever known, so that for a little while he was almost able to forget the dark quest on which he rode.

And when the time came for sleep, the squires took him back, making a candle-lit procession of it, to the guest chamber, and left him with a goblet of spiced wine beside the bed.

Four days passed, with all the singing and feasting and rejoicing that goes with Christmas time; and always the lady of the castle stayed close to Gawain and talked to him and smiled upon him and attended to him in all things.

But on the evening of the fourth day Gawain knew that he must stay no longer from his quest. When he told the knight and the lady of this, they grieved, and would have had him stay longer. But Gawain held to his purpose. 'I have stayed too long already, happy in your company, and my quest calls me. I must meet the Knight of the Green Chapel by noon of New Year's Day; and as yet I do not even know where this Green Chapel may be.'

Then the lord of the castle laughed, and slapped his great hand upon his broad knee. 'That makes good hearing indeed; for the Green Chapel I know well; it is not two hours' easy ride from here! Bide with us then until the morning of New Year's Day, and then one of my squires shall guide you to the place, and have you there before the sun stands at noon.'

'Then gladly will I bide here,' Sir Gawain said, 'and warm me with your kindness, and do in all things as you will.' (For he thought, if these be the last three days of my life, it were sweet that I should spend them among friends.)

'So then, we have three good days to spend,' said the lord of the castle, 'and I shall spend them as always I spend the three last days of the Old Year, hunting in the forest. But you, who have ridden so far and hard, and have, I doubt not, some great ordeal to face at the Green Chapel, shall abide here and take your ease, and keep the company of my lady who ever complains of her loneliness when I leave her to follow the boar or the red deer. And in the evenings we will make merry together.'

'That will I do most willingly,' said Gawain.

The lord's eyes flickered with laughter in his weather-beaten face. 'And since this is the time for games and jests, and I have a fantastic mood on me, let us make a covenant together – that each evening I will give you whatever I have gained in my day's hunting; and you shall give me in exchange whatever you have gained here in my castle. This exchange let us swear to, for better or worse, however it may turn out.'

'That is a fine covenant, and gladly will I swear to it,' said Gawain; and they struck hands like men sealing a bargain.

Next day the lord of the castle summoned his companions and his hounds and rode away to hunt the red deer through the forests of Wirrel and Delamare. But Gawain lay abed, with a most unusual drowsiness upon him, for he was not used to late lying. And presently the lady of the castle came, stepping lightly, and sat down on the edge of the bed, as blithe as a linnet on a hawthorn spray, and began to tease him. And by little and little, from teasing she slipped into love-talk, and spoke sweet words as though half in jest. And Gawain took them as though they were all in jest, and turned them aside lightly and courteously as though they played some kind of game. And at last the lady rose to go. 'God save you for a pleasant hour,' she said. 'But I find it hard to believe that you are Sir Gawain, as you claim to be.'

'Why so?' asked Sir Gawain, startled.

And she laughed. 'Would Sir Gawain ever have tarried so long with a damosel and never once asked for a kiss?'

'Faith, lady, I feared to displease you,' said Sir Gawain, 'but since it seems that you give me leave, I do indeed beg you most humbly for a kiss.'

So the lady took his face between her hands, and kissed him most sweetly, and went her way. And Gawain called for the chamber squires, for he would get up.

At evening, the lord of the castle came home with the carcass of a fine red deer slung across the back of a hunting pony. And he bade his huntsmen lay it before Gawain, who had come to meet him in the courtyard. 'See, now, here is the fruit of my hunting, which I give to you according to our bargain.'

'I accept the gift with all thanks,' said Gawain, 'and bid you to sup with me, though in your own Hall, tomorrow, when it is cooked. And now in return I give to you the thing that I won here in the castle this day.' And he set his hands on his host's shoulders and kissed him, once.

'So; that was a fine gift, and much do I thank you for it,' said the lord of the castle. 'Yet gladly would I know who gave you that kiss.'

'Nay,' said Sir Gawain, 'that was no part of the bargain.'

And presently they sat down to supper in great good fellowship.

Next morning the lord of the castle sent for his boar hounds and rode hunting again. And again Gawain lay in his bed with the sweet unaccountable drowsiness upon him, until again the lady of the castle came and sat down on the edge of the bed, with the little dog pattering after, to cuddle in the floor-folds of her gown. And again she fell to teasing him softly, playing with words and trying to coax words of love from him in return. But Sir Gawain continued to turn them all aside, lightly and with courtesy that held no unkindness nor rebuff; and at last she left him, though this time with two kisses instead of yesterday's one.

That evening, the lord of the castle returned home at dusk, and his huntsmen laid at Gawain's feet the grizzly carcass of a boar. 'Here, guest of mine, I bring you the spoils of my day's hunting.'

'I accept the spoils of your hunting,' Gawain said, 'and bid you to sup with me again tomorrow night.'

'And what have you to give me in return?'

'These, that I have come by since you rode out this morning,' said Gawain; and putting his hands on the other's shoulders, he gave him two kisses. 'This, and no more, I have gained, and now I give them to you.'

And together, with the rest of the castle knights, they supped royally on the red deer that had been Gawain's gift of the night before. And the lady, coming in with her maidens, smiled at Gawain and sent him sweet dark glances that he pretended not to see.

That night, Sir Gawain thought that for other reasons beside his quest it would be better if he rode on his way next morning. But when he said so to his host, the big man said, 'Nay, but why?'

'Tomorrow will be the last day of the year; and by noon of the next day, I must be at my meeting-place with the Green Knight.'

'Have I not sworn on my knightly honour that the place is but two hours' ride from here, and you shall come there long before noon on the appointed day? And there is yet one day of our bargain still to run.'

So the next morning, the morning of New Year's Eve, the lord of the castle called for his huntsmen and his hounds and rode away into the dark forest, while Sir Gawain still lay sleeping, tangled in troubled dreams of his meeting with the Green Knight that was now so cruelly near.

He woke to find thin winter sunshine streaming into the chamber, and the lady of the castle bending over him. When she saw that he was awake, she gave him one kiss, lingering a little, then stood back, looking down at him, laughing still, but a little sadly under the laughter. 'But one little kiss,' she said, 'does your heart freeze in the winter? Or have you a damosel waiting for you at court?'

'No damosel,' Sir Gawain said gently, 'and my heart is still mine to give; but lady, fairest and sweetest lady, I may not give it to you, for your lord and the lord of this castle is my host. If I were to love the wife, that would be to shame my knightly vows.'

'But my lord rides hunting and will not be home till dusk, no one will ever know, not even he, and so he will feel no hurt. Can we not love in this one day, that all my life may be sweeter remembering that Gawain of Orkney once held me in his arms?'

Gawain shook his head. 'The wrong would be none the less because no one knew of it. No, lady, it cannot be.'

For a long while she besought him, but he turned her pleas aside; and at last she sighed as one admitting defeat, and kissed him again, and said, 'Sir Gawain, you must be the truest to your vows of all knights living. So – I will plague you no more. But give me something of yours to remember you by; that I may cherish it, and it may comfort me a little in my sorrow.'

'Alas,' said Sir Gawain, 'I have nothing to give, for I travel light upon this quest.'

'Then will I give you something of mine. Take this green girdle and wear it for my sake.'

'Lady, I cannot be your knight and wear your favour.'

'Such a little thing,' said the lady, 'and you need not wear it openly as my favour, but hidden where no man shall see, and only I shall know of it. Pray you take it, for you ride into sore danger, that I know; and there is magic woven into it, that while you wear it you shall bear a charmed life. Only keep it hid, and tell not my lord of it.'

And with his meeting with the terrible Green Knight so close, the temptation was too great, and Gawain took the girdle of gold-worked green ribbons and knotted it round his neck under his shirt.

And the lady kissed him for the third time, and went her way.

That evening at dusk, the lord of the castle returned from his hunting bearing with him nothing but one fox-skin swinging from his hand.

'Alas! I have had scurvy hunting,' he said when Gawain met him in the courtyard, 'and this is all that I have to give you on the last of your three days.'

'Then it seems that my winnings have been better than yours. For I have this to give you,' said Gawain, and setting his hands on his host's shoulders he gave him three kisses.

Then with great jest and merriment, their arms across each other's shoulders, they went back into the Great Hall where supper was made ready, and feasted on the boar which the knight of the castle had brought home from his hunting the day before.

But Gawain spoke no word of the green ribbons lying round his neck under his shirt and his borrowed robe.

On New Year's Morning, Sir Gawain arose early, having slept but little, and called for the squires to arm him – keeping the green ribbons well hidden beneath the neck-band of his shirt the while. They brought him food; dark crusty bread and cold pig-meat, a cup of wine, and a platter of last summer's little withered yellow apples; but there was small wish for food in him; he drank some wine and ate one of the apples, and that was all. Then he went down into the courtyard, where the stable squires had brought out Gringolet looking sleek and well-fed.

Gringolet whinnied with pleasure at sight of his master, and Gawain fondled him a moment, then sprang into the saddle. 'Fare you well; the sun and the moon on your threshold,' he said to the lord of the castle, who had come down to take leave of him. Of the lady, there was no sign. 'If I might, I would do aught in my power to reward you for your kindness.

But I think that I shall not see the rising of another sun.'

And he rode out through the gates that had been flung wide, with the squire who was to guide him riding hard behind; out over the causeway and away through the grey light of a low sullen dawn, with sleet spitting down the wind. By forest and mire and dreary wasteland they went, until they came to the lip of a broad valley between steep rocky slopes, and reining in, sat looking down, and saw the whole valley full of swirling mist.

'Sir,' said the squire, 'I have brought you as far as I may. Down yonder under the mist is the Green Chapel you seek; and down there the Green Knight will be waiting, as always he waits to fight with and slay all who would pass him by. None who come into combat with him may escape living. Oh, sir, do not go down there! None shall ever know; I will not betray you, that I swear as I hope for knighthood myself one day.'

'My thanks,' said Gawain; 'but my honour's lost and my knighthood shamed if I turn away now from my tryst. God knows how to save his servants if he wills it so.'

'Then your death is on your own hands,' said the squire. 'Follow the cliff path yonder and it will bring you down into the deep-most heart of the valley; a stream runs down the valley, and the Green Chapel stands upon the opposite bank. I bid you farewell, Sir Gawain, for I dare come with you no further.'

So Sir Gawain gentled his horse into the cliff path,

and held on down, the rocks rising sheer on his right hand and dropping sheer into the mist on the other; and out of the mist came the sound of rushing water, rising to meet him. At last he came as it were down through the mist into the clear air below it, and reached the valley floor, and saw a deep narrow stream swirling its way in a tumble of white water among rocks and the roots of lichen-hung alder trees. But he could make out no sign of any chapel, until after a while of looking about him he saw a short way upstream and on the far side a low green mound covered with alder and hazel scrub; and as he rode doubtfully towards it, he heard above the rush and tumble of the water, a sound as of a scythe on a whetstone coming up from somewhere deep within the heart of it.

This must be the Green Chapel, he thought, and green it is indeed; and no Christian chapel but some secret place of the Hollow Hills. And within it the Green Knight is making keen his weapon that must surely be the death of me this day.

But he set his horse to ford the stream at a place where it broadened and ran for a few yards shallow over a gravel bed, and came out close below the green mound; and there he dismounted and hitched Gringolet's bridle to an alder branch. And standing in the strange grey light scarfed with mist, he called, 'Sir Knight of the Green Chapel, I am here as I vowed, to keep our New Year tryst.'

'Wait until I have done sharpening my axe,' came the great booming voice he remembered, echoing from the cavernous heart of the mound. 'I shall not be long. And then you shall have the greeting that I promised you.'

And Gringolet pricked his ears and tossed his head and showed the whites of his eyes; but Gawain stood unmoving, and waited on.

And in a while the sound of scythe on whetstone ceased, and out from a patch of darkness beneath the hazel branches came the Green Knight, just as he had been when he rode into Arthur's Hall a year and a day gone by, beautiful and terrible, and swinging lightly in his hand a long axe with a blade of green steel that looked sharp enough to draw blood from the wind.

'Now welcome, Sir Gawain!' he cried. 'Three times welcome to so brave a knight! Now off with your helmet and make ready for the stroke I owe you for the one you dealt me in Arthur's Hall a year ago last night.'

Gawain unloosed and pulled off his helmet, and thrust back the chain-mail coif from his neck. And taking a last look at the wintry world about him, he knelt and bent his head forward for the blow. 'Strike, then,' he said.

The Green Knight swung up his great axe, and as he brought it sweeping down, Gawain heard the whistle of it, as the crouching bird must hear the wing-rush of the stooping hawk. And despite himself, he flinched back and ducked out from under the blow.

The Green Knight stood leaning on the long

handle of his axe, and grinned at him, the grin of some wild thing out of the forest. 'Can this indeed be Gawain of the bold heart? When it was you that swung the axe, I never flinched from *your* blow.'

'Your pardon. My courage lacks the knowledge that I can set my head back on my shoulders when you have done with it,' said Gawain with a flare of grim laughter. 'But I will not shrink again. Come now, and strike quickly.'

'That I will,' said the Green Knight, and again he swung up the fearsome blade and again he brought it whistling down. But this time Gawain remained as still as though he had been one of the rocks of the stream-side. And the axe-blade missed his neck by the width of a grass-blade, and dug deep into mossy turf beside him.

'Strike!' shouted Gawain. 'It was no part of our bargain that you should play with me thus!'

'Why, nor it was,' agreed the Green Knight, 'and now your head out a little further . . .'

And for the third time he swung up his axe, and swung it singing around his head, and brought it down. And this time Gawain felt a sting like a gad-fly on the side of his neck, and a small trickle of blood running down inside his coif, and the axe stood quivering in the turf beside him.

Then Gawain sprang from his knees and leapt clear, drawing his sword as he did so. 'Now I have borne the blow and you have drawn the red blood, and if you strike again, I am free of my vow and may defend myself!'

The Green Knight stood leaning on his axe and laughing a little; and suddenly Gawain saw that though his garments were still green, they were but the garments in which a man rides hunting, and he was not the Green Knight at all, but his kindly host of the past week. And then he saw that he was both.

'Gawain, Gawain,' said the knight, 'you have indeed borne the blow, and I am in no mind to strike again. Indeed, had I been so minded, your head would have lain at my feet the first time I raised my axe.'

'Why, then, this game of three blows?' Gawain asked, breathing quickly.

'The first two blows that touched you not, these were for your promise truly kept, for the one kiss and the two kisses my wife gave to you while I rode hunting, and that you rendered up to me when I rode home at evening. The third blow that drew blood was for your promise broken, when you gave me her three kisses but not the green ribbons from her waist.' He saw the look on the young knight's face, and his great smile broadened. 'Oh, I know all that passed between you. It was at my will that she tempted you, and had you yielded to her tempting, and dishonoured your knighthood and my house, then indeed you would now be lying headless at my feet. As for the green girdle, you took and hid it but for love of your life. You are young, and he must be a sad man indeed who does not a little love the life

172

God gave him. So now that I have drawn blood for it, I forgive you the girdle.'

Gawain pulled the green ribbon girdle from its hiding-place and held it out to him. 'I am ashamed, none the less. I am unworthy of my place at the Round Table.'

'Nay,' said his host the Green Knight, with booming kindness. 'You are only young with the life running hot in you. And did I not say that you are forgiven? There will be few knights at the Round Table with a better right to sit there than you. Keep the green girdle in remembrance of this adventure; and come back with me to my castle, that we may end the Twelve Days of Christmas in joy.'

But Gawain, though he put the green ribbons round his neck again, would not stay. 'I must away back to my liege lord,' he said. 'But before I go, pray you tell me, noble sir, who you are, and how you came to be both lord of the castle where I have been made welcome and happy this week past, and the terrible Green Knight, who dies not when his head is struck from his shoulders?'

'My name is Sir Birtilack,' said the other. 'I was minded to test for myself the courage of Arthur's champions of the Round Table, having heard much of the High King's court, even here in my northern wilderness. For the rest – question not the ways of magic.'

So they parted as dear friends who have known each other a lifetime. And Gawain rode back through the Forest of Wirrel and the wild border country of Wales, until he came again to Arthur's court, and his own place that he had fully earned among the foremost of the brotherhood of the Round Table.

8

BEAUMAINS, THE KITCHEN KNIGHT

It became King Arthur's custom that at Pentecost, when all of the Round Table knights who were free to come gathered each year to his court at Camelot, that he would not sit down to dine until some strange thing had happened or some marvellous sight been seen or a quest begun.

And on one Pentecost, a while before noon, Sir Gawain, looking from a window of the Great Hall, saw three men enter the inner courtyard on horseback, and with them a dwarf on foot. The three men dismounted, and left their horses in the dwarf's care; and as they turned towards the keep, one of the men leaned upon the shoulders of the other two; and he was taller than either of them by a head or more.

'Here comes your strange happening, if I mistake not, my Lord King,' said Gawain, turning from the window, back to where the King and his knights were waiting; and in a few moments more, the three men came into the Hall, the young giant in the centre still leaning on the shoulders of the other two, as though he was maybe too weak from his own height to stand without them. All three were shabbily dressed and journey-stained, but the tall one, for all his seeming weakness, was the goodliest young man to look upon that anyone present had ever seen, brown-skinned and barley-haired, with eyes as clearly blue as the sky on a March morning; long limbed and broad of shoulder, and with hands that, for all their huge size, Sir Lancelot, looking at him, recognized at once for a swordsman's hands and a horseman's hands. And Sir Lancelot was a judge of such matters.

When the three of them had come the length of the Hall, and checked before the dais where King Arthur sat, the tall young man dropped his arms from the others' shoulders, and stood up straight as a tilting lance. And without waiting for the King to speak first, he said, 'Now God save you, my Lord King, and all your fair fellowship. I am come to ask of you three gifts.' The corners of his wide mouth tilted upward. 'Not unreasonable gifts, but such as you may grant with honour. And the first I will ask of you now, and the other two I will ask of you this day a twelve-months.'

'Ask,' said Arthur, who liked the look of the young man on sight, 'and you shall have what you ask for.'

'I ask that you give me food and shelter until the twelve months be up,' said the young man.

'Nay, lad, ask for something better than that.'

'There is nothing that I want – until this day a twelve-months.'

'So be it, then, food and shelter you shall have. For I never denied that to any man,' said Arthur. 'And now, tell me your name.'

'That I had rather not, until the proper time,' said the strange young man.

'It must be as you choose,' said Arthur. 'Yet I would be glad to know who you are, for you are one of the goodliest young men that ever I have seen.' And he gave the young man over into Sir Kay's keeping, bidding him to give the boy food and lodging as though he were a lord's son.

'Assuredly he is not that,' said Kay with a sniff, 'nor even a gentleman's son, or he would have asked for horse and armour. I will give him warm lodging in the kitchen, and all the food he wants. And I make no doubt he will be as fat as a yearling porkhog by the time the year is out. And since he will not tell his name, I shall give him one; I shall call him Beaumains, Fairhands, for indeed I never saw bigger and finer hands – nor ones that looked less used to work.'

At this, Sir Gawain frowned deep between his red brows, for he too liked the look of the young man, and did not much care for Sir Kay and his thin barbed wit; and Sir Lancelot said quietly, 'I'd have a care there, Lord Seneschal, for the boy looks to me to have had other uses for his hands than chopping wood and turning a spit; and I'd not be surprised if one day he used them to make you regret that mockery.'

But Arthur said nothing, for he thought, The boy has the look of endurance about him. If he must come to his knighthood by the hard way, it is of his own choosing, and I dare say he will take no harm by it.

And Beaumains said nothing at all.

So for a full year he served in the kitchens, and the other scullions jeered at him because he did not know how to do the things that were easy and familiar to them – until he learned their skills himself, and then they learned the unwisdom of such jeering. And Sir Kay made his life a misery with petty punishments and waspish jests. Both Sir Gawain and Sir Lancelot offered to take him as their squire, even without knowing who he was; but he thanked them with a courtesy that was like the gentle courtesy of a great hound, and remained in the kitchens. He had his fill of food, and a warm place by the fire at night, but the only kindness he received was from the dogs, and from Sir Gawain who clapped him on the shoulder once or twice in passing, and from Sir Lancelot, who gave him three silver pieces at Christmas to buy a warm cloak. And in all the while, he never returned evil words to Sir Kay, or complained, or seemed the least out of temper with his fellows, even when he tried, as he sometimes did, to teach them better manners by ducking one or other of them in the horse trough.

So the time drew again to the Feast of Pentecost.

And on Pentecost morning, as the knights were gathered in the Great Hall, a damosel came running, and knelt before the King and begged him for aid.

'For whom?' said Arthur. 'For yourself? What is this adventure?'

'For my sister, the Lady Lionese,' said the damosel, 'who is held captive in her own castle, besieged there by a cruel tyrant, the Red Knight of the Red Lands, who has laid waste her estates, and now demands that she gives herself to him.'

Almost before she had done speaking, Beaumains, who had been standing by the inner archway that led from the kitchen stair, came forward eagerly to stand before the King. 'My Lord Arthur, I thank you for the food and drink and lodging that I have had in your kitchens this twelve-months past. Now I ask for the remaining two of the three gifts you promised me.'

'Ask, then,' said Arthur.

'Sir, firstly I ask that you will give me the adventure of this damosel, for it is in my mind that I have earned it!'

'In mine also,' said the King, 'and the third gift?'

'That Sir Lancelot of the Lake shall ride with me until he judges that I have earned knighthood; for I would be made knight by him and by no one else.'

The King glanced questioningly at his friend, the foremost among his knights, and Lancelot nodded. 'It shall be as you wish,' said the King.

But the damosel had risen from her knees. 'So I am to have none but your kitchen page to aid me, when here in your Hall sit the best knights in Christendom?' And the colour burned in two fiery spots on her cheekbones, and her eyes were bright with angry tears. 'Then keep your aid, for I want none of it!' And she swept from the Hall, shrilly calling up the page who was walking her palfrey to and fro in the courtyard, and mounted and rode furiously away.

And while they still heard the beat of the palfrey's hooves, a page brought word to the King that the dwarf who had come with Beaumains last year stood in the forecourt, with a warhorse and a fine sword, and said that he waited for his master.

So, followed by most of the company in the Hall, Beaumains strode out, and greeting the dwarf as an old henchman, took and buckled on the sword, and mounting the great warhorse, rode away, the dwarf following on his sturdy cob.

And Sir Lancelot, sending for his own horse and his war gear, armed and mounted and in a while rode after him.

But he did not ride alone, for Sir Kay also had sent for his horse and armour, saying, 'I also will ride after my kitchen knave, though not to give him knighthood, but a good drubbing for thrusting himself forward in this way!'

'Better you bide at home, man, and eat your dinner,' said Sir Gawain. But Sir Kay was too angry to listen; and Sir Lancelot only smiled a little, his twisted half-sad smile inside his helmet.

Riding hard and alone – Lancelot had fallen behind a little to keep clear and watch what happened – Sir Kay caught up with Beaumains just as Beaumains caught up with the damosel. 'Beaumains!' he shouted. 'Hi! You kitchen knight, if you want to leave your cooking-pots and play at chivalry, here I come to teach you the game!'

And Beaumains pulled his horse round, and said in a voice quite different from the voice that anyone had heard him use before, 'First learn that game yourself! Sir Kay, I know you for an ungentle knight. Therefore, *beware of me!'*

Then Sir Kay set his spear in rest and spurred straight in upon him. But Beaumains, having no spear, drew his sword and at the last instant, wrenched his horse aside and struck up the other's spear with the flat of the blade, then thrust the sword point under the fluted rim of the other's shoulder-piece, and tipped him from the saddle, with a wound trickling red into the summer dust. Then Beaumains dismounted, and taking up Sir Kay's spear and shield, swung back into the saddle and rode on his way.

Many small cruelties and injustices had been repaid with that blow.

And Sir Lancelot also dismounted, made sure that the wound was not serious, and heaving Sir Kay on to his horse again, patted the beast's neck, saying, 'Take him home. You have more sense than he has.'

Then he too remounted and rode on.

Meanwhile Beaumains had again overtaken the damosel; but he got no kind greeting, for indeed though she was fair enough to look upon, her name, which was Linnet, was the gentlest thing about her. 'How dare you come following after me?' she cried. 'Get back to your kitchen, Beaumains. Aye, I know your name, given to you by the knight you have felled by a foul blow. Given because your hands are so big and coarse — hands for plucking geese and turning a spit!' And then, growing shriller yet, 'At least ride further off from me, for you stink of greasy cooking.'

'Say what you will,' said Beaumains steadily, 'I shall not turn back, your adventure is mine to achieve, given to me by the High King, and I shall not swerve aside from it while the life is in me!'

'Achieve my adventure, you kitchen knight?' she jibed. 'Nay, but before long you shall meet with such a foe that you would give all the rich broth you ever supped in Arthur's kitchens rather than stand your ground against him!'

'I shall do the best I may, and we will see how it turns out,' said Beaumains gently; and rode on, a little behind the damosel.

Before long they came to a dead thorn tree, from whose branches hung a black spear and a black shield. And under the tree sat a huge knight all in black armour, his raven warhorse grazing nearby.

'Now flee away down the valley before that knight can mount his horse,' said Linnet, 'for that is the Black Knight of the Black Lands, and none may stand against him.'

'My thanks for your warning,' said Beaumains, and held straight on as though she had not spoken it.

And when they drew near, the Black Knight got to his feet, and said, 'Damosel, is this your champion, brought from King Arthur's court?'

'Nay, Sir Knight, this is but a greasy scullion, who follows me whether I will or no. Therefore I beg of you, teach him to turn back from me; for I am sick of the kitchen smell of him.'

'Why then,' said the knight, whistling up his black charger, 'I will knock him out of that fine saddle, for a kitchen knave has no right but to go on foot – and his horse is a fine one and will be of use to me.'

'You make mightily free with my horse,' said Beaumains, 'and indeed he is yours if you can take him! Come then and try, or stand aside and let us pass, this damosel and I.'

'Nay,' said the Black Knight, 'that is not a fitting thing – that a kitchen knave should ride against her will with a fine lady.'

'That would depend on the kitchen knight and on the lady,' said Beaumains, stung out of his usual steady quietness. 'But indeed I am no scullion, but a gentleman born, and of nobler blood than you!'

Then the Black Knight mounted his horse and took down his shield and spear from the dead thorn tree, and the two rode apart the proper distance and turned and thundered towards each other; and the black spear shattered on Beaumains's shield; but Beaumains's spear took his foe in a joint of his armour, piercing through mail and flesh, and the Black Knight pitched from the saddle all tumbled like an arrow-shot bird. When she saw the Black Knight lying dead, the damosel wrenched her palfrey round, and striking her heel fiercely into its flank, rode off without a word.

But Beaumains dismounted, and stripped off the dead knight's armour – beautiful plain black armour with a blue-purple sheen where the sun caught it – and put it on. Only he kept his own sword and Sir Kay's spear. And while he was securing the last buckle with the help of his dwarf, Sir Lancelot, who had sat his horse quietly at a little distance, looking on, came up. 'And do you judge that you have earned your knighthood now?'

His vizor was up, and Beaumains looked him straight in his odd twisted face and smiled. 'Yes, sir,' he said, and knew that he had been right; there was nobody else from whom he would choose to receive his knighthood.

'I also, with all my heart,' said Sir Lancelot. 'But first tell me your name – I will keep it under my helmet for so long as you wish.'

'Sir,' said Beaumains, 'I am Gareth, youngest son of King Lot of Orkney – youngest son but one of Queen Margawse.'

There was a little silence in the forest clearing, and somewhere afar off sounded the alarm call of a jay.

'How comes it, then, that of Sir Gawain, and Sir Gaheris and Sir Agravane, all your brothers, none of them knew you when first you came to court?'

'It was eight years since any of them had seen me; and even a brother changes between nine and seventeen,' said Beaumains, who was now Gareth, simply. 'But truly, I think Gawain felt something for me from the first, for he has shown me kindness in this past year, even as you.'

'Kneel then, Gareth of Orkney,' said Lancelot.

And when the young man knelt before him with

his bright sandy head bent, Lancelot gave him the light buffet between neck and shoulder which, when vigil and ceremony were stripped away, was all that was really needed for the making of a knight.

'Rise, Sir Gareth, and go on your way; when you return you will surely find a place at the Round Table, for already you begin to be a worthy knight.'

Then Sir Gareth got up, and put on his helmet and mounted the black horse, leaving his dwarf to lead his own. And he and Sir Lancelot parted, one to ride back to Camelot, the other to ride on after the Lady Linnet.

When Gareth caught up with the damosel, she cried out on him, shrill as a hawk, 'You need not think to be my accepted knight because you have killed a better knight with a coward's blow! Faugh! Ride down wind of me, for your smell sickens me! But at least I shall not have to suffer that long, for in a while we shall meet with a champion who will treat you even as you have treated him whose armour you wear. Therefore flee while you may!'

'I do not flee from any man,' said Gareth, 'nor, while the life is in me, do I leave off from following you until the adventure is accomplished.'

Before long as they rode, the damosel angrily in front, Sir Gareth a little behind and his dwarf bringing up the rear, they heard the beat of horses' hooves and a crashing in the undergrowth, and out on to the track ahead of them rode a knight all in green; green surcoat over his armour, green shield and spear, green housings on his horse, and the crest of cut silk that topped his helmet fluttering green like young beechleaves in spring-time.

'God's greeting to you, damosel,' he said, reining across the way. 'Is that my brother the Black Knight who rides with you?'

'Nay,' said Linnet, 'it is a mere kitchen knave who has slain him most foully and stolen his armour.'

'Then you slew a good knight,' said the man in green, 'and I shall slay you, in payment for the foul blow!'

'No foul blow,' Gareth said, 'I slew him in fair fight – indeed the advantage was to him, for I had no armour but my jerkin. So did I take his armour which was mine by right, as the spoils of conquest.'

Then the two set their spears in rest, and fell to most furious jousting, there upon the woodland track, until their spears were all in splinters and they betook them to their swords. And when Gareth unhorsed the Green Knight they fought on foot. And all the while the damosel Linnet mocked the Green Knight and cried out upon him for being so slow to finish off a mere scullion in stolen armour, until in his rage he struck such a blow at Gareth that his shield was hacked in half.

Then Gareth shook the broken halves from his arm and, taking both hands to his sword, leapt in upon his foe, swinging the bright blade high, and brought it down in such a buffet upon the green crested helm that he dropped like a stoned hare, and lay half stunned, with his wits away. And lying so, he cried quarter.

'Whether you have quarter of me is for the damosel to decide,' said Gareth, standing over him. 'For unless she plead for you, you shall surely die.'

'Then he must die,' said Linnet, 'for never will I plead with a scullion!'

'Fair Sir Knight,' said the fallen man, 'spare my life, and I will forgive you the death of my brother; I will be your man, and my thirty knights who follow me.'

'Willingly will I spare it, if the damosel begs me.' And slowly Gareth raised his sword as though for the death stroke, the eyes of the Green Knight straining up after the blade.

'Stop!' cried Linnet. 'Do not slay him! I beg it of you, you – kitchen knave!'

Gareth lowered his sword, and bowed his head to her in all courtesy. 'It could have been asked more kindly, but you have asked it, damosel, and it is my pleasure to do your will.' Then to the fallen man, he said, 'Sir Knight of the green harness, I give you your life. Go free and get you to Camelot, your thirty knights with you. Swear allegiance of King Arthur and tell him that the Knight of the Kitchen sent you to him.'

'Truly I thank you for your mercy,' said the Green Knight. 'But the day draws on to evening. Come back with me to my manor and rest for the night; and in the morning we will go our ways, I and my knights to Camelot, and you and the damosel on the road of your adventure.'

So that night they lodged with the Green Knight; and the damosel cast scorn upon Sir Gareth and would not suffer him to eat with her at the same table. 'Shame it is, to see you treat this scullion as an honoured guest,' said she.

But the Green Knight said, 'Worse shame would it be to treat him with dishonour, for he has proved himself a better fighting man at least than I am.' And he set Sir Gareth to eat at a side table, but himself ate there with him.

Next morning they set out upon their separate ways. And as before, Linnet jibed at Sir Gareth for his kitchen smell and big hands, and bade him ride downwind of her. And as before, Sir Gareth bore it all quietly, giving her no angry retort, but saying only, 'Damosel, you are uncourteous to mock me so; for I have served you well till now, and it may be that I shall serve you better in time to come.'

'That,' said the damosel, 'we shall see!' But for the first time she looked at him as though he were human, and she herself a little puzzled; and she bit at her lower lip.

Presently the track they followed led out from the trees, and in the distance rose the walls and towers and crowding roofs of a fine city; and between the woodshore and the city was a fair meadow, newly scythed, and all about the meadow stood pavilions of dark blue silk, and all among the pavilions wandered knights and ladies in trailing silks and damasks of the same deeply glowing blue, and pages walking slender gaze-hounds whose collars were of fine blue leather, and squires exercising horses in rich trappings of the like colour. And in the midst of the meadow was a pavilion bigger and finer than all the rest, a blue spear standing upright beside the entrance, and a blue shield propped against it.

'Now indeed it is time for you to flee,' said the damosel, 'for there is the pavilion of Sir Persant of Inde, who men call the Blue Knight, one of the greatest champions in all the world, and his five hundred knights camped about him; and even Sir Lancelot and Sir Gawain would be hard put to face him under arms; therefore I bid you again to flee while there is yet time for fleeing.'

But she spoke a little less harshly than before.

'Almost it seems as though you do indeed fear for my skin,' said Sir Gareth; and there was a flicker of easy laughter in his voice, as he snapped his vizor shut.

'Nay, your skin is no concern of mine; but the castle where my sister is besieged is not seven miles from here, and the dread grows on me that you may be overcome, now that we are so near.' And then it was as though she heard what she had said, accepting him for her champion after all. And she looked at him quickly, but could see nothing of his face behind his closed vizor; and she said with her breath, still half angry, caught in her throat, 'Now what manner of man are you? A gentleman indeed? Or a mere spirit-less creature of dumpling-broth after all? For never did woman treat knight so shamefully as I have treated you, and yet always you have answered me courteously and never departed from my service.'

'Damosel,' said Sir Gareth, 'your harsh words have

served a useful purpose; for they angered me, and anger strengthened my arm against those whom I must fight. As to whether I am gently born – I have served you as a gentleman should, and whether or not I am one, you shall know when the time comes.'

Then out from the tall pavilion appeared a squire, and he came to Sir Gareth, saying that his master bade him ask the Black Knight whether he came in war or peace.

'Go back to your master and tell him that is for him to choose,' said Sir Gareth.

And the squire went away. And in a short while another squire came from behind the pavilion leading a tall iron-grey warhorse, who trampled the ground beneath his hooves and fretted at his bit; and out from the pavilion came Sir Persant himself, in armour that took the sunlight with the blue flash of a beetle's wing, and mounted the horse, and taking shield and spear, turned to where Sir Gareth waited.

'So, he chooses war,' said Sir Gareth, and he struck spur to the black stallion's flank and broke forward to meet the Blue Knight.

And with the shock of their meeting, each had his spear shattered into three pieces, and both horses were brought down. Both knights sprang clear of the lashing hooves, and drawing their swords fell upon each other, hacking and hewing till the sparks flew; and at last Sir Gareth got in a blow to the Blue Knight's crest that burst the lacings of his helmet and tore it off and flung him to the ground.

Then, without waiting for the demand, the

damosel begged for mercy on the fallen knight, and Sir Gareth instantly lowered his upswung blade, and said, 'Mercy you shall have, because this damosel asks it; and because you are such a knight as my heart warms to, and sad pity it would be to slay such a one. Therefore do you take your knights and ride to Camelot, and there do homage to King Arthur, saying that the Knight of the Kitchen sent you.'

'That will I surely,' said the Blue Knight, 'but first, since the shadows are already lengthening, do you and the maiden you ride with sup and sleep here as my guests.'

So that night they were the guests of the Blue Knight; and the damosel Linnet no longer railed at Sir Gareth; but when the meal was over, she told Sir Persant how they rode to save her sister besieged in her castle by the Red Knight of the Red Lands, and of her companion's fights along the way. And 'Sir Persant,' she said, 'pray you make this gentleman a knight before we ride on, that he may be able to challenge the Red Knight as one of equal rank challenges another.'

'Most gladly will I do that,' said Sir Persant, 'if he will receive his knighthood at my hands.'

'And right gladly would I receive it of you,' said Sir Gareth, 'but that I received it yesterday at the hands of Sir Lancelot of the Lake.'

'So, and by what name, then, were you knighted?' asked Sir Persant.

'By my own, I am Gareth of Orkney, son to King Lot and Queen Margawse.'

And the damosel looked at Sir Gareth, and opened her mouth as though to speak, and shut it again, saying no word.

And the Blue Knight looked at both of them, and smiled a little.

Next morning they parted and rode their ways, Sir Persant towards Camelot with his knights, Sir Gareth and Linnet on towards the castle of the Lady Lioness; and well before noon the seven miles were behind them, and they came to the edge of a great level plain, and Gareth saw a little way off a fair castle, whose turrets rose up tall and proud in the morning sun. And between them and the castle was a spreading camp of tents and pavilions all of scarlet red, and knights coming and going among them whose armour, like their weapons and the trappings of their horses, were all the colour of cornfield poppies. A fair sight it would have been, save for a dark thicket of trees in the midst of the camp, from the branches of which, Sir Gareth saw as he rode closer, the bodies of some forty knights hanging as though from a gibbet. Still fully armed, their shields round their necks, their gilt spurs on their heels; and all dead, long and shamefully dead.

'Yonder is an ugly sight,' said Sir Gareth.

'Alas! There hang the bodies of those who came here before you, to save my sister,' said Linnet. 'Have you enough courage to succeed where they failed?'

'I can but try,' said Sir Gareth between his teeth, 'and that without delay.' And seeing a great ivory horn hanging from the branch of a sycamore that was the tallest tree in the thicket, he made towards it.

'Nay!' cried the damosel, behind him. 'Do not touch that horn! Not yet!'

And when Sir Gareth turned to look at her questioningly, she told him, 'When that horn sounds, the Red Knight comes out to do battle with him that sounds it.'

'So I had supposed.'

'But all morning long, the Knight waxes in strength until at noon he is stronger than seven men, but when noon is past his strength wanes until by sunset he is a strong and terrible champion indeed, but no more. Let the horn sleep until noon be past, or by sunset you will hang among those others.'

'I should deserve no better,' said Gareth, 'if I were to lie in wait to come upon him at his weakest time.'

And he took down the horn, the greatest he had ever seen or handled for it was carved most wonderfully from a whole elephant's tusk, and set it to his lips and sounded a note that rang back from the castle walls and brought all those within running to the windows, and the followers of the Red Knight from their pavilions to see who sounded such a blast. And the Red Knight himself came striding from his pavilion, armed and armoured all as red as blood; and two squires brought him his roan warhorse, and he sprang into the saddle.

But Sir Gareth was looking up at one of the windows of the castle, from which looked back at him a girl's face, as pale as a windflower and lit with a sudden wild hope. A pair of white hands fluttered to him beseechingly. And it was as though something in his breast took wing and flew up to the girl in the window that he knew would never return to him again.

'That is my sister, the Lady Lionese,' said Linnet, seeing where he looked.

'I knew that it must be she,' said Gareth, still looking. 'And truly I ask for nothing better than to fight for her and call her my lady.'

'And there,' said Linnet, 'comes the Red Knight!'

And Gareth pulled his gaze back from the face at the window, and looked round to see the Red Knight spurring towards him, all ablaze in the morning sun.

'Aye, leave your looking at yonder maiden, and look at me!' shouted the Red Knight. 'For I am the last thing that you shall see before you join the carrion hanging from those branches!'

Sir Gareth urged his horse forward, clear of the dark trees with their sad and dreadful burdens; and in the clear space between the camp and the castle, they parted their horses the proper distance; then turned with spears in rest, and hurtled towards each other so that they came together with a clash like noontide thunder. Each spear struck true to the heart of the other's shield, and splintered into kindling wood, and their horse-harness burst as though it had been but strands of silk, and horses and knights fell in one great tangle to the ground. Both horses were dead, and both knights stunned and lay so long unmoving that

all the watchers thought that they had broken their
necks, and marvelled at the stranger knight in the
black armour, who even in the moment of his own
death, could so overcome the Red Knight while the
sun was yet an hour short of noon.

But in a while, both knights stirred, and got them
to their feet, staggering, and drew their swords, and
so crashed together that it was like the last struggle of
wounded lions. For an hour they fought, and the
walls of the castle rang with their blade-strokes as
with the ding of hammer on anvil, and the sparks
flew red in the sunlight. And at the hour of noon the
Red Knight struck Sir Gareth's sword from his hand
and hurled himself upon him and by sheer weight
brought him crashing down.

For Sir Gareth the world began to spin and grow
dark; but then through the confusion in his head, he
heard Linnet's voice crying to him, 'Oh, Sir Beaumains, what of your courage now? My sister weeps at
her window to see you down and all her fair hopes
with you!'

And the last of his strength rose in him, and he
heaved himself up from under the Red Knight, and
got him in a mighty grip, and wrested the sword
from his hand, and tore off his helmet to end the
fight.

'Mercy!' groaned the Red Knight. 'I cry your
mercy! If you are a true knight, spare my life!'

'Did you spare the lives of those who hang yonder
from your death trees?' roared Sir Gareth, and raised
his sword.

But the other choked out, 'Not yet! Hold your hand and I will tell you all the reason for that!'

'The reason had best be a very good one!' said Sir Gareth.

'You shall judge. Once I loved a maiden. Never loved man more than I! But she told me that her brother Carrados had been slain by Sir Lancelot of the Lake, and she would have none of me until I had avenged him by slaying a hundred of King Arthur's knights and hanging them up like carrion. Then and only then would she be my love.'

Then the maiden Linnet added her plea to his. 'All this has been wrought by Queen Morgan La Fay, hoping to bring grief and shame upon Arthur and the flower of his knights; but through your strength and courage she has failed. And indeed this man fallen at your feet did all that he did under her spell, though this I might not tell you until now. His death will not bring back to life the men he has slain; therefore, pray you let him live.'

So Sir Gareth lowered his sword, and stood leaning on it, breathing hard. 'I spare your life,' he said. 'Get you to King Arthur and swear fealty to him, saying that the Knight of the Kitchen sent you.'

And the Red Knight stumbled to his feet. 'As you command, so I obey, for you have vanquished me in fair fight.'

Then they went to the red pavilion, where the afternoon sun shining through the silken walls made all to glow like the heart of a ruby. And the maiden Linnet salved and bound the hurts of both of them.

And while she did so, a chaplain came out from the castle, and the poor broken bodies were taken down from the dark thicket and given Christian burial.

Then horses were brought, and the Red Knight mounted, his head hanging low on his breast; and with his knights behind him, he rode off towards Camelot.

And the damosel said to Gareth, 'Come you.'

And together they went up to the castle and across the echoing drawbridge that had been lowered for their coming, and into the outer court. The people of the castle thronged about them, loud in their rejoicing, but to Sir Gareth they all seemed like the people of a dream, as he followed Linnet into the inner courtyard. And there on the threshold of her hall, in a gown of green worked all over with little flowers like a summer meadow, stood the Lady Lionese.

'Sister, here is the champion I brought to save you,' said Linnet.

And the Lady Lionese held out her hands in greeting, and said, 'Ah, Sir Champion, by what name shall I thank you?'

'I am Gareth of Orkney, son to King Lot and to Arthur's sister, brother to Sir Gawain,' said Gareth, and he knelt, and took the hands she held out to him, and felt how little and soft they were; but the world was swimming under him, and he heard the Lady Lionese weeping, as though from a long way off. 'Oh, his wounds! He is fainting – he is dying! What shall we do?'

And Linnet's voice saying, 'Call the squires and have him carried to a guest chamber, and send to the kitchen for hot water and clean linen. And broth afterwards. I will tend him.'

For several days he lay sick of his wounds, while Linnet dressed them with evil-smelling salves until the heat went out of them and they began to heal. And the Lady Lioness came and sat beside him with sprays of honeysuckle and dove-winged columbine in her hands, while her minstrels played beneath the window for his pleasure.

But in truth he needed no more pleasure than to lie and look at her.

One day when his wounds were on the mend, he said to her, 'Maiden, these have been the sweetest days of my life; and when I am well enough to ride from here, I shall leave all joy behind me unless you promise me what I ask.'

'And what is that?' said she, looking low under her eyelashes.

'That you come back with me to Arthur's court and marry with me there.'

Then Lioness put her arms round his neck and kissed him gravely, and spoke no word; but none was needed.

That night as the sisters sat together braiding their hair, she said, 'Dear sister, I wish you could be as happy as I. It should be you he loves, not me, after all the dangers that you have shared together for my sake.'

'After all my foul words to him?' said Linnet; and

she laughed. 'Nay, for all that he is so big and strong and valiant and faithful, he is too gentle for me. I should be weary of him in a twelve-month!'

'But you will come with us to Arthur's court?'

'That will I,' said Linnet. 'It may be that I shall find there a knight with a temper to match my own.'

And so, when Gareth's wounds were far enough healed, they rode together for Camelot, with Sir Gareth's dwarf riding behind.

And at Camelot they found the Green Knight and the Blue Knight and the Red Knight, each with their followings, already there. And all had sworn fealty to the High King, saying that the Knight of the Kitchen had sent them. And the King and Queen and all the fellowship of the Round Table greeted them warmly; and Sir Lancelot said, 'Would you think that the time is come now, for telling all men who you are?'

So, standing before them all, Sir Beaumains the Kitchen Knight said simply, 'I am Gareth of Orkney.'

Gawain let out a shout. 'What of your Knight of the Kitchen now, Sir Kay? I knew it! Did I not feel kinship with him from the first? Did I not always say the lad had good blood in him?' And he came to fling his arms round his young brother and beat him joyfully on the shoulders, and Gaheris and Agravane with him.

And when the cheerful tumult had somewhat died down, and by one and another the story of Gareth's adventures had been told, he took Lionese by the hand, and asked the King's leave to marry her.

'My dear nephew and my youngest knight,' said the King, 'if the maiden pleases, your wedding shall be in three days' time.'

And so three days later Sir Gareth and the Lady Lioness were wed. And after the ceremony in Saint Stephen's Church, came the wedding feast in the Great Hall; and when the feasting was done, the squires cleared back the tables in the lower part of the Hall for minstrelsy and dancing. And as the evening wore on, finding themselves together in a corner with a cup of wine between them, Lancelot and Gawain fell to watching the dancers led by Gareth and Lioness. And Gawain said, 'If it had been me, I would sooner have taken the younger sister.'

'The golden shrew?' said Sir Lancelot. 'Aye, well, the heart makes its own choices, though sometimes they be unlikely ones.' And he sounded as though he were forty instead of twenty-four. And he took good care not to let his eyes go to the Queen where she sat beneath her silken canopy looking on.

Instead, he watched where Gaheris and Linnet danced behind the bride and groom, and saw how their eyes flicked and flashed upon each other, every time the circling pattern of the dance brought them together. A fine fierce wooing they would make of it, those two, he thought; but he said only, 'I think Linnet will come to another of your kin before the leaves turn brown.'

And so indeed she did.

9

LANCELOT AND ELAINE

Before the wedding of Gaheris and Linnet, Sir Lancelot was off and away, riding errant on another adventure. Of all the knights of the Round Table, he was the one who most often rode away; and people thought that it was to gain honour that he went, sometimes up to the castle of Joyeux Gard in North Wales, which he held from the High King, but more often simply disappearing into the wilderness in search of danger and adventure. But in truth it was to save his honour and the Queen's that he went. For his love for Guenever and hers for him grew stronger as the springs and summers and winters went by; and when he could no longer bear to be at court, seeing her every day, talking with her, hawking with her, touching her hand in the dance, and knowing all the while that she was Arthur's Queen, then he would send for his horse and his armour, and ride away, lonely, leaving his heart as though pulled out by its root-strings behind him.

So in the autumn of Gaheris's wedding, he was far away, and riding through a strangely barren land, where the fields about the few settlements had a threadbare look, and the trees that in other parts of the forest would have been glowing with autumn fire of gold and copper, raised only a few withered brown leaves against the buttermilk sky. And so he came by chance over the bridge of Corbenic, and saw before him a tall tower, and huddled about the tower, the roofs of Corbenic town. And as he crossed the bridge, people came flocking from their houses and their work; and they gathered about his horse clinging to the bridle and stirrups and crying out to him as someone who they knew and respected. 'Welcome, Sir Lancelot, flower of knighthood! Now our lady will be saved from her dreadful fate!'

'What fate is that?' said Sir Lancelot, hard put to it among so many voices to make out what they said.

'Here within this tower she lies imprisoned in a bath of scalding water,' the townsfolk told him, 'and has been so for five long years, bound by the spells of Queen Morgan La Fay and the Queen of Northgalis, from jealousy because she is fairer than they – so fair that men call her Elaine the Lily – and there she must remain until the best knight in the world shall come to set her free!'

And all the while they told him this, they were urging his horse on up the street towards the tower.

'I see not why I should succeed, if other good knights before me have failed,' said Sir Lancelot. 'But I will do what I may.' And he dismounted before the arched entrance of the tower, and went on up the winding stair within, the townspeople still flowing at his heels. And so he came to an iron door at the head of the stair. It was bolted and barred from within, but the bolts and bars flew back as he set his hand to it; and he thrust the door open, and went in. The chamber was full of steam which lapped about him; but there in the midst of it he could make out a great butt of seething water, and in the butt, the Lady Elaine, holding out her hands to him imploringly. He strode forward through the eddying steam that was thinning in the draught from the open door; and he took her by the hand, and she rose up and stepped out of the scalding water. Then the women who had come up behind him gathered round her, and one took off her own smock and slipped it over her head, and another wrapped her in her cloak, for she was as naked as a needle.

And when she was clad, she put her hand back into Sir Lancelot's, and said, 'Sir, I thank you for my deliverance. And now, if it please you, let us go to the chapel that is near here, and give thanks to God.'

So they went down the stair and along the narrow way to the chapel, the people still crowding after, filled with silent joy. Then Sir Lancelot and Elaine the Lily knelt together before the altar to give their thanks. And for a little Sir Lancelot wondered again whether this was his miracle that God had given to him; and again he knew that it was not, but only the undoing of a magic spell.

And when they came out into the sunlight again, he looked at the maiden now that the flush of the boiling water was gone from her and her hair was drying to pale gold; and he saw why men called her Elaine the Lily, for it seemed to him that she was the fairest lady that ever he had seen – saving only Queen Guenever.

`She turned her head and smiled at him, very gravely and sweetly, and said, 'Sir, now that we have given thanks to God, will you take me home?'

'Most gladly,' said Sir Lancelot, 'if you will tell me where that may be.'

'It is but at the other end of the town,' said the maiden. 'For it is the Castle of Corbenic, and my father is the king of this land.'

Then Sir Lancelot understood the withered trees and the air of desolation, for he had heard, as all men had heard, of King Pelles of Corbenic who was also called the Maimed King because of a wound that he had from long and long ago, that never healed; and how, at the same time as he got his wound, his land itself had been wounded, so that there had been droughts and lean harvests and a shadow as of grief lying over it ever since. Strange stories he had heard, also of Corbenic Castle itself . . . But it was no time to be standing and thinking of such things, with the maiden standing looking at him, with her hand in his, and waiting to be taken home.

So he mounted his horse and took her up before him, and rode with her through the town, the people following quietly after, and some beginning to drift away, until he came to the tall grey castle crouched at the highest point, where the rocky hillside fell away to the half-dried bed of the great looping river far below.

In the broad outer courtyard, the castle people

were waiting to greet them, and Elaine's women came with soft cries of joy and concern to carry her away to her own apartments, while squires came to take Lancelot's horse to the stable, and others to lead Lancelot himself to the guest chamber to help him unarm, and then later to the Great Hall of the castle, where the tables were already set up and spread with white linen for the evening meal, and King Pelles, looking like the gaunt shadow of a man, lay on a gilded couch with the knights and ladies of his court about him, and Elaine sitting close at his side holding one of his wasted hands in hers.

'Ah, Sir Lancelot of the Lake,' said King Pelles – for like his people, he knew who the strange ugly knight was – 'God's blessing upon you, and my everlasting thanks for that you have saved my daughter when so many others have failed, and brought her back to me.'

Then all the gathered company followed him in thanks and greeting to Sir Lancelot, and he was given an honoured place at the High Table, and so they all sat down to supper.

And then, while the tables before them were still bare, a strange thing happened – or seemed to happen. Lancelot was never sure afterwards whether it was all a dream; one of those strange waking dreams he had had as a boy, and which he sometimes thought had to do with those lost years of his childhood that made him feel not quite like other people.

He thought that he looked up at the great window in the far gable-wall, and saw there against the sunset light a dove hovering on outspread wings, and hanging from her bill a little censer all of gold; and the faint smoke that wafted from the censer about the Hall was fragrant with all the sweetest spices of the world. And suddenly the great doors that were below the window opened wide, and in came a maiden all robed and veiled in white, and bearing in her hands a cup veiled also in white samite. And from the cup, even through its veiling, there shone a light so dazzling that none might look upon it fully. And the maiden, seeming to float rather than touch her feet to the ground, came up the Hall, holding the cup high before her, and passed about the tables, and so out of the door again. And the doors closed of themselves behind her.

And in the quiet that followed the cup's passing, it seemed to Lancelot that he had eaten and drunk better than ever mortal man. Indeed he could never afterwards remember that any other food came to table that night, nor that anyone there felt the need of it.

He lifted his face, which he had bowed into his hands as the cup passed, and asked, 'My Lord King of the Waste Land, what is this marvel?'

'A marvel indeed,' said King Pelles, 'for this that has passed before you is the Holy Grail, the cup from which Our Lord drank at the Last Supper, before His crucifixion, and in which, afterwards, was caught His holy blood. You know, as all men do, that this cup was brought to Britain by Joseph of Arimathea; and first it was lodged in Avalon of the Apple Trees in the holy place that he founded in this land. And after, it was lodged here at Corbenic, and I, who am kin to Joseph of Arimathea, and who men call the Maimed King, am also called the Grail Keeper. In time to come, the Grail shall pass about Arthur's table at Camelot, as tonight you have seen it pass around mine, summoning all the knights of the Round Table to the greatest and the last quest of all. And then shall be the flowering time for Arthur's Britain, and the flame of Logres shall shine at its brightest, before the darkness closes over it once more.'

For several days Lancelot remained at Corbenic, though he never saw the passing of the Grail again. He had ridden out from Camelot to escape his love for the Queen, but he had only brought it with him. And since by riding he could not outride it, it seemed to him, for a little, that there was no reason to be riding anywhere else. And the maiden Elaine was often in his company, as they rode together and played chess together, and talked much in the unkempt castle garden in the last warmth of the autumn sunshine. And with his heart full of Guenever, Sir Lancelot never knew that she was falling in love with him, nor guessed how many nights she wept herself to sleep.

But Brissen, her old nurse, knew.

And Brissen spoke with King Pelles, and heard what he had to tell; and she was of the Old People, the Dark People, and had skill with herbs and the spells that women use, and like many of her kind she had, too, something of the second sight. And from the King's chamber she went to Elaine, and said, 'Little bird, never weep so sorely, for though he loves only Queen Guenever, you shall have him for your loving lord for a little while; and you shall bear him a son and call him Galahad which is his father's first name, and he shall be the best knight in the world and heal your father's wound and bring the Waste Land out from the shadows.'

And she set herself to bring the first of these things about.

Next evening Elaine and her old nurse went secretly from the castle. And a while later a man, who Lancelot did not know was the husband of Dame Brissen, came to him privately and put something into the hollow of his hand; and when he looked, it seemed to him that it was a ring Queen Guenever often wore. And his heart began a slow drubbing beat that shook his rib cage, and he asked without looking up, 'Where is my Lady the Queen?'

'In the Castle of Case, not five miles through the forest. She is alone, and she bids you come to her.'

Then Sir Lancelot called for his horse, and rode wildly through the night and the autumn gale, with one of the grooms to guide him. And the bare trees lashed and moaned overhead, and always it seemed that Guenever's face with its soft hair streaming glimmered in the dark ahead of him.

In the courtyard of the Castle of Case he dropped to the ground, and asked the first person he saw, 'Where is the Queen?'

'She was weary, and has gone to her bed,' said Dame Brissen. But he was deaf and confused with the gale and the beating of his own heart, and he had scarcely seen her at Corbenic, and so he did not know her for Elaine's nurse, nor think it strange that she should be there.

'Come you first into the Hall, and drink a cup of wine by the fire,' said the old woman, 'for you are wet and must be weary with hard riding on such a night as this.'

He followed her; and there was warmth and quiet in the Hall, and no light but the flame-flicker of burning apple logs on the hearth. And then there was a crystal cup of warm spiced wine in his hands, and he drank it; and as soon as he had done so, a warm glow spread through him and it was as though he saw everything through a golden haze, and a great joy swelled in his breast because Guenever was so near . . .

'Come now,' said Brissen, and led him up a winding stair.

The great chamber above the Hall was in black darkness, so that he could not even see the window slits. He said, 'Guenever?' and walked forward into the dark.

In the morning when he woke, the cobweb grey of dawn was seeping in through the chinks in the shutters; and he turned to find the Queen his love in the bed beside him. And saw instead that Elaine lay there still asleep. Then a great bewilderment rose within him; and as he remembered all that had happened the bewilderment changed to grief and rage.

He shouted, 'Traitress!' and sprang from the bed and caught up his sword from the chest where it lay, and drew it from its sheath. 'You have betrayed me! I will kill you for this!'

And Elaine woke, and lay looking up at him with frightened eyes, never seeking to move as he stood over her with the naked sword.

'I have lived too long, and now I am shamed!' he said. And then, as still she did not answer, he cried out again like one in mortal pain, 'Elaine, why did you do this thing to me?'

'Because of the prophecy,' she said then, 'because we have to make Galahad, who shall heal my father and lift the shadow from this land and achieve the Quest of the Grail. And because – oh, Lancelot, I did it all for love of you; because I might not live without you, and save in courtesy you never looked my way!'

And she knelt up in the great bed, weeping.

Then Lancelot flung his sword into the corner, and said, but as though the words strangled in his throat, 'I will not kill you. It was not your fault, and I forgive you. See – I will kiss you to show that I forgive you.' And he took her in his arms and kissed her awkwardly between the brows.

But when she tried to kiss him in return, the grief and horror rose again in him, and with a great cry he sprang for the window, and flinging back the shutters leapt out. He landed in a bed of late sad roses, and sprang up, bleeding where the thorns had lashed his face and body – for he was clad only in his shirt – and still making his strange heartbroken outcry, ran for the half-fallen wall at the foot of the castle garden; and scrambled over, and fled on, down the rocky hillside and across the dried-out river, and was lost in the dun shadows of the autumn woods.

Christmas passed, and Easter, and the woods were shouting with cuckoos. But no word of Lancelot came back to Camelot; and then when a year was gone by, Sir Bors his cousin determined to wait no longer, but to go seeking him. And in his search, it happened by chance that he came to the Castle of Corbenic, and there he was made welcome by King Pelles, and by his daughter, the Lady Elaine.

And the Lady Elaine carried a very young baby in her arms.

And when, bowing before her in all courtesy, Sir Bors came to a closer view of the babe, it stirred from sleep and opened its eyes at him; and he recognised the wide grey eyes in its small sleep-crumpled face; and he looked at Elaine, startled, and knew that the babe at her breast never had those eyes from his mother.

And the Lady Elaine smiled a little, both proudly and sadly, and said, 'Yes, Sir Knight, this is Lancelot's son as well as mine; and his name is Galahad, and he shall be a better knight even than his father, for he shall be the perfect knight of all Christendom.'

'Sir Lancelot?' said Bors. 'Is he here?'

'He *was* here,' said the Lady Elaine. 'Alas, no

more.' And she told Sir Bors how Sir Lancelot had come to Corbenic, and how he had run mad and fled into the forest, and no one had been able to find him or gain any word of him since.

Then Sir Bors was sorely grieved; and next morning after hearing Mass he rode sadly away, turning his horse's head back towards Camelot.

And back at Court, when the Queen asked him if he had gained any news of Lancelot, he told her no, not wishing to cause her the grief that his news must bring. Yet the thing was too heavy and too sore in his breast for him to carry it alone, and so in a while he told Sir Ector of the Marsh and Sir Owain the Bastard and certain others; and a secret once told to two or three is a safe secret no more; and so, none knowing quite how it came about, it began to be known through the court that Sir Lancelot had a son by King Pelles's daughter, and that he had run mad. And so it came to the Queen after all.

For a while, Guenever herself was half mad with grief and anger, which tore at her all the worse because she must keep it hidden, while King Arthur, forced to stand by and pretend even to himself – above all to himself – that she was but grieving for the loss of a friend, came near to breaking his own heart without anybody noticing.

And so another year, and part of a third year went by; and though Sir Ector and Sir Gawain and many others of the Round Table rode out in search of him, none brought back any word.

Then one day – it was Candlemas, and the first chill snow-drops were in flower in the tangled garden of Corbenic Castle – the Lady Elaine and her maidens came out into the garden to pass an idle hour. They had a ball of gilded leather to play with, for it was too cold to sit in the overgrown arbour or stroll to and fro along the half-lost paths. And in a while, as they played, tossing the ball from one to another, it fell into the midst of a clump of bushes by the old half-empty well at the garden's foot. One of the maidens ran to fetch it, and came back without it, and with her eyes wide in her startled face.

'Madam!' she said. 'There is a wild man asleep by the well! – oh, madam, it must be the Man of the Woods, let us run away!'

'Nay,' said Elaine, 'first I will look upon him for myself.' And a great quietness came upon her. It was as though she knew, even before she parted the bushes and stood beside the well . . .

She knew him at once; Sir Lancelot lying there with his head pillowed on his arm, asleep with the deep-spent exhaustion of a creature that has been run far and fast by the hounds. He was gaunt as a wolf after a famine winter, clad only in the rags of the shirt that he had been wearing when he disappeared into the forest, and the skin of some animal bound about him; and his hair was grey.

And Elaine sank to the ground beside him, weeping as though her heart must surely break.

Then came Brissen her nurse, and bent over her, saying, 'Do not wake him, for it may be that the dregs of the madness are still there, and if you rouse him now, he may run mad again.'

'What shall we do?' whispered Elaine. 'Oh, my love, my love, what shall we do?'

'I will cast a sleeping spell upon him, so that he shall not wake for an hour,' said the old nurse. 'And while he sleeps, we will bear him within doors, out of this cold, and lay him in the tower chamber, where he may be warmed and cared for.'

So she wove her magic, a small magic made with the fingertips and a singing-charm. And the maidens brought a fine deer-skin rug, and they muffled Lancelot in it, and bore him by a private stair into the tower chamber, and laid him on the bed there. And while some kindled scented apple logs in the brazier to warm him, Elaine and her old nurse stripped him of his rags, and bathed and salved his hurts. He was scarred and gashed like an old hunting dog, with the thin silver scars of ancient spear wounds from his knightly days, and the bruises and briar scratches he had got only that morning, and one great scar, scarce healed over and still darkly purple, on his flank.

'That was a boar's tusk,' said Dame Brissen, 'and must have come near to letting out the life.'

And Elaine wept again as she looked upon him; the gaunt man lying on his deer-skin, the famine hollows under his ribs and the scars he carried, and the marks of grief on his sleeping face.

Then they laid him under warm covers, and left him with Dame Brissen to watch beside him, while

Elaine went to tell her father that Lancelot was with them once more.

And save for Elaine herself, the King her father, her old nurse and her maidens, no one in Corbenic knew who lay in the tower chamber.

The magic sleep that Brissen had laid upon him passed back into true sleep, and it was not until far on into the next day that Sir Lancelot awoke. He lay looking straight above him at the canopy of the bed, where a white hart with a golden crucifix glimmering between its antlers ran endlessly through a green silk-worked forest, pursued by white hounds. There was a deep frown between his eyes, and they were shadowed with bewilderment, but the madness that had held him two years and more was all gone from them, and they were clear again. In a while, he began to look about him, and as Elaine came swiftly from where she had been sitting in the window embrasure, to bend over him, he strained up on to his elbow and cried out to her, 'How did I come here? For God's sweet sake, lady, tell me how did I come here?'

'Sir,' said Elaine, 'I scarcely know. There have been stories in these last months, of a man of the woods . . . If you were he, as you look to be, you have been wandering through the Waste Land like a madman, your wits all gone. But yesterday your wanderings brought you back to Corbenic, and we found you sleeping by the well in the garden. But now the madness is passed, lie still, and eat and sleep, and soon you shall be well again.' And almost before she had done speaking, he was asleep once more.

For two weeks Sir Lancelot lay in the great bed, tended by the Lady Elaine and her old nurse. For two weeks he lay gazing up at the white hart for ever fleeing from the white hunting dogs; then as he grew stronger, sitting in the carved and cushioned chair in the window and gazing out on the wintry country-side. He was courteous and grateful in all things to the Lady Elaine; but she had hoped that he would come to show her more than courtesy and gratitude; and he never did. Nor did he ever ask to see his son.

And when he was strong enough to ride, he asked for clothes and a horse, and took his leave of King Pelles, and of Elaine the Lily.

'My father would give us a castle,' said Elaine, 'and I will love you always. I will live for you if that pleases you even a little. I will die for you if by that I can serve you better.'

'Neither live nor die for me,' said Sir Lancelot. 'One day there will come another knight who will love you as I cannot.'

And the Maimed King on his gilded couch said nothing, for Galahad was born, and to him that was the only thing that truly mattered.

And Elaine watched from the ramparts as Sir Lancelot rode away. And she wept no more, for it was as though all her tears were dried up, like the living rain that never fell on the Waste Land.

★

Sir Lancelot rode straight back to Camelot, and all the court rejoiced and marvelled to see him return to them out of his long, lost darkness. Only the Queen, though she stood beside her lord the King to welcome him back, showed no joy in his coming.

For three days she nursed her coldness towards him. But after that she could bear it no longer, and sent one of her maidens with word that the Queen would speak with him in her own apartments. There was nothing strange in such a summons, for often Guenever would invite those she liked best among the Round Table knights to come and talk with her in her chambers or in the castle garden, or ride hawking with her or hear the music of her harper. But Sir Lancelot knew that no pleasantly idle hour was before him, and his heart beat hard in his throat as he climbed the stair to the Queen's apartments.

The Queen's maidens were gathered about the fire, playing with a gaze-hound puppy and listening to the music of a little Welsh harp played by an old grey harper in their midst. But the Queen had drawn aside into the tall west window of the chamber to catch the last light of the evening on her embroidery. She glanced up as Sir Lancelot entered, and moved her hand towards the wall-seat opposite her. Then she went on with her stitching. She was working a fiery crimson dragon upon golden damask; a new shield-cover for the King.

The window embrasure was almost like a little room in the thickness of the wall, full of the pale clear winter sunshine, while the rest of the chamber was already shadowy. Even the struck notes of the harp sounded shadowy. Sir Lancelot knelt at the Queen's feet, holding himself still, until at last she looked up from her stitching, and said in a small clear voice as though she were speaking to a stranger, 'And so you have come back to us, Sir Lancelot.'

'I have come back,' Lancelot said. 'It has been a long time.'

She saw his grey hair and the marks of grief on his strange crooked face, and her heart whimpered over him. But she only agreed, 'It has been a long time,' and pulled a new strand of scarlet thread from the tangle beside her. 'Truly, I wonder that you have come at all.'

'I had to,' said Sir Lancelot.

'I do not see why. Surely once your senses returned to you, you had all that you could wish for at Corbenic. They say King Pelles's daughter is very fair, and indeed it must be so, that they call her Elaine the Lily.'

'She is very fair,' said Sir Lancelot, 'but it is you that I love.'

And that was the first time that ever the words had been spoken between them. And while the sudden silence lasted, the harper struck three lingering chords on his harp.

Then Guenever said, 'It is Elaine that you gave your son to.'

And Sir Lancelot said, 'Guenever, it was not as you think. They brought me a ring like the one you wear, and told me that you bade me come. They gave me something to drink; and the room was wolf-dark. And I thought that it was you.'

The thread of scarlet silk snapped in Guenever's hand, and she looked up from her embroidery and met his gaze; and so they remained looking at each other. And not another word was spoken between them at that time.

But from that day forward, the love between Lancelot and Guenever was changed from what it had been before. It was stronger than ever, but it was no longer as simple as it had been, for doubt and jealousy and regret had been added to it; and before long, guilt, for it was from that time that they gave up trying to keep apart from each other. And from their coming together, there came sorrow and loss and darkness, upon themselves and upon Arthur and upon Arthur's kingdom, even as Merlin had foretold before he went to his own darkness under his magic hawthorn tree.

And Elaine? After Sir Lancelot was gone she drooped and dwindled away like a lily starved of the sun and rain. And the spring went by, and summer ripened and fell. And the snowdrops came again in the castle gardens; and when the second summer came, she knew, and all those about her, that her life was almost sped. Then she sent Galahad to a certain abbey, bidding the nuns of the place to care for him and bring him up in the ways of God; and when he grew older, to see that he was schooled by men who could train him in all things fitting to a knight.

And she spoke to her father and her old nurse and all those about her, telling them what she would have them do when the life was gone from her. Weeping, they promised that all things should be as she wished. Then she called for parchment and ink and quill, and she wrote a letter. And when the letter was written, there was nothing more that she must do, and so, like a bird taking wing, her spirit flew from her body and was gone.

Then her attendants did all that she had bidden them. They dressed her in her finest silken gown, and laid her in a litter, with the rolled parchment in her hands, and bore her from the Waste Land and away through the late summer forest, until they came to the looping narrow waterway that joined itself at last to the broad river that flowed past Camelot on its way to the sea. And there they made ready a barge hung all over with black, and laid her in it, scattering the flowers of late summer over all; and with one old dumb manservant to steer the barge, they left her to the river.

And the river carried her on until it joined the other that flowed by Camelot, and still on, through dark stretches over-arched by alder trees and out into open meadow stretches between banks thick with meadowsweet and tall purple loosestrife, until the barge came to rest at last, against the bank below Camelot town.

Arthur and the Queen were speaking together at a window that looked far down upon the river – the same window where she and Lancelot had spoken together after his long absence – and they saw the black-draped barge come down on the quiet silver flood, and settle into the bank above the bridge. And Arthur called to Sir Kay, 'See you that black barge? It is in my mind that there is a strangeness about it. Take Sir Bedivere and Sir Agravane, and go and look more closely, and bring me back word.'

So Sir Kay went, and the other two with him; and in a while he returned and said, 'Sir, in that barge there lies the body of a fair damosel, and there is no one else in the barge but an ancient man at the steerboard, who will speak no word; and indeed I think that he is dumb.'

'Here is a strange thing indeed,' said the King. 'We will come now and look upon the body of this lady.' And he held out his hand to the Queen, and together, with many knights following, they went down through the narrow streets of Camelot town where the swallows still darted among the eaves, and across the water meadow to the river bank. And there lay the black barge at rest, and in it the body of the lady, clothed in cloth-of-silver, and with her fair hair parted and combed upon her breast, and she lying as though she smiled in her sleep.

'This is a sorry sight,' said the King. And he asked the old man who she was, but could get no answer.

And the Queen said softly, 'How fair she is. Like a lily cut down by an early frost.'

And then they saw the letter in the lady's hands that lay folded on her breast; and the King climbed aboard the barge and gently took the parchment and broke the seal and read what was written within.

'Most noble knight, Sir Lancelot, my most dear lord, now has death taken me as you would not. I loved you truly, I that men called Elaine the Lily; and therefore to all ladies I make my moan, and beg them pray for me. Give me honourable burial and pray for my soul, Sir Lancelot, as you are a true knight above all knights.'

And that was all.

Now Sir Lancelot was among those who had come down with the King and Queen; and he had taken one look at the lady's face and then stood as though turned to stone and deep-rooted there in the riverside grass. And when Arthur had done reading the letter and while all the company were murmuring for sorrow, he covered his face with his hands and groaned. And when he took his hands away, he said, 'My Lord Arthur, I am sorry at heart for the death of this lady. God knows I never desired her death, but I could not love her as she loved me.'

'Love comes as it chooses, or does not come; nor can it be fettered,' said the King, half as though he answered Sir Lancelot, and half as though he spoke to his own heart. And he gave orders for the bestowing of the lady's body until the time of her burial, and turned away.

And as the Queen turned also, she said to Sir Lancelot, 'You might have shown her something of gentleness, to save her life.'

And Sir Lancelot felt the world reel under him, for

he was in many ways a simple man, and he never understood women, least of all the Queen.

Next day the Lady Elaine was buried worshipfully in the Church of Saint Stephen, and Sir Lancelot offered the Mass Penny for her soul, and strewed the last of the summer's roses and strands of honeysuckle on her grave.

And when all was done, the old dumb servant turned again to the river where the barge waited for him, and pushed off from the bank, and poled back upstream.

And Sir Lancelot was left with a new grief and a new guilt to carry. He thrust it deep down into himself and grew a scar over it; but he carried it all his days.

10

TRISTAN AND ISEULT

The years went by and the years went by, and the names on the high backs of each seat at the Round Table changed as knights died in battle or upon some hazardous quest and new young knights took their places. And among the lost names were those of King Pellinore and his son Lamorack, slain in a family feud by Gaheris and Agravane in vengeance for the death of their father King Lot of Orkney. And after that, four seats beside the Seat Perilous were empty for a while; for though King Arthur knew that he must bow to the old laws of the blood feud, he sent both slayers away on a long and difficult quest by way of penance. And his heart was sore within him, and he wished that he still had the good counsel of Merlin beside him.

That year, on the Eve of All Hallows, the knights gathered about the Round Table were deeply aware of the empty places in their midst. For on that night of the year, the time of Ingathering, when the cattle were brought in to their winter quarters, many people set a place at their table and left it empty for the ghosts of their dead if they should come wandering home in search of shelter for the dark months ahead.

On this particular Hallowe'en, winter was coming in with a gale of wind and rain that beat like dark wings about the walls of Camelot; and at the height of the storm, just as they were ending supper, a squire entered with word that a stranger stood outside, asking shelter for himself and his horse.

'Bring him in,' said the King, 'on this night of the year all men are welcome at all firesides.'

And so the stranger came in. A tall man, and dark, dark as the storm outside as he came into the torch-light; wet and windblown, he might have been some creature of the storm. Yet about him there was a great stillness.

He came up the Hall, and as he thrust back the heavy folds of his cloak, all men saw that he carried under its shelter a harp in its bag of finely broidered mare's skin.

'God's greeting to you,' said the King as the man knelt at his feet. 'Both for your own sake and for the sake of the harp you carry, for a harper with a new song to sing, a new tale to tell is most welcome on such a night as this. Eat and drink, and warm your-self, and then maybe of your courtesy you will wake the magic of the harpstrings for us.'

'That will I, most willingly,' said the stranger.

He was given a place beside the hearth, and food freshly brought from the kitchen, and a cup of wine. And when he had eaten and drunk and his cloak had ceased to steam in the warmth of the fire, he took his harp from its bag; a beautiful harp of black bog-oak with strings of findruim, the white Irish bronze, and began to tune it, and when every string sang true, he asked, 'Now, what would you have, my Lord King? A song of war? Or hunting? Or love?'

'Any song, so that it be a new one,' said the King.

'Love,' said Queen Guenever, who had come in with her ladies to listen.

The harper was silent a little, his face in the firelight looking as though he listened to something very far off, or deep within himself, as his enquiring fingers woke random note after random note from the shining strings. Then he said, 'I will give you the tale of Tristan and his lady Iseult.'

Then there was a murmuring and a stirring of interest up and down the Hall, for Sir Tristan's name and his reputation as a knight-at-arms were known to many there. They settled themselves to listen, and sometimes telling it as a story, sometimes letting it drift into song in time to the haunting harp-music, and then back to story again, the harper wove for them this tale.

When King Marc of Cornwall was young and new to his kingship, there was war between Cornwall and Ireland. And word of it came to another King, Rivalin of Lothian. And for no other reason than that it was the sea-faring season and he thought it time his young men were blooding their spears, he called out his ships and his warbands and they coasted round Britain to King Marc's aid. Then together they won a great victory over the Irish; and when all was over, King Marc gave his sister in marriage to Rivalin for a bond between their two peoples.

For a year Rivalin lived happily with his Cornish princess, but at the end of that time, bearing their son, she died. And for Rivalin it was as though the sun went out. For a long while he could not bear even to look at the child. He called him Tristan which means Sorrow, and gave him to the Queen's old nurse to rear. And when the boy was seven, he took him from the nurse and gave him to a young knight called Gorvenal to train as a prince should be trained. And from the first, Gorvenal loved him as a much younger brother, and taught him to ride and handle sword and spear and hawk and hound, to sleep hard and bear pain unflinching, to think for himself and to keep his word, and many other lessons beside. And from somewhere deep within himself he learned to play the harp so that it was as though he played upon the very heartstrings of those who heard him.

One day when Tristan was sixteen years old, he and Gorvenal were sitting beside the fire; and Gorvenal looked across at the boy who was leaning elbows on knees and gazing into the heart of the flames. 'What do you see in the fire?' asked Gorvenal.

'I see far countries,' said Tristan.

And Gorvenal knew that this was the time he had long expected. 'Tristan,' he said, 'I too have been thinking of far countries. Here in Lothian there is no man now who can outmatch you in the princely skills – but for a prince to be foremost among his father's subjects might be a somewhat easy glory, after all.'

'I do not care for easy glory,' said Tristan.

And next day he went to his father and asked him for a ship, that he might go seeking adventure.

The King his father agreed, and the ship was made ready, and when the sailing weather came after the winter storms, Tristan and Gorvenal and a handful of young companions set sail.

Now it had long been in Tristan's heart to visit his mother's country, for his old nurse had often told him stories of the land and its magic; and so they made the long coastwise voyage and came at last to the southern coast of Cornwall; and there they landed and bought horses and rode north towards Tintagel.

So they came at torch-lighting time to Tintagel Castle on its rocks high above the sea, and stood at last before King Marc in his Great Hall. And he and Tristan looked at each other and their hearts warmed together in that first moment. Then the King greeted his guests and asked them from what land they came.

'From Lothian,' said Tristan.

And the King looked at him more closely, as though suddenly he were seeing another face within his, and said, 'Did ever you see my sister, the Queen of Lothian?' and then he sighed. 'Fool that I am, you would not have been born when she died.'

'I was born on the day she died,' said Tristan. 'I am her son.'

And the King put his arms round him, and would have wept, had he been a man for tears.

For two years Tristan and his companions were of King Marc's court; and as it had been in Lothian, so it was in Cornwall, there was no one who could ride swifter on the hunting trail than Tristan or master him at sword play; the King's harper could not make music so sweet, and he could throw any wrestler in the kingdom.

And then a sore trouble fell upon the land; and this was the way of it.

The war with Ireland, that had first brought Rivalin from Lothian, had flared again a few years later, and the patched-up peace had left Cornwall pledged to pay a yearly tribute to Ireland in corn and cattle and slaves. Cornwall had paid the tribute for a year or two, and then both sides had let the matter drop. But now the Queen of Ireland's own brother, the Morholt, mightiest of champions, sent word that the time had come for paying the old debt, and that because it had been owing fifteen years, it must be paid all in slaves; one child in every three born in Cornwall in all those years. If they would not pay, then let them make ready to defend themselves in battle, for he was coming with a fleet of ships – or else let them find a champion to fight him, the Morholt, in single combat.

Then Marc's fighting men began to make ready for war, though with little hope of victory, for Ireland had grown strong under the Morholt's leadership;

and the women, weeping, began to seek out places to hide their children.

Then Tristan sought out the King his uncle, and said, 'Better than all this ready-making for war, if we were to send the Morholt his champion for single combat.'

'Much better, if we had such a champion. But the Morholt has the strength of four men,' said King Marc.

'I have skills that you have not seen me use as yet,' said Tristan. 'I will go out as Cornwall's champion, if you will have me.'

'You are only a boy! To let you go would be to throw your life away!'

'It is my life,' said Tristan, 'and I am your nephew, your nearest kinsman, I have the right to go!'

And King Marc knew that this was true. So he sent word to the Morholt that a champion of the royal house of Cornwall would meet him in single combat. The place was set – a small island just off the Cornish coast – and on the appointed day Tristan and the Morholt came together upon the island. They landed there alone, Tristan from the shore, the Morholt from the Irish ships that lay waiting out to sea. The Morholt moored his boat where the dark rocks gay with tufted sea-pinks came down to the water's edge. But when Tristan had landed he pushed his boat off and let the tide take her.

The Morholt stood watching, dark and menacing as thunder in his black armour. And 'That was surely a strange thing to do,' said he, when Tristan drew near, 'to push your boat off again when you landed.'

'Two of us came to this island,' Tristan said, 'but only one will need a boat to carry him away.'

Then the Morholt laughed sharp in the back of his throat, and drew his sword; and together they went up to the level space in the midst of the island. And there they fought, all the long day. Tristan was the swifter swordsman, but the Morholt had the strength of four men, and his blows fell so thick and fast that at times there was nothing Tristan could do but cover himself as best he might behind his shield. At last, in trying to guard his head, he raised his shield too high, and the Morholt lunged beneath his guard and got in a great blow to the thigh that laid it bare to the bone.

But the fire of his wound and the blood-flow that should have weakened Tristan, seemed to wake a desperate valour in him that he had not found before. And, yelling, he leapt forward with blade upswung, and brought it down in a whistling stroke that bit so deep through the mail and into the bone beneath, that when he jerked it free a fragment of the blade was left in the Irish champion's skull.

With a great cry the Morholt turned and fled, leaving a crimson trail, towards where his boat was tied and other boats from the Irish ships were already putting in for him.

And Tristan walked down the landward shore of the island, trailing crimson also; and he could hear the Cornish warriors rejoicing, but it all seemed far off, and his blood soaked and soaked into the grey shingle.

As soon as the ship that carried the Morholt reached Ireland, messengers were sent for the King's daughter, the Princess Iseult; for in all the land there was none that had her skill in the healing craft. But not even she could bring a dead man back to life, and by the time she reached him the Morholt was dead of his wound. But she drew out the jagged piece of sword blade from his skull, and laid it carefully by, in case she should ever meet a man whose sword lacked a splinter that shape . . .

Meanwhile Tristan lay for a long while sick of his wound in Tintagel Castle. And when at last it was healed the King, rejoicing, gave him knighthood and determined to make him his heir. But his lords urged him to marry and have sons of his own. And when he would not listen to them, some, who were jealous of Tristan, began to whisper among themselves that it was his doing. And Tristan, knowing this, also urged his uncle to marry. 'Give me three days to think the matter over,' the King said at last, 'and on the fourth morning you shall have your answer.'

And on the fourth morning as he sat, his mind still not made up, waiting for his lords and nobles, in the sunshine before the entrance to his Great Hall, two swallows fell to quarrelling about something high over his head, darting and circling, snatching it from one to the other, until even as the King looked up, they dropped it. A thread like gossamer, but red as flame; it drifted to his outstretched hand, and he saw that it was a long hair from a woman's head; and such a colour as the King had never seen before, so dark as to be almost purple in the shade, bright as fire where the sun caught it. Surely only one woman in the world could have hair that colour; and one woman in the world would be hard to find!

So when the lords came for their answer, Marc showed them the hair, and told them, 'I will marry, as you wish, but only the woman to whom this hair belongs.'

Then Tristan stood forward from the rest, and said, 'My uncle, give me the hair and a ship, and I will go and seek this woman, and if she lives, bring her back to you.'

So a ship was made ready for a long voyage, and Tristan gathered his closest companions, Gorvenal among them, and set sail, to search all the countries of the world, save Ireland, where since the Morholt's death, the King had ordered death for any Cornishman who landed on his shores.

Yet a man's fate is a man's fate. The ship was caught in a great storm and driven hither and yon, and when the storm blew itself out at last, they found their vessel driven hard aground on the shore of a great river-mouth. Far off were other boats, and beyond, hearth smoke and the glint of pale sunshine on roofs and church spires. Then Gorvenal, who had travelled far in his own youth before Tristan came to him, said, 'Now God help us, for yonder is Wexford, and we are held fast upon Ireland's shore!'

And with the folk of the nearby fisher village already coming down in curiosity they took hurried counsel and determined to claim that they were storm-driven merchants from Less Britain. This story they told, and the people believed them, and as they were helping them to get their horses overboard and up through the shallows, the bells of Wexford began to toll; and one said to his neighbour, 'Another good man dead for the Princess's sake.'

And when Tristan asked his meaning, they all told him, taking up the story one from another, how a terrible fire dragon was laying waste the land, and how in despair, for with the Morholt dead they had no champion who could stand against it, the King had offered his daughter the Princess Iseult to any man who could slay the monster. 'Many good knights have tried and failed,' said the last man, sadly. 'It is for the latest of them that the bells of Wexford are tolling now.'

Then Tristan thought, It is I who led my comrades into this sore danger, and if I can slay the dragon, then the King can scarcely have us killed, even if he discovers that we are from Cornwall.

So in the dark hour before the next day's dawn, he got into his mail shirt and bade farewell to his companions and, taking his own horse from among those grazing under guard close by, he rode away.

He knew that he was travelling in the right direction, as the light grew round him, by the scorched desolation of the countryside; and presently he heard a terrible roaring far ahead of him, and across his path came galloping a knot of horsemen who shouted to him to turn back and fly for his life.

But Tristan turned his horse into the way they had come, and rode on. All the country looked as though a heath fire had swept through it, and all around were the blackened snags of tree stumps and the scorched and half-eaten bodies of cattle. And then, rounding a rocky outcrop, he saw before him a cave mouth dark in the side of the hill, and before the cave mouth, coiling itself to and fro in anger, long as a troop of horse and wicked as sin, was the dragon he had come to seek.

He crouched low in his saddle and, levelling his spear, struck spurs to his horse and charged in to meet it. His spear point took it in the throat as it reared up to meet him, wounding the creature sore; but horse and rider plunged on into the heat and poison fumes that made a cloud about it; and crashing against the spiked and glowing breast-scales, the horse dropped dead. But Tristan sprang clear, as the dragon, still with his spear in its throat, roaring in agony and coughing out great gouts of steaming blood, made for the rocks that choked the hillside. And Tristan sprang after it with his sword upraised.

There among the rocks and the scorched hillside scrub they came together. Tristan's shield was charred to cinders in the first onslaught and his ring-mail seared his flesh; but the dragon was weakening as the spear dragged at its throat and breast; and its fire was sinking. And at last, seizing his chance, Tristan sprang

235

in and drove his sword between the breast scales and found the monster's heart.

The dragon reared up with a death-roar that echoed like thunder among the hills, flailing the air with its tail and savage claws, then crashed to the ground, its fire dying out.

With his last strength, Tristan wrenched open its jaws and hacked off the venomous black tongue. But his own hurts were very sore, and he had scarce dragged himself a spear's throw from the great carcass when the ground seemed to rise beneath his feet and a roaring blackness engulfed him.

Now one of the men whom Tristan had seen fleeing from the dragon's lair was the King's steward, who had long desired to marry the Princess Iseult though she had no liking for him at all. And when he saw that Tristan rode straight on despite their warning, he slipped away and turned back also, to see what should befall and whether there might be any gain for him in it. And so he was near at hand when he heard the monster's death-cry; and made bold by that and the silence that came after, he pressed on. And among the rocks he found the dead horse and then the dead dragon, and of the dragon slayer no sign at all. And he thought, The dragon must have eaten him before it died, and there lies my chance. And drawing his sword he fell to hacking at the monster's carcass until his blade was reddened to the hilt. Then he galloped back to Wexford and gathering his henchmen and a cart, returned again with them to hack off the dragon's head and fetch it into the town. And when they had brought it in, he made for the King's Hall to show him the battered head and his blood-stained sword, and claim the Princess in marriage.

The King was torn between joy that Ireland was delivered from the terror that had laid it waste, and grief that his daughter must marry a man she loathed. But he had given his word, and he sent to the women's quarters to bid her come down for her betrothal to his steward.

When she received this word, the Princess thought more quickly and desperately than ever she had thought in her life before. And she sent back word to the King that she was unwell and could not come down to her betrothal that evening or the evening after, but that on the third evening she would come. For she was sure that the steward had not himself slain the dragon but was stealing some other man's glory; and she must play for time.

Then she sent for Brangian, chief among her maidens, and bade her have horses ready at the postern gate before dawn, that they might ride out and look at the place where the dragon had been slain. 'There is some mystery here, and it may be that by seeking we shall find the answer to it,' she said. 'We *must* find the answer to it, for sooner than wed with that man I will die!'

So in the dark of next morning, the Princess and her maiden slipped out and rode away towards the hills. They found the torn remains of the horse, and then the headless carcass of the dragon; and searching further, they found Tristan lying among the rocks and the blackened thorn-scrub. And at first they thought him dead. But when they had stripped off his mail, they found him clawed and scorched from head to foot, but with seemingly no death-wound upon him. And stowed in the breast of his mail shirt the Princess found what she and Brangian both knew for the forked tip of the dragon's tongue.

'Dear mistress,' said Brangian, 'you will not go to your betrothal to the steward tomorrow.'

'Nor any day,' said the Princess; and she put back the hair from Tristan's forehead and looked long into his shut face. Then they set to work to get him across Brangian's horse, and Brangian mounted behind him; and so they returned in the dawn to the King's palace.

When Tristan came back to himself he was lying in a strange chamber with two women bending over him, and one had hair as black as midnight and the other had hair the colour of hot coals. And he knew that whoever she might be, this was the maiden he was seeking, for no other in all the world could have hair quite that colour, the colour of the single hair in the silken packet he wore round his neck. And then as he raised himself on his elbow and looked about him, he saw a silver bowl beside the bed, and lying within it the forked tip of the dragon's tongue.

In a voice that seemed not to be his own, he croaked, 'Well for me that you found and kept that wicked thing, for it is my only proof that it was I who slew the dragon.'

'Well for me also,' said the red-haired maiden. 'For my father the King promised me to whoever could rid Ireland of the monster, and his steward claims that it was he.' And then they both heard what she had said, and there was a startled silence between them.

Then the Princess, when she had done salving Tristan's wounds, gave him a healing broth, and when he had drunk it and was asleep, she and Brangian took his mail shirt and his sword into the next room that they might clean them without disturbing him.

And when the Princess drew his sword, she saw that a small piece was broken out of the blade halfway down.

She laid the sword on the table without a word, and going to a carved chest, brought from it a small packet wrapped in crimson silk; and from the packet she took the fragment of sword-iron which she had taken from the Morholt's skull, and held it to the gap in Tristan's blade. It fitted perfectly.

Across the table she and Brangian looked at each other. 'This is the slayer of my kinsman,' she said in a small cold voice. 'And he lies in my hands for killing or curing.'

Brangian cried out, 'No! Oh no, my mistress! You cannot kill a man lying helpless at your mercy!'

'I can,' said Iseult, 'but I have no need to. I have only to show this to my father.'

'And destroy the dragon's tongue! If this man who slew the Morholt can prove that he also slew the dragon, the King must forgive him. And oh, my lady, remember he is all that stands between you and marriage to your father's steward!'

The Princess stood a long while looking down at the sword blade. Then she said, 'Yes, that is worth remembering.' And began to laugh. And later that night she went to her father and told him of the knight she and Brangian had found, and of her certainty that the steward's claim was false.

'As to that,' said the King when he had heard her out, 'here are two men, both claiming the same thing. Their claims must be heard before the Assembly.'

'Then let the Assembly be called for three days' time,' said the Princess. 'In three days I can heal his dragon wounds and he will be ready to prove his right to the kill.'

Meanwhile, word of how the King's steward had slain the dragon reached Tristan's men waiting beside their ship, but of Tristan himself no word at all; and even when Gorvenal went in secret to the dragon's lair, he found no clue that he could bring back to them, and they could only think that his venture against the monster had cost him his life. But even as they were debating what they should do next, word spread from the palace that another warrior had claimed the dragon-kill, and that his claim and the steward's were to be tried on the next day but one. And before they had drawn breath from that, came a letter from Tristan to Gorvenal written with much difficulty, but telling him what had happened, and bidding them all to be present at the trial, clad in their best, and bearing themselves as befitted bold and honest merchants of Less Britain.

The day came, and the great timbered council hall was made ready for the Assembly, and when the lords and nobles were gathered, and the supposed merchants of Less Britain also, the eyes of all were drawn to the monstrous head that had been dragged in on its cart and set up in the midst of the place. Then the King entered and took his place in the High Seat; and after him came the Princess Iseult walking proud under the royal goldwork that bound her hair.

Then the Horns of Summoning were sounded; and from the door on the right of the hall the steward strutted in, and from the door on the left, Tristan, still weak from his wounds but carrying himself less like a merchant than a king's son, none the less.

Then the King raised the silver rod in his hand for silence, and when all the gathering was hushed, he spoke to them of the dragon that had ravaged their land, and his promise of the Princess's hand to any man who could rid them of this horror, and how many of their best and bravest knights had died in the attempt. 'Now the evil is ended, and the dragon's head lies here before you, and two men claim the kill. Therefore, before you all, I call upon both to prove their claims. And since my steward was the first to make it, let him now be the first to speak.'

The steward stood forward boldly enough, and said, 'My Lord King, I slew the dragon in long and bitter struggle for the love of the Princess; and here lies the monster's head to prove my claim as clearly as though it could speak!'

'And yet a man might come upon such a carcass, slain by another, and cut off the head to claim the kill for himself,' said the King.

'And what man would slay this dragon and walk away?' demanded the steward.

'Let the second claimant answer that,' said the King.

And Tristan stood forward also. 'My Lord King, merchant as I am, I have some skill with weapons. And hearing of the evil fallen upon this land, I thought that if I could slay your dragon for you, it might be good for trade! By God's grace I slew the creature; but being myself sorely hurt, a great blackness came upon me; and it must be that while I lay in the blackness, this fellow came and found the dead dragon and thought to gain the reward that another man had done the bleeding for.'

'Lies! All lies!' shouted the steward.

'One of us lies indeed, but it is not I! My Lord King, has this head been closely guarded so that none might come near it unseen?'

'Night and day,' said the King.

'Then let some of your men force open its jaws. Maybe it could indeed have spoken to prove your steward's claim, *if it were not lacking the tip of its tongue!*'

And when four strong warriors had forced the jaws open, there for all to see, was the black stump of the dragon's tongue! Then Tristan sprang up on to the cart and held aloft the forked tip of the tongue which he had brought with him in a napkin. 'My Lord King, nobles of Ireland, is the proof enough?'

'The proof is enough,' said the King, and the great gathering echoed him.

And when they looked round for the steward, he had slipped away.

But there was yet one more matter to be set right. And going to the King, Tristan knelt at his feet, and said, 'My lord, there is one more thing to be told, and better I should tell it now, than that you should hear it in another way.'

'Tell on,' said the King.

'It is this: four days since, it was I who slew the dragon; two years since, it was I who slew your kinsman, the Morholt.'

A great gasp ran through the Hall, and the King's brows drew almost to meeting. 'You killed Ireland's champion? Do you know what you say?'

'It was done in fair fight,' said Tristan.

'That is true,' said the King, 'and true it is also that the Morholt was slain by no merchant but by Tristan of Cornwall.'

'I am Tristan of Cornwall.'

'Then what brings you of all men to our shores?'

And Tristan told him the whole story of the quest for the Princess of the swallow's hair.

'Then,' said the King, when all was told, 'if I give you my daughter, you will take her not as your own bride, but to be Queen of Cornwall.'

'That is so,' said Tristan, and looked at the Princess; but though she had been watching him ever since he entered the Hall, she never looked back at him now.

The King thought a long while with his chin in his hand. At last he said, 'Maybe it is time that old scars were healed, and there was friendship once more between Ireland and Cornwall . . .'

And so the thing was settled; and beside Tristan's ship, another was made ready, and furnished with all rich things, to take the new Queen of Cornwall to her kingdom. And after three days of feasting and merry-making, they set sail.

At first they had fair weather, but within a day they ran into rough seas, and the Princess and Brangian and all her maidens were direly ill; so at last Tristan bade the shipmaster to put in to the nearest shelter he could find along the Welsh coast, while Gorvenal in the Cornish ship held on to carry word of their coming to King Marc.

At noon, the Irish ship came under the shelter of a long headland, and dropped anchor in a little cove where a stream came down from the steep woods inland; and Tristan and the other men sprang overboard to carry the women ashore. And Tristan held up his arms to the Princess as she came over the side, and carried her up through the shallows and set her down on the white wave-rippled sand. Now this was the first time that ever they had touched each other since she had tended his wounds, and that was a different kind of touching; and as he set her down, their hands came together, and their eyes also, and in that moment it was as though something of Iseult

entered into Tristan and something of Tristan into
Iseult that could never be called back again as long as
they lived.

Before evening Tristan and his companions built a
little cabin of green branches up the streamside for
the Princess and Brangian, and another for her
maidens. And when morning came, the storm was
over and the sun shone in a clear sky; but the seas
were still running high. They would have to wait
another night for the seas to gentle. And Tristan,
though he was careful not to be with the Princess
again, was glad. He wandered off by himself, and sat
among the sand dunes of the headland.

And there the Princess found him after all, and she
carrying a little packet of crimson silk in her hand. 'I
have something to show you,' she said, and undid the
packet and held out the splinter of metal in her palm.
'Draw your sword that I burnished for you while you
lay sick.'

And when he did as she bade him, she fitted the
sharp fragment into the gap in the blade; and they
looked at each other with the sword lying between
them. 'So you knew,' said Tristan. 'Even before I told
your father, you knew.'

'I knew,' she said.

'Why did you not kill me, Iseult?'

'And marry my father's steward?' But they both
knew that was not all the truth. And she tossed the
fragment away into the sand as something that no
longer mattered, and walked away.

That evening at moonrise, with taper-light glimmering softly from the little branch-woven cabins up the streamside, the shipmaster came to Tristan where he was walking to and fro on the edge of the men's camp, and said, 'The wind has gone round and already the seas are gentling; it will be fine sailing weather tomorrow.'

'Then make ready to sail on the morning tide,' said Tristan.

And he went to tell the Princess.

She was alone in the bothie, and combing her hair by the light of a honey-wax candle. 'I hoped that you would come,' she said.

'I came only to tell you that the seas are gentling, and tomorrow we sail with the morning tide.'

Iseult stopped combing her hair. 'I would that the seas might never gentle,' she said, and made room for him on the cushions beside her; and he sat down.

'Lady,' he said, 'that thought is best forgotten. You will be happy in Cornwall, and King Marc will be a kind and loving lord to you.'

'Kind and loving he may be,' said Iseult, 'but this is the last day that ever I shall be happy, and already the moon is up.'

'You will forget today.'

'Never,' said the Princess. 'Whoever takes me to wife, you are my lord as long as I live; and you know it.'

And Tristan bent his head into his hands and groaned.

'Do you love me?' said the Princess.

'Iseult, I am the King's man.'

'But do you love me?'

And Tristan said, 'Though it is like to be the death of both of us, I love you, Iseult.' And he put his arms round her and they clung together as the honeysuckle clings to the hazel tree.

But they sailed for Cornwall with the morning tide.

And so they came at last to the landing-place below Tintagel; and the King himself with all his court came down to greet the Princess of the Swallow's Hair.

'Until now,' said King Marc, with Iseult's hands in his, 'I thought that this marriage would be for the binding together of the rift between Cornwall and Ireland. But now I know that it is for making music in my heart . . . Your hair is as red as fire, but your hands are so cold; yet mine are big enough to warm them.'

And Tristan, turning aside to greet old friends and old enemies, thought, Dear God! He loves her too!

The wedding day came and went, and Iseult of Ireland was now Queen of Cornwall; and for a long time – or it seemed a long time to them – Tristan never looked her way nor she his.

Autumn and winter went by, and the year turned to spring; and one day Tristan came upon the Queen in the little garden that clung to the rocks below the castle; and she was looking towards Ireland and weeping; and all his love for her that he had pushed down into his dark and inmost places came rushing up to the light again, and he put his arms round her and held her close and kissed her. And after that, there was no going back for either of them to where they had been before.

And as ill luck would have it, they were seen by another nephew of King Marc's, Andret by name, who was jealous of Tristan. And from that day forward he spied upon them, waiting his time.

Again the summer turned to autumn, and the winter passed and the golden gorse flamed along the headlands. And the love between Tristan and Iseult would not let them be, dragging at them as the moon draws the tides to follow after it, until at last, whether they would or no, they came together again.

And all the while, Andret watched.

One night in early summer, the Queen went early to her apartments, saying that her head ached, for there was thunder in the air, and she would be alone. And soon after, Andret saw that Tristan's place in the King's Hall was empty. Then he too slipped out. Soon after, a palace servant with a gold coin hidden in his closed hand came to the King with word that the Queen begged him to go to her instantly in her bower.

And when Marc came striding into the bower, brushing aside Brangian who tried to hold him back, he found Tristan and Iseult held close in each other's arms.

Then the King's wrath was terrible; all the more terrible because of his love for his Queen and his kinsman. And waiting for no excuses, he shouted up the guard. And Tristan, for all that he fought like a wildcat, was taken and dragged away, while the Queen was held captive in her own chamber – until next day they were brought before a council of the chiefs and churchmen and lawmakers of the kingdom.

And Iseult was condemned to die by fire, which according to the law of the land was the proper fate for a queen who had betrayed her lord, and Tristan was condemned to be broken on a great wheel.

By dawn on the appointed day all the preparations had been made; and great was the grief and loud the wailing throughout the land, for Tristan was the champion and the hope of Cornwall, and the Queen had made herself beloved in her husband's kingdom as she had done in her father's.

Tristan was to die in the morning, Iseult after noon, and so he was led out first by men of the King's bodyguard. Now the chosen place of his execution was some distance from the castle; and on the way to it, they passed a little chapel set high on the edge of the cliff. And when they came to it, Tristan asked leave to go in and pray, saying that he had had no time to make his peace with God before they fetched him out that morning.

And after a little counsel-taking among themselves, the men agreed, and let him go in alone and unbound, seeing that there was no way in or out but the one door, and a high window that no man could get through, above the sheer drop to the rocks beneath.

But Tristan was a slight man and a desperate one,

and he got through that window all the same, and dropped into a furze bush below the clifftop that caught and held him from the long fall; and by little and little, using every finger- and toe-hold among the black rocks, he worked his way along below the edge, until he came to a place where he could regain the cliff-top out of sight of the chapel and the body-guard watching its door. Then he set off back towards Tintagel.

He had not gone far, when round a tump of wind-shaped thorn scrub he came face to face with Gorvenal. They wasted no time in exclaiming nor in greetings. 'Is the hunt behind you?' Gorvenal said.

'Not yet, I will tell you all later.'

'Meanwhile, the sooner we are many miles from here the better. See — here are your sword and your harp. I could not bide in Tintagel, and I could not be leaving them behind me.'

Tristan took his sword and hurriedly belted it on. 'Let you keep my harp for me until maybe I come for it,' he said, and set his hand an instant on Gorvenal's shoulder, and then walked straight on.

Gorvenal swung round after him. 'Are you mad? This is the way back to Tintagel!'

'I cannot leave Iseult to die in the flames,' Tristan said. 'I must save her or die with her.'

Gorvenal drew a deep breath. 'Two swords are better than one. If you are for Tintagel, then so am I.' And they went on together.

Soon they came in sight of the castle; in sight also of the Queen's execution place outside the gates, with the pyre already built and the people crowding round. And they settled down behind some hawthorn bushes to wait. It was no good to make any plan; they could only trust that when the moment came, God would show them what to do. Presently the castle gates opened, and King Marc with the rest of his bodyguard came out. And at the same moment, down the woodland track behind Tristan and Gorvenal, came a small terrible company wearing the long hooded cloaks and carrying the wooden clappers that marked them for lepers.

Gorvenal drew aside, as all men did from such company, but Tristan knew that God was showing him the way, and stepped out into their path and spoke to the leader of the band. 'Where are you away to, friends?'

'To Tintagel, though with heavy hearts, to see them burn the Queen,' the man croaked.

'Would you save the Queen, if you could?'

'That would we – and doubly, if it were made worth our while.'

'Lend me your cloak and clapper, and there will be no burning in Tintagel today,' said Tristan; and to Gorvenal, 'Have you any money?' And he took the gold piece his friend brought from the breast of his tunic, and dropped it into the bandaged hand the leper held out for it.

The man took off his stinking rags, and Tristan flung them on, pulling the hood forward over his face. 'Bide here in hiding, while I go on with your companions.'

'I also,' Gorvenal said.

'No. If aught goes wrong, you must be still free, to get the Queen away.'

And he went on with the lepers, swinging his clapper and crying, 'Unclean! Unclean!'

When they reached the execution place, the Queen had been brought out, and was being bound to the stake, the King standing by with a frozen face to see it done.

'Come,' said Tristan, to the sad creatures behind him, and they went towards the King, all men falling back to let them pass. And kneeling before him, Tristan cried out, making his voice dry and cracked, 'Lord King, a boon!'

'This is a strange time to come asking a boon,' said the King in a voice of stone.

'Not so strange, for we ask that you give us the Queen to be of our company.'

A gasp ran through the crowd. 'If she is to die a shameful death, we can offer her one more shameful than the fire. Slower, but maybe uglier.'

And the lepers clamoured, 'Give her to us! Give! Give!'

And the King's stone face broke up in a sudden agony and he shouted to the executioners, 'Cut her loose and give her to these creatures!'

Iseult began to scream and scream, and when Tristan sprang on to the pyre to seize her, she fought him like a wild thing, while all the crowd shouted in angry protest; and then she heard his urgent whisper in her ear, 'Iseult, it is I. Do not betray me!'

252

She went on screaming, but she ceased to fight, as though accepting despair, and allowed herself to be dragged down from the pyre into the midst of the lepers, and away up the track towards the woods, while again the people parted to let them through.

When word of Tristan's escape was brought to the King, his wrath was terrible, and he sent out the hunt for him in all directions. They found the lepers, but the Queen was no longer with them and they told how a terrible warrior had torn her from their midst and made off with her across his saddlebow. And of Tristan and Iseult they found no sign. They and Gorvenal had vanished as completely as rags of morning mist when the sun rises.

They held eastward and eastward away from Tintagel towards the sunrise, and so came at last to a little lost valley through which a stream threaded down from the high moors, shaded over by hawthorn and elder, and the small thick-set oak trees of the ancient forest reached up towards it from below. And between the moors and the forest the stream broadened into a little pool where the wild things came to drink at dawn and sunset.

'Surely here we shall be safe,' said Tristan. 'We are full three days from Tintagel, and it is many years since the King hunted these hills.'

'The hunting will be good here,' said Gorvenal, 'and we must hunt if we are to live.'

And Iseult said, 'This is such a place as our valley in Wales. We shall be happy here – for a while.'

So they built a hut beside the stream, and Tristan

and Gorvenal made themselves bows from forest yew, with strings braided from the red hairs Iseult plucked for them from her head, and went hunting when they needed food; while Iseult with her knowledge of herbs gathered plants and leaves and berries that were good to eat.

And they were happy – for a while.

It was young summer when they came to the hidden valley, and three times the bracken turned to russet, and three times winter came and they huddled about the fire, while Tristan woke the music of his harp and sang to them the haunting story-songs of Lothian and Ireland. Three times the hazel catkins danced in the March winds, and the hawthorn was curdled with white blossom, and the blossom fell.

And then one evening on the edge of another autumn, Tristan and Iseult sat before their hut at twilight. They were alone, for Gorvenal had gone off on one of his long solitary hunting trips. And suddenly Iseult drew close against Tristan, and said, 'Do you feel anything?'

'A little stirring of the wind,' said Tristan.

'No, not that.'

'A night moth brushed my cheek.'

'No, not that.'

'What, then, Iseult?'

'A shadow,' she said, 'there is a shadow fallen over us. Hold me close.'

Now that very day, far off in Tintagel, King Marc called for his horses and hounds to ride hunting next dawn. And he said to his Chief Huntsman, 'I am weary of the old hunting runs. Are there no hills in Cornwall where we have not hunted before?'

'There are the moors eastward beyond the Tamar River,' said the Chief Huntsman. 'It is many years since we hunted that way, so far afield.'

So the next day King Marc and his companions rode eastward – and three days later they set up their hunting camp below the high moors. They had good hunting, and killed three times, but when the hound pack was counted at evening, one of them was missing. It was a good hound, and the King's favourite, and the Chief Huntsman called out some of his men and set off at once to find it.

All night long they searched until, a while before dawn, he came to a stream threading down from the high moors; and among the stream-side hazels and elders he caught the glimmer of a fire. He hitched his horse's bridle over a low-hanging branch and turned upstream towards the light, meaning to ask whoever was up there if they had seen or heard a strayed hound.

He came to the last red embers of a fire and saw that it glowed before the doorway of a hut, and peering in, he saw a man and a woman asleep on the piled bracken of the bed-place. And the woman's outflung hair was flame red in the dying firelight, and the naked sword lying ready to the man's hand had a small piece broken out of the blade.

The Chief Huntsman turned away and went back to his horse and set out towards the hunting camp; and before he had gone three bowshots on his way, there was a rustling in the undergrowth and the lost hound came bounding out to follow at his horse's heels.

The camp was still asleep when he reached it, but he roused the King's squire, and went in to the King and told him what he had seen.

The King was silent a long moment when he had done; and then he said, 'Bid them fetch my horse, for I would see this man and this woman.'

So the King's horse was brought, and he and his huntsman set out. It was dawn when they came to the foot of the stream, and the King bade his huntsman wait with the horses, and went on alone up the stream side, his sword naked in his hand.

He came to the hut and looked in, and saw the two sleeping there in the grey dawn light. And he knew that he had only to step over the threshold and quickly use his sword, for they were completely at his mercy. He stood unmoving, looking in; and it seemed to him that he had never seen Iseult so beautiful, and his old love for her and for his kinsman knotted in his belly.

Then he stooped and took up Tristan's sword and laid his own in its place, and he stripped off one of his hunting gloves and laid it lightly on Iseult's breast; and he turned and went his way, sheathing the notched sword in place of his own.

When Tristan and Iseult awoke, they found the King's sword and his glove, and knew that they were discovered. And Iseult would have fled again, leaving a sign for Gorvenal to follow. But Tristan said, 'If we

256

do that, now that he knows we are together, the King will surely hunt us down. And yet he found us here and could have slain us and did not.'

'What does it mean?' said Iseult.

And Tristan remembered how, on the day he brought Iseult to Tintagel, the King had taken her hands and said that they were cold but that his were large enough to warm them. And he said, 'For you, it means a way back, and forgiveness, Iseult.'

'And for you?'

'The sword for me — it means that I must put myself at the King's mercy.'

'And will there be mercy?'

'He would surely have slain me, else.'

'We have been happy here — for a while,' Iseult said.

And in a little, Gorvenal appeared, and flung down the buck that he had killed. And when Tristan told him what had happened, he too said that it was time to be returning to Tintagel.

So they went back.

'You read my message,' said the King, sitting in the High Seat in his Great Hall, when they stood before him.

'We read your message,' Tristan said, 'and we came.'

'That is well,' said King Marc. 'Listen now. I will take the Queen back into my Hall and into my heart. But to you, Tristan, I say that the world is wide. I give you three days to leave Cornwall behind you. *Never come back!*'

Tristan said, 'In three days I will be gone from Cornwall. But if ever hurt or sorrow comes to Iseult at your hands, and I hear of it, *I shall come back!*'

Then Iseult spoke for the first time. 'If I am to be your wife again, I must end what has been between my Lord Tristan and me, not leave it flying like a torn sleeve. Grant us a little time to take leave of each other.'

The King pointed to a log on the fire, already crumbling into white ash. 'I give you until that log burns through.' And he rose and went into an inner chamber. But they knew that from there he would hear when the log burned through and fell.

Then Iseult slipped from her finger a ring of heavy gold, curiously serpent-twined and twisted. 'If ever you are in sore enough need of me,' she said, 'send me back this ring, and I will come to you. But beware how you send it, for if you do, then I will surely come, though it be the death of both of us.'

And Tristan took the ring and kissed it, and pushed it on to his finger.

And the burning log collapsed with a slipping and rustling and a last shower of sparks into the red heart of the fire.

In the Great Hall at Camelot, also, a log slipped on the hearth and fell with a shower of red sparks. And the voice of the harper fell silent; and even the dark wing-beating of the storm died away.

The High King sat gazing into the fire. Sir Lancelot stared at his own bony hands clenched on his knees, while one tear trickled down unheeded beside his ugly nose.

'Is that the end of the story?' asked the Queen, pitifully.

'It seems so.'

'What became of Sir Tristan?'

'There was war in Lothian soon after, and his father was slain, and when he had driven out the enemy and avenged his father, he left Gorvenal to rule the kingdom. And now he wanders the world with his sword and his harp, and the heart-space empty within him, for Iseult's sake.' The harper moved to return his harp to its embroidered bag. And as he did so, the light jinked on the ring he wore; a heavy gold ring curiously twisted like a serpent.

'Thank you for your harp-tale,' said the King gently, 'and welcome to Camelot and to our fellowship, Sir Tristan.'

A murmuring ran round the Hall, and then Sir Bedivere cried, 'Look!' and pointed. And when they followed the direction of his outstretched finger, they saw on the back of one of the empty seats Sir Tristan's name glimmering in the torchlight in letters of new and burnished gold.

So Sir Tristan became one of the knights of Arthur's Round Table. And for a while he came every year to the gathering at Pentecost, and other knights would bring back stories of his deeds up and down Britain and in Less Britain across the Narrow Seas.

And then one year he did not come, and all the stories ceased.

Nothing more was heard of Tristan, until one day Sir Lional, returning from a quest that had taken him into Cornwall and back to his native Benwick in Less Britain, said, blunt and heavy with sorrow, 'Sirs, I have seen Tristan's grave.'

All faces in the Hall turned to him. 'How did he die?' said the King. 'Is it known to you?'

Lional bent his head. 'I gathered the story, a little here and a little there. It seems that in his wanderings in Less Britain, he came to the castle of King Hoel, who was sore besieged by one Duke Jovelin, because he would not give him his daughter, against her will. Tristan aided the King and his son Karherdin against Duke Jovelin, and when they had the victory over him, the King offered his daughter to Tristan in gratitude. He could not shame her in her father's Hall, and they say she is very fair – she is an Iseult, too; Iseult of the White Hands, and – maybe he hoped for a little happiness . . .'

'So he married her?' said Guenever, half under her breath.

'He married her, and he was a true and loyal lord to her, though he could not love her as she loved him . . . The old King died, and Karherdin was the new King; and there was deep friendship between him and Tristan. And in the end – there was some feud; something to do with a maiden Karherdin loved and who had been torn away from him; and in the feuding Karherdin was killed, and fighting at his shoulder Tristan was sore wounded.

'And for all his wife's tending, and the physicians whom she summoned from far and wide, the wound sickened and he grew weaker day by day.

'He knew that his death was upon him, and that only one person in the world might save him. But whether she could heal him or no, he longed to see her face before he died. At last he sent for his squire and gave him Iseult's ring, and bade him go to the Queen of Cornwall in secret and show it to her, and beg her to come if she would save his life. "And when you return," said he, "if she be with you, cause your ship to show white sails; and if she will not come, then let the sails be black, for it will be time to put on mourning for me."

'So the squire went, disguised as a merchant, and gained speech with the Queen in private, and gave her the ring and Tristan's message, and she gathered up her salves and healing herbs and went with him without a backward glance.

'But the voyage was a slow one, for the ship was becalmed in the Narrow Seas; and all the while Tristan grew weaker, as the fever of the wound burned him up; and all that held him to life was his longing for Iseult and his waiting for the ship that would surely bring her to him.

'And Iseult of the White Hands had always known that his heart was left in Cornwall, and she saw when the ring was gone from his hand. And she heard his fevered mutterings while she tended him in the long nights, and so she knew of the ship, and the signal of the black or white sails. And jealousy tore at her, though she never let him see it, even when he begged her a score of times a day to look from the window and tell him if she saw a ship putting in from the sea.

'And then one morning as she looked from the chamber window, she did see a ship heading in for the harbour, and the sails of it as white as a swan's wings. She told Tristan what she saw, but when he asked her with seemingly the last breath that was in him as to the colour of the sails, for one fatal moment the bitter jealousy flared up in her, and she told him that they were black.

'So for Tristan there was nothing left to hold on to his life for, and he turned his face to the wall and let it go out of him on a great sigh.

'Then she cried out that they were white, white as swans' feathers, but she was too late.

'So the first thing that Iseult of Cornwall heard when she came to shore was the sound of bells tolling. And Tristan lay in the great church with candles burning at his head and feet; and the other Iseult standing beside his bier.

'When she came into the church and saw this, Iseult of Cornwall said, "Lady, stand further off from him, I pray you, for I loved him more than you." And she laid herself down on the bier beside him, and took him in her arms and kissed him. And they say that with the kiss her heart broke.

'When word of all this was brought to King Marc,

he took ship for Less Britain, and brought their bodies back to Cornwall. They say he spoke no word of grief or forgiveness, but he had them laid together in one grave.

'And when I stood beside it, a hazel sapling had begun to grow from Tristan's side of the grave, and from Iseult's honey-suckle, and they were already reaching out to intertwine with each other.'

'And that truly is the end of the story,' said Queen Guenever, very softly.

11

GERAINT AND ENID

And the years went by and the years went by, and every Pentecost the High King's knights, new-made or old, gathered still to Camelot, where the Round Table stood in the Great Hall. But at other times of year, Arthur would hold his court in other parts of his realm, at Carlisle or London or Caerleon, that he might keep close touch with all parts of the kingdom.

One Easter he held his court at Caerleon, and on Easter Day as he and the knights who were with him were sitting down to dinner, there strode into the Hall a tall young man who carried his red-gold head as high as though it were a torch; and he was clad in silk, with fine dyed leather boots upon his feet, and a gold-hilted sword hanging at his side. He strode up the length of the Hall to kneel at the King's feet, but still without lowering his head, and said, 'Greetings, my Lord King.'

'Greetings to you also, and God's welcome,' said the King. 'I seem to know your face, and yet I do not know your name.'

'I am Geraint, son of Erbin whose borders march with King Marc of Cornwall. You saw me once when I was a child and my father fought in your wars.'

'And what brings you to me now, Geraint, son of Erbin?'

'I have been biding this while past in the Forest of Dean,' said the young man, 'and this morning in the forest ways I saw a stag such as I never saw before, pure white, and proud-going above any other stag in the forest. Therefore I marked where the beast harboured, and came swiftly to bring you tidings of it.'

'That was well done,' said the King. 'Tomorrow at the young of the day, we will go and hunt this wondrous stag.' And he sent orders to the huntsmen and grooms.

And the Queen said, 'My lord, give me leave tomorrow to ride out to watch this hunting.'

'Gladly I give you leave,' said Arthur, 'and any of your maidens who care to ride with you.'

So the matter was agreed, and the feasting went forward with harp-song and merriment, until it was time to sleep.

But when morning came and the hounds were brought round from their kennels, there was no sign of Geraint, and Guenever lay sleeping late in her bed. 'Let them sleep,' said the King. 'They may follow when they wake, if they are so minded.'

And with Kay and Gawain and others of his knights for hunting companions, he mounted and rode away into the forest in search of the white stag.

Soon after, Queen Guenever awoke. She called to

her maidens, and while some of them helped her to dress, she sent a page to the stables to see what horses were left that were suitable for ladies to ride. But the hunting party had taken all the palfreys save for the Queen's own mare and one other. So the Queen, half laughing and half out of humour, chose one of her maidens, and said, 'What selfish creatures are men! You and I will ride after them together.'

So the horses were brought, and the Queen and her maiden rode away, out through the castle gate, and following the broad trail of men and hounds and horses, towards the forest. And presently as they rode, they heard the sound of horses' hooves coming hard behind them, and as they looked round, Geraint ranged up beside them riding a tall willow-grey horse. He was clad as he had been last night, in a damasked silken tunic, and a cloak of blue-purple worked with gold apples at the corners, that blew out behind him on the wind of his going.

'God's greeting to you, lady,' he said, 'I slept late, and so missed the hunting party.'

'I also,' said the Queen, 'but it will not be long before we find them – for if we take our stand up yonder on the ridge, we shall hear the horns when they sound, and the music of the hounds.'

So together they crested the ridge, and found open country beyond. They checked on the woodshore to listen for sounds of the hunt. And while they waited, they heard hoofbeats again, and three riders came by along the track below them.

And first there came a dwarf riding a tall prancing

horse and carrying a long wicked looking whip in his hand. And then there came a lady clad all in blue and golden silk, and mounted on a fine cream-coloured palfrey of proud and even pace; and behind her came a tall knight, fully armed and riding a big roan warhorse.

'Geraint,' said the Queen, 'do you know who that knight may be?'

'Not I,' said Geraint, 'for he rides with his vizor closed, and the badge on his shield is strange to me.'

'Angharad,' said the Queen to her maiden. 'Do you go down and ask of the dwarf who his master may be.'

So the maiden rode down to meet the dwarf, and asked him in all courtesy the name of the stranger knight.

'I will not tell you,' said the dwarf.

'Then I will ask him myself; maybe his manners are better than yours.'

'That you will not, by my faith!' said the dwarf.

'And why?' said the maiden.

'Because you are not worthy to speak with such as my master.'

But none the less, she turned her horse's head towards the knight; and at that, the dwarf struck her savagely across the face with his whip, so that the bright blood sprang out.

Sobbing, the maiden returned to Queen Guenever and told her what had passed.

'That dwarf shall tell *me* who his master is,' said Geraint, firing up on the maiden's behalf, and he touched spur to his horse's flank, and went full tilt down the grass slope to the dwarf, and demanded the name of the knight who rode behind him.

'I will not tell you,' said the dwarf, and made to ride by.

'Then I will ask it of your lord himself.'

'That you shall not,' said the dwarf.

'And wherefore shall I not?' demanded Geraint.

'Because you are not worthy to speak with such as my lord!'

'I have spoken with greater men than your lord,' said Geraint, wrenching his horse round and heading towards the knight.

But the dwarf also flung round and came after him with a shrill cry; and the long whiplash cracked across his face, drawing blood as it had done from the maiden's.

Geraint's temper was as swift to flare even as Gawain's, and his hand flew to his golden sword-hilt. But there remained a cool grain of common sense in him; and he thought, It will be but a poor vengeance if I slay this atomy, and then, being without armour, am slain myself by his knight.

And he rode back to Queen Guenever.

'Lady, with your leave, I will ride after that knight until we come to some place where I can borrow armour and a spear. He *shall* tell me who he is, and make amends for the insult done to you and your maiden.'

'Go,' said the Queen, 'but I shall be sorely anxious until I have tidings of you.'

'If I live,' said Geraint, 'tidings you shall have within two days.'

So Geraint followed the dwarf and the knight and the lady; all day, through steep valleys and over high moors, and along woodshores where the wild cherry trees were in Easter bloom, until towards evening they came to a walled town by a river, and in the heart of the town stood a strong and proud fortress. And as they rode through the narrow streets towards the fortress, the people came thronging to greet them; and it seemed that in every house and court-yard were men and horses, shields being polished and armour furbished and horses shod. And everywhere it seemed to Geraint that amid all the uproar he heard men exclaiming to each other over and over again, 'The sparrowhawk! The sparrowhawk!' And when they came to the castle, the gates were open wide; and the dwarf and the knight and the lady rode in.

But there was no friendly face turned towards Geraint, no one that he knew in all the town, and despite all the armour that he saw, he found no likely place to borrow any. And so, with the day already thickening to dusk, he came to the far side of the town. And there across the open meadow land, almost where the forest closed in again, he saw an ancient manor house, half in ruins, with the long-stranded ivy clothing roofless towers; and only one part of the building that seemed to be weatherproof and still lived in, for a gleam of light shone from it. And as he drew near, thinking that here at least was none of the bustle of the town, and maybe he would

269

find someone to advise him where he could borrow armour and a spear, he saw an old man, grey haired and clad in garments that were faded and tattered but must once have been as rich as his own, sitting at the foot of a broken marble staircase that led to the upper chamber.

Geraint reined in his horse, and sat for a few moments looking down at him; and then the old man looked up and smiled. 'You seem heavily thoughtful, young sir?'

'I am thoughtful.' Geraint returned the smile. 'Because I am a stranger here, and do not know where to go this night; and yours is the first kind look that has come my way since I entered the town.'

'Come in with me, and you shall have the best that I can offer – both you and your horse.'

'God be good to you for your kindness,' Geraint said, and slid wearily from the saddle and, leading his horse, followed where the old man led, first into the half-ruined Hall, and then, leaving his horse there, up the stairway to the chamber from which the light shone.

The chamber must once have been fair, but now, in the light of the fire on the hearth and a few tallow dips, it showed shabby and smoke-darkened, with damp patches on the once gaily painted walls. And beside the fire, in a tall upright chair, sat an old gentlewoman in the threadbare remains of a silk gown that had once, like the old man's, been fine. And looking at her, Geraint thought that when she was young and before sorrow touched her, she must have been as fair as a wayside rose. And beside her on a cushion on the floor sat a maiden in an old tattered smock and mantle; and it seemed to Geraint, looking at her face in the firelight between the soft curtains of her hair, that she was fairer even than the old gentlewoman must have been.

'Daughter,' said the grey-haired man, 'there is no squire but you to tend upon this stranger whom I have brought home, and no other groom to see to his horse.'

'The best tending that I can,' said the maiden, rising, 'I will give to him and to his horse.'

And when Geraint sat down where she bade him on a bench beside the table, she pulled off his boots of fine leather. And then she went down to the Hall to water the horse and give him straw and a measure of corn. Then she returned and set the table for a meal, and put before them boiled meat and plain dark bread, with a little white manchet loaf that Geraint guessed was in his honour, and a flask of thin wine.

And as they ate, the maiden waiting upon them, Geraint asked the old man with all courtesy how he and his ladies came to be living in that half-ruined place with no one to tend upon them. 'Surely,' said he, 'it has not always been so?'

'Indeed no,' replied his host, 'once I owned the town and the castle yonder, and a great dukedom beside.'

'And how in God's name did you come to lose it?'

'Through pride of heart,' said the old man. 'I have

271

a nephew, my brother's son, whose dukedom I held with my own while he was a child. But when he came to strength and manhood and laid claim to his own dukedom, I would not believe him yet ready for so great a charge, and refused him. Then he made war on me, and indeed he proved himself the stronger of us two, and seized not only his own dukedom but mine as well, leaving me nothing but this half-ruined house in which to shelter my wife and my daughter who was then but a child.'

'That is a grievous story,' said Geraint, 'and sorry I am to hear it. But now, pray you tell me the meaning of the great uproar and ready-making of arms in the town as I rode through, and the coming of the knight and the lady and the dwarf, who rode into the castle and were made gladly welcome?'

'The ready-making was for a great joust to be held tomorrow. Every year on the second day after Easter, the young duke my nephew sets up a silver rod between two hazel forks in the meadow below the town, and a fine sparrowhawk fastened to the rod by its jesses, and from all parts, knights flock in to joust for the sparrowhawk, that the victor may give to the lady he loves best. The knight you speak of has won the sparrowhawk for two years, and if he wins it this year also, then he will gain great honour, and be called the Knight of the Sparrowhawk henceforth.'

'Then I would fain joust with him, if I had the armour and spears – indeed it was for that purpose that I followed him here, before ever I heard of the sparrowhawk,' said Geraint, touching his gashed cheek. And he told his host, Duke Ynwl, of the injury done to the Queen and her maiden, and to himself.

'My own armour you should have most willingly,' said the old Duke, shaking his head. 'It is old-fashioned now, and battered, and maybe rusty, for it is long since I had the heart to look at it; but before age and sorrow bowed me, I was about your size. But alas! That will not help us, for you have no maiden with you, and you will not be admitted to the lists unless your lady-love ride with you, and you proclaim her the fairest lady in the world, and do battle in her name.'

Geraint was silent a moment; and then he looked up and saw the maiden Enid in her shabby gown in the firelight, and he said, 'Sir, if it pleases her, will you give me leave that your daughter ride with me tomorrow? If I come out of the jousting alive, then my love and loyalty shall be to her as long as I live; and if I come not out alive, then she will be in no worse case than she was before.'

'Enid?' said the Duke.

And the old Duchess looked at her daughter with a small questioning smile.

And the Lady Enid blushed as pink as a foxglove, and said, speaking to Geraint directly, for the first time, 'Gladly will I come with you tomorrow.'

So the old Duke brought his armour from the worm-eaten chest where it was kept; and before they slept, he and his daughter and Geraint burnished off the worst of the rust and replaced here and there a worn strap. And Geraint thought that indeed if she had not been a maiden, Enid would have made a good squire to some knight; and when their hands met on the battered armour, they glanced up and smiled at each other.

Next morning they rose early, and with the help of the old Duke, Geraint put on the armour while the maiden groomed his horse and the aged palfrey that was the only mount they possessed. And while the shadows were still long, they came to the broad meadow below the castle, which was already crowded with knights and their ladies, and pages walking tall warhorses up and down; and the silk-hung stands below the castle walls were filled with onlookers; and at the far end of the meadow the sparrowhawk already sat with her leash made fast to the silver rod between the hazel forks.

Trumpets sounded golden upon the morning air, and the tall knight on the roan horse whom Geraint had followed yesterday came forward to where his lady sat beneath a silken canopy, and cried in a great voice for all to hear, 'Lady, will you come with me and take the sparrowhawk which awaits you, for it is yours by right of your beauty which outshines the beauty of all other ladies. If any knight shall say you nay, then let him do battle with me!'

'Wait!' Geraint shouted, taking up the challenge. 'Do not touch the sparrowhawk, for my lady here with me is yet more fair than yours, and in her name I lay claim to it!'

Then the knight laughed. 'You? Some country

churl who has found a suit of battered armour in a ditch? Come then and we will do battle for it, if you wish to have your head broken!'

Then the two drew apart to the furthest ends of the meadow, and wheeled their horses and came thundering down upon each other so strongly and truly that at their meeting both spears were shattered. Then the dwarf brought another spear for his knight, and the old Duke another for Geraint; and they came together again, and again their spears broke, and a third time yet again. But for the fourth encounter, the old Duke came to Geraint with a spear that was not new as the others had been, but old and battered and stained, and said, 'Sir, this spear was put into my hand on the day that I was made knight, and it has never yet failed me in a joust.'

Geraint thanked him, and set the spear in rest; and a fourth time they thundered together from the far ends of the meadow; and this time, though his antagonist's spear shattered as the others had done, the ancient spear in Geraint's hand took him in mid-shield so strongly that his girths broke and he and his saddle together flew over his horse's crupper to the ground.

Geraint too flung himself from his horse, and as the other scrambled to his feet, he drew his golden-hilted sword and was upon him. So they fought up and down the meadow, blade against blade, until their armour was hacked and hanging loose, and the blood and sweat ran from them, and the light began to fade from their eyes. And at last it seemed that the defender of the sparrowhawk was gaining on Geraint, and the old Duke cried to him, 'Remember the insults done to you and to Queen Guenever!'

And the red flame of his rage sprang up bright and fierce again and the darkness fell from his eyes, and summoning up the last of his strength, he swung up his sword and brought it crashing down upon the other's head in a blow that cut through crest and helm, and mail coif and flesh, and bit to the very bone.

The knight crashed to the ground, his sword spinning from his hand; and there on his knees he cried quarter, and asked mercy of Geraint.

'Mercy you shall have,' said Geraint, standing over him, 'on this condition, that you go to Guenever the Queen, and make amends to her for the injury done to her maiden by your dwarf; and tell her that Geraint, son of Erbin, sent you. For the injury done to myself – ' he smiled grimly inside his battered helmet – 'I have taken enough payment. Yet I demand one thing more, that now you tell me your name, which at the first I asked in all courtesy.'

'I will go to the Queen as you bid me,' groaned the knight. 'And as for my name, Geraint, son of Erbin, I am Edern, son of Nudd.'

Then came squires to help him away to have his wounds tended; and after, he was put back upon his horse, and drooping in his saddle, with his dwarf and his lady, he set out for Caerleon.

Meanwhile, Geraint said to the maiden Enid, 'Go

now and take up the sparrowhawk on its silver rod, for it is rightfully yours.'

Then came the young Duke with his people, and greeted Geraint and bade him to come back with him to the castle. 'My thanks to you,' said Geraint, 'but where I spent last night, there will I spend this night also.'

'That must be as you wish; but at least you shall have more comfort there than you had last night, and my uncle and his ladies also.'

And when Geraint with the old Duke Ynwl and his wife and daughter came again to the ancient manor house, they found the young Duke's servants had come there before them by a shorter way and were making ready the living chamber as though for a feast, and water was heating on a blazing fire for Geraint to wash off the blood and sweat of his fighting.

And when he came from his bath, the young Duke was there with his household knights and guests from the jousting for the sparrowhawk. And the old Duke in a new furred gown was looking about him as one in a dream, at the fine food and drink upon the table and the fresh water-mint strewn upon the floor, and the rich stuffs being spread over the poor furniture, and everywhere the glint of gold that had been his long ago. But of the old Duchess and the maiden Enid there was no sign, and when he asked where they were, the chamberlain told him, 'They are in the upper chamber, putting on the new gowns that the Duke has brought for them.'

And Geraint said, 'Pray you send and ask the maiden to wear her old gown until she comes to Arthur's court, that the Queen may dress her in gowns of her choosing.'

So Enid came down to the great chamber in her old threadbare gown; but in that, she looked as fair to Geraint as the other ladies in their brilliant silks and damasks.

They all sat down to supper. And over the table that night, peace was made between the old Duke and the young Duke; and the young Duke restored to the old one all the lands and riches that were his aforetime.

And next day the Lady Enid bade goodbye to her father and her mother; and still in her threadbare gown, but riding a sweet-paced bay palfrey which the young Duke had had brought for her from his own stables, and carrying the sparrowhawk on her gloved fist, she rode out with Geraint upon the long road back to Caerleon.

Meanwhile, the King and his knights had had good hunting and slain the white stag; and on the morrow, the Queen had look-outs set on the ramparts to watch for Geraint's return. Some while after noon they saw coming across the bridge of Usk a dwarf on a tall horse, and behind him a maiden on a palfrey, and last of all a knight in hacked and battered armour, who sat slumped in the saddle of his warhorse with his head hanging down between his shoulders.

And one of the watchers went and told Guenever

what he had seen; a dwarf and a lady and a sorry and battered knight. 'But I know not who they may be.'

'But I know,' said the Queen. 'Bring the knight and the lady to me when they have entered the gate.'

So Edern the son of Nudd and his lady-love were brought to the Queen in the Great Chamber. And kneeling at her feet, Edern told her all that had passed. And how Geraint had overcome him and sent him to her to make amends for the injury done to her and her maiden; and he humbly asked her pardon.

And the Queen granted it, and ordered that he be taken to the chief guest-chamber, and Morgan Tudd who was Arthur's own physician summoned to tend his many hurts. And she greeted his lady kindly, and gave her into the keeping of her maidens.

And she bade the look-outs on the ramparts continue their watch for Geraint.

On the edge of dusk, Geraint came riding, and the Lady Enid with him in her threadbare gown, drooping a little with weariness, but the sparrowhawk still on her fist.

And when word of this was brought to the Queen, she gathered all her maidens and went to greet them in the inner courtyard. 'Now welcome and God's greeting to you,' she said, 'and to the maiden who rides with you, for whom you won the sparrowhawk.'

And by her knowing so much of the story, Geraint knew that Edern, son of Nudd, must have kept his promise and reached Caerleon ahead of him. And he dismounted and lifted the maiden down, and while squires took their horses and the sparrowhawk, he took her by the hand and led her to the Queen; and as she sank low before the Queen, Guenever stooped and took her in her arms.

'Lady,' said Geraint, 'I have kept my promise, and the name of the knight is Edern, son of Nudd; but I am thinking that you know that already.'

'Surely,' said the Queen, 'for not many hours since, he rode in, asking my pardon and saying that you had sent him to make amends for the injury his dwarf did my maiden. And he told us all the story of the jousting for the sparrowhawk, so far as he knew it.'

'Is it well with him? He was a good fighter,' said Geraint.

And the Queen smiled, 'As well as may be. He is in the guest chamber while the many wounds you gave him are tended to; and his lady is with him now.'

Then came Arthur with his knights; and Geraint presented the maiden Enid to him, and told the rest of the story, and asked the King's leave that they should be married the next day.

'Assuredly you have my leave,' said the King, 'and seldom saw I a fairer maiden than this duke's daughter, even though she is so poorly clad.'

But the Queen said, 'I am thinking that my Lord Geraint brought her to me in her old gown, that I might have the joy of finding her gowns from among my own, that are more fitting to her beauty.'

And she swept Enid away with her to her own

apartments, while Geraint went with the King and his knights to the feasting in the Great Hall. And that evening it was decided that the head of the white stag should be awarded as a bride-piece to Geraint's lady.

Next day, in a gown of golden damask, Enid went to the castle chapel, and there the High King himself gave her hand into Geraint's before the high altar, and so they were wed. And after the marriage there were three days of rejoicing; jousting and hunting by day, and feasting with harpsong and dancing in the Great Hall by night.

But on the fourth morning Geraint went to the King and said, 'My Lord Arthur, now it is time that I was away into Cornwall, to my own place, to bring my Lady Enid before my father, that the sight of her may gladden his autumn days.'

Then the King was sad, and the Queen and her maidens grieved for the loss of the Lady Enid, for in those three days her sweetness and gentleness had made her dear to all of them. But they knew that it was right that Geraint should take her back to his own people and his own place.

So all things were made ready, and the next morning after they had heard Mass, they rode out, with a knot of the King's best knights headed by Sir Lancelot and Sir Gawain to company them on their way. They crossed the Severn by the flat-bottomed barges that always lay there ready to ferry travellers and their horses to the other side, and they turned their horses' heads towards Upper Cornwall, and rode until in two more days they came to the castle of Erbin, Geraint's father.

The old lord greeted his son and his son's wife with great joy; and for three days there was hunting and hawking and jousting by day, and feasting and harping in the Great Hall at night, just as there had been at Caerleon; and then Arthur's knights took their leave and went back to their own lord.

And Geraint set himself to strengthen his borders, which his father, being old, had allowed to grow weak, and set to rights all things that were in need of it, and help his father in the ruling of his domain. And when ever and where ever there was a tournament or jousting or other such trials of skill, there he would be, eager to pit himself against the best knights that could come against him. But the time came when the borders were strong and secure and all was well with his father's lands and people, and he had overcome all the knights who came against him in joust or tournament, so that there seemed nothing to fight for and no one to try his skill against any more. And he began more and more to forsake his old companions and pass his time in his own apartments or in the castle gardens, with Enid, for being with the Lady Enid was the one thing that he never grew weary of.

So he began to lose his people's hearts, and there was a murmuring among his household knights, some saying that Enid had bewitched him, and others that he was no true son of his father after all. And the murmuring came to the ears of the old Lord

Erbin, and he sent for Enid to his own chamber and told her of it, and asked her was it by her wish and her doing that Geraint had forsaken his heart-companions and a man's proper way of life, to spend all his time with her.

Grief and shock struck through Enid when she heard this, and she gripped her hands together and raised her face to the old man's, and said, 'Truly, my lord, I am to blame in this, for I have thought only that it was sweet to have your son by me, when I should have found means to send him from my side. I had not thought that he was forsaking his companions and his courage and his proper way of life for love of me. But I swear that never have I asked this of him; and it is hateful to me that it should be so, for I would have him the valiant knight I loved and left my home and kin for.'

'Then tell him so,' said the old lord, gently.

But though she tried and tried again, Enid could not tell him so; she could not give him the wound that she knew it would be to him. And she was afraid of him too, a little; afraid of his fiery temper that was hotter even than Gawain's.

And then one summer morning, lying wakeful as she had lain all night, she looked at Geraint lying asleep beside her, the first sunlight lying across his breast, where he had pushed the coverings down; and she raised herself on her arm to look the better, and saw his sleeping face among the tangle of bright hair, and the way his breast rose and fell, and the way, even in his sleep, he had reached out towards her.

And suddenly all her love for him seemed to rise into her throat and choke her, and she began to weep.

'Alas and alas!' she whispered. 'If through me you have lost your valour and your strength as men say! Alas and alas that you are no more the knight that first I loved! An ill day for both of us, when I consented to wed with you!'

And her tears fell on Geraint's bare chest and roused him, so that he heard what she said, confusedly between sleeping and waking, and thought both that she accused him of having lost his knightly valour and that she wept for love of some other knight who she would have wed. And he sprang from the bed, blinded by rage and grief, and flung her aside when she would have clung to him, and shouted for his squire to bring him his armour and have his warhorse saddled and made ready.

Then looking down at Enid still crouching where he had flung her to the ground at his feet, he said, 'Lady, have your mare saddled also, for we are going riding. And we shall not return until you have come to know whether or not I have altogether lost my knighthood. Until also, you have decided whether I am not so well worth loving as him you were weeping for just now.'

And he would pay no heed to her weeping nor her protests that she loved no other man. And he strode off to seek his father and tell him that he was setting out upon a quest.

'So suddenly?' said the old lord. 'And who rides with you?'

'Enid my wife,' said Geraint, harsh in his throat, and strode out with no other word, back to the place where his squire waited for him with his armour.

Meanwhile Enid, not summoning any of her maidens for she could not bear anyone with her in her grief and bewilderment, had gone to the small chamber where her clothes-chest was kept. And first she thought, I will put on my finest gown and my golden bracelets for my pride's sake. But then she drew out the old threadbare smock, carefully treasured, and she thought, If he sees me in this gown, maybe he will remember how he first saw and loved me, and how I left my home and parents in it for his sake, and his heart will gentle and turn to me again.

And she put on the shabby gown and went down into the courtyard.

But when Geraint had been armed by his squire, and came down and found her waiting with her mare at a little distance from his own great warhorse, the face he turned to her was as though it had been carved from stone.

'Mount,' he said, 'take the road that leads uphill, from the tower gate, and ride ahead of me – *well* ahead of me. And do not turn back for anything that you see or hear.'

And when she would have spoken one last plea, he cut her short, 'And speak no word to me unless I speak first to you.'

So Enid mounted and rode sadly out through the gate and turned into the track that led northward up on to the high moors.

Presently the road dipped towards a valley choked with forest, and as they came towards the woodshore, Enid saw two armed men sitting their horses in the shadow of the trees, hedge-knights who lived by robbery. And one said to the other, 'Now here comes a fine chance for us! Two horses and a maiden, aye, and a fine suit of armour off that knight who rides with his head so sunk on his breast; for I am thinking that he will not be one to hold his own against us!'

And hearing, Enid thought, He bade me not to turn, nor speak with him; but I must warn him of this! And she turned her horse and rode swiftly back to Geraint and told him what she had heard.

But Geraint only said, 'No need that you come back to me with such warnings, when I know that in your heart you would gladly see me dead at the hands of these men. Only one thing I require of you – that you obey me and keep silent!'

And at that moment the foremost of the hedge-knights came charging towards him. But Geraint wrenched his horse aside at the last instant, so that the other's spear-point passed him by, then turned and with his own spear laid crosswise swept him from the saddle, so that he crashed to the ground head down with his neck broken under him. Then charging to meet the second, he ran him through the throat-mail with his point, and hurled him to the ground as dead as his comrade.

Then Geraint dismounted and stripped the knights of their armour and bound it upon their horses' backs, and knotted up the reins. Then he remounted, saying to Enid, who had sat her mare looking silently on the while, 'Now ride ahead of me once more, driving these horses ahead of you. And whatever you hear or see, do not turn back or speak to me unbidden, for I vow before God that you shall be sorry if you do!'

And the Lady Enid did as she was bid.

Presently they left the forest country, and the road that they followed led out across bleak and open moors. And as they rode, Enid saw, small in the distance, three knights riding towards them through the heather and low thorn-scrub; and the wind was blowing from them towards her, and brought her the words of the foremost rider as they drew near. 'Now this is our well-starred day! Four horses and three suits of armour – and the woman too, for it's little that lack-lustre knight will be able to do against us!'

Then Enid thought, He bade me not to speak to him; but if I do not, it may be his death, and I had rather that it was mine. And again she rode back to Geraint and warned him of what she had heard.

'Truly your warning means less to me than your disobedience to my orders!' said Geraint.

And in the same moment the first of the three hedge-knights came clattering down upon Geraint with levelled spear, but he swung his horse aside so that the spearpoint only glanced off the rim of his shield while his own drove true to its target and flung the man back over his horse's crupper, dead before he hit the ground; and in the same way Geraint served the second man and the third. Then he dismounted and, stripping the dead men of their armour, bound it across their horses' backs, and knotted up the reins, and gave them into Enid's keeping with the same grim orders as before. 'Now ride ahead of me, driving these five horses, and do not again disobey me, for I think that I shall kill you if you do.'

So they rode on, the land growing rough and thickety about them, and it grew more and more difficult for Enid to drive the five horses before her, but she held on, making no complaint. And Geraint saw the trouble she had, and his heart stirred within him for her sake, but he would not listen to the stirring of it, only rode on with his head on his breast.

And presently as they went, Enid became aware of four hedge-knights skulking on the tangled fringes of a blackthorn thicket. And as they drew near, one of them shouted with laughter, and cried out to the rest, 'Now here is a fine chance come our way! Horses and armour – aye, and a maiden, too, and seemingly the knight who rides behind so spent with capturing them all that he'll have little more fight left in him for keeping them!'

And a great cold and a great fear came upon Enid when she heard the words, and she thought, If I disobey him again, my lord will surely kill me. And then she thought, But if I do not warn him assuredly he must be killed. And she turned as best she could with her five driven horses, and rode back to Geraint and told him what she had heard.

'Is there nothing I can say that will make you obey

me?' said Geraint. 'I see these men, and their purpose is plain, and I do not fear them.'

And this time he did not wait for them to attack but struck heel to his horse's flank and spurred towards them, his spear in rest; and the foremost of them he took in mid-shield, flinging him from the saddle, and the second in the breast, piercing his armour and driving to the heart. And the third he took in the throat, breaking his neck before ever he touched the ground, and the fourth, by way of an ending flourish, he took by the hardest stroke of all, the crest stroke that tore his helmet from his head and broke his neck in the doing of it.

Then he dismounted, and disarmed the fallen knights and bound their armour upon their horses' backs, and again he handed the horses over to Enid and bade her drive them ahead of her as before.

Night came upon them while they were in forest country, and at last Geraint spoke to Enid of his own accord. 'Turn aside under the trees; it grows too dark for safe riding, and in the morning we will be on our way again.'

'Whatever you will,' said Enid, and they headed in among the trees, where as they went deeper it was already night. Then Geraint dismounted and lifted Enid from the saddle; but there was no gentleness in his hands as he set her down, and none in his voice. 'Here is a wallet with food in it. Eat, and watch the horses, and take care that you do not sleep lest any of them stray.'

And he stretched himself out with his head on his

shield to sleep, while Enid, the food wallet untouched beside her, sat watching, and the moon rose and shone silver all about her, and the night sounds of the forest woke and an owl swooped by on furred wings, and somewhere a vixen cried to her mate, and something rustled in the undergrowth. And Geraint lay still, but slept no more than his lady whom he had left on watch. And as the horses stirred, Geraint's helm clanked softly where it hung from his saddlebow.

And the moon-watered darkness warmed to the summer dawn, and the ferns and foxgloves grew out of the shadows and somewhere a crack-voiced cuckoo called.

And Geraint shifted, cramped in his armour; and speaking no word of greeting to Enid, he set her on her mare again, and said, 'Take the horses and ride on ahead as you did yesterday.'

That day they rode through gentler country, and from time to time passed by meadows where long lines of men with scythes were getting in the hay. And they met with no more adventures. But towards evening they came to a town of many thatched roofs and the slender spire like an iris bud of a church, and at the end of the town a strong castle that looked as though it had grown from the ground on which it stood. And at the castle gate Geraint asked for lodging for the night.

The porter passed them through into the court-yard, looking somewhat aside at the damosel in the threadbare gown driving nine horses before her, and the knight who rode like a thundercloud behind.

And then, while squires and pages came to help them dismount and take the horses, the Earl of the castle and the town came out from his Great Hall to bid them welcome.

Presently they sat down to eat, and at table Geraint and Enid were set close to each other, but as soon as the meal was over and the Earl's household broke up and began to move and mingle about their evening pastimes, the two shifted far apart. First the Earl spoke with Geraint, asking him the purpose of his journey.

'No purpose save to look for adventure and follow any quest that pleases me,' said Geraint, looking down at his hands that hung lax across his knees. And his face was the face of a man who would find little joy in any quest that came his way. And as he talked with Geraint, the Earl looked across the Hall to where Enid sat sadly by herself with her face turned to the fire, and it seemed to him that she was the fairest maiden that ever he had seen. And presently he said, 'Sir, have I your leave to go and speak with yonder maiden who sits sad and alone?'

'If you wish. It is nothing to me,' said Geraint, not looking up from his hands.

So the Earl went, and drew up a cushioned stool, and with a 'By your leave,' sat him down beside Enid. 'Sweet lady,' he said, speaking to her gently as though she were a falcon that he did not wish to startle into bating from his fist, 'forgive me – I am thinking that you have little pleasure in following yonder knight.'

'His journey is my journey,' said Enid.

'With neither servants nor maidens to accompany you?'

'It is pleasanter to me to ride with my lord than to have servants and maidens.'

'Yet he must be a churl to treat you so,' said the Earl. 'I would not treat you in such a way, if you were to remain with me.'

Enid looked at him as though she were not sure she had truly heard his words. And when she saw that she had, she said simply, 'My troth is pledged to that man, and I have no thought to break faith with him.'

'Think again,' said the Earl. 'If I slay yonder man, I can keep you for myself as long as I will, and when I weary of you I shall turn you away. But if you come to me of your own free will, you shall be my wife and the lady of all my lands, and I will keep faith with you and love you as long as I live.'

Then Enid was silent a long while, her mind scurrying this way and that as she thought what she must do. And it seemed to her that the best thing would be to pretend to come to the Earl's way of thinking. So she said, speaking quick and low, 'Then this must be the way of it. Tomorrow I must ride on with that knight as before, but in a little I shall contrive it so that it seems I am lost; and do you and a few of your men follow quickly to take me while I am parted from my lord, and bring me back here before he can seize me again. Then I shall be yours, and he will never know that it was by my own will.'

And with that, the Earl was satisfied.

So the next day they set out as before, Enid riding ahead and driving the nine captured horses. But as soon as they were well clear of the town and its castle she drew to the side of the road, and waited for Geraint to come up with her. And at first, when he saw her do so, Geraint made to rein back; but in the end, though darkly as ever, he rode on until he came up with her, and she heeled her mare round and rode beside him.

And as she rode, she told him all that had passed between her and the Earl on the night before. 'At any moment he will be after us, and I fear with more armed men than even you can withstand. Therefore, my dear lord, let us turn these captured horses loose, and take to the forest, where we may escape from him.'

And this time, though still with a brooding face, Geraint heard her out, and when she had finished, he spoke less harshly to her than he had done during the two days of their journey. 'Now despite all my orders it seems that you are determined to save my life. But I will not run like a coursed hare from the hounds. If they come after us, here will I wait their coming – but do you make for the forest, and if I should be overcome, get you back to Arthur's court, for you will be safe there.'

'I have disobeyed you often enough to disobey you once more!' said Enid with a sudden flash of spirit that made him look at her for the first time in those two days. And as he looked, he saw her eyes go past him down the road that they had come; and looking the same way, he saw in the distance a rising dust-cloud turned to gold by the morning sun. And as the cloud rolled nearer he could make out at the base of it the forefront of many horsemen coming at full gallop, the sun glinting on crests and spearpoints.

'Give me the horses,' he said, 'and do you at least draw aside from the road to give me fighting room.' And he pulled down his vizor.

'You cannot! Even you, my lord. There must be four score of them and you are but one!' cried Enid.

'Do as I say,' ordered Geraint, hollow behind his vizor. 'There are ways to even the odds a little.'

'What are you going to do?'

'An unknightly thing. Now, into the trees with you!'

And Enid did as he bade her.

Geraint remained waiting in the midst of the road, looking towards the nearing dust-cloud out of which began to sound the drum of many hooves. And at the right moment he loosed the captured horses, slashing his spear butt across the rumps of the hindmost so that they sprang forward snorting from the blows and sweeping the rest in panic along with them, so that all nine went bucketing along the road, the armour clattering and ringing on their backs, towards the on-coming knights.

The Earl and his companions cursed and strove to

pull their steeds aside, and then the runaways were in their midst, spreading confusion on all sides.

And while his pursuers fought cursing with their startled mounts and all was a snorting and clashing turmoil, Geraint set his spear in rest and charged down upon them. He crashed into their midst and had picked the first man from the saddle on his spear-point before they knew what was upon them; then reversing his spear, swept three more from their saddles with a broadside blow before their own points were ready for him. Then as his spear broke in his hand he flung the splintered butt away and drew his sword.

The dust-cloud rose and swirled about the battle, and out of it, to Enid watching on the woodshore, came the clash of weapons and the shouts of men and the neighing and trampling of horses, and the flash of blades in the sunlight, and the blades growing red. And again and again riderless horses broke free of the tumult and fled away; but none of them was Geraint's willow grey.

Long and desperately he fought, grimly savage as a wild boar brought to bay with the hounds snapping and snarling at its flanks. But they were four score to his one, and there could be but a single end to that fight. He was struck down with many wounds, and lay for dead, save that dead men do not bleed so redly, upon the stained and trampled ground.

Then his attackers stood back from him, and Enid slid from her saddle and came and knelt in the dust at his side, bending over him and seeming not to heed the Earl and his men all around. She gave a low wailing cry, 'Alas! Now the only man I ever loved lies slain, and it is through me that he came to his death!'

'Nay now, what of your promise to me?' said the Earl, lifting her up. 'Come back now to the castle, and we shall soon find means to heal your grieving.'

And he set her again on her mare, and gave orders for the carrying back of the bodies of the knights that Geraint had slain. And Geraint himself he caused to be carried back lying in the hollow of his shield with his sword beside him.

And himself, he took the bridle of Enid's mare, and so led her back to the castle. And all the way she spoke no word, but gazed straight before her as though she looked at some dreadful sight that had struck her dumb.

When they came into the Great Hall, the bearer-knights laid Geraint, still on his shield, on the dais at the upper end of the place. And then the Earl called for a chamber to be made ready and rosewater warmed for washing and fine silks brought out of the clothes-chests, that Enid might change her thread-bare and dusty gown that was now stained also with Geraint's blood.

'I have no taste for emerald damasks and rose-scarlet silks when my lord lies dead,' said she.

'Nay, sweet lady, be not so sorrowful,' said the Earl. 'What though yonder knight be dead? Have you not a rich earldom and its lord along with it to replace him? I shall make you happy again if you will but let me.'

'I shall never be happy again in all my life,' said Enid; and she did not change her gown.

'At least come and eat,' said the Earl, when the tables were set for the noonday meal. 'See, your place shall be here by me.' And he took her hand and led her to the table.

'Eat,' he said again, and himself set the best and most delicate morsels of food on the white manchet bread before her.

But Enid said suddenly in a clear cold voice, 'I swear to God that I will not eat until my lord rises from where he lies upon his shield and eats with me.'

'That is an oath you cannot keep,' said the Earl, 'for that man is already dead.'

'Then I shall not eat again in this world,' said Enid in the same cold clear voice.

'Drink, then,' said the Earl, pouring golden wine into the cup beside her. 'Drink at least, and the fire of the wine will warm you to another way of thinking.'

'I will not drink until my lord rise and drink with me.'

At that, the Earl lost his hard-held temper and shouted at her as he would have shouted at a disobedient hound, 'Since fair words are nothing to you, let us be seeing what this will do!' And he struck her across the face, so that the imprint of his hand sprang out crimson on her white skin.

She let out a wild shriek, and sprang up. 'If my lord were yet living, you would not have dared to strike me so!'

Now a while before this, Geraint had begun to

come back to himself, like someone lying in dark water rising slowly towards the light and the world of living men; but though he heard what passed between Enid and the Earl, he did not know whether he lived, or whether everything about him was real or all a dream; and he lay a while unmoving, as though between two worlds. But Enid's shriek when the Earl struck her pierced through to him like a sword-thrust, and he broke surface from the darkness in which he had lain. And at the sound of Enid's weeping the strength rushed into him, and he sprang to his feet, snatching up his sword that lay in the hollow of his shield beside him, and hurled himself upon the Earl and dealt him such a blow that the keen blade split his head in two and was not stopped in its downward sweep until, as he sagged forward among the platters and wine cups, it was stayed by the table edge.

Then a great tumult broke out, and everyone except Enid fled from the Hall, not fearing one living man with a sword, but believing that a dead man had risen up to slay them by some wizardry.

And alone in the empty Hall, Geraint stood cleaning his blade on the white table linen, and looking at Enid who stood unmoving and white as the linen, her eyes clinging to his face. And suddenly his heart smote him with a pang of love for her that was sharper than the pain of his wounds. But there was no time for soft words now; all that must wait.

'Enid,' he said, and the tone of his voice was all the

soft words that she needed. 'Do you know where the stables are?'

'Yes,' she said, and then, 'Will you have me go and fetch the horses?'

'We will go together,' said Geraint, 'and swiftly before the Earl's men find their courage again and return, for I am in no state now for another fight.'

So they went swiftly to the stables, found their horses and saddled them and, mounting, rode out from the castle whose gates stood wide, and not a soul to stand in their path or question their going.

They took the road towards the forest which lay dark as a cloud shadow across the distance; and in the open country the midsummer heat was great, and Geraint's armour stuck to him with blood and sweat, and the heat of it seared his wounds and his head swam and there was a darkness before his eyes. And when they had reached the forest and ridden a short way further, they turned aside under the trees and struggled on further yet, until they judged that the Earl's men would be hard put to it to find them. Then, under a great oak tree, they dismounted and hitched their horses to a low-hanging branch, and the Lady Enid set herself to help Geraint unarm. And she could not hold herself from weeping as she saw the wounds upon him. And while she was helping him with the laces and buckles, they heard hunting horns among the trees.

The meaning of the horns was this: King Arthur and his company had ridden out from Camelot, hunting far into the south-western hills; and their hunting camp was pitched close by in a pleasant clearing of the forest. And it was the horn of the King's huntsman gathering in his hounds that Geraint and Enid had heard. And almost in the same breath of time they heard the sound of a rider brushing through the trees, and out on to the deer-path that led beside the oak tree rode Sir Kay the King's Seneschal.

And Geraint knew him, but he did not know Geraint without his shield which he had left in the Earl's Hall, for even though his helm was off and his face bare, he was so battered and bloodstained and like a man half dead that scarce anyone save Enid would have known him. And Enid had turned away to gather up his armour, so that her face was hidden.

So Sir Kay demanded of him to know what he did, standing there so close to the King's hunting camp.

'I am standing here in the shade of a tree out of the sun,' said Geraint, swaying a little on his feet.

'Who are you? And on what journey are you bound?'

'As to who I am, that is my own concern, as for my journey, I am bound wherever adventure leads me.'

'And by the look of you, it has led you into some unchancy places,' said Sir Kay. 'So now leave off your adventuring a while, and come you to King Arthur, whose pavilion is pitched nearby.'

'That I will not, unless I choose,' said Geraint, who was in no mood to be taking Kay's orders.

'It is not for you to choose!' shouted Kay. 'By God, you shall come when I say so!' And he rode at Geraint with his drawn sword. But Geraint reached for his own sword which leaned against the tree-trunk, and with the flat of it, not even drawn from its sheath, caught him a buffet under the chin that tipped him from the saddle all flailing arms and legs on to the carpet of last year's oak leaves.

And at that moment Lancelot, who had been riding close behind him, also came out into the deer path. The sunspots through the leaves dappled on his grey hair, and his one black brow was grave and level while the other flew even more wildly than usual, as he reined in and looked at the scene before him. 'Ah, Sir Kay, Sir Kay,' he said as the King's Seneschal scrambled to his feet, 'will you never learn to judge your man?' And then to Geraint he said, 'Forgive me, Sir Knight, you are somewhat battered – though I judge that there are others in worse case somewhere in these parts this day – but are you not Geraint, son of Erbin?'

'I am,' said Geraint.

'And Enid your lady with you. In a glad day you are returned to us. Now pray you come with me to the King, that he too may be made glad by your return.'

'Right joyfully will we come,' said Geraint, 'since you ask in courtesy.'

By now other knights and squires had appeared; and they took the two weary horses, and would have gone to help Geraint who was almost beyond walking; but he shook them off, and took Enid's hand in his. And together, with the rest about them, they walked into the King's hunting camp, to the big striped pavilion set up in the midst of the clearing, close to the cooking pits where the carcass of a deer they had slain that day was roasting over the flames. Arthur sat on a pile of fern before the entrance, leaning against his saddle, and Cabal, the latest of his hounds to bear the well-loved name, lying at his feet.

Lancelot said, 'Sir, we have had noble hunting this evening, for see, we have found the Lord Geraint and his lady come back to us again.'

Then the King made them joyfully welcome, and Geraint, trying to kneel at his feet, almost fell, but that Enid had her arms round him on the instant and supported him against herself.

'Later,' said the King, 'I shall ask for the story of this adventuring; but it seems that there are other things that must be seen to first.'

And he called for Morgan Tudd, and had Geraint taken to a tent where he could rest and be alone with only Enid and the physician to tend him. And the King and his companions remained in the hunting camp until Geraint was well enough to ride; and then, all together and as blithe as linnets in a haw-thorn tree, they rode back to Camelot. And Enid no longer rode ahead of Geraint, nor yet behind, but side by side with him among all the rest.

And when they reached Camelot, and Queen Guenever came out to greet them – for they had sent messengers ahead, and she knew of their coming –

she said to the High King, 'My Lord Arthur, now let you and all this company come into the Great Hall, to the Round Table, for there is a thing that you must see.'

And when they came into the Great Hall, there on the high back of one of the Round Table seats that had been empty since the last knight to sit there had died, was Geraint's name in letters of fair bright gold.

So Geraint became a knight of the Round Table; and when he had gone back to his own place and people, and become a strong and wise ruler after his father's time, he never failed to return to the gatherings at Pentecost, so long as he lived, and so long as the Round Table lasted.

12

GAWAIN AND THE LOATHELY LADY

One year, when there had been Saxon raiding, and a joining of spears between them and the Old People from the North, and when the barbarians had been driven back and the North was quiet again, the High King and his companion knights kept their Christmas at Carlisle, and Guenever and her ladies with them.

And on Christmas night when they were all gathered in the Great Hall, and the squires and pages were bringing in the feast, the boar's head wreathed in bay leaves before all, there came a clatter of hooves and a beating on the door. And when the door was opened, into the Hall, her hair pulled down and her cloak mired with her wild winter riding, ran a damosel who flung herself down at Arthur's feet. 'My Lord King!' she cried. 'Give me your help and save my lover from the black fate that has come upon him!'

'What I can do, that I will,' said the King. 'Tell me quickly what it is, this fate, which has caused you so much weeping.' And he stooped to raise her, but she would not rise, only crouched the more closely.

'I was betrothed to a knight who was more dear to

me than my own heart. But yesterday as we rode out
making plans for our marriage, through the deep
ways of the Forest of Inglewood, we came upon a
place where the trees fell back, and in the midst of it
a dark lake all jagged with rocks along the shore, and
on an islet in the lake, a castle, with black banners
flying above the keep and the drawbridge down. And
as we lingered there, wondering, for we had never
come upon the place before, a terrible creature in full
armour, twice the size of a mortal man and mounted
on a horse twice the size of a mortal horse, came full
gallop across the bridge towards us, and called upon
my love to leave me to him and ride on his way
alone. My love drew his sword to defend me, but
some evil magic lies in that place, and in that
moment the spell of it fell upon him so that the
sword dropped from his hand and he was powerless
against the wicked knight. And the knight hurled
him from his saddle and took and bound him and
flung him across his horse's back, while I must look
on powerless. I tried to fight him, and got this in
payment.' She touched her bruised face and torn
garments and showed her hands cut and bruised.
'But he only laughed his terrible laughter and
dragged my love's horse round to ride away. I called
after him that I would go to Arthur's court and tell
my wrongs and beg for a champion to save my love –
or avenge him – maybe even the King himself. But
he only laughed the more, and shouted at me, "Tell
your cowardly king that here at Tarn Wathelan he
may find me when he will; but much I doubt that

even he will find the courage to come against me!"
And so he went, driving my dear love on his horse
before him. And so do I come to you, my Lord
Arthur, kneeling at your feet and praying for your
aid!'

Then an angry murmur ran round the Hall, and
men looked at each other and their hands moved
towards their daggers, and many a one was already
half out of his seat.

But the King sprang to his feet and cried in a great
voice, 'Now by my knightly honour, I vow that the
King indeed shall ride upon this matter, and avenge
this maiden's wrongs in full measure!'

And some of the knights, especially the young
ones, beat upon the table and gave tongue,
applauding the vow. But Gawain said, 'Uncle, let me
ride upon this quest; for I smell some evil beyond
what the maiden has told, and Britain cannot long be
doing without her King!'

But though Lancelot also, and Bedivere and
Gareth, and even in a rash moment Sir Kay, offered
themselves to go in his stead, the King refused them.
'My thanks to you all, but it is over long since the
King himself rode on a quest instead of watching his
knights ride out.' And then, looking round on them,
on a sudden, he added half in anger and half in something that was like appeal, 'God's truth, my brothers,
I am not yet old!'

And there was something in his voice that held
them from protesting any more.

Only the Queen was not happy; for like Gawain, it

seemed to her that she could catch the smell of some evil that she could give no name to.

Next morning when the King had heard Mass, his squires armed him and buckled on Excalibur and brought him Ron his mighty spear; and his most fiery-hearted warhorse was fetched from the stable. And with the maiden to guide him, he left Carlisle and headed deep into the Forest of Inglewood, the dark fleece of trees that covered all those parts.

Mile after mile they rode, until at last they came out from the trees into the fierce yellow flare of a stormy sunset; and before them spread the waters of a lake giving back its answering fire to the fiery sky; and all around rose the dark rocks of the shore; and set on its islet, a storm-dark castle with its banners streaming crow-black from the turret tops against the sunset light.

'This is the place,' said the damosel. 'Oh, my Lord King, save my love for me and avenge my wrongs!'

Then Arthur took the horn that hung at his saddlebow, and winded a long-drawn mighty call that echoed back from the rocks of the lake shore and set the ravens whirling on black wings from the crannies and ledges of the castle. Again he sounded his horn; and yet a third time, until the note seemed to fling back from the high sunset clouds above the ramparts, but no other answer came. Then he drew his sword, and cried out in his battle voice, 'Come, Sir Knight of Tarn Wathelan! Your King bides here, and is not used to be kept waiting!'

And as he hurled his challenge, the great drawbridge dropped slowly to span the narrow gap of water between the castle and the shore; and there in the gate arch appeared the Knight of Tarn Wathelan, huge beyond the size of mortal man and armed from crest to toe in black armour, and mounted on a giant red-eyed warhorse the colour of midnight. 'Now welcome, King Arthur!' he shouted. 'For long and long I have wished for your coming, that I may defy you to your face as always I have defied you in my heart!'

Then anger rose in the King, and he spurred his horse full gallop down the track to the water's edge, while the huge knight-spurred out as swiftly to meet him. 'Yield you now to me!' shouted back Arthur, above the drum of horses' hooves. 'Yield and make amends for your evil doing, or fight!'

But in the same moment his horse stopped dead, all but flinging him over its head, and stood stock still, neighing in terror; and as the King sought to urge it forward again, he felt it trembling under him. And like an icy shadow, a great fear fell upon him, the more terrible because it was not of the knight or of anything in this world; a black terror of the soul that came between him and the sky, and sucked the strength from him so that sword arm and shield arm sank to his sides and he was powerless to move.

'This is Devil's work!' said something deep within him. 'Devil's work . . .'

And the Knight of Tarn Wathelan reined in his own horse not a spear's throw away, and fell to laughing, until his laughter rang and boomed back from the castle walls. 'Now it is for *you* to yield or fight, my Lord King!'

And Arthur struggled to raise his sword arm until the cold sweat started on him, but could not move a muscle.

'You see!' bellowed the huge knight.

'What – would you – of me?' gasped Arthur.

'As to that, I could kill you now, or fling you into my dungeons to rot among other valiant knights who lie there, and take your realm for my own by means of the magic that is mine to wield. But I am minded to sell you back your life and freedom. How say you to that?'

'What is the price?'

'That you return to me on New Year's Day, bringing me the answer to this question: What is it that all women most desire? Swear on the Holy Rood to return, with or without the answer to the question, for if you have it not, then you will be still my prisoner, your ransom unpaid. And if it pleases me I shall slay you and fling your body into the dark waters of the lake.'

And there was nothing that Arthur could do but swear, with shame and rage and humiliation battling with the terrible fear that held him captive like a fly meshed at the heart of a spider's web.

Then the Knight of Tarn Wathelan made a quick gesture with his spear; and Arthur's horse reared up and spun round on its hind hooves, and dashed off at such a desperate gallop that they were far and far into the trees before Arthur could rein it to a trembling halt.

It was then that he realised that there had been no sign of the maiden since they first rode out into the clearing and saw Tarn Wathelan ahead of them.

With the shame of what had happened eating into him, the King rode on his way. But not back to Carlisle. He could not look his companions in the face again until he had paid his ransom – if indeed his ransom was ever to be paid.

All that week between Christmas and the New Year, he rode the forest and moorland ways, North and South, East and West. And whenever he saw a girl herding geese, or an ale-wife in the door of a wayside tavern, a great lady amidst a train of servants, riding by on a white palfrey whose harness rang with little bells, or an aged nun by a holy well, telling her beads, he asked her the question that had been put to him by the Knight of Tarn Wathelan.

'What thing is it that all women most desire?'

And every one of them gave him a different answer. Some said riches and some said beauty, some said pomp and state, some power, some laughter and admiration, some said love.

And the King thanked each one of them courteously, and wrote down her answer on a long strip of parchment which he had obtained from an abbey on the first day of his quest, that he might forget none of them when he came again to Tarn Wathelan. But he knew in his heart that none of them was the right answer. And so at last it was the morning of

New Year's Day, and he set his horse's head once
more towards the castle of Tarn Wathelan with a
heavy heart. And his thoughts turned back to
Merlin, so long asleep under his magic hawthorn
tree, for nobody else could help him now.

The hills looked darker than they had done when
last he rode that way, and the wind had a keener
edge. And the way seemed much longer and rougher
than it had done before, and yet it was all too quickly
passed.

But when he was not far short of his journey's
ending, as he rode chin on breast through a dark
thicket, he heard a woman's voice, sweet and soft,
calling out to him, 'Now God's greeting to you, my
Lord King Arthur. God save and keep you.'

The King turned quickly in the direction from
which the voice had come, and saw, close beside the
track, a woman in a scarlet gown. She sat upon a turf
hummock between an oak sapling and a holly tree;
and her gown was as vivid as the holly berries, and
her skin as brown and withered as the few winter
leaves that still clung to the oak tree. At sight of her
shock ran through the King, for in the instant
between hearing and seeing, he had expected the
owner of the soft voice to be fair. And she was
the most hideous creature that ever he had seen, with
a piteous nightmare face that he could scarcely bear
to look upon. Her nose was long and warty and
bent to one side, while her long hairy chin bent to
the other. She had only one eye, and that set deep
under her jutting brow, and her mouth was no more

than a shapeless gash. On either side of her face her hair hung down in grey twisted locks, and the hands that she held folded in her lap were like brown claws, though the jewels that winked upon them were fine enough for the Queen herself.

In his amazement, the King could not at once find his tongue to answer her greeting. And the Loathely Lady raised her head and looked at him, a long full look that seemed to hold grief and anger and an old pride. 'Now by Christ's Cross, my Lord Arthur, you are an ungentle knight, to leave a lady's greeting lying unanswered so! Best remember your manners, for I know on what dark adventure you ride, and proud as you are, it may be that I can help you.'

'Forgive me, lady,' said the High King. 'I was deep in thought, and that, not lack of courtesy, was the reason I did not return your greeting. If you do indeed know the adventure that I ride on, and the question that I must answer, and if you can indeed help me, I shall be grateful to you all my life.'

'It is more than your gratitude that I must have, if I am to help you,' said the Loathely Lady.

'What, then?' said the King. 'Whatever you ask, you shall have it.'

'That is a rash promise,' said the Lady, 'and you shall swear it on Christ's Cross, lest later you repent. But first, let you listen to me. You are pledged to tell the Knight of Tarn Wathelan this very day what it is that all women most desire, or else yield yourself up to his mercy. And mercy he has none. That is so?'

'That is so,' said the King.

'You have asked many women, in these past seven days, and all of them have given you answers; and not one of them the right answer. I alone can give you that; the answer that shall pay your ransom. But before I give it to you, you shall swear by the Holy Rood, and by Mary the Mother of God, that whatever boon I ask of you, you will grant it.'

'This oath I take upon me,' said the King, with his hand on the cross of his sword.

'Then bend down to me – closer – closer, that not even the trees may hear,' said the Loathely Lady. And as he did so, she got awkwardly to her feet and whispered the secret in his ear.

Then the King caught his breath in laughter, for it was such a simple answer, after all. But in a little he grew sober again, and asked the Lady what was the boon that she would have in payment. But she said, 'Not yet – when you have given his answer to the Knight of Tarn Wathelan and proved that it is indeed the true one, then come back to me here, where I shall be waiting for you. And now, God go with you on your way.'

So the King rode on towards Tarn Wathelan. And now the hills seemed less dark and the wind less keen, for he was sure that he had the true answer to the Knight's question.

In a while he came to the clearing in the forest, and sitting his horse on the lake shore, he sounded a long note on his horn. This time he did not need to sound more than once, for the master of the place was ready for him, and while the echoes still hung among the rocks, the drawbridge came clanging down, and over it the huge Knight on his huge black horse came riding, and reined up within a spear's length of the King.

'Well, now, little King, do you bring me the answer to my question?'

'I bring you many answers, given to me by many women, and among them must surely be the true one,' said Arthur, and tossed the roll of parchment into the giant's mailed hand.

And sitting his horse there on the lake shore, the huge knight read them from the first to the last. And when he had read them all, he burst into a roar of laughter, and flung the scroll over his shoulder into the deep sky-reflecting waters of the Tarn. 'Here be many answers indeed! Some bad, some good, but none of them the true answer to my question. Your ransom is unpaid and your life and your kingdom are forfeit to me. Bend your neck for the stroke, oh, most lordly Arthur Pendragon, High King of Britain!' And his hand went to the hilt of his sword.

Then Arthur said, 'Give me leave to try one more, before I yield up to you my life and kingdom.'

'One more, then, but be quick,' said the Knight.

'This morning as I rode here,' said King Arthur, 'I met with a lady clad in a scarlet gown and sitting between an oak and a holly tree, and she told me that the thing all women most desire is *their own way*!'

Then the Knight of Tarn Wathelan let out a great bellow of rage. 'It must have been my sister Ragnell who told you this, for none but she knew the true answer. And a curse upon her for the telling! Was she hideous and misshapen?'

'She was indeed the most unlovely lady that ever I saw,' said the King.

'If ever I catch her, I will roast her alive over a slow fire, for she has cheated me of the kingdom of Britain!' roared the Knight. 'Nevertheless, go your way in freedom, for your ransom is paid.'

Back over the moors and through the forest depths rode the King, all at once so weary that he could scarcely even feel relief. And when he came to the place where he had met her before, there between the oak and the holly tree sat the Lady Ragnell, waiting for him.

He reined up beside her, and this time was the first to speak in greeting. 'Lady, your answer was indeed the true one. And I have my life, and kingdom, thanks to you. Now ask your boon, and I will assuredly grant it.'

'Assuredly,' said the Loathely Lady. 'If you are a man of honour as well as a king. So then, this is the boon I ask: That you will bring to me from your court at Carlisle, one of your knights brave and courteous, and good to look upon, to take me for his loving wife.'

At her words, Arthur felt as though he had taken a blow to the belly. 'Madam,' he said, 'you ask a thing impossible.'

'Then Arthur is not, after all, a man of honour?' said the Lady.

And the King said, 'You shall have your boon, lady.'

And with his head sunk on his breast, he rode away. And never knew how the Lady looked after him with a mingling of hope and fear and desperate pain in her one bleared eye.

On the second day of the New Year the King returned to Carlisle. Wearily he dismounted in the courtyard, and went through into the Great Hall, where his companion knights were gathered and the Queen came to greet him with hands held out and eager questions, for she had been torn with anxiety through the past eight days.

'I have boasted too much of my strength in arms, and I come back to you a beaten man,' said the King heavily.

'My lord, tell us what has come to pass?' said the Queen, her face turning white under the golden circlet that bound her hair.

'The knight whom I rode against was more than a mortal man, and his castle and all the land about it held by black enchantments which suck the courage from a man's heart and the strength from his arm. So I fell into his power and was forced to yield myself to him. And he – bade me go, but return to him on New Year's Day with the answer to a certain question, or forfeit to him my life and kingdom.'

For a moment there was no sound in the Great Hall but the crackle of the logs blazing on the hearth, and a hound under a table scratching for fleas. And then Lancelot said gently, 'But, sir, you are returned to us, so it must be that you gave this wizard knight the true answer that he sought. And therefore you are honourably redeemed.'

'I gave him the true answer, by the help of a lady; but her help was dearly bought, and I cannot pay *that* ransom myself.'

Then Gawain spoke up, 'So – what is it that must be paid to this lady?'

'She asked a boon, to be given her when the question had been answered; and I – I promised her whatever she asked. I swore that I would grant it.' The King groaned. 'And when the question was answered and I was free, and returned to her and bade her ask her boon – she asked that one of my knights should marry her.'

Again there was silence in the Hall; and then Gawain said, 'Och well, that might be none so ill a thing. Is she bonnie?'

'She is the most hideous and misshapen woman that ever I saw,' said the King. 'Crooked of nose and chin, old and withered, and with but one eye. A twisted thorn-tree woman, like something out of an evil dream.'

And for the third time there was silence in the Hall.

'Would to God that I might pay the price myself,' groaned the King. And Guenever reached him her hand like a mother reaching a consoling hand to her child. But she was careful not to look at Sir Lancelot, who was as careful not to look at her.

And a faint breath of relief was running through

the knights who already had wives of their own and so were safe from what was coming.

'But you cannot, dear uncle, and so to keep your honour clean, another must pay it for you.' Agravane, always a mischief-maker, leaned forward into the light, his eyes flickering. 'How about you, dear brother Gawain? You are for ever protesting your loyalty to the King, as though it were greater than other men's; protesting yourself the King's champion as Lancelot is the Queen's!'

Lancelot was half out of his seat before the words were well spoken; but even swifter than he, Gawain sprang up, his hot blue eyes blazing and his red hair seeming to lift like the mane of an angry hound. 'Little brother, you speak my very thoughts! My Lord Arthur, I will wed your beldame for you, and quit you of your ransom!'

'My thanks be to you for the offer,' said the King, 'but I shall not – I cannot – accept it until you have first had sight of her.'

'Nay, my lord and uncle, my mind is set to do this in your service, for am I not the King's champion, as my brother Agravane says?' And Gawain caught up his wine-cup from the table beside him, and held it high, thrusting his defiant gaze among his fellow knights. 'Drink, friends, to my bride!' And standing there, he drained the cup and crashed it down upon the table.

Nobody echoed the toast.

'Not without first seeing her,' said the King again, his voice dull and hoarse but with no yielding in it.

And Cabal, his huge grey wolfhound, nuzzled into his hand; and he looked down and gently pulled the great hound's ears. Then, abruptly, as a man making up his mind, he raised his head and looked around at the faces turned to him in the torchlight.

'Tomorrow, we ride hunting towards Tarn Wathelan, and Gawain shall see the Lady Ragnell in the cold light of day, with a cooler and clearer head on him than he has at this moment. And all of you who are not yet wed, shall look upon her too, before any of you choose her for his bride!'

So next day, in the first light of the winter morning, the horses were brought from the stables and the hounds from the kennels, and King Arthur and his companions rode hunting. The morning was crisp with frost, and they put up a noble stag and chased him far into the depths of Inglewood Forest, the winding of the horns mingling with the music of the hounds. He led them through dense thickets of holly and yew and bare oak and hazel; and at last, not so far from Tarn Wathelan, they made the kill.

And when the carcass of the deer had been graillo-ched and flung across the back of a hunting pony, and they turned back towards Carlisle, they rode merrily along with jest and laughter, though the led palfrey in their midst reminded them all too clearly why they had come hunting that way. And for that very reason they laughed the louder and called to each other under the trees to silence the trouble in their own hearts.

And then suddenly Sir Kay, riding out alone

beyond the rest as he often did, caught a glimpse of scarlet among the trees; and ducking under the branches of a great forest yew, he reined back and stayed looking at the woman who sat there in a gown of blazing scarlet, between an oak and a holly tree.

'God's greeting to you, Sir Kay,' said the Lady Ragnell.

But the King's Seneschal was too much astonished to answer. He had heard what the King had said of the Loathely Lady, last night in Carlisle Castle. But he had not imagined anything so terrible as the face he saw turned towards him. He crossed his fingers for fear of witchcraft, and did not even hear her salutation. But by this time most of the other knights had joined him; and in their company Sir Kay felt bolder; and because he had been afraid, his manners were worse than usual, and he began to jibe at her most cruelly. 'See now, here if I mistake not our King's description of her, is the lady we have come to seek. So now, which of us shall woo her to wife? Come, think of the sweetness of her kisses and do not be hanging back!'

And then King Arthur rode up, with Gawain at his side, and at sight of them Sir Kay fell silent; and the Loathely Lady, who had bowed her face, weeping, into her hands, looked up again, with a kind of pathetic and desperate pride.

'Since one of you must indeed marry her,' said the King, harsh in his throat, 'here is no cause for jesting, Sir Kay!'

'Marry her!' cried Sir Kay. 'Well, it shall not be I!

By the boar's head, I had sooner mate with the witch of Cit Coit Caledon!'

'Peace, Sir Kay!' said the King. 'This is churl's treatment of a lady! Mend your speech, or you shall be knight of mine no longer!'

And the other knights watched in silence, sickened and in pity. Some looked away; even Sir Lancelot pretended to be busy with some adjustment to his horse's bridle.

But Sir Gawain looked steadily at the Lady, and something in that pathetic pride and the way she lifted her hideous head made him think of a deer with the hounds about it, and something in the depth of her bleared gaze reached him like a cry for help. And he glared about him at his fellow knights. 'Nay now, why these sideways looks and troubled faces? Kay was ever an ill-mannered hound! The matter was never in doubt, for last night did I not tell the King that I would marry this lady; and marry her I will, if she will have me!'

And so saying, he swung down from his saddle and knelt before her. 'My Lady Ragnell, will you take me for your husband?'

The Lady looked at him for a moment out of her one eye, then she said in that voice so surprisingly sweet, 'Not you, too, Sir Gawain. Ah, not you, too.' And as he looked at her in bewilderment, 'Surely you do but jest, like Sir Kay?'

'I was never further from jesting in my life,' said Sir Gawain, with stiff lips.

'Then think you before it is too late. Will you

indeed wed with one as ugly and misshapen and old as I? What sort of wife should I be for the King's own nephew? What will Queen Guenever and her ladies say when you bring such a bride to court?'

'No one will say anything that is not courteous to my wife,' said Gawain. 'I shall know how to guard you from that.'

'Maybe so. But yourself? You will be shamed, and all through me,' said the Lady, and wept again, more bitterly than before, so that her face was wet and blubbered and yet more hideous.

Gawain took her hand. 'Lady, if I can guard you, be very sure that I can guard myself also,' he said, and glared round him at the others with his fighting face upon him. 'Now, lady, come with me back to Carlisle, for this evening is our wedding time.'

'Truly,' said the Loathely Lady, 'though it is a thing hard to believe, you shall not regret this wedding, Sir Gawain.'

And she rose and moved towards the white palfrey they had brought for her, and then they all saw that there was a hump between her shoulders and she was lame in one leg, beside all else. But Sir Gawain helped her into the saddle and mounted his own horse beside her; and the King ranged up on the other side. And so, with the rest of the company strung out behind them, the knights on their horses and the huntsmen with the hounds in leash, and the hunting pony with the carcass of the deer across its back, they wended their way back to Carlisle.

Word ran ahead of them from the city gates, and

the people came flocking out to see Sir Gawain
and his hideous bride go by; and as they passed, the
voices of the crowd sank away, and here and there
men made the sign of the Cross, or an old woman
cried out 'God save us!' in dismay. And so they came
to the castle gates and rode inside.

That evening in the castle chapel, Gawain and the
Lady Ragnell were married, with the Queen herself
to stand beside the bride, and the King to act as
groomsman; and after, Sir Lancelot was foremost of
the Round Table company to come forward to kiss
the Lady's withered brown cheek, followed by Sir
Gareth and Sir Gaheris, Sir Ector of the Marsh and
Sir Bedivere, Sir Bors and Sir Lional and all the rest;
but the words strangled in their throats when they
would have wished her and Sir Gawain joy of their
marriage, so that they could scarcely speak. And the
poor Lady Ragnell looked down upon bent head
after bent head, and at the ladies who came forward
to touch her fingertips as briefly as might be, but
could not bear to kiss her cheek. Only Cabal came
and licked her hand with a warm wet tongue and
looked up into her face with amber eyes that took no
account of her hideous aspect, for the eyes of a
hound see differently from the eyes of men.

At the feasting that followed in the Great Hall, the
talk and laughter all along the tables was feverish and
forced; a hollow pretence at gladness, and through it
all Sir Gawain and his bride sat rigidly beside the
King and Queen at the High Table. And when at last
the feasting was over, the squires set back the tables

and began to make the Hall ready for dancing. And then the company thought that now Gawain would be free for a while to leave her side and mingle with his friends. But he said, 'Bride and groom must lead the first dance together,' and offered his hand to the Lady Ragnell.

She took it, with a hideous grimace that was the nearest she could come to a smile, and limped forward to open the dance with him. And throughout the long and stately measure that followed, with the King's eye upon them and Gawain's also, no one in the Hall, not even the youngest page, dared to look as though anything was amiss.

At long last the evening wore to an end. The last measure had been danced, and the minstrels departed, the last wine-cup had been drained, and the bride and groom were escorted to their chamber high in the keep. The great chamber was full of flickering lights and shadows from the fire upon the hearth and the candles that burned in tall sconces either side of the carved and curtained bed, so that the creatures in the woodland scenes upon the walls seemed to move and come and go, and the whole chamber seemed part of some enchanted forest. And when all the company that had brought them there were gone, Gawain flung himself into the deeply cushioned chair beside the fire, and sat gazing into the flames, not looking to see where his bride might be. A sudden draught drove the candleflames sideways and the embroidered creatures on the walls stirred as though on the edge of life. And somewhere very far off, as though from the heart of the enchanted forest, he fancied he heard the faintest echo of a horn.

There was a faint movement at the foot of the bed, and the silken rustle of a woman's skirt; and a low sweet voice said, 'Gawain, my lord and love, have you no word for me? Can you not even bear to look my way?'

Gawain forced himself to turn his head and look at the speaker – and then sprang up in amazement; for there between the candle sconces, still wearing the Lady Ragnell's scarlet gown, and with the Lady Ragnell's jewels on her fingers, stood the most beautiful maiden that he had ever seen. Her skin as white as milk in the candlelight, her hair as darkly gold as corn at harvest time, her huge dark eyes waiting to meet his, and her hands held out to him while a little smile quivered at the corners of her mouth.

'Lady,' he said at half-breath, not sure whether he was awake or dreaming, 'who are you? Where is my wife, the Lady Ragnell?'

'I am your wife, the Lady Ragnell,' said she, 'whom you found between the oak and the holly tree, and wedded this night in settlement of your King's debt – and maybe, a little, in kindness.'

'But – but I do not understand,' stammered Gawain, 'you are so changed – '

'Yes,' said the maiden, 'I am changed, am I not? I was under an enchantment, and as yet I am only partly freed from it. But now for a little while I may be with you in my true seeming. Is my lord content with his bride?'

She came a little towards him, and he reached out and caught her into his arms. 'Content? Oh, my most dear love, I am the happiest man in all the world; for I thought to save the honour of the King my uncle, and I have gained my heart's desire. Indeed you spoke truly when you told me I should never regret this marriage, though at the time I could not believe you.' He drew her hard against him and kissed her, while she put her arms round his neck. 'And yet from the first moment I felt something of you reach out to me, and something of me reach back in answer . . .'

In a little, the lady brought her hands down and set them against his breast and gently held him off. 'Listen,' she said, 'for now a hard choice lies before you. I told you that as yet I am only partly free from the enchantment that binds me. Because you have taken me for your wife, it is half broken; but no more than half broken.'

'What is this? I do not understand.'

'Listen,' she said again, 'and you shall understand all too well. I am half free of the spell, half still held by it; for half of each day I may wear my true form as I do now; for the other half I must be as I was when you took me from under my oak and holly trees. And now it is for you to say, whether you will have me fair by day and foul by night, or fair by night and foul by day.'

'That is a hard choice indeed,' said Gawain.

'Think,' said the Lady Ragnell.

And Sir Gawain said in a rush, 'Oh, my dear love, be hideous by day, and fair for me alone!'

'Alas!' said the Lady Ragnell. 'And that is your choice? I must be hideous and misshapen among all the Queen's fair ladies, and abide their scorn and pity, when in truth I am as fair as any of them? Oh, Sir Gawain, is this your love?'

Then Sir Gawain bowed his head. 'Nay, I was thinking only of myself. If it will make you happier, be fair by day and take your rightful place at court. And at night I shall hear your soft voice in the darkness, and that shall be my content.'

'That was indeed a lover's answer,' said the Lady Ragnell. 'But I would be fair for you; not only for the court and the daytime world that means less to me than you do.'

And Gawain said, 'Whichever way it is, it is you who must endure the most suffering; and being a woman, I am thinking that you have more wisdom in such things than I. Make the choice yourself, dear love, and whichever way you choose, I shall be content.'

Then the Lady Ragnell bent her head into the hollow of his neck and wept and laughed together. 'Oh Gawain, my dearest lord, now, by leaving the choice to me, by giving me *my own way* you have broken the spell completely, and I am free of it, to be my true self by night and day. And my brother also – '

'Your brother?' said Gawain, his head whirling.

And seeing his bewilderment, the Lady Ragnell drew him back to the great chair beside the fire, and sank down beside him on to the rushes, her arm across his knees. 'My brother the Knight of Tarn Wathelan,' she said. 'Both of us were spell-drawn from our true seeming by the magic of Morgan La Fay, my brother because she thought to use him in one last attempt against the King her half-brother, me because – I have a little power of my own – I sought to withstand her.'

'But how did you know the way to save the King?' Gawain asked.

'To every spell there is a key, though one that is almost beyond the power of human kind to use.' Gawain was taking down her hair so that it fell in a curtain of harvest-coloured silk about them both. 'I was the key to save the King; and in saving the King, it was given to me also to call to you for aid for myself and my brother. But if you had not answered my call, no one could have saved me, for the name of *that* key is Love.'

Next day there was much bewilderment but even more joy when Sir Gawain led the Lady Ragnell into the Great Hall. And the wedding feast was renewed; a true wedding feast this time, and a fitting end to the Christmas festivities.

For seven years Gawain and Ragnell knew great happiness together, and during all that time Gawain was a gentler and a kinder and a more steadfast man than ever he had been before. But at the end of that time the Lady Ragnell went from him. Some say that she died, some that she had the blood of the Lordly People in her – had she not herself said that she had a little power? – and the Lordly People cannot live for more than seven years with a mortal mate.

In one way or another way, she went; and something of Gawain went with her. He was a valiant knight still, but his old blazing temper returned upon him and he was less steadfast of purpose and less kind than he had been; and he went hollow of heart for her sake, all the remaining days of his life.

13

THE COMING OF PERCIVAL

When King Pellinore was slain, his queen wanted no more to do with the world of men; and she took their young son Percival and disappeared with him into the wilderness. And there among the mountains and forests of Wales, she found an abandoned charcoal-burner's bothie, and made a home for the child, where he might grow up far from wars and feuds and the cruelties of men towards men which are different from the cruelties of the animal kind.

So from that time forward until he was seventeen, the boy grew up never seeing another human face save his mother's, knowing nothing of the outside world or the ways of men and women. At first he remembered his father's court, the ladies smelling of musk and civet and oil of violets, whose fine gowns trailed along the floor behind them, the shine of knights in armour, the strength of his father's arms when he swung him up from the ground to sit upon his shoulder; the old man in the castle armoury who had begun to teach him how to cast a light spear. Above all, the splendid high-stepping horses in the stables, and the great deerhounds in the kennels who had accepted him as a friend. But little by little the memories faded until they were no more than a brightly coloured blur in the back of his head; until they were so faint that he thought they were only the memories of a dream.

The forest and the mountains were his whole world, and the forest creatures were his friends. He knew where every vixen in his home valley had her lair and cubs, and could whistle so like a thrush or a blackbird that the birds would answer to his call. And he grew strong and hardy and brave and simple-hearted. One day he found an old battered spearhead lying where the winter rain had pulled down the earth between the roots of a tree. The shaft was rotten and crumbled at his touch, but when he bore it home and rubbed it up, the spearhead came up bright as new. He showed it to his mother, and a shadow came over her face as she looked, and over her heart as well. But she said nothing, and he honed the blade on a stone until it was keen enough to cut the wind, as the old man in the lost dream had once shown him how to do, and he found a straight ash sapling to make a new spear shaft, and he practised with it until he could make it do whatever he willed. Then he turned hunter; but he never hunted for pleasure, only for food, as the animals of the wild hunted for food themselves.

But as the years went by and he grew towards manhood, Percival began to find something lacking in forest life. He needed other companionship than his mother's and the wildlings', he wanted other sounds than the birdsong and the wind in the trees and the voices of the hill-streams. He did not really know what it was that he wanted, but he wandered further and further afield in search of it.

And one spring day, wandering further from his home than ever he had been before, he came into a valley down which wound something that was like a deer path, but many times broader and more deeply trodden than any deer path that ever he had seen before.

And as he checked beside it, wondering, he heard sounds that were not any of the forest sounds he knew; and round the bend of the track where it skirted a tangle of elder and wayfaring trees, came four shining figures mounted upon a dun horse and a roan, a grey and a bright chestnut. Percival knew what the horses were, for he had seen the wild Welsh ponies often enough, though these were far bigger and more splendid and high-stepping; and their riders seemed to be shaped like men – or at least, like himself – he had seen himself often enough in the pool under the old willow tree near his home where the bitter dark willow-water was a fine medicine and the wild things came to drink when they were sick; but instead of brown skin and rough yellow hair, and the hides of animals, they each had some kind of hard shining skin – shining like the blade of his beloved spear – and the flash of gold and brilliant colours about them, so that it almost made him blink to look at them. And so with the clopping of their horses' hooves on the beaten ground, and a jingling of chain-mail and harness, they came on towards him along the track.

'God's greeting to you,' said the foremost rider when he drew level with Percival standing at gaze at the side of the track. And he reined in the chestnut, the others behind him, and sat looking down at the boy.

His head was bare, for his helmet hung at his saddlebow, and his mail coif was pushed back on to his shoulders. And Percival saw that his thick hair was grey, though he did not look to be old, and he had a strange crooked face that became all the stranger and more crooked when he smiled, and yet seemed to Percival very beautiful.

'Nay, now,' said the stranger, 'pull your eyes back into your head, I pray you! Have you never seen our like before?'

Percival shook his head. 'That have I not. And truth to tell, I do not know whether you be men from the world of men or angels out of Heaven. My mother has told me about the angels in Heaven; and you are so shining-bright. She said that the angels are shining-bright.'

The others laughed, but not unkindly, and he of the crooked face said, 'No angels we, alas! Though maybe there is something of the angels in all men, aye, and something of the Devil's brood as well.'

'Then if you are men – ' Percival began doubtfully. Memory was working in him; the half-lost memories of fine horses, and men who shone like this, that he had seen before. Suddenly the answer came to him. 'Then you must be knights!'

'We are knights indeed, and our fealty is to King Arthur, who made us knights of his Round Table.'

'King Arthur?' said the boy. 'Round Table?'

'Arthur Pendragon, the High King of all Britain,' said the man with the crooked face, gravely now. 'And the Round Table is the order of knighthood which he founded. We who are part of it are vowed always to fight for the right, to defend the weak from oppression, to keep our swords free from tarnish and at the service of Britain, to truly serve the Lord God.'

Percival was silent a long moment, looking up with shining eyes into the ugly face above him. Then he said, 'I would be a knight.'

'Maybe you will, one day,' said the other, kindly.

'What must I do to become a knight?'

'Come to the King at Caerleon, and tell him that I sent you – I, Sir Lancelot of the Lake, who under him hold the Castle of Joyeux Gard beyond the mountains yonder. If you prove worthy, he will make you a knight, when the time comes.'

And bowing his head to Percival with as grave a courtesy as if he had been a duke, he rode on his way, and his companions after him.

And Percival remained standing on the edge of the track, hearing the beat of their horses' hooves and the jingle of harness die away into the distance, with a strange mixture of feelings rising within him.

It was long after dark when he reached the charcoal-burner's bothie that was home to him, and firelight shone from the doorway to meet him, and his mother was tending the supper cooking among the hot ash, fish that he had speared in the shallows of a hill pool. She looked up and saw his face, and a great stillness took her. But Percival had no time for stillness. The news that he carried was blazing within him.

'Mother – I have met with men! At first I thought that they might be angels, for they shone as you have told me the angels shine, but they were knights. The one who seemed to be chief among them – Sir Lancelot of the Lake – told me that they were knights in the service of King Arthur of Britain, and he said that if I went to the King and proved myself worthy, one day he might make me a knight, too.'

'One day,' said his mother. 'There is time enough.'

'No! Mother, you do not understand, I must go tomorrow – I must go to Arthur at Caerleon and show him that I am worthy to be a knight!'

'You?' she said desperately. 'You, a boy out of the woods, clad in deerskins and carrying an old spear?'

And Percival squatted on to his heels beside her and put a big brown hand gently on her knee. 'But that is not all I am, is it, Mother? I used to think that it was only a dream I remembered – shining men and great horses and my father with a golden circlet on his head – but when I saw them, I knew it was no dream.'

And his mother wept in her heart, for she knew that the time had come when she must lose him. But she put her own hand over his, and said, 'No, it was no dream, your father was King Pellinore of Wales. But it is more than ten years since he was killed.'

'Who killed him?' said the boy, turned for a moment from his eagerness to be away after his knighthood and the great world by something that he saw in her face.

'Sir Agravane and Sir Gaheris, in vengeance because he had first killed their father Lot, King of Orkney, though that was done in battle. And after, when your half-brother Lamorack would have avenged your father, they killed him also.'

'When I am a knight,' said Percival, 'I will avenge my father and my half-brother on Agravane and Gaheris.'

But his mother cried out, 'No! Oh, no! It was in part to keep you from the horror of a blood feud that I brought you here and bred you up far from the world of men! And now you would go to the very place where you will find them!'

'Are they also at Caerleon?' asked the boy after a moment.

'They and their brothers Gawain and Gareth are knights of the Round Table.'

Then it seemed to Percival that the shining world of men, the world beyond the forest was less simple than he had thought it would be. But even in the moment that he realised that, he remembered the strange crooked face of Sir Lancelot smiling down at him, speaking of the honour of knighthood, and knew that he wanted above all things in the world to be one of that company.

And he said, 'Mother, as to the thing between our house and the house of Orkney, it must be as God wills. But I must go to Caerleon and to the High King. I know here – ' he put his free hand on his belly – 'that it is the thing that I must do.'

So his mother sighed, and yielded. She had always known that the day would come, and the thing that he must do . . .

So early next morning that the birds were scarcely awake, Percival made ready to set out.

His mother took his face between her hands and kissed him for the last time, knowing that she would not see him again, and said, 'Remember that your father was a true knight as well as a king, remember that I love you, and be worthy of us both. Have a care as to the friends you choose, and in whose company you travel, for you are simple-hearted, and so like to be over trusting. Let no woman ever have cause to cry out against you for your treatment of her. Pray to God daily as I have taught you, that He may be with you in all your ways, and I think that one day you will indeed be a knight, and the knight that you would wish to be.'

Percival promised, and returned his mother's kiss, and picking up his spear from where it leaned against the doorpost, went his way.

He had not forgotten the things that she had told him last night; but the blackthorn was in flower, for it was Easter time, and as he went, the willow wren who is always the first to feel the coming day, began his faint silvery whisper-song, and then the thrush joined in, and the robin, and the linnets among the gorse in the open places. And the sun at his back sent his shadow streaming out long and eager before him; and Percival went on his way, travelling at the long loose-limbed wolf-lope that eats up distance; tossing up his spear to watch the early sunlight on the blade, and whistling joyously in answer to every bird in all the forests of Wales.

All day he walked; and at dusk he ate the food that his mother had given him, and lay down to sleep in a sheltered hollow between the roots of an ancient ash tree. And next morning before sun-up he was on his way again.

Well before noon on the fifth day he came to the gates of Caerleon. Never having seen such a thing before, he checked for a little, and watched the people coming and going through the archway under the great gatehouse; but nobody seemed to come to any harm, so after a while he walked through, and no harm came to him either. And the crowds in the narrow streets were only men and women like himself and his mother, though they wore garments of coloured cloth instead of skins, and some of them stared as he went by. And so he kept on walking up one street and down another, until he came to another gate arch, and again passed through. One of the men in the gateway asked his business, and he said that he had come to see the High King because he wanted to be a knight, and the men laughed, and one of them tapped his own forehead, but they let

him through; and so he came at last to the entrance
of the Great Hall.

Arthur and his knights were at their midday meal,
and Sir Kay stood beside the King at the High Table,
pouring wine into the golden cup in which, though
Percival, watching from the shadows just within the
doorway, could not know that, it was Arthur's
custom to pledge his knights before it passed from
hand to hand among those of the brotherhood
present, until all had shared the same cup. It seemed
to him that he had never seen anything so brilliant or
beautiful as the crowded Hall with the spring sunlight slanting down through the high windows upon
the tables where the knights and their ladies sat, with
the King, his Queen beside him, under the gold-
worked canopy at the high table. He gazed at the
splendid distant figure, and thought how wonderful
it must be to be one of his knights, and his gaze went
up and down the tables in search of the strange face
of Sir Lancelot.

But in the same instant, before the King had even
taken the goblet from Sir Kay, there came a jingling
tramp of mailed feet, and a man all in red-gold
armour glistening like a noon-day pheasant, came
striding past Percival into the Hall and made for the
high table, all men struck with astonishment to see
him go by. 'Hai! You wine-bibbing dogs!' he shouted
in a great voice. 'If wine-bibbing be a part of knighthood, here stands a better knight than all of you!'
And he seized the cup from Sir Kay and drained it
at one long gulping draught. Then, bellowing with

laughter, he turned and strode out the way he had come, still gripping the precious cup. And they heard his horse's hooves strike sparks from the cobbles outside as he galloped away.

Then the frozen stillness that had seemed to hold the Hall in bonds snapped and Arthur sprang to his feet, and every one of his knights with him. 'Now by my faith!' cried Arthur. 'Here is an insult that shall not go unpaid for! Who will bring me back my drinking cup?'

'I will!' cried a hundred voices. 'Let *me* go!' 'Sir, I claim this quest!'

'No!' said Arthur. 'For none of you, is this quest. The fellow is a churl, for all his golden armour, and not worthy to fall to a knight's spear. Let one of the squires who seeks for knighthood ride after him. And if he returns with my goblet, and wearing the fellow's game-cock armour, I will make him knight that very hour!'

Then Percival sprang forward from his shadowed corner. 'My lord, King Arthur, send me after your cup! I was needing a suit of armour, and the golden gear that one was wearing will do me finely!'

They all looked at the speaker, seeing a tall, strong young man, brown as an acorn, thatched with shining yellow hair, but wearing only a deerskin and carrying a home-made spear. And Sir Kay, with his customary ill manners, let out a thin bark of laughter. 'Here's a fine champion for you, my Lord King! Pah! You stink of goats; get back to your herding, boy.'

'No need for that,' said the King to his Seneschal;

and then to Percival, 'Come, if we are to speak together, we cannot well do it with the whole length of the Hall between us!'

And when Percival came and stood before him, he looked into the young face as though he found something suddenly interesting there. 'Pray you, tell me who you are?'

'I am called Percival, and my father was King Pellinore of Wales. But after he was killed, my mother and I lived alone in the forest, until now I come to you, that one day if I am worthy, I may ask you to make me a knight.'

'That's a fine fairy story,' said Sir Kay.

But the King, still looking into Percival's face, said, 'Your father was a friend of mine, and an honourable knight of my Round Table. I thought there was something in your face . . . Very well, the quest is yours. Bring me back my cup, and return flashing in that game-cock armour, and presently you shall take your father's place.'

'I will be the truest knight to you that ever – ' Percival began, his blue eyes blazing with eagerness.

'I am sure you will,' said the King. 'But first you must eat.'

Percival shook his head. 'Nay, I'll not wait for that, my Lord King. Pray you give me a horse – '

'There shall be a horse ready for you when you have eaten. Also armour and a spear.'

Percival would have none of the armour and weapons. 'I have my own spear,' he said. 'And armour I can do without, until I can put on the golden beetle-skin of the man who stole your cup.'

But he was hungry and he did eat a little, though in haste, then rose, and bowing to the King and the company, turned to go. But midway down the Hall, a damosel slipped out from among the Queen's maidens at a lower table and stood before him. 'God go with you, Sir Percival, best of knights!' she said.

But Sir Kay, following close behind, struck her across the face, knocking her sideways. 'Out of the way, you witless wench, and hold your peace!'

Percival looked round at him. 'Beware of me, when I return in my golden armour!' he said. 'For I will repay that blow on the maiden's behalf; and you shall not easily forget the repayment!'

And he strode on out of the Hall to the courtyard, where a fine dun horse was waiting for him, and scrambling into the high unfamiliar saddle, he rode away. At the city gate he asked which way the golden knight had gone, and headed in the same direction, giving the horse full rein. He had caught and ridden wild ponies among the Welsh hills, until they bucked him off, but never a tall horse such as this before. But the horse that had been chosen for him by Arthur's order was a wise one, and with no weight of armour to carry, he and his rider made better speed than the churlish knight in his golden harness; and about the time of long shadows they overtook him as he was riding up an open valley.

'Turn! Thief of gold cups!' Percival shouted as he drew nearer. 'Turn and fight!'

The knight checked and looked round, all the light of the westering sun blazing on his red-gold armour. And at sight of the half-naked boy on the warhorse, he laughed. 'And who are you, beggar-brat on a stolen horse, to bid me turn and fight?'

And he swung his horse round on the track and sat watching as the other came up to him.

'No beggar-brat, at least,' said Percival. 'But come from King Arthur's court, on a horse out of King Arthur's stables, to take back the cup that you stole from the King this day.'

'And *you* will take it back?' said the knight. '*You?*' And he rocked with laughter in his high gilded saddle.

'Also you shall yield to me, and strip off, for I've a mind to that fine golden armour that you wear so proudly.' Percival gentled his fidgeting horse with one hand and made ready his spear with the other, and added reasonably, 'Quickly now! Otherwise I shall kill you first and take both the cup and the armour afterwards.'

The golden knight ceased to laugh. He sat silent a moment as though not believing his own ears, and then let out a roar like a wild bull. 'Insolent whelp! You have asked for death, now you shall have it!' And he couched his spear and drove in his spurs and came charging down the steep track upon the half-naked stripling who had dared to stand against him.

But Percival leapt from his horse's back, so that the spear point whistled through the empty air where he had been; and as horse and rider thundered on,

he whirled round, shouting after them, 'Coward!
Chicken-heart! First you would spear an unarmed
man, and then you run away down the hill! Come
back and fight!'

Below him the man in the golden armour
wrenched his horse round and came charging back,
his spear levelled at Percival's breast. Percival waited
until the last possible moment, poised lightly on the
balls of his feet, then side-ducked, and as the mur-
derous spear again whistled by him, drove in the
point of his own weapon between the bars of
the knight's vizor, so that it took him between the
eyes and pierced through flesh and bone to the brain.

For a moment he swayed in the saddle, then slid
over and pitched to the ground, as his horse fled on
without him.

Percival, with a strange feeling in him between
awe and triumph, knelt down beside the body and
pulled out his spear, then took the golden cup from
the wallet at the man's waist. Then he set about
getting the Golden Knight out of his armour. He
contrived to unlace the crested helmet and pull it off;
but he could not think how to deal with the rest of
the armour, for he did not understand the compli-
cated straps and buckles and laces, and thought that it
was all made in one piece. He was trying desperately
to pull the Golden Knight bodily through the neck-
hole of his harness, when he heard horse's hooves
again, and looking up, saw an old man in plain dark
armour, his helmet hanging from his saddlebow,

sitting his horse and looking down at him, half smiling.

'That was a valiant kill,' said the old man. 'And this robber-knight deserved death if ever a man did; but what is it that you seek to do with him now?'

'I try to get him out of his armour, so that I can wear it myself. For I am sworn to King Arthur to bring him back his cup, which this man stole from him, and return in the robber's golden armour. The King promised me that if I did that, and showed myself worthy, he would make me a knight, by and by.' He gave another tug. 'But the neck-hole is not big enough!'

'Nay, it is not made all in one piece,' said the old knight, the smile deepening in his eyes and in his voice. And he dismounted, and kneeling beside Percival, showed him how to unbuckle and unlace the shining pieces and draw them off one by one.

'And now,' he said, getting to his feet when the task was finished, 'do you tell me your name.'

'I am Percival, son of King Pellinore of Wales.'

'And one day you hope to be Sir Percival, of the Round Table? I am called Gonemanus, and I live close by; so now, come back with me a while, that I may have the training of you in the ways of knight-hood, as I would train a son of my own, for more than one skilful man-killing goes to the making of a worthy knight. Then you may go back to Arthur ready for his service.'

So Percival went with Sir Gonemanus to the ancient manor house that was his home, and remained with him all summer. And there he learned to ride, and the proper use of sword, shield and spear, and all the skills of knighthood. There too he learned of gentleness and chivalry and faithkeeping and all those qualities that should be a part of all true knights; though indeed much of that he had learned already from his mother in the charcoal-burner's bothie, just as he had learned from her how to pray.

He was a ready pupil, and by autumn he had learned all that Sir Gonemanus could teach him. So he bade the old man a grateful farewell, and set out, wearing the splendid golden armour and carrying a long spear, for Camelot, where the High King was at that time holding his court.

He rode through a world of gold and brown and russet, the bracken dead and sodden on the high moors, though here and there a strand of honey-suckle still in flower along the bank of some sunken green-way, and the fallen leaves muffled his horse's hoof-beats as he rode. But his heart was as high as springtime within him, and wherever he stopped and asked a night's lodging at some hermitage or lonely steading, or even paused to ask his way of a passing hunter or fellow traveller, always they felt when he had gone by, as though the sun had come out.

At last he came one early morning riding down the aisles of a beech wood, and knew from the for-ester at whose hut he had spent the night that Camelot was only a few miles ahead of him. It was a misty morning, and on every side the straight trunks of the great beeches rose up so that almost he seemed to be riding down the aisles of some vast many-pillared church. And all the world was quiet, with a solemn quiet as though it were waiting for something.

Presently he came out on to the verge of a broad track that showed signs of much coming and going of horses and men. The forester had told him that he would find such a track hereabouts, and that it led down to Camelot. Here, where there was open sky, he could see that the mist was thinning and faint blurs of blue beginning to show through the milky greyness of it. And so near his journey's end, he reined in his horse and pulled King Arthur's cup from its pouch, wondering suddenly whether he should have taken it back at once, and not kept it all this summer while he learned to be a knight; suddenly anxious lest there should be some dent or scratch on its bright surface. And as he sat turning it over in his hands, the first gleam of early sunshine struck through the mist and caught the cup, so that it flashed into his eyes with a radiance that was almost blinding; and in the same instant, from somewhere a lark leapt up singing towards Heaven, heralding the new day. And something pierced Percival as with a spear of light. A memory? A message? It was gone before he could lay hold of it to discover what it was. Only he knew that it was to do with another cup, and another sunbeam . . . And like the lark, there was something that he heralded, some word that he had to bring . . . something beautiful and terrible . . . Then the mist drifted back again and the lark fell silent, and he was left looking down at the King's golden cup, and trying to lay hold of the memory that was already lost, like the memory of a dream that fades on waking.

Scarcely aware of it, he put the cup back in its pouch. But he made no move to urge his horse forward, but sat on by the side of the track, still trying to find again the lost and lovely moment . . .

He was not even aware of the four knights who came riding up the track towards him, just as the four had come on that spring day that now seemed so long ago. Sir Kay and Sir Gawain and Sir Lancelot, and one who bore on his shield a blood-red dragon on a golden ground.

'Ride forward,' said the King to Sir Kay, 'and ask yonder knight with the plain shield his name and why he sits thus lost in thought by the side of the road.'

So Sir Kay pricked forward ahead of the rest, and when he drew near to Percival, shouted with his usual lack of courtesy, 'Ho! Sir Knight! What is your name and what brings you on this road?'

But Percival, still seeking his lost moment, did not even hear him.

'Are you dumb?' demanded Sir Kay, and ranging alongside he struck Percival in the face with the back of his mailed hand.

Percival came back to himself with the crash and pain of the blow, and jerked his head back inside his helmet. 'No one strikes me such a coward's blow and rides away unscathed!' he told the angry knight he saw beside him. Then, recognising him, 'Aye, and there is a blow I promised you for another matter, too,' and wheeled his horse away, closing his vizor and setting his spear in rest. 'Defend yourself, Sir Kay!'

Sir Kay had also pulled his horse back, and for a moment they sat facing each other, then struck in their spurs and came thundering together. But Sir Kay checked a little at the final moment, which was a fault of his in jousting, while Percival pressed in his charge unhesitating; and so Kay's spear had lost force and was turned by the other's shield, while Percival, travelling like a thunderbolt, took him in the shoulder, and carried him clean over his horse's crupper and hurled him to the ground.

Then reining in his horse, he sat with lance in rest once more, defiantly confronting the other three. 'If any more of you would joust with me, come on!' he shouted. 'I am ready to defend my right to sit my horse by the roadside and think my own thoughts, without insults or blows from such a churlish knight as that one.'

Gawain said suddenly, 'That is Percival, I'll swear, wearing the armour of that other churlish knight who stole your cup at Easter!'

'Go forward, and ask him to come and speak with us, nephew Gawain,' said the King, and added with a flicker of laughter his tone, 'and ask it in all courtesy!'

So Gawain rode forward, with spear reversed in token of friendship. 'Gentle Sir Knight,' said he, 'yonder is our Lord the High King, and he is wishful to speak with you.'

And looking, Percival saw for the first time the red dragon on the golden ground, and knew that the bearer of that shield must be the King. 'I will beg the King's pardon that I have felled one of his knights,' he said. 'But I am not sorry that I did it, for I owed him that blow he gave to the damosel on the day I first came to Caerleon.'

'As to Sir Kay,' said Gawain, scarcely looking at the battered Seneschal, who was just getting back his wind and clambering slowly to his feet, 'he rides through life asking for what he gets, and often enough he gets it.'

'Then I am glad,' said Percival, 'for now I have kept both my promise to him, and my promise to the King that I would return to him with his golden cup and wearing the golden armour of the knight who stole it.'

And he rode back with Sir Gawain to where the King waited, and dismounted and knelt at his stirrup. 'Sir, my Lord King Arthur, here is your cup again. Now pray you make me one of your knights.'

Sir Gawain spoke, not unkindly, but quickly jealous to guard what he valued, 'It takes more than the slaying of one robber and the unhorsing of the King's Seneschal to make a man worthy of knighthood, let alone the Company of the Round Table!'

But the King said, 'Gawain, I know what I do. His name is already on his waiting place at the Table; it is so that I rode out to meet him.' And to Percival he said, 'Take off your helmet.'

And when that was done, he leaned down from the saddle and gave the kneeling young man in the golden armour a light blow between neck and shoulder. 'Rise, Sir Percival of Wales.'

So they returned to Camelot, with Sir Kay bringing up the rear and nursing his bruises. And when Percival had told his story to the rest of the assembled knights, and the five of them had been unarmed, and all went to take their places, there indeed was Sir Percival's name shining in fair new gold on the tall back of his waiting seat, the seat between Sir Gawain's and the Seat Perilous.

Sir Percival looked at the name, and then at Sir Gawain; and a stiffness came over his face. Gawain saw it, and said steadily, 'Aye, I am Gawain of Orkney, and yonder are my brothers Gaheris and Agravane and Gareth.'

Sir Percival looked at the other three, with the stiffness still in his face; and the other three looked back. And the talk about the Table drifted into silence. All knew that it was for Sir Percival to take up the old feud or leave it lying. And for a long moment Sir Percival himself did not know which he was going to do. He had told his mother that it must be as God willed; but now it seemed that God was leaving the choice to him. And after three slow heartbeats of time, he made it. 'God's greeting to you, sirs – I pray you grant me your friendship.'

'That will I,' said Sir Gareth warmly. 'God's welcome to our midst.'

'And I,' said Sir Gawain. 'And here's my hand on it.'

'And I,' said Sir Gaheris, bringing his own hand down with an open-palmed crash upon the table.

Even Sir Agravane smiled thinly.

And on the surface, that was all. But all those about the Table knew well enough what lay beneath. That what their youngest knight had really said was, 'My father killed yours and you killed mine; and nothing can change that. Therefore let us leave the old feud sleeping.'

And that the Orkney brothers had said, 'We understand, and we accept the peace-making.'

Later that day, the King said to the captain of his knights, 'Gawain was right when he said that it took more than the slaying of one robber and the unhorsing of the King's Seneschal to make a knight. But now I think the boy has proved his worth in a more difficult way.'

'It cannot have been easy to leave the old feud lying,' Lancelot agreed.

They were walking together in the narrow orchard below the western walls of the castle, the autumn sunset making a bonfire blaze beyond the distant hills. There were fallen apples lying in the grass, and a few still clinging to the trees that were almost bare of leaves. When they had first come out through the postern gate, the broad loop of the river below had been flashing back the singing gold of the westering sun. But now the mist was rising . . .

Arthur said suddenly, 'Do you remember Merlin?'

Lancelot thought. 'Yes,' he said at last, 'but not well. I only saw him once, when I was a boy in Less Britain before ever I became your man. It was he that sent me to you.'

'He said once – it was when Guenever came to me and brought the Round Table for her dowry, and when we first gathered to it as a brotherhood – he said then, that when Percival came to join us, it would be as though he were a herald.'

'A herald?'

'A sign, then. For by his coming we should know that within less than a year the Mystery of the Holy Grail would come – will come, upon us here at Camelot, bringing the final flowering and fruiting time of Logres; and the knights will leave the Round Table and ride out upon the greatest quest of all.'

'We shall come together again,' said Lancelot, trying to console him.

'Some of us,' said the King. 'But it will not be the same; never the same again.' He narrowed his eyes into the blazing sky over the western hills. 'We shall have done all that is in us to do. For Britain, for the kingdom of Logres. For all that we have fought and built for and tried to make secure . . . We shall have served our purpose; made a shining time between the Dark and the Dark. Merlin said that it would be as though all things drew on to the golden glory of the sunset. But then it will all be over.'

Lancelot said, 'We shall have made such a blaze, that men will remember us on the other side of the Dark.'

And the mist was rising, rising now all round the orchard, creeping almost among the feet of the apple trees and shutting out all things beyond, so that they might have been on an enchanted island.

Merlin's remembered voice, clear across twenty years and more, was in Arthur's memory, and it was the day that he received Excalibur. 'Away over yonder – away to the West – there lies Ynys Witrin, the Glass Island; Avalon of the Apple Trees, that is the threshold between the world of men and the Land of the Living . . .' Merlin's voice seemed actually in his head. 'And not far off is Camlann, the place of the last battle . . . Nay, but that is another story, for another day as yet far off . . .'

The voice faded, and he was back in the orchard below Camelot, and it was not Merlin with him, but Lancelot. And the voice in his ears was his own. 'It grows late,' he said, 'let us be going in to the feasting, to make welcome our newest-come knight of the Round Table.'

THE LIGHT BEYOND
THE FOREST

The Quest for the
Holy Grail

1

THE NEW-MADE KNIGHT

On every side, Camelot climbed, roof above coloured roof, up the steep slopes of the hill. About the foot of the hill the river cast its shining silver noose; and at the highest heart of the town rose the palace of King Arthur. And in the Great Hall of Arthur's palace stood the Round Table, which could seat a hundred and fifty knights, each with his name written in fairest gold on the high back of his chair behind him: the Knights of the Fellowship of the Round Table, which had been formed long ago when Arthur was new and young to his kingship, for the spreading of justice and mercy and chivalry and the upholding of right against might throughout the land.

Wherever the knights might be at other times – for they had lives of their own to lead, and quests of their own to follow – it was their custom always to gather to the King for the great feast days of the Church. And so one Pentecost Eve they were assembled and just sitting down to supper, when a maiden came riding into the hall on a horse all lathered with sweat from the speed that she had made.

And she called upon Sir Lancelot of the Lake, who

was the greatest of all the Round Table knights, to ride with her, in the name of King Pelles, whom she served.

'What thing is it that King Pelles wants of me?' asked Sir Lancelot.

'That you shall know in good time.'

Sir Lancelot sat looking at his big bony sword hand on the table, while the past stirred within him, and his heart twisted a little with old sorrows and new foreshadowings. Then he rose from his place, all his companions looking on, and called for a squire to saddle his horse and another to bring his armour.

And he rode with the maiden as she asked, down from the palace and across the three-spanned bridge, and into the green young-summer mazes of the forest.

Soon he found that they were following a path that he had never followed before in all the years that he had known those forest ways; and after a league or less it brought them out into a broad clearing that was strange to him also; where the grey buildings of a nunnery sat peacefully among orchards and herb gardens beside the way. As they drew near, the gates were opened as if those within had been watching for them; and convent servants came to take Sir Lancelot's horse, while others led him to a fair and high-ceilinged guest chamber.

There was a bed in the middle of the chamber, and on it two knights lay asleep, and looking at their russet-brown heads burrowed into the pillows, Sir Lancelot saw that they were two young kinsmen of his, Bors and Lional, who he supposed must be on their way to the Round Table gathering. He laughed, and shook each by the shoulder to rouse them, and they plunged awake, reaching for their daggers before they saw who it was.

And while they were still exclaiming and greeting each other, the abbess and two of her nuns came into the chamber, bringing with them a very young man. At their coming, the laughing and the horseplay ceased; and a great quiet came with them into the chamber.

'Sir Lancelot,' said the abbess, 'we bring you this boy whom we have raised up and loved as our own, ever since his mother died, before he stood as tall as a sword-blade from the ground. Now it is time that he becomes a knight, and his grandsire, King Pelles, would have him receive his knighthood from your hand.'

And the quiet closed in again after her words; and in the midst of it Sir Lancelot and the boy stood and looked at each other.

Now Sir Lancelot of the Lake was an ugly man, with an ugliness such as women love. His dark face under the thick badger-streaked hair looked as though it had been put together in haste, so that the two sides of it did not match. One side of his mouth was grave with heavy thought, while the other lifted in joy; one eyebrow was level as a falcon's wing and the other flew wild like a mongrel's ear. He had lived forty-five summers and winters in the world, and loved and sorrowed and triumphed and fought to the utmost, and every joy and sorrow and striving had set its mark on him.

The boy's face was pale and clear, waiting for life to touch it, and his hair made a smooth cap as of dark silk on his head. He was like his mother, Elaine, the daughter of King Pelles; and Sir Lancelot saw that in the first moment that they turned to each other. But the look which had made men call Elaine 'The Lily' in him made them think of a spear-blade or a still tall flame.

Yet from the strong chaos of Sir Lancelot's face, and the waiting quietness of the boy's, the same wide grey eyes looked long and steady out at each other.

And Sir Bors and Sir Lional, watching, exchanged quick startled glances.

'What is your name?' said Sir Lancelot, at last.

'Galahad,' said the boy.

There was a sudden wild weeping deep down in Lancelot where no one but he could know of it. All the years of his manhood he had loved Guenever, King Arthur's queen, and for her sake had never looked towards another woman. But there had been a time, long ago, when King Pelles' daughter had set her love on him and, being desperate, had won him to her by a trick for just one night. And of that one night she had borne a son, and called him Galahad.

'My name also was Galahad, before I gained my second name that now men call me by,' said Lancelot. And then knew that he need not have said it, for his son already knew.

To the lady abbess he said, 'Madam, let him keep

his vigil in the church tonight, and it shall be as his grandsire wishes in the morning.'

So that night Galahad kept his vigil, kneeling before the high altar of the nunnery church; and when the birds woke to their singing in the first light of Pentecost morning, Sir Lancelot dubbed him knight.

'Now come with us to King Arthur's court,' he said, when it was done.

But the abbess shook her head. 'Not yet. Go you back to Camelot; and when it is the right time, he will come.'

So Sir Lancelot and his young cousins rode back to Camelot alone. And all the way Sir Lancelot looked straight between his horse's ears and spoke not one word.

When they reached Camelot, the King and Queen had gone with all their court to hear morning Mass, and it was too late to join them. So the three knights went into the Great Hall to wait for their return. And there they found a most strange thing.

This was the way of it.

Long before, when the Fellowship was formed, Merlin the old and wise, the master of secret knowledge, who had taught Arthur those things which a king should know, had made for him by magic arts the Round Table with its places for a hundred and fifty knights. But no more than a hundred and forty-nine had ever sat down at that table, while always the last seat remained empty. And this seat was called the Seat Perilous, for no man might sit in it that disaster did not befall him. Now Merlin, who had forgotten his wisdom and given his heart to an enchantress because she smiled at him and was beautiful, slept where she had locked him in a magic hawthorn tree; and for twenty years and more, Arthur and his brotherhood had sat at his Round Table with the empty seat among them. And some of those who had sat there in the early years were dead now, and new young knights come to fill their places; and others were scarred by old battles and had grey in their hair that had been black or gold or brown when first they gathered there. And still the Seat Perilous remained empty and waiting.

But now the sun falling through one of the high windows touched the carved and beautiful chair, and on its high back something glinted in the light. And drawing near, the three knights read, in letters that seemed that moment to have been set there in new-fired gold: 'Four hundred and fifty years have passed since the Passion of Our Lord Jesus Christ. And on the day of Pentecost this seat shall find its master.'

'That is today,' said Sir Lancelot, at half breath.

And Sir Bors, scarce knowing why he did so – and he was not one to do things without clear reason – spread his cloak over the back of the Seat Perilous, so that the words were hidden until their moment came.

In due time the King and Queen and all the court returned from Mass, and greeted the newcomers; and the King asked Sir Lancelot how his venture of the day before had gone. Sir Lancelot told how the maiden had taken him to a nunnery, and how there he had knighted a young man who was King Pelles' grandson. But he said no more as to the boy, for he thought, 'Every one will know, soon enough.' Yet the Queen must have guessed, for she bade them all God's greeting and withdrew quickly to her own chambers, her ladies going with her.

Then the pages began to set the table for dinner; but just as the knights were about to take their places, a squire came running, crying out as he burst upon them, 'Sirs – my Lord King – there is a great wonder – '

'And what wonder is that?' said the King. He was hungry.

'A stone – a great stone floating as light as a leaf along the river; and in the stone a sword standing upright! With my own eyes I saw it!'

The King remembered another sword in another stone, and how he had pulled it out and so proved himself the true fore-chosen King of Britain; and he forgot his hunger. And with all his knights behind him he went down from the palace to the river bank. There, caught by an out-thrust of rooty bank, they found a block of red marble, and standing upright in it a sword with a pommel formed of a ball of amber as large as an apple. And engraved on the quillions in letters of gold they read: 'None shall take me hence, but he at whose side I am to hang. And he shall be the best knight in the world.'

Arthur knew that his own sword and its stone

were past and behind him; and he called to Sir Lancelot who was nearest and dearest to him of all his knights, 'This sword all but has your name on it.'

'Not mine, my lord the King,' Lancelot did not know why he said it. It was not modesty. He knew his own reputation as well as the world knew it. But he knew that it had to be said.

'Try,' said the King.

'No,' said Lancelot, and his hand went to the hilt of the sword at his side. 'I have Joyeux; why should I turn faithlessly to seek another blade?' And his mouth shut like a trap and he moved no nearer.

Then at the King's bidding Sir Gawain of Orkney, who was the King's nephew and loved him well, set his two hands to the sword-grip and pulled until the veins stood out on his neck, but could not shift the blade; and then young Sir Percival of Wales spat on his hands and tried, more to keep Sir Gawain company than anything else, for he was a large, kind, simple-hearted young man and had no high opinion of himself. After he, too, had failed, no one else came forward; and so after a while they left the sword in its block of red marble among the alder roots, and went back to the Great Hall to dinner.

But another marvel was to come upon them before they ate that day.

For when they were all seated, and with a ringing and singing and sounding of horns the first dishes had just been borne in, suddenly, and without any hand touching them, all the doors and window-shutters slammed to as in a squall of wind. Yet there was no wind. And the Hall was still lit as though with the clear brightness of the day outside.

All round the table men looked at each other with startled faces. And in the same instant, none seeing how they came, there were two strangers among them; an old man robed in white, and beside him a knight whose surcoat over his armour blazed red as though he were a tongue of flame, but with no shield over his shoulder and only an empty sheath hanging from his sword belt.

'Peace be with you,' said the old man to the King.

'And with you, stranger,' returned the King. But his gaze went to the knight in the scarlet surcoat.

'Sir,' said the old man, 'I bring before you this knight of the line of King Pelles, and through him of the line of Joseph of Arimathea; he who brought to this land the Holy Grail, from the land where Our Lord Jesus Christ drank from that wondrous cup, and shared its wine with his disciples when they gathered to the Last Supper. That was the beginning of the mystery of the Grail's sojourn among men; and many wonders and many sorrows have followed therefrom; and because of it King Pelles himself lies maimed of a wound that never heals and his land is a wilderness; but now the time comes for the ending of all these things. And with the time, comes the knight who shall bring them to fulfilment and surcease.'

'If it be as you say,' said the King, 'there was no man ever more welcome.'

Then the old man, serving the knight as though he were his squire, helped him to disarm and put his flame-red surcoat on again over his white tunic. And now that his head was bared, many were the eyes that went from his face to Sir Lancelot's and back again. And the old man led him straight to the Seat Perilous, and pulled aside Bors's cloak, so that the golden lettering shone out once more. But the words had changed since Bors had covered them, and now they read: 'This is the seat of Galahad.'

The young knight sat down in it, very grave and still. He looked at the old man and said, 'Faithfully you have done what was demanded of you. Now go back to Corbenic as you came. Greet my grandsire, and tell him that I will surely come when the time brings me.'

And the ancient man went to the great door, and opened it, no one daring to move or follow him, and went his way.

Behind him, the King and all his knights set themselves to making Sir Galahad welcome. They would have done the same for any newcomer to their brotherhood. But from the old man's words, they had added reason for gladness at his coming. They knew well enough, all of them, of King Pelles, who men called the Grail Keeper, the Fisher King, and who they called also the Maimed King because of the wound he had in his thigh that never healed; and they knew that because of this wound, his land suffered also, bound by drought and lean harvests and the shadow of sorrows and strange happenings that hung over it like a cloud. Now, it seemed, through the new young knight in their midst, all this was to be mended; and so they rejoiced.

But for another reason also they were glad. For a long while they had felt, the older knights especially, that in Camelot the high and shining days were over, that the long struggle for right against might was behind them, and the dreams were done with, and life had settled into a solid mould; and there was a weariness of heart among the Fellowship of the Round Table. Now there was something ahead of them again, instead of all in the past. Something coming; joy or grief, maybe death, but something coming . . .

'A light beyond the forest,' thought Sir Lancelot, 'but the dark forest to be traversed first.' And was not quite sure why he had thought it.

'If I were a tree, and spring was coming – a long way off, but still coming – this is how I should feel,' thought Sir Percival, and his wide serious gaze was on the young knight who sat so gravely and calmly in the forbidden seat. Sir Percival was a born follower, and to such a one there is nothing better in the world than to find the leader his heart goes out to.

'How is it that he can sit there, and no harm come to him?' said Sir Bors, worried, to Sir Lancelot beside him. 'He has had no time yet to prove his worthiness.'

And Sir Lancelot said, 'Did you not see his name on the back? I am thinking it could only be because God would have him sitting there.'

2

THE THUNDER AND THE SUNBEAM

As the meal drew to its end, the King was telling his newest knight of the wonder that they had all seen that morning before his coming. 'Since the seat is for you, it may be that the sword is for you also,' said the King. 'Come, and we will put the matter to the test.'

So again the knights went down through the steep narrow streets of Camelot, where the swallows darted between the eaves in the summer air; and again they gathered on the river bank.

The block of red marble still lay stranded among the alder roots, and the strange and beautiful sword still stood fast in it.

And Sir Galahad stepped down among the wet roots where the water ran shallow under the bank, and drew the sword from its stone as sweetly as from a well-oiled sheath.

A gasp broke from the watching knights; and the King said, 'Surely here is a wonder indeed! Two of my best knights have failed in that attempt.'

Sir Galahad stood looking at the sword in his hand, feeling its balance. 'The adventure was not theirs, but mine,' he said, not boasting but simply stating the simple fact, and slid the blade into the empty sheath at his side. 'I am no longer a knight without a sword. All that I need now is a shield.'

'God shall send you a shield, even as he has sent you the sword,' said the King.

And Sir Lancelot remembered the words on the hilt, and beat down a bitter sense of loss, telling himself that no man could be for ever the best knight in the world, able to tell himself that, because he did not yet quite believe it.

Then the King spoke again, 'My brothers, the thought is on me that soon we are to scatter, and never again shall I see you all here with me as you are now. Therefore, for the rest of this day, let us hold a joust here in the meadows below Camelot, and do such deeds that after our time is past, old men shall tell of it to their grandsons by the fire on winter nights, and the children's eyes shall shine at the hearing, and they shall tell of it to their grandsons in turn.'

So the lists were set up, and men sent for their horses and weapons, and all the rest of that day while the sunlight lasted the knights jousted on the level ground below Camelot. And men looked to see how Sir Galahad would show, seeing that he had had so strange an upbringing and had maybe never learned to carry arms. But he proved himself so well, both as a horse-master and with sword and lance, that by sunset, of all those who had come against him, Sir Lancelot and Sir Percival were the only two he had not been able to unhorse.

And when the dusk thickened over the river

meadows, they made an end, and rode back up the streets of Camelot town, with all the townsfolk who had come down to watch straggling home again behind them. And so they went back into the palace, for it was time for the evening meal.

But the wonders of that day were not yet over.

When the knights had unarmed and sat themselves once more at table, when the torches had been lit and the linen board-cloths were spread, there came a clap of thunder so loud that it seemed the very roof must fall. And after the thunder there came a sunbeam that struck like a sword through the Hall, dimming out the torches and lighting every corner to seven times the radiance of broad day. And it seemed to all those about the table that the light shone into their very souls; and a great awe fell upon them; a great stillness so that they could neither move nor speak.

And as they sat so, the Holy Grail came in to the Hall, no man seeing the hands that carried it.

It entered through the great door, veiled with a cloth of fine white samite as every man there had seen the Communion Cup veiled upon the altar at the celebration of the Mass. And so the knowledge came into their hearts of what it was they looked upon. It seemed to float of itself, light and still as a sunbeam upon the air; and at its coming the high Hall was flooded with a thousand fragrances, as though all the flowers and spices of the world had been poured out before it. Slowly, it circled the vast table, hovering before each man, and passing on; and each man, after it had passed him by, found spread before him food far more delicious than any that ever came out of the palace kitchens.

And when it had circled the table, as silently as it had come, the Grail passed from their sight.

The sunbeam faded and the torches brightened again in the smoky shadows, and the stillness passed from the men sitting there. And the King said, but still quietly, 'My brothers, now our hearts should be lifted up for joy, that Our Lord has shown so great a sign of his love, in feeding us with his grace from his own cup at this high feast of Pentecost. Now indeed we know that the time is come of which the old man spoke, who brought Sir Galahad among us.'

And Sir Gawain, who was ever among the quickest to take fire of all the Round Table brotherhood, sprang to his feet and swore that next morning he would ride out upon the Quest of the Holy Grail, and never return to court until he had looked openly upon the mystery which that day they had been allowed to glimpse; and until the freeing of King Pelles' Waste Land had been brought about, as the old man had foretold.

And on hearing him, every knight in the Hall sprang up and took upon himself the same oath.

But the King bent his face into his hands, and the tears ran between his fingers. 'Gawain, Gawain, you fill my heart with grief. For now indeed I know that we are to scatter; and I must lose the best and truest companions that ever a man had. And well I know that many of you, the flower of those who ride away, will not return to me again.'

And yet he knew that if it were not Gawain, then another must have done the thing, for it was foreordained.

'Sir,' said Sir Lancelot, striving to comfort him, 'if every one of us is to meet death upon this quest, we could meet it in no sweeter nor more honourable way.'

But the King was not comforted.

Now word of Galahad's coming, and of his taking the sword from its stone, had reached the Queen's apartments, and she had gone out with her ladies to watch the jousting from the rampart-walk. Guessing who the new young knight must be, she longed to see him, but dared not see him too close, for she knew that the seeing would be like a dagger in her heart. And back in her own apartments at supper she had heard the thunder, and one of the squires had brought her word of the coming of the Grail, and the oath that Sir Gawain and all the knights after him had sworn.

'Sir Lancelot, too?' she said, and drove the needle through the lily that she was embroidering, deep into her finger.

'He would not be Sir Lancelot else!' said the boy.

And the red blood sprang out and made a crimson fleck on the lily petal.

Next morning when the knights were arming and their horses being walked up and down in the great courtyard, the Queen bathed her eyes that no one might know she had passed the night in weeping, and went out to bid them God speed. But at the last, her courage broke in her hand, and she turned back into the castle garden, to hide her grief, and flung herself down full-length on a low turf-seat under a pleached vine arbour.

Sir Lancelot, standing harnessed and ready to mount, saw her face in the moment that she turned away, and left his horse to the nearest squire, and went quickly and quietly after her.

The King was not looking that way. Sometimes he found it hard not to know how it was between his wife and his best friend. But so long as he did not know, he had no need to hurt the two people dearest to him on earth. He prayed, so deep down within him that he was not even aware of it, that nothing would ever happen that would force him to know.

And Sir Lancelot went through the narrow door into the garden.

He stood over Guenever, and touched her silken sleeve, and she cried out to him, 'You have betrayed me and given me up to death!'

'Would you have had me hang back, when the others swore to take up the Quest?'

'Yes! Rather than quit the service of my lord the King to go to strange lands from which only God can bring you safely back!'

'If it is his will,' said Lancelot, 'then God will bring me safely back.'

'I am sick with dread!' cried the Queen, not listening. 'If you loved me truly, you could not go without my leave!'

'Madam,' said Sir Lancelot, 'the horses are stamping in the courtyard. Give me your leave to go now.'

She was silent a moment, and then she said, 'I have seen Galahad, as he rode up from the jousting. He is very like you.'

'He is beautiful,' said Lancelot.

'So are you — so are you!' and she broke into weeping laughter, and turned and took his strange face between her hands. 'I grieve for his mother, for though she bore your son, I have had more joy of you than ever she had!'

'Lady,' said Lancelot, and his voice cracked in his throat, 'give me leave to go.'

'Go,' she said, 'and God be with you.'

And Lancelot went back to the courtyard where all the rest were mounted and ready to be off. There with the rest, he took his leave of Arthur, his liege lord and his dearest friend; and that, too, was sharp pain within him, the more so for that he was torn with guilt because of the Queen.

'God be with you,' said the King.

And they mounted and rode away, Sir Percival as close as might be behind Sir Galahad.

And all Camelot wept to see them go.

Sir Galahad, who had been born in the Castle of Corbenic, and bred there through his first years, and whose grandsire was King Pelles, knew well enough where the Grail was lodged. Sir Lancelot knew it too.

But they knew also, as did every knight setting out from Arthur's court that morning, that simply to ride to Corbenic and beat upon the castle gate, demanding to see the mystery within, would serve but an empty purpose. They must cast themselves on fate, welcoming whichever way it took them, and trusting that when the time was right, if they proved worthy, the quest they followed would bring them to the place of their hearts' desire and the thing that their spirits reached out to.

So they parted from each other when they had crossed the river, and took to the forest singly, wherever the trees were thickest and there was no path. And the forest closed over behind them as though they had never been.

3

THE SHIELD OF KING MORDRAIN

Now the story tells that when Sir Galahad had parted from the rest, he rode four days, meeting with no adventures. But on the evening of the fifth day he came to an abbey of Cistercian monks; and there he found two more of the Companions of the Round Table: King Bagdemagus and Sir Owain the Bastard. They greeted each other joyfully, and that evening, when they had eaten with the brothers, they went out into the abbey orchard, and sat themselves down under an apple tree to talk and exchange any news of the past few days.

'This is a happy chance that brings us all three to the same place at the same time,' said Sir Galahad, for courtesy's sake.

'No chance brought *us*,' said King Bagdemagus, 'but word of the shield.'

'The shield?' said Sir Galahad.

And Sir Owain told him, 'We have heard that in this abbey there is a shield, with a strong magic upon it, that any man who takes it down from its place and hangs it about his neck, unless he be worthy of it, will be slain or sore wounded within three days; and we are come to put the matter to the test.'

'Tomorrow morning,' said King Bagdemagus, watching a brown furred bee among the last of the tarnished apple blossom, 'I shall shoulder this shield, and ride upon my fortune.'

'If you fail – ' began Sir Galahad, then turned to Owain the Bastard, 'Pray you grant me next turn, for I have as yet no shield of my own.'

So the matter was agreed between them; and next morning, when they had heard Mass, King Bagdemagus asked one of the monks where the shield of which they had heard might be.

'Are you yet another who comes seeking to bear it?' said the monk, sadly; but he took them behind the high altar of the abbey church; and there on the wall hung a great shield, white and blazoned with a cross as red as fresh-spilled blood on fresh-fallen snow.

When they had looked at it, Owain said, 'Indeed, Galahad, I will yield you my turn, if our brother here fails, for surely this is a shield to be carried by the best knight in the world; and I shall not seek to take it up. I have neither the valour not the virtue to carry it. And I value my neck!'

But King Bagdemagus took it down and slipped the strap over his head and settled it on his shoulder, and strode out, calling for his horse.

A young squire belonging to the abbey saddled and brought it for him, and he mounted and rode away, followed by the squire on a sturdy cob, who was to attend him, and bring back the shield if that should be the way things went.

Galahad and Owain returned to the orchard, and sat down again under the apple tree, without a word between them. And Owain made a great business of burnishing his helmet. But Galahad sat with his hands round his updrawn knees, and gazed straight before him as though at something a very long way off.

King Bagdemagus rode some two leagues or more, until he came to a meadow sloping gently down to a willow-fringed stream. And there the adventure of the shield came upon him, for among the stream-side willows a knight in white armour sat his horse, head turned as though to look for his coming, and in the instant that he rode out from the woodshore, the waiting knight struck in his spurs and with levelled lance came thundering towards him across the open ground.

The King spurred to meet him, and they came together with a crash that rang all up and down the valley. But the combat was a short one. Bagdemagus's lance shattered on the White Knight's shield, while the point of the other's weapon took him below the shoulder, driving through the iron rings of his hauberk and on deep into the flesh, and hurled him backwards from the saddle.

Then the stranger knight dismounted, and took from the fallen King the white shield with its blood-red cross. 'That was foolish of you,' said he. 'For it is granted to no man to bear this shield save he that is the best knight in all Christendom.' He beckoned to the squire. 'Take this shield and carry it back to Sir Galahad; but having given it into his hands, bring him here again to me. Since this is the shield that he will bear henceforth, it is right that he should hear the truth concerning it.'

So the squire hung the shield from his own saddlebow, and going to King Bagdemagus where he lay, got him across his horse, and mounted behind him to hold him secure. Then, leading the cob, he rode back the way they had come.

When they reached the abbey, Galahad and Owain and the brethren saw them and came running. They lifted King Bagdemagus down from his horse and bore him to one of their guest chambers, and the Father Infirmarer brought warm water and salves and fine linen to tend to his gaping wound.

Then the squire brought the shield from where he had left it hanging at the cob's saddlebow, and gave it to Sir Galahad. 'Sir, the knight from whom King Bagdemagus got his wound sends you this, and bids you bear it from now on, for you alone have the right. Also he bids you come to him, that he may tell you all that you should know concerning it. He bids you come now, for he is waiting.'

So Galahad's harness was brought, and Owain and the squire helped him to arm. And he took the great shield on his shoulder. Sir Owain would have ridden with him, but Galahad bade him remain with King Bagdemagus, and rode out alone, save for the squire to show him the way.

So they came to the meadow, and found the

White Knight sitting his horse among the willow trees, as still and timeless as though he and his mount were painted upon the quiet of the summer air.

And when they had greeted each other in all courtesy, Sir Galahad asked him for the story of the shield.

'Gladly I will tell it,' said the knight, 'for it is yours to know.'

And he began the telling.

'Two and forty years after the Passion of Christ, that same Joseph of Arimathea who took his body from the cross and gave it burial, left Jerusalem, bearing with him the Holy Grail, his son and many of his people following. By God's command they set out, not knowing where; and their wanderings brought them at last to the city of Sarras, far towards the sunrise, beyond any other city of men.

'Now when they came there, they found the king of that place, Mordrain by name, at bitter war with a neighbouring king who sought to overrun his frontiers. He was set to go into battle; but Josephus the son of Joseph, who was a priest and deep-sighted beyond other men, told him that the fighting would go ill for him, for he was an infidel and could not call upon the help of God. Josephus told him of what is in the Gospels; and then he had a great white shield brought, and on its face he painted a cross, blood red; and he had a shield-cover made for it of fine white sendal. And he gave it to the King, saying, "Carry this into battle with you, and at the point in the fighting when all seems lost, uncover it, and pray to God, the semblance of whose sacred death you bear, that you may return victorious, to receive in faith his holy law."

'King Mordrain did as he was bidden, and at the crown of his battle, when defeat and death seemed sure, he took the cover from his shield, praying for deliverance. And the enemy broke and crumbled before him as a sand wall where the tide sweeps in. Then he returned to Sarras with great rejoicing, and was baptized a Christian. And he remained true to that faith, and the shield ever his most honoured and beloved possession.

'The time came when, again at the bidding of God, Joseph and his son Josephus left Sarras, and brought the Grail to Britain. This you know. And here they fell into the hands of a cruel and wicked king who threw them into prison. And when at last word of this came to King Mordrain, he gathered his fighting-men and set sail for Britain, and overthrew the wicked king and set Joseph and his son and their followers free.

'So the Christian faith came to Britain; at first to Avalon of the Apple Trees, and from there spreading throughout all the land.

'And Mordrain loved Josephus so deeply that for his sake he remained in Britain and never returned to his own city. And when the time came that he must lay aside his shield, he had it lodged in the abbey where you first saw it; for it was told to him in a dream, that, after him, only the best knight in Christendom might carry it without coming to disaster, for the power there is in it.'

And when he had finished the story, suddenly the White Knight was no longer there.

When they had come back to themselves from the daze in which he left them, the boy from the abbey knelt down before Sir Galahad, and begged to ride with him as his squire, the squire of the best knight in all Christendom.

But Galahad looked down at him, troubled, and said, 'If I had need of company, be sure that I would not refuse you.'

'I would be to you the best squire in Christendom,' said the boy.

And Sir Galahad said, 'But I ask of you a harder thing.'

'I will do anything!'

'Then go back to the abbey, and be with King Bagdemagus while he mends of his wound, that Sir Owain may be free to follow his quest.'

And the squire ceased his pleading and rose from his knees. 'I will do the harder thing,' he said, though the words choked within him.

And so they parted.

Sir Galahad rode for many days, wherever the forest took him, and without meeting any other adventure, until one morning he came out on to the slopes of a broad and pleasant valley through which a river wound its shining way; and saw in front of him a castle, tall and turreted, that seemed to float above its own reflection in the water, as a swan will do. As he sat his horse, looking down towards it, an old ragged man came by, and gave him God's greeting in the passing. Galahad returned the greeting, and asked the name of the castle.

'Sir, it is called the Castle of Maidens,' said the old man.

'That is a fair name.'

'Maybe so, but it casts a dark shadow on the land.'

'How is that?' asked Sir Galahad.

'Because of its custom. Its evil treatment of those who pass by. Better that you turn back and follow another way.'

'I do not like to turn from my chosen road,' said Galahad, 'but assuredly I shall not pass by.' And he flicked the reins, and rode on, making sure of his weapons as he went, while the old man, wagging his head and grumbling to himself about the rashness of youth, hobbled on into the forest.

When Galahad drew near to the castle, a mounted page came out to meet him, and bending his wild-eyed mare side-on across the track, demanded to know his business, in the name of the lords of the castle.

'I seek only to learn the custom of this place,' said Sir Galahad peaceably.

'Bide here, and truly you may learn it, and find the lesson little to your taste,' said the page insolently, and, making his mare dance and snort, he wheeled about and rode full gallop back to the castle.

Galahad sat his horse in the dust of the track and waited, and in a little while there burst out from the castle seven armed and splendidly mounted knights, who shouted to him, as with one voice, 'Sir knight, put up your guard, for the answer to the question that you ask is death!'

And all seven together, they set their lances in rest and came charging straight down upon him.

Sir Galahad pricked forward to meet them, and felled the firstcomer with a blow that came near to breaking his neck. Six more lance points rang against his shield, but he remained as firm as ever in the saddle, and the shield was not even scratched, though the weight of the thrusts flung his horse back on its haunches. He flung aside his own splintered lance, and drew his sword, and the fight went on; one against seven, so that the seven thought to have an easy victory. Yet it seemed that the lone knight did not know how to tire, and their weapons could not scathe him; and when the fight had raged till noon, and the seven were all sore wounded and weary beyond lifting sword arm, a cold fear fell upon their hearts, and they turned and fled.

Galahad sat his weary horse to watch them go; and when the dusk had sunk behind them, he turned to the castle bridge; and there in the gateway stood an old man in the habit of a priest, who held out to him a bunch of massive keys.

'Sir,' said the old man, 'this castle is yours now, by right of conquest, and all within it, to do with as you will.'

So Galahad rode into the castle; and as soon as he was within the walls, a great crowd of maidens came thronging about him, many-voiced and fluttering as bright birds in a cage, crying, 'Welcome! Sir knight,

we have waited long and long for one to come who
could free us from our captivity!'

And while some took his horse, others led him to
the inner court, and helped him to unarm as though
they had been his squire. And when he was
unhelmed, a maiden tall and fair beyond all the rest
came out through an inner door, carrying an ivory
horn, wonderfully carved and bound about with
gold. She held the horn out to Sir Galahad, saying,
'Gentle sir, let you sound this, to summon all the
knights who will hold their lands from you, now
that you are lord of this castle. Then, when they are
gathered here before you, let you have them swear on
the crosses of their swords that the old evil custom of
this place shall never return to it again.'

Sir Galahad took the horn, and stood with it in his
hands. 'First, do you tell me what custom that is; and
why so many maidens are captive here.'

The old priest took up the story.

'Ten years ago, the knights who today you vanquished and put to flight came to this castle asking
hospitality of Duke Lynoor, the lord of all these parts.
Now the Duke had two daughters; and as soon as
they saw them, these same knights would each and
every one have had the eldest and most beautiful for
his lady. So there burst out a great quarrel among the
knights and between them and the Duke. And
the Duke and his son were slain, and the maidens
made captive. Then the knights having other things
to think of, ceased their quarrel among themselves
and made common cause to seize the castle treasure,

and summoning all the fighting men of these parts, they fell to waging war on their neighbours, until they had forced them all to submit and become their vassals. Then the Duke's elder daughter said to them, "In truth, my lords, as this castle was captured because of a maiden, so, because of other maidens, it shall be lost again; and one knight shall be the down-fall of seven."

'At this, the seven knights were greatly enraged. And from that day forward, in revenge for her words, and also that none should have the chance to bring them true, they have taken and held captive every maiden to pass beneath the castle walls.'

'And the Duke's daughters?' said Galahad, and looked towards the maiden who had brought him the ivory horn.

'Nay,' said the maiden, 'my sister is dead long since. I was but a child when they came.'

Then Sir Galahad set the horn to his lips and winded a call that sent the echoes flying ten forest leagues away.

Presently, men came from far and wide to answer the summons. And when all were gathered, he said to the Duke's younger daughter, 'Lady, this castle is mine by right of conquest, to do with as I will. So now I make a gift of it to you.'

And he caused all the assembled knights to swear fealty to her, and to take oath upon the crosses of their swords, that never again should the old evil customs return to the castle, and that all the captive maidens should at once be set free and sent in safety to their own homes.

And that night he supped and slept in the castle, which was no longer called the Castle of Maidens; and next morning after hearing Mass, he rode out again on his way.

But now the story leaves Sir Galahad a while, and tells of Sir Lancelot.

4

SIR LANCELOT FAILS HIS TESTING

For many days after parting from his companions, Sir Lancelot rode alone through the forest, waiting with an open heart for God to tell him what to do and whither to turn his horse's head. But indeed it seemed to him that in that forest there was neither time nor place, so that a man might ride many days towards the sunset, and find himself at the last back in the place from which he had set out; almost, he might bide quiet beneath a tree and let the forest shift around him, like the country of a dream.

And then one morning he came down to a stream, and found a big warhorse that he thought he knew grazing on the bank, its bit slipped free and its reins carefully knotted up to be out of its way. And sitting with his back to an alder tree, helmet off and his yellow head tipped back against the rough bark, Sir Percival, whistling soft and full-throated to a blackbird, and the blackbird whistling back as though they were old friends. But, indeed, Sir Percival was friends with all furred and feathered things.

He got to his feet when he saw Sir Lancelot ride out from the woodshore, slowly, as men move in armour, and they greeted each other; and when Sir

Lancelot had turned his own horse loose to graze beside the other, they sat down again together beneath the alder tree. And Percival asked if he had seen or heard anything of Sir Galahad.

'Neither sound nor sight,' said Lancelot.

Percival sighed.

'Were you seeking him?'

'I was hoping we might ride together a little while,' Percival said, 'but it was a foolish hope.'

It seemed to Lancelot that the knight beside him was young to be riding errant and alone in the dark forest. And yet that was foolishness, for Percival had shown himself in the jousting to be no green boy. He was older than Galahad by at least a year, and no one would be thinking Galahad young to ride errant, no matter through what dark forest.

'Would I serve, until we can come by word of Sir Galahad?' he said. There was a smile in his voice; and if it was a crooked smile, that was hidden in the shadow of his helmet.

And Percival said, 'If it be not Sir Galahad, there is none that I would rather ride with.'

So when they went on again, they rode together.

For many days they kept each other company, and then one evening, in a wild dark country of rocks and twisted low-growing trees, they met with a knight bearing a great white shield blazoned with a blood-red cross; and because the device was strange to them, they did not know him for Sir Galahad, lately come from freeing the Castle of Maidens.

Sir Lancelot called out to him to know his name,

but Sir Galahad never answered, for indeed he was away inside himself in some desert solitude of his own, as was often the way with him, and had no thought to come back and greet and be greeted by other men.

So when he did not answer, but would have ridden on across their path, Sir Lancelot called out a warning; and when still he neither checked nor answered, shouted the final challenge, 'Joust!' and couching his lance, rode straight at him. Galahad looked round, then, and swung his horse to meet the charge; and the lance took him full on the shield and shattered into a score of pieces; but he remained rock-firm in the saddle, and his own lance in the same instant took Sir Lancelot under the guard, and hove him clean over his horse's crupper, but did him no other harm. Then Percival came thundering down upon the unknown knight, but Sir Galahad wrenched his horse aside, and as the other missed his thrust, took him with the sideways lance stroke as he hurtled past, and swept him from the saddle, so that he plunged down all asprawl beside Sir Lancelot, not knowing if it was day or night.

And Sir Galahad went back to the solitude within himself, and turned his horse and rode away.

By the time the two he had felled had gathered themselves together and caught their horses and remounted, he was long out of sight.

'We have no hope of catching him now,' said Percival, 'and this wilderness of rocks is no good place for us, with the dusk coming down. Let us turn back to the hermitage we passed a while since, and beg shelter for the night.' For truth to tell, his bruises ached.

But Sir Lancelot was in a deeper pain. For this was the first time since he took valour that ever he had been unhorsed. And again, and achingly, he was remembering the words on Galahad's sword. Two things were most dear to him in life; one was his love for the Queen, and one was knowing that he was the best knight in the world; not merely the strongest, but the best, and not only that other men should say it of him, but that he should know it of himself. And the knowledge was beginning to grow most painfully within him that of these two things, he could not have both.

Sir Percival felt the trouble in his companion, and said, quick and warm, 'It was surely a chance stroke.'

Lancelot shook his head, 'It was as clean a fall as ever I saw one knight give another. That is why I must press on after him. I must know who he is – '

'Wait until morning,' Percival said, 'and then we will seek him together.'

'No,' said Lancelot, 'I must know – I must find out – '

'Then God go with you,' said Percival, 'but I will ride no further this night.'

So they parted, and Percival turned back to the hermitage, while Lancelot pushed on through the rocks and the stunted trees and the gathering dusk, after the glimmer of a crimson cross on a white shield.

When it was full dark, he came to a rough stone cross that stood on the edge of wild heath country at the parting of two ways; and close beyond it saw an ancient chapel. He dismounted, and, leading his horse, walked towards the chapel, for he hoped there might be someone there who could tell him which way the knight had gone. But when he had looped the reins over a branch of the ancient hawthorn that grew beside the place, and turned himself to look more closely at the chapel, it was no more than a ruin, with nettles growing thick about the door sill; and coming within the porch, he found a rusty iron grille to bar his way.

And yet the place could not be deserted after all, for light flooded out to him through the grille, and within, he could see an altar richly hung with silken cloths; and before the altar, six candles glimmered crocus-flamed in a branched silver candlestick. But no man moved within the lighted sanctuary – nothing stirred save the night wind blowing from the heath; and though a great longing came upon him to go in and kneel before the altar, there was no way in. No way at all.

For a long time he knelt there outside the grille, hoping that someone would come, but no one came, and at last he rose and turned away, and unhitching his horse from the thorn branch, led it back as far as the wayside cross, unsaddled it and turned it loose to graze. Then he unlaced his helm and set it on the ground, unbuckled his sword belt, and lying down with his head on his shield, fell into a fitful sleep full of ragged dreams and uneasy wakings, and always the vision of the knight with the white shield glimmering far ahead of him, out of reach.

By and by, as he lay so, a late moon began to rise; and by its light he saw coming towards him along the track two palfreys with a litter slung between them; and in the litter a knight, sick or wounded, and moaning aloud in his pain. The mounted squire who led the foremost palfrey halted close beside the cross. And the knight broke out from his dumb moaning into piteous words: 'Sweet God in Heaven, shall my sufferings never cease? Shall I never see the Holy Cup which shall ease this weary pain?' And he stretched out his hands in anguished pleading.

And all the while, Sir Lancelot lay without speech or movement, so that he seemed to be asleep, yet seeing all that went on. And lying so, he saw the silver candlestick issue from the chapel, no hand carrying it, and with its six tapers burning clear and still, move towards the cross. And behind the candles, floating in the same way, lightly as a fallen leaf floats on still water, came a silver table; and on the table, half veiled in its own light, so that his eyes could not fully look upon it, the Grail that he had seen in Arthur's court at the feast of Pentecost.

No thunder this time, no sunbeam, but the great stillness, and the blaze of white light.

And when he saw the wonder coming towards him, the sick knight tumbled himself from his litter, and lay where he fell, his hands stretched out to it, crying, 'Lord, look on me in thy mercy, and by the power of this holy vessel grant me healing from my sickness!'

And with his eyes fixed upon the light, he dragged himself towards it, until he could touch the silver table with his hands. And even as he did so, a great shudder ran through him, and he gave a sobbing and triumphant cry, 'Ah, God! I am healed!'

And with that cry, it was as though he sank into sleep.

And all the while, in his strange half-waking state, Sir Lancelot saw and heard, yet could feel *nothing*. He watched the Grail come, and stay a while, and presently move back into the chapel again; and he knew that it was the Grail of his quest, and his heart should have leapt in awe and exultation, and he should have been kneeling in worship beside the other knight; and still he could feel *nothing*. It was as though his spirit within him was turned to lead.

When the Grail was gone back into the chapel again, and the six-branched candlestick after it, and there was no light but the moon, the knight of the litter awoke, strong again and filled with life as though he had never known a day's sickness; and his squire came from where he had been waiting at a little distance all the while, and said, 'Sir, is it well with you?'

'It is well and more than well with me, thanks be to God!' said the knight. 'But I cannot but wonder how it is with yonder man who lies sleeping at the foot of the cross, and did not rouse once at the marvel that has been here this night.'

'Surely it must be some wretch who has committed a great sin, so that God deemed him unworthy of the mystery that you have been allowed to share,' said the squire.

And he brought the knight's armour, which had lain beside him in the litter, and helped him to arm. But when it came to the helm, the squire came across to where Sir Lancelot lay, and took up his helm, and his sword Joyeux that lay beside him, and caught and saddled his horse, and took all to his master. 'You will make better use of these, for sure,' said he, 'than that worthless knight who must have forfeited all right to such honourable gear. Now mount, my lord, and let us ride.'

So the knight mounted Sir Lancelot's horse, and the squire again leading the litter palfreys, they rode away.

Soon after, Sir Lancelot stirred and sat up, like a man rousing from deep sleep; and at first he wondered whether he had indeed seen, or only dreamed, what had happened. Then he got up and went back to the chapel. But the grille was still across the doorway, and though the tapers glimmered within, he could see no sign of the Grail.

For a while he stood there, waiting, he did not know for what, and hoping – hoping – And then there came a voice from somewhere, maybe out of his own heart. It was a cold and terrible voice that said, 'Lancelot, harder than stone, more bitter than wood, more barren than the fig tree, get thee gone from this holy place, for thy presence fouls it.'

And he turned away, and stumbled back to the foot of the wayside cross, weeping as he went, for what he had lost without ever finding it. And so he saw that his horse and sword and helm were gone, and he knew that it was all bitter truth and none of it a dream. And he crouched down at the foot of the cross, and came near to breaking his heart within him.

The day dawned at last, sun up, and the sky ringing with lark-song above the open country. Sir Lancelot had always taken great joy in such mornings; but now he felt that nothing could ever bring him joy again; and he turned away from the wayside cross and the chapel and the open heathland, and set out again through the dark forest, unhorsed and unhelmed, and with his sword sheath hanging empty at his side.

The day was still short of noon when he came upon a small wattle-built woodland church, in which a solitary priest was making ready for the service. He went in and knelt down, and heard Mass; and when it was over, begged the priest for council, in the name of God.

'What manner of council do you seek?' asked the holy man. 'Is it that you would make your confession?'

'I have sore need to do that,' said Lancelot.

'Come then, in the name of God.'

He led him to the altar, and the two of them knelt down side by side.

Then the priest asked Lancelot his name, and

when he heard that the stranger with the crooked grief-stricken face was Sir Lancelot of the Lake, he said, 'Then, sir, if all I have heard of the foremost of Arthur's knights be true, you owe God a great return, for that he has made you the man you are.'

'Then ill have I repaid him,' said Lancelot, 'and this he has all too clearly shown me, in the thing that befell me last night.'

'Tell me of last night,' said the priest.

And Sir Lancelot told him of all that had passed.

When he had finished, the priest said, 'Now it is clear to me that you bear the weight of some mortal sin upon your soul. But the Lord God holds out his arms to all sinners who repent and make amendment. Now therefore make your confession to God, through me, and I will give you all the help and counsel that I may.'

But Lancelot knelt there silent, with bowed head. He had made his confession as often as any other man. But he had never made it fully; for the love between himself and the Queen was not his alone to confess. Yet he knew in his heart that it was the thing that was shutting him out from God. He had never known that so clearly as he knew it now, and his heart was torn two ways. And still the priest begged him to confess his sin, promising that if he did so and renounced it utterly God would let him in again. And at last it was as though something cracked within him, and he said like a man in mortal pain, 'For more than twenty years I have loved my Lady Guenever, the Queen.'

'And you have won her love to you?'

Lancelot bowed his head lower yet.

'And what of King Arthur, her lord?'

'The marriage was made between them for the good of the kingdom, after the way of marriages between kings and queens. After, she grew to love him as a most dear friend. To me also he is the best-loved friend I have ever had. We would not that any hurt should come to him.'

'Yet you wrong him by your love for each other, every hour of every day.'

'I am a great sinner,' said Sir Lancelot, 'and the weight of my sin is on my head and on my spirit. I am shut out from God.'

'So then, your sin is confessed,' said the priest. 'Now swear before God, as you hope for his forgiveness, that you will turn from the Queen's fellowship, and never be with her again, save when others are by.'

'I swear,' said Sir Lancelot, seeming to tear something raw and bleeding from his breast.

'And that from now on, you will not even wish for her presence, nor be with her in your inmost thoughts,' said the priest; and his words fell single and pitiless as axe blows.

'I — swear,' said Sir Lancelot. But he prayed within himself, 'God help me! For unless you help me, I have sworn an oath which I cannot keep. I will try, with all the strength that is in me. More, I cannot do. And sweet God in Heaven, help and comfort my lady also.' And so he was already a little foresworn.

Then the priest gave him absolution and his blessing.

And they rose from before the altar, and turned to leave the church. And seeing how the knight stumbled as though for mortal weariness, the holy man said, 'My cell is close by; come with me and rest, and when you are rested, we will speak of what is next for you to do.'

'I thank you; and glad would I be to rest,' said Lancelot. 'As to what is next for me to do, that I already know; I must find some way to come by another sword and helm and another horse, that I may ride forward again on the Quest.'

'In that I can help you,' said the priest, 'for I have a brother, a knight-at-arms, rich in this world's goods, who lives not far from here. And he will furnish all these things gladly, as soon as I send to ask for them.'

'Then my thanks to you, and to your brother. And most surely I will stay a while.'

And now the story leaves Sir Lancelot of the Lake, and tells again of Sir Percival.

5

SIR PERCIVAL: KINGS AND DEMONS

When Percival left Sir Lancelot to ride on alone, he went back to the hermitage, and the holy woman who lived there gave him shelter for the night. And in the morning when they had prayed together, and she had fed him on black bread spread with golden honey from her own bees, he buckled on his armour and rode out again.

All day he rode, through a wild country of rocks and blackened heathland and dark drought-stunted trees, along the fringes of King Pelles' Waste Land; and all day long he met never a soul. But towards evening he heard the deep tolling of a bell, a warm bronze sound, a sound with a bloom on it like the bloom on dark grapes, summoning through the trees. And he made his way towards it, hoping for shelter for that night also.

Almost at once he came to a large abbey, ringed around with walls that looked as though they were meant to keep out the world. But when he sat his horse before the gate and shouted cheerfully, the monks came running to open it and make him welcome. They took his horse to the stables and himself to a fair guest chamber; and there he supped and slept; and when he woke, the bell was ringing again, for it was the morning hour of Prime. He got up and went quickly to the abbey church, where the brethren were already gathered, to hear Mass.

Midway up the church there was an ironwork screen, and beyond it the Mass priest was making ready. Percival went towards it, expecting to pass through and join the rest. But there seemed to be no gate in the screen. So he knelt down outside it, and looking through saw beyond the Mass priest a bed richly spread with silken coverings, all of the purest white. Someone lay on the bed, under the coverings; but in the shadows he could not make out whether it was a man or a woman. And then the thought came to him that he was not there for staring and wondering, and he set himself to listen to the Mass.

But when the priest held up the Host, the figure on the bed sat up, and Percival saw that it was an ancient man, his hair as white as the silken coverings, and on his head a golden crown. As the coverings fell away, he showed naked to the hips, and his body and face and arms were striped with wounds and gashes enough to have killed three men. When he stretched out his hands towards the Host, even the palms of his hands were wounded.

He cried out, 'Most gracious and loving Father, be not unmindful of my dues!' and remained sitting with his hands stretched out, until Mass was over and the priest brought him the communion bread. And after that he lay down again under the white silken coverings, and was as he had been before.

Percival was filled with compassion and curiosity. He followed the brethren when they came by some side way from behind the screen, and outside, in the cloisters, he drew the one he thought had the kindest face apart, and said, 'If it is not unseemly of me to ask, let you tell me of the old wounded man with the gold crown upon his head who lies beside the altar.'

'Gladly I will tell you,' said the monk, who had told the story many times before, but still found it painful and still a marvel in the telling. 'That is King Mordrain of the city of Sarras, over beyond the Holy Land.' And he told Percival of Joseph of Arimathea and his son Josephus, and King Mordrain, and the great white shield with its blood-red cross, just as the White Knight had told it to Sir Galahad. And he told also, how, after the battle to free Joseph and his people from the wicked British king, when they came to unarm King Mordrain, they found him covered with wounds enough to kill three men, but he swore that he felt no pain and all was well with him.

'Next day,' said the monk, 'the Christians gathered before the Holy Grail to make their prayers and thanksgivings. And King Mordrain, who since he became a Christian had longed above all things to enter into the mystery of the Grail, drew too near. Then a voice in their midst, and no man speaking, said, "King, go no closer. It is forbidden thee." But the King's longing was so great that still, as the service of the Grail went on, he drew by little and little nearer yet.

402

'And suddenly the brightness of the Grail engulfed him; and he fell to the ground. And when he awoke, as if from a swoon, there was neither strength in his limbs nor sight in his eyes.

'Then he prayed, "Gracious Lord Jesus Christ, I would have looked upon that which you forbade me; and this punishment is just, and I accept it willingly. Yet grant me this, that I may not die until that knight born of the line of Arimathea, he that is to enter at last into the mystery of the Grail, shall come to set me free."

'And the voice said, "King, Our Lord has heard thy prayer, and it is granted. When the knight Galahad comes to thee, thy sight shall be restored that thou shalt see him clear; and thy wounds shall be healed that will not close before; and thou shalt be set free."

'Then King Mordrain ordered that his shield with the blazon of the blood-red cross upon it should be taken and lodged at a certain abbey where it was told him in a dream that the knight Galahad should come for it, five days after he received knighthood.

'And for four hundred years, he has lain as you saw him but now, touching no food but that which the priest brings to him at the sacrament of the Mass, and waiting for the knight who bears his own shield to set him free.'

'That has been a long waiting time,' said Percival, in awe.

'But now it seems that it is nearly over, for word

has come that the shield has been claimed, and its new master has been seen carrying it in the forest.'

And Percival saw again in his memory the knight who had unhorsed both himself and Sir Lancelot, two days since; and the last level light of sunset burning on the blood-red cross of his shield. And so he knew who the knight was, and could have wept that he had not known before.

'Now he is two days ahead of me,' he thought. And he was in such desperate haste to be gone that he would not even wait to eat with the brethren, but begged for his horse and armour, and giving them courteous but hurried thanks and farewell, mounted and rode away, his morning shadow out ahead of him like an eager hound in leash.

About noon, the track that he was following led down into a wooded valley; and there he saw coming towards him a score of armed men.

And as they drew towards each other, the foremost of the band called out to him to know his name and fealty.

'I am called Percival of Wales, and my fealty is to King Arthur.'

As soon as they heard this, they shouted, 'Have at him!' one taking up the cry from another, and, ripping out their swords, thrust their horses forward against him.

Percival's own sword seemed to leap from its sheath into his hand, as he made ready to meet them. But they were twenty to his one, for all the skill and swiftness of his swordplay. His horse was killed under him, and as he sprang clear, he was beaten to his knees, and the blows crashed in on him from all sides, gashing through his helm and shoulder mail. A few more panting breaths of time, and it would have been all over with him. But as the struggle began to darken before his eyes, suddenly, as an ill dream flies at waking, the yelling press about him broke and crumbled; and above him, high on his great horse, he saw a knight whose sword seemed kin for swiftness to the summer lightning, and whose white shield blazed with the blood-red cross it bore.

The enemy knights were scattered and galloping for the shelter of the forest. And as young Percival, sobbing for breath, his head swimming inside his hacked and battered helmet, struggled to his feet and turned to thank his rescuer, the knight of the red-cross shield struck spurs to his horse and was gone also, making in the opposite direction, as one who has done what he came to do, and has nothing more to stay for.

Percival shouted after him, desperately, 'Sir knight! For God's sweet sake let you stay and speak with me!'

But the other showed no sign of having heard. Only a flicker of red and white showed for an instant through the stunted trees, and then was gone into the brown glooms of the forest. The beat of horse-hooves died away. Somewhere a jay gave its alarm call, and then all was still.

Percival stood where he was, his moment of incredulous joy chilling to despair. Blood from the wound in his head trickled into his eyes, and his heart felt as though it must burst his breast-cage. Then, having no horse, he began to run, like a child running desperately after his heart's desire.

For a long time he ran, blundering against trees, falling into the hollows where the old and rotten forest floor gave way beneath him, sobbing as he ran, long after he knew that it was no use to run any further. Until at last he fell headlong over a hidden root, and pitching down onto the wound in his head, knocked himself dizzy. There he lay still, and heard the silence of the forest all about him, save for the mocking laughter of a green woodpecker somewhere among the trees.

Then he tore off the wreck of his helmet, and flung aside sword and shield, and fell to the sorest weeping that ever he had known, until at last, forsaken and desperate and with an aching head, he wept himself to sleep.

When he awoke, it was far into the night, and the moon was riding high and cold and uncaring above the tangled branches. And a woman was bending over him.

'Percival.' Her voice was soft and warm on the lonely places of his mind. 'Percival, what are you doing here?'

He was too confused and miserable even to wonder how she knew his name. He was grateful that she sounded kind, and that was all. 'Alas, I do nothing,' he said, sitting up and getting slowly to his feet. 'And truth to tell, lady, if I had not lost my horse, I would not be here at all.'

'If you would promise to do my bidding whenever I call on you,' said the lady, 'I could find you a horse; one that has no equal for fire or beauty or speed of foot.'

Hope leapt in Percival. 'As to that, I am a knight, and one of Arthur's court, and so sworn to be the true and faithful servant of all women who need my help.'

'Wait for me, then, and in a little I will return.'

And suddenly, she was not there any more.

Percival did think it a little odd that he had not seen her go; but it was very dark under the trees; and before he had had time to do much thinking, she was back. And she was leading a great warhorse, black as sin itself from proud crest to sweeping tail. Its round hooves trampled the forest floor as though it scorned the earth beneath it, and there was a fire in its eye that Percival had never seen in even the most mettle-some horse before. For as long as he could remember, all horses and all hounds had been his friends, and he had never known what it was to fear even the wildest of them. But at sight of this one, something shot through him that he thought was fear, though in truth it was a shaft of warning. Still, it was a horse, and a fine fleet one, and the thing he most needed in all the world, just then. So he shea-thed his sword and laced on his battered helm again and catching up his shield, swung into the high saddle and settled his feet in the stirrups with a reck-less joy.

'Go now,' said the lady, 'but remember what you have promised me.'

'I will remember,' said Sir Percival, not at all sure what he *had* promised. 'My thanks to you, lady.'

And he struck spurs to the horse's flanks, and felt the surge of pride and power beneath him as the great beast bounded forward.

Then began the wildest ride that ever was ridden by mortal knight.

They were off and away at full gallop, crashing through the trees, faster and faster. Low, hanging branches tried to sweep Sir Percival from the saddle, the ground was a dark blur that fled backwards beneath the pounding hooves; and when he would have reined in something of their headlong pace, the black horse snorted and leapt forward against the bit. And then it seemed to the young knight that they were no longer galloping at all but borne upon the air. On and on over hills and valleys, the night rushing past on either hand. The forest was behind them now, and it seemed to Percival that they must have covered many days of distance in that wild midnight ride. On and on, the foam flying back like spindrift from the black muzzle, the wind of their going screaming by. And then ahead of them was a wide and rushing river; and the black horse neighed in triumph, making straight towards it. Now indeed Percival thought the moment of his death was upon him, and desperately put his hand to his forehead and made the sign of the cross.

And in that instant, feeling the weight of the

cross upon it, the thing that wore the shape of a black horse gave itself a violent shake, and flung its rider from the saddle; and so plunged into the flood, howling and shrieking as it went; and instead of spray, bright sheaves of flame shot up on either side of it, as though the river itself were on fire.

And sprawling on the bank where he had fallen, Percival gave thanks to God, who had saved his soul from damnation.

When morning broke, and he could look about him, there was no sign of the river at all; no sign of the country of his wild night ride. He was on a rocky island, girt about on all sides by sea; and the sea stretching away to the sky's edge with no other sight of land. There was no trace anywhere of men and women, no dwelling places nor cultivated land; but the island was not empty of life, for wherever he looked among the tawny rocks prowled the striped and speckled shapes of wild beasts; lions and leopards and strange winged serpents.

'Now I am in deadly peril of another kind,' thought Percival, and felt for his sword, and then he saw that in the very middle of the island a great crag thrust heavenward. If he could reach the crest of it, the sheer rock-faces below might be some protection against attack from the wild animals. So, at the best speed he could make, he set off towards it.

But as he began the climb, the most terrible uproar broke upon his ears, and a vast shadow swept between him and the sun; and looking up, he saw one of the great winged serpents with a lion cub in its jaws, making for the rocky summit like an eagle carrying home its kill. But the cub was still alive, and crying out in terror, and hard behind came a lioness, tearing the day apart with her roaring, and striving to leap into the air after the winged horror, desperate to save her young.

Percival began to run, drawing his sword as he went, but the lioness passed him and was first to gain the crest; and when he also reached it, lioness and serpent were locked in battle, she tearing at the monster's throat, the scaly tail tightening about her body. Percival ran in among the lashing coils and caught the creature a glancing blade-blow on the head, at which it rounded on him, spewing out great gobbets of flame. He sprang aside, then thrust in again. The struggle was long and desperate; but at last his sword found a second time the place on its head where the first blow had landed. There the scaly hide was laid open and the bone cracked, and the second blow broke the slim, savage head apart, and the great coils ceased to lash, and the fire sank away, as the monster dropped dead at his feet.

Then Sir Percival sheathed his sword and flung aside his scorched shield, and pulled off his helmet to feel the cool wind on his head. And the lioness, when she had made sure that all was well with her cub, came and fawned on him like a great dog, bending her proud neck against his knee, her tail sweeping behind her in gratitude and delight. And Percival fell to stroking her head and shoulders.

'The Lord does not mean that I should be lonely

in this place, for he has sent you to keep me company.'

All day the lioness stayed with him, until, when dusk came, she took the cub by the scruff of its neck, and bounded away down the steep slopes to her lair in some place unknown to him among the rocks. Then the young knight was very desolate, thinking that she had deserted him, and feeling himself now quite alone. But before the dusk had deepened into the dark, having seen the cub safely lodged and fed, she returned to him, friendlywise as before, and lay down beside him. And Percival put his arm round her neck and fondled behind her ears as he would have done to a favourite hound, while she rubbed her head against him. And at last he propped himself against her, his head on her flank for a pillow, more glad of her company than almost ever he had been of company before. And so he fell asleep.

When he woke in the morning, the lioness was gone; but looking out to sea, he beheld a ship with sails spread like dark wings, flying straight as an arrow towards the island.

Hope leapt in Percival, for surely a ship must mean the promise of rescue, and he caught up helm and sword and shield, and went scrambling and leaping down through the rocks towards the shore.

Even as he went, he kept his gaze on the ship winging in towards him. And surely she was the strangest vessel that ever man saw, for she came as though all the four winds of heaven were in her sails, and ahead of her raced a whirlwind that parted the waters and beat up great waves curling back from her on either side. And as she drew close in to the land, he saw that she was clad from stem to stern with draperies that formed a pavilion of fine black silk. She slackened speed as the wind dropped from her sails, and settled lightly as a bird against the shore where the rocks rose straight from deep water. And Percival, reaching the shore at the same moment, saw that seated in the black-draped entrance amidships was the most beautiful maiden he had ever beheld, with a mouth as silken red as harvest poppies, and eyes and hair as dark as midnight.

Just for a moment he thought that he had seen such blackness somewhere not long ago; but he could not think where. And the maiden was holding out her hands to him, saying in a voice as sweet as wild-wood honey, 'Sir knight, how come you to be here on this island, so far from the haunts of men that but for the chance wind that has brought me to your aid, you must surely have died of hunger or been slain by wild beasts before any help could find you?'

'That is a long story that I scarcely know myself,' said Percival, 'but I think that whatever happens to me, it is God's will.'

The lady made a movement with her hands, as though to brush something aside, and she laughed a little. 'Then it must be by God's will that the winds blew me here, Sir Percival of Wales.'

'You know my name!' said Percival, surprised.

'I know it well, I know you better than you think.'

'Then if you know so much of me, grant that I may know something of you.'

'Know then,' said she, 'that I am one who would have been the greatest lady in my land, if I had not been wrongfully driven from it.'

Instantly pity and indignation rose in Percival, and he said, 'Damsel in exile, tell me who has used you so cruelly.'

'A great lord,' she said, 'a mighty king who chose me for my beauty and placed me in his household. For I was beautiful; more beautiful than you see me now with my sorrows come upon me. And being so fair, alas, I grew a little vain and spoiled, and spoke to my lord one day foolishly and light-heartedly in a manner that he took amiss, though indeed there was little harm in it. Then his wrath flared out against me as though I had done some monstrous ill, and he drove me forth with a few who were loyal to me, into exile. And now, that by the wind's chance I have found you, who I know to be a valiant and honourable knight, I beg you to help me against this cruel lord who has so misused me. Indeed, you cannot refuse me, for you are of the Round Table, and so bound by your oath, sworn there at King Arthur's bidding, to be the champion of all distressed ladies who ask your aid.'

'Indeed I am bound by that oath, but even if I were not, still would I give you all the help in my power,' said Percival.

And she thanked him very sweetly; and they sat

talking for a while, she on the deck of her ship and he on the rocks alongside.

Noon came and the sun beat down, and the rocks gave back their heat in shimmering waves; and Percival felt like to fry inside his armour, but was too courteous to tell the lady so.

But at last, of her own accord, she turned behind her into the ship, and spoke to someone out of sight, and two servants brought out a tent of black silk lined with crimson, and set it up on a small patch of shore-grass, very pretty to see, with every silken edge of canopy and curtains dagged like black flower petals, and little gay pennants that fluttered overall. And when all was ready, and the curtains looped back to let every movement of air pass through, she called to Percival, 'Come now, and sit here with me in the shade, for it is too hot out there on the bare rocks.'

So Percival came; and in the blissful coolth of the shade under the awning, she helped him to unharness, and bathed his hurts, crying out softly at sight of them, and he lay down on soft cushions and slept.

When he woke, a low table had been set up beside him, and the servants were bringing food from the ship; the most choice and delicate of food in bowls and dishes of such intricate beauty that he could scarce believe they had been made by human hands.

'Eat with me,' said the lady. And Sir Percival sat up and thanked her, and began to eat, he on one side of the table and she on the other, their eyes often meeting. Then the servants brought cool wine clouding in crystal goblets; and it was such wine as

Percival had never drunk before, and went to his head like no wine that he had ever drunk before; so that soon he began to see everything through a golden haze. And the lady seemed kinder and more beautiful with every moment that went by. And when he stretched his hand to meet hers across the table, it was the softest thing that he had ever touched, and her fingers curled round his so that his heart turned over in his breast for the sweetness of the moment.

'Love me,' said the lady. 'It is so long since any loved me, and I am sorely alone.'

'I will be the truest lover to you that ever lady had,' said Percival.

And the table was no longer between them, but she was beside him on the couch of soft cushions. But even as he put his arms round her to draw her close, it happened that Sir Percival's eye fell upon the hilt of his sword, where he had laid it down beside him, and as with all knightly swords, it formed a cross.

Instantly the golden haze turned grey, and a cold and shuddering fear seized upon him. Desperately he fumbled one hand to his forehead and crossed himself; and as he did so, a great howling and shrieking broke out all around; and he was choked by a filthy stench that had caught him by the throat. The tent collapsed into bat-wing tatters, and all things seemed whirling away into nothingness. And he cried out like one drowning, 'Lord Jesus Christ, help me or I am lost!'

He found that his eyes were clenched shut, and when he opened them, he was lying among the baking rocks, and of the tent and the soft cushions, the food and the servants, there was no sign. But looking seaward, he saw the black-draped ship putting off from the shore; and in the entrance where he had seen her first stood the lady. But now all her beauty and sweetness were gone, and she screamed at him, 'Percival, you have betrayed me!'

Then the ship was racing out to sea, with such a storm springing up in her wake that it seemed at any moment she must founder, and the whole sea aflame to engulf her. But before the flames and the tempest the black ship sped on her way faster than any wind could blow.

Percival watched until ship and storm were out of sight, then sank down on his knees, weeping most bitterly, and thanking God for his deliverance and praying for forgiveness, and then weeping again for shame and misery and near despair.

All that night he passed on the rocky shore, not even caring now if the wild beasts of the island came and killed him. But none came near. Nor did his lioness come to comfort him, and he supposed that he was no longer worthy of her. It seemed the longest and darkest night that ever he had known.

But dawn came at last, and with the dawn he saw another ship making into land; a very different vessel, with sails of white samite, gliding in among the rocks as quietly as a swan on calm water. And when he got up and went to look closer, there was no one on board. But as he stood marvelling at this, a voice spoke to him out of nowhere.

'Percival, go now aboard this ship, and follow wherever adventure leads thee. And have no fear of anything, for wherever thou goest, God is with thee. Thou hast been near to disaster, but thou hast prevailed, and, therefore, one day thou shalt meet again with Galahad, for whose company thou longest, and with Bors also, for ye are the chosen three.'

The voice died into the light shore wind. And Percival took up his arms and went aboard the waiting ship, and pushed off from the rocks; and the wind filled the sails and carried him swiftly out to sea.

But now the story leaves Sir Percival, and tells for a while of Sir Bors.

6

SIR BORS FIGHTS FOR A LADY

For three days after parting from his companions of the Round Table, Sir Bors rode through the forest ways alone. And at evening on the third day he came to a tall, strong-built tower rising dark against the sunset, in the midst of a clearing. He beat upon the deep arched gate, to ask for a night's lodging, and was welcomed in. His horse was led to the stables and himself up to the Great Chamber high in the tower, full of honey-golden sunset light from its western windows that looked away over the treetops. There he was greeted by the lady of the place, who was fair and sweet to look upon, but poorly clad in a patched gown of faded leaf-green silk.

She bade him to sit by her at supper; and when the food was brought in, he saw that it was as poor as her gown, and was sorry for her sake, though for his own it made little difference, for he had taken a vow at the outset, that he would eat no meat and drink no wine while he followed the Quest of the Holy Grail; and so he touched nothing but the bread set before his place, and asked one of the table squires for a cup of water. And seeing this, the lady said, 'Ah, sir knight, I know well that the food is poor and rough, but do not disdain it, it is the best we have.'

'Lady, forgive me,' said Bors, and flushed to the roots of his russet hair, 'it is because your food is too good and your wine too rich that I eat bread and drink water, for I have vowed to touch nothing else, while I am on the quest that I follow.'

'And what quest is that?'

'The Quest of the Holy Grail.'

'I have heard of this quest, and I know you, therefore, for one of King Arthur's knights, the greatest champions in the world,' said the lady; and it seemed as though she might have said more, but at that moment a squire came hurrying into the room.

'Madam, it goes ill with us — your sister has taken two more of your castles, and sends you word that she will leave you not one square foot of land, if by tomorrow's noon you have not found a knight to fight for you against her lord!'

Then the lady pressed her hands over her face and wept, until Sir Bors said to her, 'Pray you, lady, tell me the meaning of this.'

'I will tell you,' said the lady. 'The lord of these parts once loved my elder sister, never knowing what like she was — what like she is — and by little and little, while they were together, he gave over to her all his power, so that in truth she became the ruler. And her rule was a harsh one, causing the death and maiming and imprisonment of many of his people. Learning wisdom on his deathbed, and listening at last to the distress of his folk, he drove her out and made me his

successor in her place, that I might undo what could
be undone of the harm. But no sooner was he dead
than my sister took a new lord, Priadan the Black,
and made alliance with him to wage war on me.' She
spread her hands. 'Good sir, the rest you must know.'

'Who and what is this Priadan the Black?' said
Bors.

'The greatest champion and the cruellest and most
dreaded tyrant in these parts.'

'Then send word to your sister, that you have
found a knight to fight for you at tomorrow's noon.'

Then the lady wept again, for joy. 'God give you
strength tomorrow,' she said, 'for it is surely by his
sending that you are come here today!'

Next morning, Sir Bors heard Mass in the chapel
of the tower, and then went out to the courtyard,
where the lady had summoned all the knights yet
remaining to her, that they might witness the coming
conflict. She would have had him eat before he
armed, but he refused, saying that he would fight
fasting, and eat after he had fought; and so the squires
helped him to buckle on his harness; and he
mounted and rode out through the gate, the lady
riding a grey palfrey at his side to guide him to the
meeting place, and all her people, even to the castle
scullions, following after.

They had not ridden far when they came to a level
meadow at the head of a valley, and saw a great
crowd of people waiting for them, with a fine striped
pavilion pitched in their midst. And as they rode
out from the long morning shadows of the trees, out

from the shadow of the pavilion appeared a damsel in a gown of rose-scarlet damask mounted on a fine bay mare.

'That is my sister,' said the lady, 'and beside her, look, Priadan, her lord and champion.'

The sisters pricked forward to meet each other in the centre of the meadow; and beside the damsel of the pavilion rode a huge knight in armour as black as his tall warhorse; and beside the lady of the tower rode Sir Bors, feeling the balance of his lance.

'Sister,' said Sir Bors's lady, 'as I sent you word last evening, I have found a champion to fight for my rights, in the matter between us.'

'*Rights!*' cried the elder sister. 'You played upon my lord when he was in his dotage, until you had wheedled out of him what is truly mine. These are your *rights!*'

'Damsel,' said Sir Bors, 'your sister has told me the other side of that story. It is she whom I believe, and it is she whom I will fight for this day.'

And the two champions looked at each other, each searching out the eye-flicker behind the dark slits of his opponent's helmet.

'Let us waste no more time in talking,' said Priadan the Black, 'for it was not to talk that we came here.'

So the onlookers fell back, leaving a clear space down the midst of the meadow, and the two champions drew apart to opposite ends of it, then wheeled their horses and with levelled lances spurred towards each other. Faster and faster, from canter to full gallop, the spur clods flying from beneath their hooves, until at last they clashed together like two stags battling for the lordship of the herd. Both lances ran true to target, and splintered into kindling wood, and both knights were swept backward over their horses' cruppers to the ground.

With the roar of the crowd like a stormy sea in his ears, Sir Bors was up again on the instant, the Black Knight also. And drawing their swords they fell upon each other with such mighty blows that their shields were soon hacked to rags of painted wood, and the sparks flew from their blades as they rang together and slashed through the mail on flanks and shoulders to set the red blood running. They were so evenly matched that it came to Bors that he must use his head as well as his sword arm, if he was going to carry off the victory. And he began to fight on the defensive, saving his strength and letting his opponent use up his own powers in pressing on to make an end.

The crowd yelled, and the lady he fought for hid her face in her hands. And Sir Bors gave ground a little, and then gave ground again, Priadan pressing after him, until at last he felt the Black Knight beginning to tire, his feet becoming slower, his sword strokes less sure. Then, as though fresh life was suddenly flowing into him, Bors began to press forward in his turn, raining his blows upon the other man, beating him this way and that, until Sir Priadan stumbled like a drunk man, and in the end went over backwards on the trampled turf.

Then Sir Bors bestrode him, and dragged off his

helmet and flung it aside, and upswung his sword as though he would have struck Sir Priadan's head from his shoulders and flung it after his helmet.

When Sir Priadan saw the bright arc of the blade above him, he seemed to grow small and grovelling inside his champion's armour, and cried out shrilly, 'Quarter! You cannot kill me, I am crying quarter!' And then as Sir Bors still stood over him with menacing sword, 'Oh, for God's sweet sake have mercy on me and let me live! I will swear never again to wage war on the lady you serve! I will promise anything you ask, if only you will let me live!'

And Sir Bors lowered his blade, feeling sick, and said, 'Remember that oath. And now get out of my sight!'

And the Black Knight scrambled to his feet and made off, running low like a beaten cur.

And the elder sister gave a shrill, furious cry, and set her horse at the onlookers who jostled back to let her by; and so dashed through them and away, rowelling her mare's flanks until the blood on them ran bright as her rose-scarlet gown.

When all those who had come with her and Sir Priadan her lord saw what manner of champion they had followed, they came and swore allegiance to the lady of the tower. And so, with great rejoicing, she and her household rode back the way they had come. And in the Great Chamber of the tower, Sir Bors sat down and ate and drank at last, though still only bread and water; and the lady herself bathed and salved his wounds.

And after he had rested for a day or so, he set out once more on his quest.

And now the story leaves Sir Bors a while, and tells of Sir Gawain.

7

SIR GAWAIN SEE A VISION AND SLAYS A FRIEND

After Sir Gawain of Orkney left his comrades of the Grail Quest, he wandered from Pentecost until St Magdalen's Day, which is late into July, without ever meeting with any adventure worth the setting down, and it was the same with all his fellows, with whom he crossed paths from time to time. And this he found most odd, for he had expected the Quest for the Holy Grail to provide more strange and marvellous adventures than any quest on which he had ridden before.

Then one day he met with Sir Lancelot's brother, Sir Ector of the Marsh; and that was a fine meeting for both of them, for they were old friends; and gladly they shouted each other's name and beat each other on the shoulders. And when they had done with their greetings, Sir Gawain asked Sir Ector how it went with him.

'Well enough, in body,' said Sir Ector, 'but I grow weary of riding these forest ways and finding no adventure.'

'You too?' cried Sir Gawain. 'I swear to you that not one adventure worth the name has come my way since we parted beneath the walls of Camelot. Ten knights have I met and fought with at different times, and ten knights have I slain in fair combat; but there is neither strangeness nor adventure in that.'

So they decided that as neither had met with any adventure riding alone, they should ride together for a while, and see if that would change their luck.

And presently, as they rode, Gawain asked his comrade if he had heard any word of Sir Lancelot, his brother.

'No word,' said Sir Ector, 'it is as though he had ridden out of the world of men; and indeed, my heart is uneasy for him.'

'And Galahad, and Percival, and Bors?'

'No word of them either. Those four have vanished, leaving neither wind nor wake behind.'

'God guide them, wherever they be,' said Sir Gawain.

For a week they rode together, and still met with no adventure. And then towards evening of the seventh day, they came on an ancient chapel. The place was forsaken and half-ruined, and they had hoped for some habitation of living men, where there might be food to be had, for they had not eaten all that day. But the evening was darkening early, with rain in the wind, and any shelter was better than none. So they dismounted and stood their shields and lances against the outer wall, before unsaddling their horses and turning them loose to graze. Then they went into the chapel, and unbuckling and laying aside their swords, they knelt down before the age-worn altar, to make their evening prayers.

And when their prayers were done, hungry as they were they lay down on the chancel floor to try to sleep.

But sleep they could not, for their empty bellies and the wind and rain outside. And as they lay half-wakeful in the darkest hour of the night, they saw a hand and a forearm clad in a sleeve of flame-red samite enter through the chapel door; and no man or woman whose arm it was but just the arm; and in the hand a tall candle, and hanging down from the wrist, a bridle, plainly and serviceably fashioned. And despite the wind that whistled through the crannies in the ancient walls, the candle burned bright and clear, straight-flamed as a laurel leaf, shedding its light all around.

The vision passed between them, and on up the chancel to the altar; and as suddenly as it had come, was gone again, leaving the chapel to the stormy dark.

And as they strained their eyes to make out what had become of it, they heard a voice, 'Oh ye, weak in faith and dull in belief, these three things that ye have just now looked upon are the three things that ye lack. And for this reason ye ride up and down the forest ways and will never attain to the high adventure of the Holy Grail.'

Then the voice was silent. And when the two knights, awe-struck, had listened a while for it to come again, they turned towards each other in the dark. And Sir Gawain said, 'Did you see what I saw?'

And Sir Ector said, 'Did you hear what I heard?'

And both had seen, and both had heard, but neither could make any guess as to the meaning of the thing.

So they passed the rest of the night with little sleep; and in the morning when the storm had passed, saddled up and rode on, determined to seek a hermitage or an abbey where there might be some wise and holy man who could rede them the riddle.

But before ever they found such a place and such a man, they came out into a rich and open valley, and saw at a little distance a knight in full armour; but the sun was behind him, still low, and everything of a trembling dazzle after the night's rain, so that the device on his shield was dark to them.

As soon as he saw them, he shouted, 'Joust!' in challenge, and turned his horse in their direction.

'Give me leave to take him first!' said Sir Ector.

But Sir Gawain was already galloping to meet his challenger. The clash of their meeting sent the birds bursting up from the woodshore, crying and calling in alarm; and both knights were lifted clean out of their saddles by the other's lance. But while Sir Gawain had taken no more harm than a dint to his shield, the other knight was speared right through the body, and the shaft snapped off as he fell, so that he lay transfixed, too sorely wounded to move.

Sir Gawain was on his feet before a man's heart might beat twice, and drawing his sword, called to the other to get up and fight if he would not lie there and be slain.

But the other answered, choking, 'Alas, Sir Gawain, you have slain me already.'

And when, with Sir Ector's help, Sir Gawain had unlaced and taken off the helm of the fallen man, he saw the white agonised face of Sir Owain the Bastard, who he had often jousted with in friendship at Camelot.

'Now curse the sun that flashed off your shields and hid the blazon,' said Sir Owain. And then, 'Here is an end, for me, of the Quest of the Holy Grail. Therefore take me to the abbey near here, that I may die among holy men and have Christian burial.'

'There is no abbey in these parts, that I know of,' said Sir Gawain; and the words strangled in his throat for the grief and horror that was upon him.

'Nay, but I passed by such a place, further down the valley,' said Sir Owain. 'Get me upon your horse, and I will guide you to it.'

So Sir Gawain and Sir Ector lifted him up to the saddle, coughing blood when they moved him, and Sir Gawain mounted behind him to hold him from falling, while Sir Ector followed, leading Sir Owain's horse beside his own. And so, slowly and sorrowfully, they rode on until they came to the abbey. And there the monks gave them kind greeting, and Sir Owain was laid on the bed in the guest chamber.

And when he had prayed and made ready, he said with his last strength, 'Now I am where I would be. When you go back to court, give my greeting to all of our brotherhood who you find there – though indeed it is in my heart that many will not return from this Quest – and bid them to remember me in their prayers. Now pull the lance-head from me, for I can bear this pain no longer.'

So Sir Gawain, weeping, took hold of the broken lance-head, and quickly and strongly pulled it out from between his friend's ribs. And Sir Owain gave a groan and stretched himself all along, and the life went from him.

The monks brought a cloth of fine silk in which to wrap his body, and the funeral rites were performed, and he was buried in the abbey church.

Then Gawain and Ector would have ridden forward once more, though indeed the heart was gone out of them. But at the last moment, Sir Gawain bethought him of the vision that they had had in the deserted chapel, and that had been for the time driven from their minds. So he asked that they might speak with the father abbot. And while their horses waited in the outer courtyard, they stood before him in his chamber, and told him of what they had seen and heard, and asked him for the meaning.

The abbot was very old; and when Sir Gawain had done speaking, he sat for a long while with his chin sunk on his breast, so that they thought he dozed, and Sir Gawain began to fidget with his feet until the spurs jingled faintly on his heels. At last the father abbot looked up, and they saw that indeed he had not been dozing. 'It is very simple. You saw a hand with a candle and a bridle, and a voice told you that these were the three things lacking in you. The hand is charity, and the vermilion sleeve is the Grace of God, which burns in charity with a constant flame, so that he that has it is filled with the love of Our Lord in Heaven. The bridle stands for self-control, for even as a man governs his horse with a bridle, so must he govern himself. The candle? The candle stands for truth, what else? The truth of Christ. Lacking these three things, as the voice told you, you will not attain to the adventure of the Holy Grail.'

Then Sir Gawain grew very thoughtful, and said, 'Holy Father, if that is so, then it is useless for us to continue this quest any further.'

The old man bowed his head.

'So, sir,' said Ector, heavily, 'if we take your word for it, it would be as well for us to turn about, and return to Camelot.'

'That is my advice. You will serve no purpose by going on. No better purpose than you have served already.' And he gestured towards the little window in the chamber wall, that looked down into the church towards Sir Owain's grave.

But Sir Gawain and Sir Ector did not turn back, not yet; for Sir Gawain was a stubborn man who did not easily turn back at another's bidding from any path that he had started out upon. And Sir Ector would not leave his friend to go on alone.

And now the story leaves Sir Gawain, and tells again of Sir Lancelot.

8

A HAIR SHIRT AND AN UPHILL ROAD

Sir Lancelot remained with his holy man for three days; and at the end of that time a squire came riding out of the forest with a raking bay horse, and the helm and sword for which the priest had sent to ask of his brother. So next morning Sir Lancelot laced on the helm and belted the unfamiliar sword at his side, and thanking the priest for his goodness and asking him to pray for him, that he might not again fall into evil doing, he mounted the bay horse and rode on his way.

Towards noon he came upon a small chapel with a hermitage beside it. And drawing closer, he saw the black scar of a fire on the grass before the chapel, and an ancient man in a monk's white habit kneeling in the chapel doorway, beside the body of another who lay there dead. And the kneeling monk was crying out in grief and protest, 'Dear God, why have you allowed this to be? He has served you heart and soul these many years, and could you not have kept him from this?'

Sir Lancelot dismounted and, hitching his horse's reins on a branch, came close and said, 'God keep you, sir, you grieve most sorely for this man's death.'

'Not for his death,' said the aged monk, 'but for the manner of it. For see the fine soft tunic that he wears, and his own garment cast aside.'

And looking where the old man pointed, Lancelot saw a horrible hair-cloth shirt lying tumbled close to the dead feet. And still he did not understand.

'He was of my Order,' said the monk, 'though a fighting-man in his youth, and to us the wearing of fine linen is forbidden. Therefore, finding him like this, I know that the Devil must have come upon him at the last, and tempted him to the breaking of his vows, so that it was no godly death he died, and I cannot but fear that he is lost to all eternity.'

And Sir Lancelot did not know what to answer, to comfort the old man.

But out of the sorrowful silence, another voice answered, quiet as a little wind through the treetops but clear as a trumpet call, 'Nay, he is not lost, but most gloriously saved.'

And looking round, Lancelot could see no one there; but clearly the old monk could see the speaker well enough, for he looked upward from his kneeling, as though at one standing tall above him; and wonder and the beginning of relief were on his face.

'Listen,' said the voice, 'and I will tell the manner of this man's death. Thou knowest that he was of noble birth, and still has kinsmen in these parts. Two days since, the Count of the Vale went to war with one of these kinsmen, Agoran by name. And the man who lies here, knowing his kinsfolk outnumbered and their cause just, took his sword from the place where he had laid it by, and turned fighting-man again on their behalf. So by the feats of valour that he performed, his kinsman had the victory; and the good man came back here to his hermitage to take up again his true life where he had laid it down.

'But followers of the Count knew at whose door to lay their defeat, and came after him, and called him out and would have cut him down with their swords. But though he was clad only in his habit and hair shirt, their blades turned and rebounded as though on the finest armour that was ever forged.

'This threw them into a mindless fury; and they fetched branches and lit a fire, saying they would see if the flames could do what their blades could not. And they stripped the old man to the skin, he making no resistance, but saying, "If it be God's will that my time on earth is accomplished, then I shall die, and that will please me well. But if I die, it will be by God's will, and not the fire; for the fire has no power to burn a hair of my head; nor is there a garment in the world, whether it be my own hair shirt or of the finest linen ever woven, that would be so much as scorched, if I were to put it on now."

'At this they cried "Moonshine", with much laughter. And one of them tore off his own fine shirt, and they thrust it upon the old man in mockery, and cast him upon the flames.

'That was yester morning; and when they returned at night, the fire was newly burned out, and the old man lying there as peacefully as on a bed;

and dead indeed, but with no mark nor scorch upon him when they dragged him from the hot ash; and the fine shirt upon him fresh and unmarked as thou seest it.

'Then great fear came upon them, and they ran, leaving him as thou didst find him here. Now therefore bury him in the white fine shirt, for it is no shame to him but the garment of his victory. And for the hair shirt he wore so many faithful years, there is another wearer waiting.'

Then came a sudden gust of wind, and a dazzle of sunlight in and out between the swaying treetop branches; and when all was quiet again, the voice spoke no more.

And the old monk brought his gaze down to look at his dead friend in joy and relief.

He asked Sir Lancelot to bide with him in keeping watch beside the body, and help him next morning to bury it. So Sir Lancelot remained with him through the rest of that day. And again he made his confession, and the old monk gave him much good advice. And next day, when they had buried the holy man before the altar of his little chapel, and the knight was making ready to arm and ride away, the monk said to him, 'Sir Lancelot, last night, when I had heard your confession, I gave you absolution and blessing. Now, before you ride on, I give you your penance. It is that you shall wear this hair shirt from now on. And further, I charge you to eat no meat and drink no wine while you follow the quest on which you have started out. But above all, keep to the hair shirt, for while you wear it it shall keep you from further sin.'

So Sir Lancelot stripped, and took up the hair shirt of the man he had just helped to bury, and pulled it on, with its rasping bristles next to his bare skin, and then put on his tunic and then his harness. And so he took his leave of the old monk, and mounted and rode away.

That night he came to a woodland shrine where two ways parted, and laid him down there with his shield for a pillow. Watching and fasting had wearied him out, till not even the prickling and chafing of the hair shirt could keep him awake. But his sleep was restless and broken with dreams, and with the first cobweb light of dawn he was glad to be up and riding on.

Noon found him in a valley between wooded cliffs, all shut in and murmurous with small winged things among the young bracken. And there riding towards him he beheld the knight who had robbed him of horse and helm and his well-loved sword Joyeux before the chapel of the Grail.

The knight saw him in the same instant, and shouted to him to defend himself or he was a dead man, then struck spurs to his horse – Lancelot's horse – and rode at him full tilt. Sir Lancelot spurred to meet him, anger and gladness mingled in his answering shout. The point of the other knight's lance took him in the shoulder; but though it broke through the links of his hauberk it did little more than gash the skin, and he crouched low in the saddle, and gathering up all his strength, got in a blow that brought the horse crashing down and all but lifted the rider's head from his shoulders, as he galloped past. Without pause, he wrenched round and came thundering back on his tracks; but although the horse was already struggling up, the knight lay where he had fallen among the bracken, and the fight was over.

Then Sir Lancelot dismounted and took Joyeux from the fallen man's sheath, leaving the blade that he himself had carried since yesterday in its place. The battered helmet was not worth the taking back. He tied the bay to a birch tree where the knight would find it when he came to himself and was fit to ride, and took back his own horse, that came at his whistle and was dear to him like his sword – it had been a bad moment when he saw the horse go down – and rode on.

And as he rode, his heart lightened and warmed within him, and the prickling and chafing of his hair shirt where his armour pressed it against his skin was a kind of sharp joy to him, for he thought that the winning back of his horse and his sword was maybe a sign that God's face was no longer quite turned away from him, and the strength and potency of his knighthood were given back to him once more.

Sir Lancelot rode for many days in the forest and along the fringes of the Waste Land, sleeping now beneath the roof of a holy man or a forester or a hurdle maker, now under a tree or at the foot of a wayside cross, or on open heathland, where the night wind searched him to the bone. He dreamed strange dreams in his solitude as he slept by night and rode by day, of men with stars between their eyes, and trees that bore bright and bitter fruit, and knights who turned into lions, and lions who grew sky-wide wings. And still he looked and listened for tidings of the knight with the red cross on the white shield. For he knew in his heart that that knight had some special meaning for him. And always he looked and listened for tidings of Sir Galahad, not knowing that they were one and the same. And always he rode with his heart wide open, waiting for God to tell him what next to do in the following of his quest.

One day he came out into a vast clearing in the forest, and saw in the midst of it a strong and splendid castle. Between him and the castle lay a wide meadow; and clustered all round the meadow verges, bright as the small flowers of spring time, were tents and pavilions, striped and chequered, blue and violet, green, red and yellow, each blinking with goldwork on fluttering pennants. And in the open midst of the meadow a great tournament was going forward.

Five hundred knights at least, he judged, were taking part; and half of them were cloaked and armed in black as glossy midnight-deep as ravens' feathers, while the other half were cloaked and armed in white; the proud fierce white of swan's wing or lightning flash. And the white knights had taken up the side towards the castle, while the black had the side towards the forest, so that their backs were to Sir Lancelot as he sat his horse and watched them.

And as he watched, it seemed to him that the raven ranks were getting the worst of the contest. He saw that they were beginning to fall back towards him; and his lance hand itched and his knees tightened their grip on his horse's flanks, and instantly he was on their side, as he had always been on the side of anyone hard pressed by a stronger man. And next moment, scarce knowing what he did, he had struck in his spurs and, couching his lance, was out from the woodshore to their aid.

He took the first knight to come against him with such force that he brought down both horse and rider; the next he got with the point to the helmet-crest, the most difficult stroke of all and only to be attempted by a master. Then thundering on, he broke his lance against a third man's shield, yet unhorsed him all the same; and drawing his sword, plunged on into the thick of the struggle. And there he fought so valiantly, dealing out such skilled and mighty blows, that he should surely have carried off the crown of any tournament. Yet it seemed that not all his strength and skill and valour could avail against the ranks of the white champions. His blows might have landed upon mighty tree trunks, or Joyeux have been no more than a sword of plaited rushes, for all the harm he seemed able to do the men he fought with, and he was powerless to check their forward thrust that drove the black knights back and back.

Again and again he charged them, striving to

break an opening in their ranks, again and again he failed, until he could barely lift his sword arm for weariness, and though there was no scathe on him, his whole body was drained of strength as a man sore wounded may be drained of his life's blood.

At last a band of the white knights surrounded him and bore him down by main force, and dragged him off into the forest; while without his aid the raven ranks were quickly overwhelmed and put to flight.

Once in the forest, Sir Lancelot looked for death and did not care; but his captors simply turned him free, and that was the worst shame of all.

'Let you remember,' said one of the white knights, 'that though it comes about by our strength and not by your choosing, you are of our company now. Remember that, and ride on your way.'

One of them gave him his sword again, and he sheathed it, fumblingly, at his side. And, slumped wearily in the saddle, his head on his breast, he rode away.

Never before, no matter how long or hard the fighting, had this dreadful weakness sapped his sword arm; never before had he been captured and then turned free in casual mercy. And what was left of his pride was bleeding-raw within him. 'Now,' he thought, 'I have lost everything; my love, and the strength of my knighthood; and God's face is still turned away from me.'

That night he passed in a wild and craggy place far from the haunts of men, dividing the dark hours between little sleep and much prayer. And in the morning, when the sky was clear-washed with light in the east, and the birds began to sing, he prayed again; and as he prayed, and the sun rose and dazzled into his eyes, a new feeling came upon him. Not hope, quieter than hope, but a kind of peace, an acceptance that what had happened to him yesterday, whatever happened to him henceforth, it was God's will for him; even if it was God's will that he should remain shut out.

And he saddled his horse again and rode on.

He came at last to a valley running down between sides of sheer black rock, to a mighty river. And on the bank of the river, mounted on a great warhorse of his own colour, waited a knight in armour so black that the blackness had a bloom on it like the bloom on a thundercloud, and cast its own darkness over the daylight all around. At sight of Sir Lancelot he struck in his spurs and came for him full tilt, at such speed that there was no chance of avoiding him, nor of getting in the first thrust. His levelled lance took Sir Lancelot's horse in the breast, so that it screamed and reared up, then came crashing down with its scarlet heart's blood fountaining from the wound. And the black rider on his black steed whirled on unchecked, and in a few breaths of time was lost to sight.

Sir Lancelot scrambled to his feet, and stood looking down at his dead horse; and grief was heavy in him, for they were old friends and had been through many adventures together. But for himself, he cared nothing that he had been worsted yet again. All that was over with him. He accepted it as the will of God, and unslung his shield from the saddlebow, and started walking towards the river.

When he reached it, he saw how wide and deep and fast it ran, so that there could be no way over without a boat or wings. The rocky bluffs on either side of the valley were beyond any man's scaling, and to turn back into the forest would be a backward-going over the way he had come. So he laid aside helm and shield, and lay down in the lee of a mossy outcrop of the rocks on the river bank, for the daylight was fading fast, to wait until God should show him the way forward.

And so he fell into the deepest and quietest sleep that he had known for many a long night.

And now the story leaves Sir Lancelot and tells again of Sir Bors.

9

SIR BORS MAKES A HARD CHOICE

For many days after he left the lady of the tower Sir Bors wandered, while the forest darkened to full summer about him.

And one warm heavy noontide he came to a place where two tracks crossed each other. And as he checked there, wondering which to take, he heard the sound of horses' hooves; and looking in that direction, he saw riding hard towards him two hedge-knights, and between them his own brother, Lional, stripped to his breeks, and with his hands bound before him. One of the knights was dragging his horse by its shortened rein, and the other had a long spiny thorn branch in his hand, with which he was viciously lashing their captive as they went.

Bors was just about to dash to the rescue when the hoof-drum of another horse ridden at full gallop came upon him from the other side, and with it the sound of a woman screaming. And snatching a desperate glance that way, he saw a knight riding furiously across the open glade, with a maiden across his saddlebow, who fought and screamed in the grip of his bridle-arm, her long fair hair flying over his shoulder like a banner of pale silk.

Seeing Sir Bors, she screamed more loudly yet, and held imploring arms to him as the horse plunged on into the trees. And, the hedge-knights drawing near, he saw his brother's face turned to him in wild hope as he was dragged past, and as they turned down the middle track, his brother's back, crimson-striped from neck to waist, and the blood oozing out between each stroke of the thorn branch.

The choice must be made, and on the instant, and the making of it felt like something within him being torn in two.

He flung a hurried prayer heavenward, 'Lord Jesus Christ, protect my brother for me until I can come back to his aid!' And before the prayer had flown, he was away full gallop after the knight and the maiden.

It was not long before he had them again in sight, and shouted after them, 'Sir knight, set the maiden down, or you are a dead man!'

At that, the knight checked, and slipped the maiden from his saddlebow; but then hitched round his shield and drawing his sword made straight for Sir Bors with a bellow of fury. But Sir Bors was ready for him, and beat up his blade, then slipped his point in under the shield and took him below the breast, bursting through his hauberk and the body-flesh beneath, so that he flung up his arms and pitched from the saddle, and was a dead man before he hit the ground.

Then Sir Bors went to the maiden, who was standing white-faced nearby. 'Damsel, you are safe

now from this knight. What more would you have
me do?'

'Accept my thanks,' said the maiden, 'and take me
home – oh, pray you take me home; it is not far from
here.'

Everything in Bors was crying out to be away back
to his brother; but he could not leave the maiden
alone in the forest; so he fetched the dead knight's
horse and mounted her on it, then remounted
himself, and led the way in the direction that she
bade him.

They had not gone far when they met with twelve
knights, who set up a joyful shout and came spurring
towards them. But when Sir Bors would have drawn
his sword again, she stayed him, saying, 'These are
of my father's household. They will have been out
scouring the forest for me.'

Then there was a joyful coming together; and the
maiden and the knights would all have had Sir Bors
return with them to her father's castle. But Sir
Bors shook his head. 'Gladly I would come; but I
have sore need to be elsewhere, and that as quickly as
may be!'

And seeing in his face that the matter was indeed
desperate, they pressed him no further, but bade him
God speed. And so he left them and headed back as
fast as his horse could carry him, to the place where
he had abandoned his brother, and on down the
track that the hedge-knights had taken.

He had followed it but a short way, when he came
upon a tall man with face half-hidden by a monk's

dark cowl, standing beside the way, and reined in to ask if he had seen them pass.

'Look for yourself,' said the monk, 'and see that which was your brother when you left him.' And he pointed down into the wayside tangle of fern and brambles. And looking where he pointed, Sir Bors saw, as it seemed, the body of his brother Lional, with the blood still fresh upon it, lying there like a broken toy that some careless child had thrown aside.

Grief broke over Bors in a wave, and he dropped from his horse, and kneeling, cradled the body in his arms. And within himself he cried out, 'Lord Jesus, I prayed to you to guard him, and you did not heed! You did not heed!' But he thrust the desperate protest aside, and said, 'Oh God, thy will be done,' and lifted the body, feeling it almost weightless in his arms, and laid it across his saddle. And to the monk standing by, he said, 'Good sir, is there a church or chapel near here, where I can bury my brother?'

'There is,' said the monk. 'Do you follow me, and I will lead you there.'

And so, leading his horse, Sir Bors followed where the cowled figure led.

Presently they came to a tall, strong-set tower rising among the trees as though it too were rooted there rather than built by the labour of men, and close beside it a moss-grown and deserted chapel. Before the chapel door they checked, and Sir Bors lifted down the body of his brother, and carrying it within, looked about for some fitting place to lay it down. The light in the chapel was dim and green, and showed him in the centre of the place a great flat-topped tomb of carved stone. And there, since there seemed nowhere else, he laid the body.

But search how he would, he could find neither cross nor candles nor any sign of Christian usage in that place.

'It grows late. Leave him here,' said the monk. 'Spend the dark hours yonder in the tower; and in the morning, come back with me, and we will bury him as befits a knight.'

So with a heavy heart, Sir Bors left the strange chapel, and followed the monk into the tower hard by.

Now from the outside, the tower had seemed as forsaken to the hoot-owl as the chapel beside it; but as he crossed the threshold he was met by the glow of torches and the music of minstrels, and surrounded by many knights and ladies in gay silken garments, who made him welcome and brought him into the Great Hall and helped him to unarm, and gave him a robe, gold-diapered and lined with the softest marten skins, to cover his shirt.

Then a lady came into the Hall, more beautiful and gracious than any woman that ever he had seen before, with eyes as softly and deeply blue as nightshade flowers, and hair that shone red-gold through the purple silken web that bound it up. She came to Bors, and bade him welcome also, for clearly she was the mistress of the strange stronghold; and led him to sit beside her on a cushioned bench, while the pages and squires made the long tables ready for supper.

And she asked him how he came to be there; and he told her of his quest, and of his brother's death, at which she made soft sounds of grief for his grief, and would have taken his hand where it lay upon his knee, but that slowly, and careful to do her no discourtesy, he drew it away.

When he did this, she started and trembled, and asked him, 'Bors, am I ugly to you?'

'No, lady,' said Bors, 'you are among the fairest that ever I saw.'

At that she sighed, and smiled a little. 'Then let you prove it to me. For so long – since first I heard account of you at Arthur's court, I have held you in my heart and waited for your coming. So long, I have waited, refusing others who might have made me happy, for your sake. And now – will you not love me in return?'

At this Bors was silent, not knowing what to say. And in a little the lady said, 'I can give you power, greater riches than any man has ever had before you.' And that made it a little easier for Bors to hold out against her beauty and the soft light in her eyes.

'Ah, lady,' he said, 'I have told you of the quest on which I ride, and that my brother, whom I loved better than anyone else in the world, lies newly dead in the chapel at your gates, I know not how or why. I am not free to love any lady.'

'Forget the quest,' said she, 'I can give you greater joy. Your brother is dead, and grieving will not bring him back.' And she leaned forward, holding out her hands. 'It is not easy for a woman to beg a man for his love, but I lay down my pride and beg for yours, for I love you as never a woman loved a man before.'

'Lady,' said Sir Bors, 'I would do anything else to make you happy, but this I cannot do.'

Then she began to weep, and rock herself to and fro like a woman keening for her dead, and pull down her bright hair all about her. And Sir Bors, suddenly weary, got up to go and seek his armour, that he might return to the chapel.

When she saw that none of this could move him, she cried out to him, 'You are cruel and heartless! A false knight; for you have brought me to such grief and shame that I will kill myself before your eyes, rather than live another hour to suffer so!'

And she bade her knights lay hold of him and bring him out to the courtyard and safe-keep him there. And she called twelve maidens from among those in the Hall; and bidding them follow her she climbed the outside stair to the highest rampart. And when they stood there between the torchlight and the moon, one of the maidens called down into the courtyard, 'Sir Bors, oh, Sir Bors, if you are a true knight, have pity on us now, and grant my lady what she begs; for if she jumps from this tower for love of you, we must assuredly jump with her, for we are hers, and cannot let her die alone!'

Bors, standing pinioned, looked up at them, seeing how fair they were, and how young, and pity tore at him; and he shouted back at them in a fury, 'If your lady jumps, and if you jump with her, that is for you to choose. I cannot and I will not love her.'

At that, with wild lamentations, they all sprang out into the empty air, and fell like so many bright birds brought down by the fowler's arrow.

And Sir Bors tore himself free, and in the horror of that moment, crossed himself.

In the instant that he did so, he seemed to be engulfed in a great cloud of stinking darkness shot through with murky flame, and a great shrieking and howling as though all the fiends of Hell whirled about him. He was beaten to his knees, deafened and dizzy as it seemed the whole castle turned upside down. And when, little by little, the cloud and the tumult cleared, and he shook his head and looked about him, the tower and the lady and the knights and maidens were all gone. Only his armour lay scattered in the moonlight on the sour grass before him, and his horse grazed undisturbed nearby; and he was crouching beside the doorway to the deserted chapel.

Still on his knees, he thanked God for his deliverance, then, getting to his feet, stumbled inside.

But there was no body lying on the ancient stone tomb, no sign of his brother anywhere; and it came to him that what he had thought was Lional's body must have been, like all else of that night's adventure, part of a snare laid for him by the Lord of Darkness.

All might yet be well with Lional, and his heart lightened with a gleam of hope; and it being by then near to dawn, he armed himself, and whistled up and saddled his horse, and set out once more along the forest ways, hoping that somewhere ahead he might get word of his brother.

Two days later he came to yet another castle; and close before it he met with a young squire, and checked to ask him if there was any news worth the telling and hearing.

'Indeed yes,' said the boy, 'tomorrow there is to be a most splendid tournament here, between our own knights and those who follow the Count of the Plain.'

Hearing this, Sir Bors determined to stay until the morrow. It might well be that other knights of the Grail Quest would gather to such a tournament, and from someone among them he might get word of his brother. Maybe Lional would even come himself. For he had begun to hope that his sight of Lional captive and beaten was as unreal as the rest of the night's adventure that had followed it.

So, thanking the squire, he made on towards a hermitage which he could just see far off on the forest verge, hoping to beg shelter there for the night.

As he drew nearer, he saw a horse that he thought he recognised grazing under the trees, and pushed forward with a quickened heart. And when he reached the hermitage, there, sitting in the doorway, was no holy man, but Lional himself, surrounded by his armour and polishing away at his sword against tomorrow's tournament. Lional looked up as he drew near, but when he saw who it was, his face set like a stone. And as Bors flung himself from his horse to greet him with joy, he made no move, but only rubbed the harder at the sword blade across his knee.

'Lional!' cried Bors. 'Oh, my brother, how is it with you?'

'It is no thanks to you, that it is not death with me,' said Lional between his teeth, 'as it would have been, but that a flash of forked lightning came out of a clear sky, and killed those two who had me in their power; and that left to myself I was able to burst free of my bonds.' He rubbed the red rope-burns on his wrists as he spoke. But his eyes never left Bors's face. 'I would have died for you, Bors, and you left me in sorest peril of my life to go to the rescue of a maiden who was nothing to you.'

To Bors, it was as though his brother had struck him. He knelt down before him with bowed head and joined hands, 'God knows I did what I thought was right. Lional, pray you forgive me.'

Lional stumbled to his feet and began to gather up his armour without a word.

'What are you doing?' Bors said, still kneeling.

'Getting myself armed, as you see. I was a fool to think I had a brother to love and trust; but even I am not such a fool as to think that I can fight you in nothing but my shirt, while you are fully armed.'

'Lional, in God's name, no!' Bors said, watching.

'There is only one way to stop me from killing you,' Lional said, 'and that is for you to kill me.'

'No!' Bors said again. 'You are my brother!'

'I *was* your brother.' Lional fastened the last buckle. He was beside himself with grief and rage. He mounted his horse and wrenched it round towards where Bors still knelt as though frozen. 'Get up!' he yelled. 'Get on your horse and fight me. If you do not, I swear I'll kill you kneeling there, and put up with the shame that will follow me afterwards.'

Bors tried once more, stretching out his hands, humbling himself as he had never humbled himself to any man before. 'Lional, have pity on us both, remembering the love between us; and do not kill me kneeling here, for I cannot and I will not fight you.'

Lional let out a harsh cry, and struck his horse so that it plunged forward, hurling Bors over backwards and trampling him under the great round hooves; and as he lay groaning and half-conscious on the ground, hurled himself from the saddle and began to drag and wrench at his brother's helmet like a madman, his sword ready in his other hand.

But at that moment, the hermit, who had heard all that passed, yet waited, hoping that they might heal the quarrel for themselves, came hobbling out from his bothie, and seeing Lional about to hack off his brother's head, flung himself down over the injured knight, crying out, 'For God's sake hold your hand! Would you kill your brother, and your own soul with him?'

'Get out of my way, old man,' said Lional, 'or I shall kill you first and him after, and my soul may pay for both!'

But the hermit only clung to Bors the closer, gripping his shoulders and shielding his body with his own.

And so Lional killed him lying there, with one

sword stroke that split his skull under the thin silvery hair; and heaving the old man's body aside, went back to work on his brother's helmet.

But it so chanced that at that very moment another knight of the Round Table, Sir Colgrevance by name, who had also heard of tomorrow's tournament, came riding up, and saw what went forward. And he flung himself from the saddle, and seizing Lional by the shoulders, heaved him backwards, shouting, 'Lional! Are you mad? Would you kill your brother?'

'Yes,' said Lional, struggling free, 'but if you meddle in the matter, I shall kill you first, as I did the old man.'

'Then I fear that you must try it,' said Sir Colgrevance, getting between Lional and his brother, and drawing his sword and hitching his shield from behind his shoulder.

The fight between them was fierce and deadly, for both were mighty champions, and had been matched in friendly combat so often that they knew each other's swordplay as well as they did their own. And it went on so long that Bors began to come back to himself. He dragged up on to one elbow, and saw the dead hermit lying close by, and his brother and his friend in desperate combat; and horror rose in him, and he struggled to get to his feet and come between them. He managed to sit up, but the world swam round him, and for pain and weakness he could get no further.

And the fight was beginning to go against Sir Col-

grevance, and seeing Sir Bors sitting up, he shouted
to him, 'Come and help me, man! It is for you I
fight; and if I die, it will be on you the shame!'

At this, Bors managed to get his legs under him,
and half stood up. And all the while Sir Colgrevance
was panting and sobbing out to him for help; but
before he could take a step towards the battling
figures, Sir Lional got in one last great blow that split
his opponent's helm and bit deep into his head, so
that he gave a great choking cry and went down
sprawling into death.

Then Lional turned on his brother, and dealt him
a blow that sent him half down again. 'Fight!' he
shouted, 'Fight, or die like the faithless coward you
are!'

Bors drew his sword. The tears were running
down his face, but he drew his sword and found his
shield. The world was steadying under him, and the
strength coming back into his arm. 'God forgive me,'
he prayed. 'Sweet Lord Jesus Christ, forgive me!' And
he raised his sword . . .

Something happened between his shield and
Lional's, as when the sun flashes off polished metal,
but a thousand times brighter; there was a crack as of
thunder, and a blast of searing heat, and they were
flung back from each other and hurled half-stunned
to the ground.

And when, in a little, their eyes cleared and their
senses returned to them, they saw the ground
between them blackened as by fire, and their shields
twisted and scorched. Yet neither of them had taken

any harm at all, save the wounds that had been on them already.

Then a great quiet came upon them; and out of the quiet, Bors heard a voice which said to him, 'Bors, get up now, and leave this place. The time has come that you must part from your brother, and make your way to the sea, where Percival waits for you.'

Then Bors went to his brother, and they put their arms round each other. 'Lional, my most dear brother,' he said, 'do you bide here, and see that these two who died for my sake are laid in the ground with all the honour that is due to them.'

'I will do that,' said Lional. 'But you? Will you not stay too?'

Bors shook his head. 'I am to go to the sea, where Percival waits for me. But I think that when all is over, we shall see each other again.'

So they parted.

And by and by, when all was done for Sir Colgrevance and the holy man, Sir Lional went back to Arthur's court, for his heart was not in the Quest any more.

But Sir Bors rode away, down to the sea.

He rode day and night until he came to an abbey on the coast; and there he lodged one night. And as he slept, the voice came to him again: 'Arise, Bors, and go down now to the shore.'

So he rose and armed himself, and saddled his horse and brought it from the stable, and rode down towards the sound of the sea in his ears.

When he came to the shore, he found a ship lying close into the rocks, seemingly empty, and set with sails of white samite, so that she was like no ship he had ever seen before. He dismounted and went on board, and instantly, before he could embark his horse as he had meant to do, she drew away from the shore, and the wind filled her sails and sent her speeding like a seabird over the waves. He looked round him, but the night was too dark to make out any details of the vessel; and since there seemed nothing else to be done, he took off his battered helm, and, commending himself to God, lay down in a sheltered corner and went to sleep.

The first thing he saw when he woke in the morning was the yellow head of Sir Percival as he sat rubbing his eyes in the early sun.

Percival saw him in the same moment, and they cried out each other's names and stumbled towards each other with joyful greetings. 'How do you come to be here?' Percival asked. 'For I was alone in this ship, as I have been for many days, when I fell asleep last evening.'

And they exchanged news of all that had happened to them since they were last together.

'Now we need only Galahad to join us,' said Percival, 'for the promise that was made to me to be altogether fulfilled.'

But now the story leaves Bors, and tells again of that same Galahad.

10

THE SHIP AND THE SWORD

Now the story runs that when Sir Galahad had left Sir Percival after saving him from the twenty knights, he took his way through the Waste Forest, and there met with many adventures.

And so he came, on a day, to the abbey where Sir Percival had seen King Mordrain lying; he that had first owned the white shield with the blood-red cross. And he heard King Mordrain's story; how that he had waited in wounds and blindness so many years, for the shield's next master to set him free.

So next morning he went at the time of Mass to the abbey church where the King lay.

And when Mass was over, he drew near, the iron grille opening to let him through. And King Mordrain rose on his bed and held out gaunt arms to him; and the light came back into his eyes, so that he saw him clear.

'Long has been the waiting time,' said Mordrain, with great gladness. 'But now it comes to its end.'

And Galahad caught him as he swayed, and sat down at the head of the bed and laid him back against his shoulder. And suddenly in that moment the old wounds were healed over, leaving not even their scars behind.

'Now I have all that my heart longed for,' said the King. 'Now, Lord God, let me come to you in peace, for my sorrows are over.'

And lying against Galahad's shoulder, he gave a long, slow, contented sigh, and his spirit went free.

And when he had been buried as befitted a king, Sir Galahad rode on his way, for he knew that the time had come for him to ride towards the sea.

But as he headed for the coast, he came one shimmering late summer noontide to a place where a great tournament was going forward. Indeed it was almost over, for those knights whom he judged to be defending their castle, were outnumbered and outmatched and beginning to be driven back.

Galahad drew his sword and spurred forward to their aid. And he performed such mighty feats of championship, and hurled so many of the attackers from their saddles, that the defenders took heart and began to press forward again, as though the Archangel Michael himself had come among them.

Now Sir Gawain and Sir Ector, who had also chanced upon the tournament and were fighting on the other side, saw the white shield with the red cross blazing in the midst of the *mêlée*; and by now most of the Quest knights knew whose device that was, and they began to think that maybe they would withdraw from the struggle and look for an adventure elsewhere. But before they could do so, by the chance of battle, Sir Galahad came straight that way, and in the close fighting, dealt Sir Gawain such a blow on the head that his sword bit through helm and mail-coif and brought him crashing to the ground.

Then he swept on, and was lost in the roaring swirl of men and horses. And the fighting had turned as a tide turns and began to shift away from the castle, while Sir Ector got his horse head-on to the flood and managed to hold him there, guarding his fallen friend and keeping him from being trampled as he lay on the ground.

The attacking knights broke and streamed away; with the defenders hot in pursuit. But presently the knights of the castle came back from their hunting, and found Sir Ector kneeling over his friend; and they gathered Sir Gawain up with the rest of the wounded, and bore him back to the castle, and sent for a physician to salve and bind his head. Then Sir Gawain opened his eyes and said, 'My head is sore hurt – and I am like to die.'

'In a month you will be fit to ride and carry arms again,' said the physician.

Then Sir Gawain said to Sir Ector, 'Now, if you are for riding on, you must ride on without me, for as soon as I can ride indeed, I am away back to Camelot. This looked to be a fine quest at the outset, but it has brought me nothing but sorrow and a sore head.' And then he added, as though that made it worse, 'There is no standing against *that one*. I am thinking that if I had got my blow in first, he would not have bled at all!'

460

'Somehow, I would scarce expect him to,' said Sir Ector, in a puzzled voice.

'Any more than one would expect it of a stone or a flame or a lily, or St Michael himself,' said Sir Gawain, with disgust. 'I had sooner the men I fight or ride with were flesh and blood!'

So in a few days they parted, and Sir Ector rode on alone.

Sir Galahad had not returned with the castle knights. When they looked for him at their turning back from the pursuit, he was simply not there. He had ridden on towards the sea.

He rode so far and fast that dusk of that same day found him not two leagues from Corbenic. But he knew within himself that for him the Quest was not yet ready to be accomplished, nor his journeying to the Grail Castle done. And so, passing a hermitage by the way, he stopped there to ask shelter for the night. And the hermit fed him and gave him a spread of fresh grass to sleep on.

But in the dark hour of the night there came the nearing sound of horse's hooves, and a light quick beating on the door, and a woman's voice calling for Sir Galahad.

And Sir Galahad rose and went to the door, and found there a maiden, holding the bridle of a little palfrey.

'What is it that you would with me?' he asked.

'Arm yourself, and mount and follow me; and I

will lead you to the highest adventure that ever a knight beheld.'

So Galahad went back into the hermitage and armed himself while the maiden caught and saddled his horse that grazed nearby. And he took his leave of the hermit, and mounted, and went with her.

They were far on their way when the sun rose and dusty-gilded the dark spreading trees of late summer. And all that day and far into the night, they rode, not stopping to eat or rest. And in the clear green half-dark of the next dawn, they began to hear the sounding of the sea. So they came down to the shore, and found there waiting for them a ship whose drooping sails were all of white samite, and Bors and Percival standing on the deck, looking for them to come.

'We must turn our horses loose here,' said the maiden, and slipped to the ground, lifting down after her a casket of rare and exquisitely carved wood, which she had carried on her saddlebow all the way. Sir Galahad dismounted also, and unsaddled both horses and turned them loose to graze. Then he went down to the vessel, and stepped aboard, helping the maiden, still with her beautiful carved casket, over the side after him. Then there were great rejoicings, as the companions greeted each other; and for Sir Percival especially, when he saw the maiden, and knew her for his sister Anchoret, whom he had not seen for many years. And a great joy and peace of heart rose in all of them, at their coming together again.

And a wind came out of the quiet dawn and filled the sails, so that when the sun rose clear of the world's edge they were far out to sea, beyond sight of any land. And still the three knights were talking; sometimes gravely, sometimes with laughter, telling each other of all that had passed since last they were together. But at last, when the sun had risen high enough to glow like a blurred golden rose through the white samite curve of the sail, a little silence fell between them. And Sir Bors said, 'Now it seems to me that if my lord Lancelot, your father, were here, there would be nothing more that we could wish for, save for the fair ending of our quest.'

'To me also,' said Sir Galahad. 'But it is not God's will.'

All that day and all the next night the ship sped before the wind; and at dayspring they came to a low rocky island alive with the crying and calling of sea birds. And as though there was an unseen hand at the steering-oar, they headed up a narrow hidden creek; and the wind fell from the sails and the ship settled to rest. And just ahead of them beyond a sandy spur of the shore, so that she could only be reached on foot, they saw another ship much richer and larger than their own.

'Good sirs,' said the maiden Anchoret, who had kept herself happily apart, and scarcely spoken since the joyful moment of greeting her brother, 'yonder is the adventure for which Our Lord has gathered you together. Do you come now, and see.'

So they sprang ashore, helping her among them,

and she still carrying the beautiful casket cradled in her arms, and went scrambling across the dunes to the strange ship. When they got there, they saw written on her side: 'Oh man who would set foot in me, take heed that thou be full of faith. For I am Faith, and if thou fail me, I shall fail thee.'

Then Bors and Percival hesitated on the shore. But Galahad stepped aboard, and the maiden with him, and so the other two followed.

In the midst of the ship, under an airy canopy, they found a bed spread with fair silks and linens. And at the head of the bed rested a golden crown, and across the foot lay the most beautiful sword that any of them had ever seen; with a handspan of its blade drawn from the sheath. And the pommel was of one great gem-stone that shone with all the colours under Heaven; and engraved on the quillions were the words, 'None was ever able to grip me, none ever shall, save one alone; and he shall surpass all who came before him, and all who come after.'

'Here is a marvellous claim!' said Sir Percival. 'Let us test its truth.' And he reached out to take up the sword. But big as he was, his hand could not encircle the grip. Then Sir Bors tried, with no better success. And then they looked to Sir Galahad. But he said, 'Not yet.' He was reading some words wonderfully etched on the unsheathed part of the blade. 'Let no man draw me from my scabbard, unless he can outdo and outdare every other. Death it is to any lesser man who draws me.'

'Why has the sword been left half-drawn from its

sheath?' said Sir Bors at last, as they stood looking down at it. 'It is not good for a blade to be left exposed so, especially in the sea air.'

'I can tell you that story,' said the maiden Anchoret. 'Long ago, when King Pelles, who men call the Maimed King, was whole and strong, he rode out hunting one day in his forest that stretches along the sea. He became separated from his hounds and huntsmen, and all his knights save one, and trying to find his way back to them, he came at last through the forest to the coast which faces Ireland. And there, lying in a deep inlet, he found this ship on which we now stand. He read the words upon the side, but he was as good as any earthly knight; he had faith in God, as strong as any other, and he knew of no sin that he had committed against his God. And so he boarded the ship, while the knight who was with him waited on the shore. He found the sword, and unsheathed it by as much as you can see; but before he could draw it completely from the sheath, there came a spear flying out of nowhere, and pierced him through the thigh, making a wound which has never healed but maims him to this day. And in the moment of his wounding, his land was wounded also, and became as it is now; a land in which the waters do not flow and the harvest fails, and trees grow stunted and men and cattle hollow-eyed. And so it must remain until the man who draws this sword shall heal the King of his wound.'

And still they looked down upon the half-drawn sword; and as they looked, they saw another strange thing: that the sheath was worthy of the wondrous smith-craft it contained, of some strange skin the colour of a red rose and wrought over with gold and blue, but where there should have been a rich sword belt for its support, there was nothing but a length of hempen rope, so poor and frayed that it would surely not support the weight of its weapon for an hour without breaking. And on the scabbard, in letters twisted among the blue and the gold so that they made part of the enrichment, they read, 'Let not any man take off this sword belt to replace it with a better. That is for a maiden's doing, and one that is without sin and the daughter of a king and a queen. And she shall replace it with another, made from that about herself which is most precious to her.'

Then the three knights fell to wondering how they were to find the right maiden. And listening to them, Anchoret smiled, and said, 'Sirs, do not lose heart. So it please God, the new belt shall be in its place before we leave this ship. As rich and beautiful and potent a belt as even such a sword as this demands.'

And as they all turned to look at her, she opened the casket that she had carried all that while, and drew out a belt woven of gold thread and silk and strands of yellow hair; and the hair so bright and burnished that it was hard to tell it from the threads of gold; and brilliant gems strung among the fantastic braids, and gold buckles to make all secure.

'Good sirs,' said she, 'I am the daughter of a king and of a queen, as my brother Percival knows. And I have never knowingly sinned; and this sword belt I braided of the most precious thing I had, my hair. Last Pentecost a voice spoke to me, telling of what was before me, and what I must do; and I obeyed the voice, and cut off my hair, which maybe I loved too much; but I cut it gladly, none the less, and wrought with it as you see.'

And while they watched, finding no words to speak, she bent over the sword and untied the hempen rope, and fitted on the beautiful belt as skilfully as though it had been her daily task.

'Now,' said Bors, drawing a long breath when it was done, and turning to Galahad, 'put on your sword.'

And Percival echoed him, 'Put on your sword.'

'First I must make sure of my right to it,' said Galahad. And he took it by the hilt, and his hand closed round the grip with the ease of familiar things, as though it were a sword of his own, long lost, and found again. And as his watching companions caught their breaths, he unsheathed it and let the light play on the blade, smiling a little. Then he slid it back into the sheath; and the maiden unbuckled his old sword, the sword that he had drawn from its red marble block in the river below Camelot, and laid it in the place left empty across the foot of the bed, and buckled on the new one.

'This is your sword,' she said. 'It has been waiting for you since the world stood at morning.'

'For your part in this,' said Galahad, looking down at her, where her veil had fallen back from her bright boy's head, 'I cannot speak my thanks. I would that you were my sister, as you are Percival's. But sister or no, I am your true knight, for ever.'

11

DEATH OF A MAIDEN

So the three knights and the maiden returned to their own ship; and as soon as they were on board the wind caught and filled the sail and carried them swiftly from the islet.

More days passed; and one morning the ship came sailing into a small land-locked harbour far to the north of any lands that they had known before. And since it seemed to them that their ship would not have brought them so surely to this landfall, if it were not for some purpose, they went ashore and took the track which ran up from the waterside and looked as though it must lead to some living-place of men.

Presently the track lifted over a moorland ridge, and they saw before them the dark mass of a castle rising like a rock-crag from the heather that washed to its walls. And as they stood looking, ten knights came riding out through the castle gateway; and behind them a maiden carrying a great silver bowl.

When they came up, the leader of the troop spoke to Sir Galahad, with no courtesy of greeting. 'The maiden you have with you is of noble birth?'

'She is the daughter of a king and of a queen,' said Sir Galahad.

'Has she ever sinned?'

'Never. That is known to all of us, by certain signs of a ship and of a sword belt.'

'Then she must obey the custom of the castle.'

'I am weary of the customs of castles,' said Galahad. 'What is this one?'

'It is that every maiden of noble birth to pass this way must pay passage dues, not in gold, but in blood from her right arm.'

'That is an ugly custom,' said Galahad.

And Percival moved closer to his sister.

'It is still the custom,' said the leader, urging his horse closer. 'The dues must be paid.'

'Not while the strength is in my sword arm,' said Galahad.

'Or in mine,' said Percival.

'Or yet in mine,' said Bors.

And as the knights came thrusting about them, they drew their swords and turned shoulder to shoulder, facing outwards all ways, with the maiden Anchoret in their midst. And when the knights charged in on them, they hurled them back. But scarcely was the fighting begun, when a score more knights came riding out from the castle and ringed them round. Then the attackers drew back a little, panting. 'You are three valiant fighting-men,' said the leader, 'and so we have no wish to kill you. But even you cannot burst out of this circle; and as to the maiden, it will be all one in the end. Yield her up now, and go free.'

'Such freedom would not taste over-sweet,' said Galahad.

'Then you are bent on dying?'

'As God wills. But it is not yet come to that.' Galahad brought up his sword.

Then the fighting burst out again, fierce and furious; and the knights drove in upon the three companions from all sides. All day they fought, until the shadows grew long and were lost in dusk, and the dusk deepened into the dark and they could no longer see the sword strokes. Then a trumpet sounded from the castle to break off the fray. And as the three stood leaning on their weary swords, the horsemen still ringed around them, more men came from the castle, bearing torches, and behind the torch-bearers an old white-haired man with a gold chain about his neck, who said to the companions, 'Sirs, the last of the fighting-light is gone from the sky. Therefore it is time to call a truce. Do you come back now with us to the castle, and have safe lodging for the night. No harm shall come to you nor to the maiden while darkness lasts, and in the morning you shall all return to this place and state in which you stand now, and the fighting shall go forward as though there had been no pause between one sword-stroke and the next.'

And the maiden Anchoret said, 'Let us go with them. We shall be safe under the truce; and I know in my heart that this is the thing we are to do.'

So they went with the old man and the castle knights, through the deep gateway into the stronghold. And there they were made welcome as honoured guests. And when supper was over in the Great Hall, the old man told them more concerning the custom of the castle.

'Some two years ago, the lady of this place, whose knights we are, fell sick of that dread disease, leprosy. We sent for every physician far and near, but none could heal her sickness. At last, a wise man told us that if she were bathed with the blood of a maiden, who was of noble birth, and who had never sinned in fact or in thought, our mistress would be instantly healed. Therefore no high-born maiden passes this way, that we do not take from her a bowlful of her blood. That is all the story.'

'And yet the blood of these maidens has not healed your lady,' said Sir Bors.

'Alas, no. It must be that none to pass this way so far has been altogether without sin.'

When the telling was done, the maiden Anchoret called her three companions to her, and said, 'Sirs, you have heard how it is with this lady, and that it lies in my power to give her healing. Now I know for what purpose the ship has brought us to this morning's harbour.'

'If you do this thing,' said Galahad, 'I think that you will lose your life to save hers.'

'That I know,' said Anchoret. 'But I know also, as I have known from the moment that I was told to cut my hair, what pathway I follow. Therefore let the three of you, who are most dear to me, give me your leave, for I would sooner do this with your leave and your blessing than without.'

Then the three bowed their heads and gave her the leave that she asked for.

And she called to all those in the hall, 'Be happy! For tomorrow your lady shall be well again!'

Next morning, they heard Mass together, and then returned to the Great Hall. And the people of the castle brought their lady from the chamber where she lay. And as she came, horror rose in Bors and Percival, and despite themselves they gave back a little at sight of her terrible leper's face when she put back her veil. Only Sir Galahad stood his ground, and bowed to her gravely in all courtesy; and the maiden Anchoret moved forward.

'You are come to heal me?' said the lady, as well as she could through her crumbling lips.

'Lady, I come, and I am ready. Let them bring the bowl.'

Then the same maiden who had followed the knights out from the castle yesterday came carrying the same silver bowl. And standing before them all as straight and sweet as a young poplar tree, Anchoret held out her arm over it, and the old man brought a little bright knife, and opened one of the veins that showed blue under her fair skin, like the branching veins on an iris petal.

The red blood sprang out, and swiftly the bowl began to fill.

When it was almost brimming, Anchoret began to sway on her feet, as though a cold wind were in the slender branches of the poplar tree. She turned her face to the lady, and said, 'Madam, to give you healing, I am come to my death. Pray for my soul.'

And with the words scarce spoken, she fell back fainting into the arms of the three companions who sprang forward to catch her.

They laid her down, and did all that might be done to staunch the bleeding, but it had gone too far with her.

She opened her eyes after a while, but they all knew that she was dying; and when she spoke to Percival, her voice had grown so faint and far away that he had to bend close to catch her words.

'Dear brother, I beg you not to leave my body buried in this country. But as soon as my life is gone, carry me back to the ship, and let me go where fate and the wind shall bear me. I promise you this, that whenever you reach the holy city of Sarras, where the Grail Quest will assuredly take you in the end, you will find me there. And in that city, and nowhere else, pray you make my grave.'

Weeping, Percival promised her.

She spoke once more, 'Tomorrow, part from each other and go your separate ways, until your paths shall bring you together again to the Grail Castle of Corbenic. This, through me, is Our Lord's command to you.'

And she gave the quietest of sighs, and the life went out from her.

And within the hour, when she had been bathed with the blood of the maiden, the lady of the castle was whole and well again, her blackened and hideous flesh restored to all its bloom; and she was young and beautiful once more, to the great rejoicing of all her people.

But Galahad and Percival and Bors set about their own tasks in sorrow. And when she had been made ready and all things fitly done, they carried the maiden's body on a litter spread with softest silks, back to the ship waiting in the harbour, and laid her there amidships. And Percival her brother set between her folded hands a letter he had written, telling who she was and how she had come to die, and setting forth on fair parchment the events of the Grail Quest in which she had taken part, that anyone who found her body on foreign shores might treat it with the more honour, knowing all her story.

Then they pushed the vessel off from the shore, and watched her drift quietly out to sea. For as long as they could still see the ship, they waited on the water's side; and when she was quite gone, they turned back to the castle.

The lady and her knights would have had them enter and rest, but they would not set foot in the place again, but asked that their arms should be brought out to them. So the people of the castle brought out their harness and weapons, and for each of them a horse, and they armed themselves and mounted, and set forth on their way once more.

But they had not gone far when great storm clouds began to gather, and it grew dark as late evening, though it was scarce past noon. And seeing a chapel beside the track, they stabled their horses in a rough shelter outside, and went in. Hardly had they done so, when the bulging black bellies of the storm clouds burst into thunder and lightning and lashing rain. And looking back from their shelter, the way that they had come, they saw the whole sky split open above the castle, and flaming thunderbolts hurtling down upon it. And above the roar of the tempest, they could hear the crash of falling towers.

All night the storm raged, but towards dawn the thunder ceased and the clouds parted and drifted away, and the sky grew clear and gentle, washed with light from the sun that was not yet risen.

Then the three companions rode back to see what had become of the castle. When they came to the gatehouse, it was scorched and ruined; and riding inside they found nothing but fallen stones and the bodies of men and women lying where the tempest of God's wrath had struck them down.

The lady of the castle had not kept her restored health and beauty long.

'The ways of the Grail Quest are indeed strange past men's understanding,' said Percival, thinking of his sister.

They dismounted and hitched their horses to some fallen roof timbers in the courtyard, and went looking from place to place to see if any living thing yet survived. And so they came at last to the castle chapel, and behind it a small enclosed burial ground, with soft green grass, and late-flowering white roses arching their thorny sprays over the gravestones, a pleasant and peaceful place, and the storm had passed it by untouched. And as they moved among the stones, reading the names on each, they knew that it was the resting place of all the other maidens who had died for the sake of the lady.

After a while, they turned away and went back to their horses, and rode together until the moor was passed and the dark trees of the forest came to meet them. And there they checked, and took their leave of each other, as the maiden Anchoret had bidden them. 'God keep you,' they said, 'God bring us all to our meeting place again at Corbenic Castle.'

And they rode their three separate ways into the forest.

But now the story leaves Sir Galahad and Sir Percival and Sir Bors and tells again of Sir Lancelot, with his horse slain, lying beside the great river.

12

SIR LANCELOT COMES TO CORBENIC

Now as Sir Lancelot lay in the shelter of his rock on the river bank, between sleeping and waking, he heard a voice in his inmost depths that said, 'Lancelot, rise now, and take your armour, and go on board the ship that is waiting for you.'

And when, startled, he opened his eyes, he found himself lying in a pool of brilliant silver light, so that he looked to the sky, thinking that the moon must have risen. But there was no moon. Then, with the words still echoing in the hollows of his head like the sea echoing in a shell, he got up and armed himself. And all the while the strange radiance was still about him, growing and spreading down to the margin of the river, showing him at last a ship lying there at rest like a great white sea bird among the reeds.

He went down the bank towards it. And as he went, the light faded, till the night was like any other. Only the blur of the ship still showed moth-pale through the reeds and alders.

He stepped aboard; and as he did so, it seemed to him that the air was full of fragrance – the scent as of all the spices in the world that had flooded through

Arthur's Great Hall at Pentecost; of other things too, that were hard to give a name to, such as May mornings and applewood fires and well-oiled harness leather when he was a boy and his first honour hard and clean within him. And for one moment he was near to weeping, and in the next, joy leapt up in him like a cage-freed bird. And he prayed, 'Lord, Lord, Lord, I have done as you bade me; I am in your hands, do with me as you will.'

And as the wind woke in the sail, and the vessel slipped downriver towards the sea, he settled himself down against the side of the ship and drifted into a sleep that was itself like a blessing.

When he woke, it was morning, and the ship was far out of sight of any land. And looking about him, he saw, behind the single mast, a low couch or litter draped in silk; and on the couch, a maiden lying as though in quiet sleep. He drew near, softly, so as not to disturb her; but when he came beside the couch, he saw that she was dead. And he saw also the letter which Percival had set between her hands. Very gently, he took and unfolded it; and read all that was written; how she was Percival's sister, and how he and Bors and Galahad had placed her there, and of all the happenings of the Grail Quest that had gone before. Then he gave the maiden back her letter, and knelt down beside her to make his morning prayer.

And the gladness was in him, that the three so far ahead of him in the Quest had been together in that ship, and the maiden with them; and that they had, as it seemed, left word for him and reached back to draw him into their company.

So for a month and more Sir Lancelot was in the ship, and the winds and tides took him where they chose. And in all that time he was never hungry, though there were no stores on board; for every morning when he had done praying, it seemed that he had been fed with all that he could need until the next morning came. And he was never lonely, for in some strange way the dead maiden kept him gentle company, as she lay unchanging like one that slept. And it seemed that they shared together the autumn storms, and the stars of quiet nights, and the singing of the seas.

And then one night the ship came to shore again, where a dark forest marched down almost to the margin of the sea. And as he waited, not sure for what, but sure that he waited for something, Lancelot heard sounds that he knew must mean a horseman coming through the forest; the soft beat of hooves on leaf mould, and a great brushing aside of low-hanging branches.

Nearer drew the sounds, and nearer yet; and out on to the open shore rode a knight, who checked at sight of the waiting ship; then dismounted and, unsaddling his horse, turned it loose to wander where it would, and came on across the shore-grass and the shingle without haste or hesitating, as though to a meeting long planned. Frosty moonlight burned on his shield as he came, and showed it white, blazoned with a cross so brilliant that even in that light, which steals all colour from the world, it blazed blood-red.

So Sir Lancelot saw again the knight with the red cross on his shield, who he had followed so long and so desperately at the outset of the Quest.

His hand moved towards his sword, but did not draw it from its sheath, for it seemed that to do so might in some way disturb the maiden. And as the newcomer climbed aboard, he said, 'Sir knight, I give you welcome.'

The knight checked, and looked towards him in the shadow of the sail. 'God's greeting to you. Pray you tell me who you are?'

'I am called Lancelot of the Lake,' said Sir Lancelot. 'Now do me the like courtesy and tell me by what name you are called.'

For answer, the other unlaced and pulled off his helm. And as the white moonlight fell upon his face, Sir Lancelot stepped out from the shadow of the sail; and they stood and looked at each other as they had done in the abbey guest chamber on Pentecost Eve.

And the young knight saw the strange crooked face with one brow level as a falcon's wing and one flying wild like a mongrel's ear, but all worn down to bone and spirit since he saw it last. And the old knight saw the boy's face that had become a man's; a face that was gravely beautiful, but yet without a soft line in it anywhere, and a look of inner certainty that he had never seen in any man's face before. And from both faces, the same eyes looked out at each other.

Then Lancelot said, 'Galahad! So it was you!'

And Galahad, who seldom smiled, smiled ruefully and said, 'Forgive me. It was I, my father.'

And they put their arms round each other and strained close. And for a while neither spoke again, for they could not find the words to say.

And then they fell to talking both at once. And all through what remained of that night they crouched in the bows of the ship, each telling the other of all that had befallen them since they set out on the Quest. And Galahad told his father of Bors and Percival and the maiden Anchoret; all those things for which there had been no room in the letter between her hands. And while they were still talking, the sun rose up, and it was another day.

For all the winter half of that year it was given to Lancelot and Galahad his son to be together in the ship, since it was the only time that ever they were to share in this life. And many times the ship put in to islands and unknown shores far from the world of men. And many were the strange and wonderful adventures that they met with when they went ashore together. But the story does not tell of these, for it would take too long in the telling, and draw no nearer to the mystery of the Grail. But always they returned to the ship, and the maiden lying there as though asleep. And there were times when Galahad left his body behind for good manners' sake, while he went away into the solitude and the desert places within himself. But now Lancelot had learned enough to let him go; and so the bond between them grew very strong.

And then the year turned to spring, and Easter was come and gone; and the leaf buds were breaking on the bare forest trees that rang with bird-song, when the ship came yet another time to land. And as they touched shore, a knight came out of the woods, riding a tall warhorse and leading in his right hand another as white as the wild pear blossom of the woodshore.

Seeing them where they waited on the deck of the ship, he came on at a hand-canter, and reining in, spoke to Galahad. 'Sir knight, you have been as long as it is permitted you with your father. Now leave this ship, and mount and ride, for the Quest is waiting.'

Then Galahad put his arm round his father's shoulders, as though he were the stronger and older of the two, and said, 'I knew that, soon or late, this was how it must be; and my heart is sore within me, for I do not think that we shall meet again in this world.'

And then he went ashore. And Sir Lancelot, still standing on the deck as though he were rooted there, with the grief in him darkening the spring day, said, 'Pray for me, that I may keep faith with the Lord God both in this world and the next.'

And Sir Galahad said, 'I will pray, because you are my father, and there is love between us, and you ask it. But your own prayers are strong, and by your own prayers you shall surely keep faith.'

And he mounted and rode away into the forest towards the cuckoo's calling, while the messenger who had come for him rode another way.

And as Sir Lancelot stood there looking after him, a rushing wind filled the sails and bore the vessel swiftly from the shore. So he was alone again, save for the body of the maiden Anchoret.

Then, kneeling beside her, Sir Lancelot prayed as even he had never prayed before, more humbly and more fiercely and with more of urgent longing, that if he was not indeed outcast from God's love, he might be allowed one more sight of the Grail, and that he might see it, not as he had done that other time beside the wayside cross, but with his heart and soul quick and answering within him.

Long and long he prayed, through nights and days, scarcely leaving off even to sleep. And then one night, when he ceased for a little from his praying, he found that he was no longer at sea, but far up the shrunken remains of what must once have been a broad river, and the ship had drifted into the deep inlet that yet remained, among rocks below a great castle.

And looking, he saw that he was below the rear towers of Corbenic.

Corbenic where he had come in his youth to the Lady Elaine, and where Galahad his son had been born. He knew it well, even after twenty years. And yet it was not Corbenic as he remembered it, but in some way strange; and looking far up the rock-cut steps that led from the shore to the river gate, he saw that the gate stood wide, and that it was guarded – the moon was very bright – by two lions standing face to face before the threshold.

And as he hesitated, wondering what he should do, a voice out of the moonlight said, 'Lancelot, for you also it is time to leave the ship. Go up into the castle, for it is the place of your heart's desire.'

So Lancelot hastily armed himself, leaving nothing behind that he had brought on board with him, and looked once in leave-taking towards the body of the maiden Anchoret, and scrambled ashore. And as he climbed up the rock stairway, the ship drifted out into mid-river and down towards the sea again.

At the head of the stairway the lions stood waiting, and Lancelot set his hand ready to the hilt of his sword. But before he had need to draw it, they pulled back from the gateway and sat down on their haunches like hounds. And so he passed through between them into the town, and went on up the steep main street until he came to the fortress itself. It was midnight, and the moon shone down, and all the people of the town and the castle were abed, and no guards anywhere, and all the gates standing open as though they waited for his coming. And his mailed feet rang hollow on the stones of the vaulted stair that led up to the Great Hall, but none came to see who walked that way.

So he went on, following his own shadow on the moonlit floors, until he came to a part of the castle that he did not know at all, and a stairway leading up once more.

Again he climbed. And at the head of the stair he came to a closed door, the first closed door that had met him in all that while. He pushed against it, but it did not open to him.

He tried again and again, but there was no latch to the door, and for all his pushing it yielded no more than if it had been part of the solid wall.

And as he stood there, desperately wondering what to do next, for he was sure that he must open that door if he was to come to the thing he sought, a strain of music reached him from beyond the unyielding timbers. It was music sweeter than any singing of this world, and braided into the shining cadences he seemed to catch the words, 'Glory and praise and honour be thine, Father of Heaven.' And then he thought that his heart must surely burst, for he knew the Grail was within the chamber beyond that door, and he was once again shut out.

He knelt down, close against the door timbers, and prayed with his head bowed into his cupped hands, 'Dear God, my sins are heavy on me. But if ever I did anything that pleased you, of your pity, do not bar me altogether from that which I have sought so long.'

He thought he heard a faint sound of something moving, and the music swelled louder on his ear. And when he looked up from between his hands, he was dazzled as though he were looking into the sun. The door stood wide, and the chamber beyond it blazed like a golden rose in the heart of the dark castle. Light flooded out from it, and a beauty that

was more than the flowers and the candles and the
singing, that pierced him through and licked him
round and drew him so that he stumbled to his feet
and was half into the chamber when the voice spoke
to him again.

'Back, Sir Lancelot. It is given to you to see, but
not to enter in.'

So Sir Lancelot drew back from the place of his
heart's desire, and knelt humbly on the threshold,
looking in.

Afterwards he was never sure whether he had
actually seen the flowers and the candles and heard
the music, any more than he was sure whether he had
actually seen the chamber full of the rainbowed
sweep of angels' wings. But he knew that, as he knelt
there, he saw again at the very heart of the blaze and
the beauty the Holy Grail, under its veil of samite.

And kneeling before the Grail there was an aged
priest. Perhaps it was Josephus himself, perhaps not;
there seemed no time in that place, no barrier
between those living in this world and those living in
Heaven; and anyway, he was beyond thinking. Only
he knew that the priest was celebrating the Mass,
and that at the crowning moment when he rose and
turned holding aloft the cup, there were three others
in the chamber; and for an instant he thought that
they must be Bors and Percival and Galahad; and
then he knew that they were not, though he could
not see them for their brightness. And two of them
were placing the Third in the upstretched hands of
the priest. And then Sir Lancelot was not sure

whether the priest held up the Third, or whether he was the Third himself, and it was something else he carried; something much too heavy for him, so that it bowed him almost to the ground.

Then Lancelot forgot that he was forbidden to enter the chamber, and knew only that he must help – must take some of the weight. And he got up and stumbled across the threshold with his hands held out.

He was met by a puff of wind laced with flame that scorched and blinded him. Darkness rushed in upon him from all sides; and he felt hands, many hands, that flung him backwards out of the chamber, so that he fell all asprawl across the stairhead; and the darkness engulfed him where he lay.

13

THE LOOSING OF THE WATERS

Next day when the castle awoke and people were once more stirring all about, they found Sir Lancelot lying as though stunned by a heavy blow outside the door of the Grail chamber. They knew who he was, for many of the older knights remembered him well across the twenty years between; but how he came to be where he was, and in his present state, they did not know, save that he must have been seeking the Grail.

They carried him to a turret chamber far from the noise and bustle of the great castle, and laid him on the bed and, unarming him, searched him all over for wounds, but found no mark upon him save for the silvery traces of old hurts, for he was scarred like an old and well-tried hunting dog.

So they laid the covers over him and let him lie, until he should come to himself, seeing that there was nothing more they could do for him but let him rest. But the days went by and the nights went by, while always somebody sat watching him by sunlight or rainlight or the light of a silver lamp; and Sir Lancelot never moved nor spoke. And here and there a lady in the Great Chamber who remembered him when she was a maiden, or the youngest scullion in the kitchens who had never seen him at all but heard stories told by the old kennelman who had, wept a little to think of the greatest knight in the world brought so low.

Twenty-four days, and twenty-four nights. And then around noon on the twenty-fifth day, Sir Lancelot opened his eyes and looked about him with an eager light in his face, as though he still thought to see what he had seen in the Grail chamber. Then the light faded, as he knew and accepted his loss.

He looked at those about his bed and asked, 'How is it that I come to be in this chamber? How long have I lain here?'

And they told him what they knew of his coming, and how long he had lain there like one dead.

Then Sir Lancelot said that he must ride; and after food had been fetched to give him strength, and he had eaten, a maiden brought him a fair new linen tunic. But he saw the cruel hair shirt that he had worn for more than half a year lying on a chest beside the bed, and took that up instead.

An old and gentle knight among those gathered about him said, 'There are those among us who know what cannot be spoken in words. There is no more need that you wear that now. For you, the Quest of the Grail is over; and you have travelled as far as you may along that road.'

Sir Lancelot looked at him, and smiled; a shadow of his old lopsided smile. 'That I know. For me, now, there is only the way back. Yet I did not take this shirt of penitence only for so long as I followed the Quest, but if it may be so, for all of life that remains to me.' And he pulled on the horsehair garment next his skin, and then the fine linen over it lest the maiden who had brought it should be hurt; and over that a gown of crimson wool that had also been brought for him.

Four days more he remained at Corbenic, gathering back his strength; and on the fifth he asked for his armour to be brought to him, for he wished to return to Arthur's kingdom, from which he had been absent more than a year.

So a squire fetched his harness and weapons and helped him to arm; and when he went down to the castle courtyard, he found a swift and fiery chestnut horse being walked up and down there.

'It is a gift from King Pelles,' they said, 'from the Grail Keeper, the Maimed King.'

'Pray you give him my thanks,' Sir Lancelot said, 'and may God be with him.'

And he mounted, and leaving the Grail Castle behind him, rode on his way.

Yet he did not at once return to King Arthur's court. He knew that for him the Quest was spent and over; yet now there was an unwillingness in him to turn round and ride home; a dread of what he would find there; the empty places at the Round Table; a dread, maybe, of seeing Queen Guenever again. After all the stress and struggle, he needed a threshold time before returning to the world once more.

Also there was a feeling in him of something still

491

to happen, still to be waited for. And so, while all that summer and autumn and winter went by, he rode errant in the Waste Land, giving himself to any adventure that came his way; and waiting, always waiting, he did not know for what, until spring came round again, the poor shabby spring of the Waste Forest.

Once he heard from a charcoal burner that Galahad and Bors and Percival had been seen riding together again; and then he knew that the fulfilment of the Quest must be near for them, and he was glad. But he did not go seeking them, for he knew that his path did not lead that way.

One night, being far from any village or hermitage or forester's hut, he lay down supperless to sleep under a half-dead willow tree by the last trickle of an all but dried-out stream, choosing the place because there was a little sparse grass there for his horse to graze.

And sleeping there with his shield for a pillow, he dreamed.

He dreamed that he was back on the threshold of the Grail chamber at Corbenic, seeing it all as it had been before. But now Galahad and Percival and Bors were there; and there also, lying on a couch, was King Pelles himself. The light and the singing and the beauty made a bright cloud in Lancelot's head, so that he could not see to the heart of the glory. But, as before, he knew that the Mass was going forward, and he saw the Grail, and beside it a spear whose blade dripped red. And he knew, though he heard no voice, that they were receiving their orders, to take the Grail back to the holy city of Sarras, from which it had come so long ago, that from there it might return to its true place. There was another order, too, for Galahad alone; and he saw Galahad take up the spear and carry it to the Maimed King, and touch the gaping wound on his thigh with the blood that dripped from the blade. And he saw King Pelles rise whole and strong once more from the couch on which he lay. And then he seemed to catch the voice at last; or maybe it was another voice; and it said, 'Now the waters are loosed and the rivers shall run, and the Waste Land shall put forth wheat and the cattle bear many young, and the birds shall sing in the trees among the broad leaves of summer.'

And then he woke; and the glory became the first sunlight slanting into his eyes, and the birds were singing as he had never heard them sing in the Waste Forest before, as though they were singing for the first morning of the world. And then another sound came to his ears; the swift purl of running water; and as he raised himself on his arm and looked about him, he saw, clear through the green mist of buds that seemed breaking on the willow branches even while he looked, that the stream below him, that had been no more than a chain of stagnant puddles, was running swift and deep. And his great warhorse went brushing down through the willow branches to drink.

And he knew that he had dreamed true; and the Maimed King was whole again, and his land whole again with him; and the Grail was away to its own place, and Galahad and his companions with it.

The waiting was over; and when he had whistled up his horse and saddled it, he mounted and turned its head towards Camelot.

And now, for the last time, the story leaves Sir Lancelot, and tells of Sir Galahad and Sir Bors and Sir Percival.

14

THE GRAIL

Now for Sir Galahad and Sir Bors and Sir Percival, all had been just as Sir Lancelot had seen it in his dream. But they had seen and heard and known all that for him had been mercifully hidden in the brightness of the glory. And their souls were raised up and sat loose within them as a sword half-drawn from its sheath.

And obeying the voice, they armed themselves and went down to the seashore out beyond the mouth of the great river.

And there they found the proud ship which had given Galahad his sword. And looking down into her, they saw under the canopy the bed with the golden crown still lying at its head. But at the foot, where Galahad had left his old sword lying in place of the other, stood the silver table which they had last seen in the Grail chamber of the castle far behind them; and on the table, the Grail itself, under a veil of crimson samite.

'Brothers,' said Galahad, 'this is the last of our journeys. May God go with us.' And they stepped on board.

And at once the great wind that they knew so well woke in the far corners of the sky and came sweeping into the sail, and drove the ship out from land and sent her skimming over the waves.

For many days they journeyed so; and their bodies were never hungry while the Grail was with them. And at last, without their having glimpsed any land between, the wind fell from their sails, and the ship came drifting into the harbour of a great city; and they knew by its beauty and by the light that shone about it, that it must be Sarras, the Sacred City, which is, as it were, the threshold of the City of God.

And as they drew alongside the quay, they heard the voice again. 'Now leave the ship, and take up the silver table with its burden, and carry it up into the city, not once setting it down until you come to the church which is the city's crown. Then set down the Grail in its old lodging place.'

So they took up the silver table between them, and stepped ashore. And as they did so, a second vessel came gliding into the harbour, and looking towards it, they saw the white samite sails shining in the morning sun, and the body of the maiden Anchoret lying amid-ships where they had laid her so many months before.

'Truly,' said Galahad, 'the maiden has kept her promise well.'

Then, with Bors and Percival in front and Galahad at the rear, they set to carrying the silver table with the Grail upon it, through steep streets between honeycomb golden houses up into the Sacred City. But with every step they took, the weight of the silver table and its burden grew greater and greater, until, by the time they drew towards the gate of the Sacred City they were near to exhaustion.

Now in the arched gateway sat a crippled beggar, all bent and twisted together, with his crutch and his begging bowl beside him. And seeing him there, Galahad called out to him, 'Friend, come and take the fourth corner of this table and help us on our way.'

'Alas,' said the man, 'gladly would I help you, but you see how it is with me. It is ten years since I walked unaided.'

'You see how it is with us,' returned Galahad, 'that we are forespent under the weight of that which we bear. Do not be afraid. Get up, now, and try.'

And the beggar's eyes were fixed on the Grail under its samite covering. And it seemed to all those watching that under the samite there began to be a glow that was not the sunlight, for the narrow street was deep in shade. And he made a little whimpering sound and got up, slowly and unsteadily, but as straight as ever he had been. And the strength rushed into him, and he came gladly and took the fourth corner of the silver table. And suddenly it seemed that there was no weight to it at all.

So they went through the gate and up into the Sacred City, with a great rejoicing crowd gathering to them, more and more at every step, as word went ringing round Sarras of what it was they carried, and of the healing of the beggar man. And when they came to the great church that was the living heart of the city, they set the Grail down before the high altar.

Then they went back to the harbour again, where the second ship waited for them.

There, too, a crowd was gathered, looking on in awe and wonder; and Galahad and his two companions went on board and lifted the litter on which the maiden lay, and carried her up through the steep, thronged streets, to the church in the Sacred City where the priests were by now gathered, and set her down beside the Grail. And the light, shining in through the high windows of stained glass, splashed her white robes with the colours of rose and foxglove and iris and all the fairest flowers of summer.

And there before the altar she was buried, with such ceremonies as befitted a king's daughter.

But when word of all this was brought to the King of the city, Escorant by name, he sent for them and demanded the meaning of what he heard. And they answered truthfully every question that he asked; and told him the whole story of the Grail Quest. But the eyes of his spirit were blind, and he believed no word of all they said, but called them vile impostors, and summoning his guards, had them thrown into prison.

'And let you lie there and rot,' said he, 'until you bethink you of a better story.'

For a year, they remained in their prison, but as it had been with Joseph and his people when they were held captive in Britain, the Lord God sent the Holy Grail to comfort and keep them all the time of their captivity.

And at the end of a year, King Escorant lay sick, and knew that he was near to dying. And he thought of the three captives in his dungeons, and his heart was changed within him, so that he sent for Galahad and Percival and Bors. And when they stood before him in their prison filth, he begged their forgiveness for his evil treatment of them.

And they forgave him fully and freely, even Bors, who found forgiveness harder than the other two. And in that same hour, he died.

Now King Escorant left no son to follow him; and so when he had been laid in his splendid tomb, the people of Sarras began to wonder among themselves who they should have for their next king. And their choice turned toward Sir Galahad, remembering how he and his companions had come bringing back the Grail, and of his healing of the lame beggar at the Sacred City gate. And they said, 'Surely we could choose no better king than this one.'

When their chief men came and told Galahad this, he said, 'That was none of my doing, but the power of the Grail.'

And the chief men said, 'Even though that be so, there is another reason. King Escorant had no blood-right to the crown; but you are of the line of Joseph of Arimathea, and you have brought back to this city the Grail which he brought here long ago. Therefore it is fitting to the end of this mighty and mysterious adventure that you should bear the golden weight of the crown, even if it be for a single day.'

So Galahad was crowned King of Sarras, though indeed he had no wish for it and the goldwork seemed as sharp as thorns upon his forehead.

On the morning after the crowning, Galahad rose in the first paling of the dawn, and put on his well-worn harness that he had carried through so many adventures. Only he left aside his helm, and let his mail coif lie unlaced on his shoulders so that his head was bare. And he called Bors and Percival to him, and together they went up from the palace to the church in the midst of the Sacred City.

When they came into the tall-towered church, where the colour was newly waking in the eastern windows, they looked towards the high altar and the Grail in its usual place. And standing there, they saw one in the vestments of a bishop. It seemed to them that he was the same priest whom they had seen in the Grail chamber at Corbenic. And indeed it seemed that he knew them also; for as soon as they had crossed the threshold, he spoke to them in greeting. And to Sir Galahad, who was now King of Sarras, he said, 'Galahad, come now, and see and share in this that you have so longed for.'

And Galahad drew near, the others moving a little behind him, and, kneeling, looked into the Cup which the priest had uncovered and held out to him.

Behind him, Bors and Percival saw nothing but the strangely wrought golden vessel. They had shared in the mystery at Corbenic, and this time it was not for them, only the awe and the joy and the reverence that they had always known at Mass. This was the last mystery that Galahad must go to alone, no matter how close they knelt behind him, as each man goes alone to his birth and his dying.

They saw his whole body begin to shake, as though a great wind were blowing through him. He looked up; and his face, with the first sunlight of the morning upon it, shone as though it were lit from within; and his eyes were full of all that the others could not see.

He held up his hands and cried out in a great glad voice, 'Lord, I give thee thanks, that thou hast granted me my soul's desire. Here is the wonder that passes every wonder, that heart cannot conceive nor tongue relate. Now grant me that I come to you!'

And he fell headlong, the clash of his armour on the marble pavement ringing through the empty spaces under the high arched roof. For he had seen into the heart of all things, where·no man may look and continue living in his body.

Bors and Percival sprang to gather him in their arms, and he looked from one to the other in farewell. To Bors, he said, 'When you come to Camelot again, greet Sir Lancelot, my lord father, for me, and take to him my love.'

And his head fell back against Percival's shoulder.

And suddenly, to the two left behind, it seemed that the emptiness of the great church was full of the sweep of wings and the glory of unheard music; and Heaven itself opened, and a hand came down and took the Grail from before the altar, and returned whence it came.

And Heaven closed in their faces, leaving only the emptiness of the great church behind. Even the man in bishop's robes was gone; and they were alone, and Galahad was dead.

And grief took them such as no grief they had ever known before.

The people of Sarras, too, mourned for Sir Galahad. They made him a grave where he had died, close beside the spot where the maiden Anchoret lay; and buried him with all the honours due to a king.

And when that was done, Sir Percival laid aside his old knightly dress, and put on the rough habit of a hermit, and with Bors's help made himself a wattle cabin outside the city walls in which to spend the rest of his life in prayer and contemplation.

Sir Bors stayed with him in faithful friendship; but he never laid aside his sword nor changed his harness for a hermit's garb, for he knew that when Percival had no more need of him, the lines of his own life would lead him back to Britain and King Arthur's court. And he knew, to his sorrow, that the time would not be long. From the first moment of their first meeting, Percival had followed Galahad, and he would follow him still.

Percival lived just one year and three days after Sir Galahad, and then was laid beside his friend and his sister, in the church at the heart of the Sacred City of Sarras.

Then Sir Bors, being alone, put on his armour, and went down to the harbour and boarded a ship sailing westward. And after many days at sea, he came to his own shores at last, and took horse for Camelot.

When he arrived there was great rejoicing, for it was full two years since Sir Lancelot had returned, and he had been the last, until now, of the Grail knights to come home; so that the King and his court had long ago given up Sir Bors as lost to them, along with Sir Galahad and Sir Percival.

He found his brother Lional there, and Sir Gawain with a scar on his head, and Sir Ector of the Marsh, and other old friends. But many more were lacking; and when they sat down to eat that evening, half the places at the Round Table were empty, and among those missing were many of the best who used to sit there. And of those who were there, many had wounds and scars, and most were changed in some way from what they had been before. And he thought that the high adventure of the Grail had been a costly one. He knew that the end had been victory, but he was too weary to see how.

When the evening meal was over, he sought out Sir Lancelot his kinsman. He had noticed that the older knight ate no meat and drank no wine at supper; and he thought that at the neck of his fine silken tunic he had glimpsed the rough edge of a hair shirt, and the redness of chafed skin beneath. He took him aside, up to the rampart above the castle garden, where it was possible to speak and be sure that no one else was by to hear. 'Sir,' he said, 'I bring you a message. Galahad got his soul's desire, and died in my arms and Percival's, for he had come into the heart of the mystery, where it is not possible for a mortal man to come, and yet remain mortal. And with his last breath he bade me greet you from him, and bring you his love.'

'I wish I could have been with him,' said Sir Lancelot, heavily.

'So did he. So did we all. Often we spoke of you, and wished that you might be among us.'

'There was a reason why that could not be,' said Sir Lancelot, 'A reason – a holding back . . . It was not all mine to give . . . Not for me alone, to renounce, you see . . .'

His voice had grown absent and inward-turning, as though he spoke to himself within himself, and not to Bors at all. And Bors saw his eyes following something that moved below; and looking in the same direction, saw through the soft thickening light of the summer evening that the Queen had come into the garden.

Next day, when Bors was rested, the King sent for his clerks, who had taken down from each returning knight the story of his adventures on the Quest. And they took down Sir Bors's story, which was the only one that went beyond Sir Lancelot's and told of the last adventuring of Sir Galahad and Sir Percival and himself, and of the taking up to Heaven of the Grail.

And then the record was complete, and the King sent it for safe-keeping to the monks of the abbey library of Salisbury; that in future years the story of the Quest for the Holy Grail might not be lost to men coming after.

THE ROAD TO CAMLANN

1

THE DARKNESS BEYOND THE DOOR

When the darkness crowds beyond the door, and the logs on the hearth burn clear red and fall in upon themselves, making caverns and ships and swords and dragons and strange faces in the heart of the fire, that is the time for story telling.

Come closer then, and listen.

The story of King Arthur is a long, long story, woven of many strands and many colours; and it falls naturally into three parts.

The first part tells how the father of Arthur, Utha Pendragon, with the help of the enchanter Merlin, won the fair Igraine to be his queen. And when their son Arthur was born, Merlin, knowing by his magic arts that Utha would die before he could count one grey hair in his beard, and that in the struggle for power among the nobles after his death his son would be trampled underfoot, took the babe on the very night he was born, and carried him away and gave him to a certain quiet knight called Sir Ector, to be brought up along with his own son Kay until the time came for him to claim his destiny. But he did not tell even Sir Ector who his fosterling was.

And as Merlin had foreseen, Utha died when his

son was but two years old, and the chiefs and nobles of the realm fell to struggling together for power; and the invading Saxons, whom Utha had driven out of Britain, seeing their chance, came storming in again.

And Merlin sorrowfully watched all this and waited, while in his foster-father's castle Arthur grew from a child into a boy and from a boy into a young man. And when Arthur was turned fifteen, Merlin went to the Archbishop Dubricius in London, and told him certain things; and so the Archbishop called a great joust, and all the knights and nobles of the realm came flocking to take part. And when they were gathered, suddenly there appeared in their midst, in the garth of the great abbey, a stone with an anvil set upon it, and driven into the anvil and through it into the stone was a splendid sword. And about the stone was written in letters of gold:

'Who so pulleth out this sword from this stone and anvil is the true-born King of all Britain.'

And when the knights and nobles had tried and failed to pull out the sword, Arthur, who was not yet even a knight, but had come to London as a squire to his foster-brother Sir Kay, drew out the sword as easily as from a well-oiled sheath.

Then Merlin told the long-kept secret of his birth, and it was known that he was indeed the son of Utha Pendragon and the rightful High King after him.

So Arthur was crowned by the Archbishop. And after, with Merlin always beside him, he gathered his war-host and in many great battles he drove back the Saxons and the Picts and the men from across the Irish Sea. And when eleven kings from the outlands and the mountain places along the fringes of Britain joined spears and rose against him, he quelled them also, and drove them back into their own mountains. And he made his capital at Camelot, and there he began to gather his court.

Now you must know that Igraine, his mother, had borne three daughters to her first husband before ever she became Utha's queen. And the eldest, Elaine, was married to King Nantres of Garlot, and the second, Margawse, was married to King Lot of Orkney, and the youngest, Morgan La Fay, was married to King Uriens of Gore. And the husbands of all of them were among the eleven outland kings.

Morgan La Fay was a mistress of black magic, and she sought always to do harm to Arthur her half-brother. But it was Margawse who did him the sorest harm in the end. And this was the way of it: she was sent by King Lot, her lord, no one knowing who she was, to play the spy in the High King's court; and she was beautiful, and nearly twice as old as he was, and skilled in the sweet dark ways of temptation; and so she made him love her for one night. Merlin could have warned him, but at that one unlucky time, when he was needed most, Merlin was away about affairs of his own. So the thing happened. And nine months later, back in her own far northern home, Queen Margawse bore a son, whose father was not Lot of Orkney, but her half-brother, Arthur of

Britain. And she sent word to the young High King, telling him who she was, and that she had borne their child and named him Mordred, and that one day she would send him to his father's court.

Then Arthur knew that he had done one of the forbidden things, and that because of it, in one way or another, he was doomed. But meanwhile he had a kingdom that must be ruled and a life that must be lived as valiantly and justly and truly and joyfully as might be; and this he set himself to do.

It was not long after that the sword which he had drawn from the stone, and which had served him well in all his fighting since, broke in his hand. And from the Lady of the Lake, he received another sword: the great sword Excalibur, faery-forged for a hero and a High King, which served him all the rest of his days. And a while after that, he saw and loved Guenever, the daughter of Leodegraunce the King of Camelaird, and took her for his Queen.

Guenever brought with her for her dowry a mighty round table and a hundred of her father's best and bravest knights to swell the strength of the High King's own following. And the High King's following was already strong, for champions were gathering to him from the farthest ends of his realm and even from beyond the seas. And so the brotherhood of the Round Table came into being; that great company of knights oath-bound to fight always for the Right; to protect the weak from the tyrants; strong to uphold the ways of justice and gentleness throughout the land.

Merlin saw only the beginning of that gathering, for his own fate was upon him, calling him down to his long enchanted sleep beneath a magic hawthorn tree.

So – the knights gathered, Sir Bors and Sir Lional and Sir Bedivere; from Orkney came Sir Gawain, the High King's nephew (though he was but a few years younger than Arthur himself) and later his brothers Gaheris and Agravane and Gareth, for all the sons of Margawse left her as soon as they could draw sword – all except Mordred. And from the kingdom of Benwick across the Narrow Seas, came Sir Lancelot of the Lake, the greatest of all the brotherhood.

Each of them brought their own story, and men have told and retold them ever since; minstrels singing to the harp in a prince's hall; monks in chilly cloisters writing upon sheets of vellum for the making of books; a Lancastrian knight called Sir Thomas Malory weaving tales and songs together in a narrow prison cell ... Tales of Sir Lancelot and Elaine the Lily, of Sir Lancelot and the Queen; tales of Geraint and Enid, and Gareth and Linnet, and Gawain and the Green Knight; the long and tragic lament for Tristan and Iseult, the short and shining account of the coming of Percival. These and many and many more together make up the first part of the great story of King Arthur, which I have told in an earlier book, *The Sword and the Circle*.

Only a year after the coming of Percival, there

follows the story of the Holy Grail, the cup from which Christ drank at the Last Supper, and which afterwards received His blood; and how the knights of the Round Table set out in quest of the Mystery, for their souls' sake and the sake of the kingdom. And that retelling I have called *The Light Beyond the Forest*.

It is a strange story, of a forest that is not like other forests, and a maimed king and magic ships and a bleeding lance, and always the Grail moving ahead like a beckoning light among the trees.

One by one the knights died in their questing, or lost heart and turned homeward, until only four were left; Sir Percival and Sir Bors, Sir Lancelot and Sir Galahad, his son. And of these four it was given only to Sir Galahad to fully achieve the quest, and in achieving it to die, for mortal man cannot come to the heart of the Mystery and yet live on in the world of men. And Sir Bors and Sir Percival, coming close behind him, achieved something of the quest, and lived on, Sir Percival for a year before he followed Sir Galahad, Sir Bors to return home. And Sir Lancelot, struggling valiantly and desperately behind them, failed the quest because of his love for Guenever the Queen, which he could not put altogether away from him, and so was allowed only a distant glimpse of the glory of the Grail and its meaning before he was turned back.

And so the great days, the shining days of the Round Table were over; and the long, many-coloured, many-stranded story of King Arthur

The Road to Camlann

Pendragon turns to its third part; the last and the darkest. The part which in this book I have called *The Road to Camlann*.

2

THE POISONED APPLE

The flowering time that had come to Arthur's Britain with the Grail Quest was over and past, though for a while a golden quietness lingered like the little summer that comes sometimes when the days are growing shorter and the autumn is already well begun.

The knights had returned to sit at their old places at the Round Table – those of them who returned at all. But many of them did not come back, and among them some of the bravest and the best. And a new generation of young knights came in to take their places: men who had never known the early days, the shining days of high adventure, of young champions gathering about a young High King, with the battle to save Britain and champion the Right still in front of them.

And among this wave of new men, his mother Queen Margawse, who had kept him always at her side, being now dead, came Mordred, half-brother to Gawain and Gaheris, Agravane and Gareth. Mordred, who was own son to the High King.

And with his coming, it seemed that the waiting

dark began to gather itself, ready for the time of creeping in . . .

Mordred was very like his father to look upon, but cast in a lighter and a slighter mould. Whereas Arthur was brown-skinned, and had been fair-headed like a hayfield at harvest time before his hair became streaked with grey, Mordred had the pallor of something reared in a dark cellar far from the light and air. Pale skin, pale hair, eyes pale and opaque and veined with brilliant blue like turquoise matrix, so that no man could ever see what went on behind them; a voice light and pleasant and somehow pale too. He was a leader of men in his way, though it was not the way of his father, but he could set fashions that men would follow; fashions for wearing black garments, for playing with a flower or a feather between his fingers; a fashion for thinking and secretly speaking ill of the Queen with a shrug of the shoulders and a little laugh.

Mordred had nothing against the Queen herself, but he had not been at court seven days before his subtle mind had divined the love between Guenever and Lancelot, the foremost of the King's knights and his dearest friend, and how the King himself took care not to know, never to recognise, even to himself, that that love existed.

Guenever was the weak place in the King's defences; Lancelot and Guenever together were the way through which he might be reached and brought to ruin, and all that he stood for with him. And Mordred hated his father the High King and coveted his throne, as Margawse, his mother and Arthur's half-sister, had taught him to do through all his childhood and his growing years.

The older and truer knights, Gawain foremost among them, held out against the new fashion. But without anyone knowing how it happened, save Mordred himself, and maybe Agravane the mischief-maker, who from the first was his follower and right-hand man, it was not long before many of the new-comers were whispering among themselves that Sir Lancelot and Queen Guenever were betraying the King by their love for each other, or that Guenever was betraying both of them; and that in any case the King should be told.

For a while it seemed that having raised the small evil wind, there was little more that Mordred could do with it; for Sir Lancelot also heard the whispers, and he said to Sir Bors his cousin, 'Now I am thinking it is once more time that I was gone from court for a while.'

'That may indeed be so,' said Sir Bors. 'Yet I think it is no time for one of your far-riding quests, lest when you are far from us and no man knowing where, the Queen may have sudden need of you.'

And they looked each other in the eye as old comrades-in-arms, neither speaking Mordred's name. And Lancelot said, 'That was in my mind also. Therefore, while the court is here in London I shall go only so far as Windsor, and beg shelter of the hermit there, he that was once of our company, Sir Brassius. None save you shall know where I am gone.

But if the Queen has need of me, do you send me instant word.'

'That will I,' said Sir Bors.

And Sir Lancelot of the Lake donned his armour and sent for his horse and, as he had done to save the reputation of the Queen so many times before, rode away.

And when he was gone, the Queen took to wearing all her jewels and laughing a great deal, to show to all men and women that she cared nothing for Sir Lancelot's going, and was as happy with him far away as she was when he was near at hand. And when he had been gone a while, she made ready to give a private supper party in her own apartments to a few chosen knights of the Round Table.

She bade come to her feast Sir Gawain of Orkney and his brothers Gaheris, Agravane and Gareth, Sir Mordred, Sir Bleoberis the Standard Bearer, Sir Ector of the Marsh and Sir Bors and Sir Kay the Seneschal, Sir Lucan, Sir Mador de la Porte and his cousin Sir Patrice, and a certain Sir Pinel the Wild, cousin to that Sir Lamorack who had been slain in blood feud by the Orkney brothers far back in the years before the coming of the Grail. These and others, twenty in all, the Queen bade to come and sup with her.

And she set herself to order and make ready a feast that should do honour to her guests.

Now all his life Sir Gawain had a great love for fruit, especially apples. This was known to all men and, wherever he was a guest, his host would take pains to see that fruit was set upon the table for his pleasure. So now, though it was late in the year, the Queen took much trouble to come by some of the little golden long-biding apples that are withered and sweet as honey at Christmas, enough to fill a dish to set close by Sir Gawain's place at table.

So then, the Queen held her feast, and those who were bidden to it made merry at her table, while her harper played for them beside the fire of scented logs. But among her guests, Sir Pinel hated the Orkney brothers, Gawain the leader of them most of all, for the sake of his kinsman Sir Lamorack, and for long and long he had brooded upon ways to do them harm; though he had done no more than brood until Sir Mordred came to court. And Sir Pinel also knew of Sir Gawain's love of apples . . .

And when the main part of the feasting was over, the wine still went round, and they fell to eating dried apricots and little honey-and-almond cakes and the like. And then as chance would have it, Sir Gawain and Sir Patrice both reached for an apple in the same instant; and Sir Gawain in courtesy held back his hand for Sir Patrice to take first. And Sir Patrice took the biggest and finest apple from the top of the pile.

If any had been watching, they might have seen that Sir Pinel began a sudden movement of protest, then checked into frozen stillness, staring down at the half-eaten honey-cake in his hand. They might have seen for an instant the trace of a startled frown between Sir Mordred's pale brows, before he took up his wine cup with a faint shrug, as one saying within himself, 'Ah well, these things happen.'

But nobody chanced to be looking their way.

And Sir Patrice ate the apple to the core, and threw the core into the fire, where it sent up a little hissing spurt of blue flame. And in the same instant he began to choke; and choking and clutching at his throat struggled to rise, then fell sprawling backwards upon the rush-strewn floor.

The men nearest to him sprang to his aid; but he was already dead, and beyond their help.

'Poison!' someone cried.

Mordred, kneeling among those beside the body, remembered small dark hints of his own, dropped into Sir Pinel's ear; remembered also that quickly frozen movement, and knew well enough that the poisoned apple had been meant for Sir Gawain, and who had poisoned it. It would have been better to have had his half-brother Gawain out of the way. Sir Gawain, living, would always be a danger to his plans and was a loyal man to Arthur. But Sir Patrice's death would serve his own purposes well enough, he thought. For the Queen had provided the apples and so suspicion must fall on her – if it were given a little guidance – and with suspicion must come danger; and when word of that danger reached Sir Lancelot, it would fetch him hot-foot back to her aid. Somewhere among all that, though he had no time as yet to see where, must lie the chance to work evil against the King and father whom he hated.

And getting to his feet, he too cried, 'Poison!' in a voice of horror, his face turned full upon the Queen.

Then a great uproar broke out in the Queen's chamber, with Sir Mador in the midst of it all, crying that his cousin had been foully slain, and that he would have blood for it, until Sir Gawain shouted him down. 'Whoever did this thing, the poison was meant for me, and not for Sir Patrice! All men know the fondness that I have for apples – '

'All men, and all *women*!' shouted back Sir Mador.

'What mean you by that?' demanded Sir Gawain. 'Now by God's teeth, speak clear!'

And a second time, into the sudden silence, Sir Mordred whispered, '*Poison!*' as one who cannot believe the horror of his own thoughts, his brilliant blue eyes wide upon the Queen, who had risen and stood as though turned to stone in their midst.

And Sir Mador looked around him at the crowding knights, and said, 'I will speak clear! No matter who the poison was meant for, I have lost a kinsman and a friend by it, and in the Queen's apartments. And before you all, I accuse the Queen of his death. Since none but she and her household have had access to the food upon this table!'

And the knights standing all about, Sir Pinel among them, looked aghast at the Queen and at each other. And not one of them spoke up in Guenever's defence, for save Sir Pinel and Sir Mordred there was not one but had suspicion of her in his heart.

And standing in their midst, Queen Guenever began to sway. Soundless and white to the lips, she slid to the ground in a swoon so deep that it was as though she also were dead.

Then while her maidens came running to tend her, word was sent to the King; and he came straightway, and strode in through the doorway just as she sighed and opened her eyes.

'I have heard a wild story,' said the King. 'Let someone now tell me the truth of it.'

And the knights parted, that he might see Sir Patrice lying dead upon the floor. And standing rigidly beside his slain kinsman, Sir Mador de la Porte repeated his accusation against the Queen.

The Queen, who had risen wavering to her feet once more with the help of her maidens, gazed wildly from her lord's face to the face of her accuser. 'Before God,' said she, 'I am innocent of this sin!' and held out beseeching hands.

Arthur crossed the floor and took her hand in his, and holding it, looked about him at his knights. 'This is a hideous matter,' he said, 'but as to your Lady the Queen's part in it, you have heard her swear that she is innocent. Do you accept that?'

'No, my Lord King,' said Sir Mador bluntly, 'I do not accept it.' And no other man spoke at all.

'Then it seems that we must put the case to trial in the Court of Honour,' said Arthur. 'If I were not the King, I would gladly take my lady's quarrel upon myself and prove her innocence in single combat against all accusers. But I am the King, and so bound by the law to be a just judge and not a champion in any such trial. But, Sir Mador, I make no doubt that another will take my place and give you battle in the Queen's name, rather than that she should suffer death unjustly.'

But no knight stood forward to take the Queen's cause upon himself, to prove her innocence in single combat; for to uphold her cause before God's judgement, doubting that it was indeed a rightful one, would be a terrible thing to do, and might set one's very soul in peril.

'My Lord King,' said Sir Mador after a long pause, 'there is no one here who will fight for the Queen. Therefore name me a day on which I shall have justice.'

And with the Queen's hand still strong-held in his, the King said steadily, 'Not all the knights of the Round Table are here within this chamber, nor even at court this day. Fifteen days from now, Sir Mador, do you come armed and mounted to the meadows below Westminster. It may be that one will come against you as the Queen's champion; then may God be with the Right. And if none comes, then shall my Queen be ready, that same day, to receive judgement of death upon her.'

'I am content,' said Sir Mador.

And silently the knights went their separate ways, bearing the body of Sir Patrice among them.

And when the King and Queen were alone, Arthur asked his wife to tell him all she knew of what had happened.

'Truly I know nothing,' said Guenever, 'but that I had a bowl of apples set for Sir Gawain, and Sir

Patrice took the finest apple and ate, and died; and that, before God, I am innocent!'

'That I believe,' said the King, 'but my belief is not enough. Where is Lancelot, who has been your champion since first he was made knight?'

Guenever shook her head. 'Would to God and his sweet mother that I knew; for if I might get word to him, he would surely come and play the champion's part for me now.'

The King thought long and heavily. Then he said, 'Gawain is too fiery, and the attempt, whoever made it, was on his life . . . Since he cannot fight for you, get word with Sir Bors at once, and ask him – beg him if need be – to do battle for your innocence.'

'He is not sure of it,' said the Queen. 'I saw the doubt in his eyes, like all the rest.'

'Beg it of him for Sir Lancelot's sake,' said the High King, the words strangling a little in his throat; and he kissed her on the forehead, and turned and strode from the room.

The Queen sent for Sir Bors, and when he stood before her in her chamber, she asked him to fight for her innocence against Sir Mador.

Sir Bors listened to her with a stiff and unhappy face, and said when she had finished, 'Madam, how may I do this? I also was at your supper table, and if I now take up your cause, the suspicion of my brother knights will fall upon me also.'

'Sir Lancelot would fight for me, were he here,' said Guenever, and Bors saw the flicker of hope in her face as she thought of her life–long champion, and he felt, as he had felt it often enough before, that she had played false by both her champion and the King, and so he gave her back harsh words.

'Sir Lancelot might have come as close as Sir Percival or myself to the Mystery of the Grail which he longed for with his whole soul. His love for you cost him that, yet still you would have him back at your call.'

Then the Queen humbled herself to Sir Bors, begging him on her knees; and at last he yielded, and swore that he would do battle for her in the Court of Honour if no worthier knight had come forward to be her champion by the fifteenth day.

In the first grey of the next morning, Sir Bors left the royal castle, no man knowing, and rode to the hermitage at Windsor, and told Sir Lancelot of the evil that was upon the Queen. Then he returned to the court, and let it be known by all men that he had sworn to fight in her defence, if no more worthy knight had come forward by the appointed day.

The day of the trial came, and the meadow below Westminster was made ready. The lists were set up, and the stands for the onlookers hung with coloured stuffs as gay as for a Midsummer jousting. But at the upper end of the meadow a tall iron stake stood stark and menacing, with brushwood piled high about its foot, ready for the Queen if Sir Mador had the victory; for death by burning was in those times the punishment for murder, as it was for many other crimes that were all called by the name of treason.

Then the High King came down with his knights

about him, and the Queen, well guarded and in the keeping of the Constable and his men-at-arms, walking to her place as proud and seemingly unshaken as ever she had been when she came down with her maidens to watch the jousting among the Round Table knights. Only she took care not to look at the stake and the piled brushwood as she passed them by.

Then Sir Mador stood out before the King, and again made formal accusation against Queen Guenever of the death of Sir Patrice his kinsman. And standing there, he swore that he would prove her guilt, before God, at hazard of his own life, against any man who came forward to maintain her innocence.

And at that, Sir Bors stood forward to give him answer. 'Here I stand in the Queen's defence, to maintain her innocence of this crime, in God's name, unless, even now, a better knight than I shall come forward as her champion.'

'The challenge is given and accepted,' said the King, looking straight before him, but not at either of them. 'Now let the champions make ready.'

And the trumpets rang in the wintry air, and both knights turned and went each to his own pavilion, where a squire waited, holding his horse. And in the waiting silence they mounted and rode to the opposite ends of the lists.

As they turned their horses to face each other the winter sunshine struck thin and clear upon the colours of their shields and their horses' trappings and the tips of their skyward-pointing spears. In another moment those spears would swing slowly down into the couched position. But in the waiting pause, three swans came flying up-river, with out-stretched necks and musical throb of wings. And the Queen turned to watch them as though they might be her last sight of beauty in this world. But Sir Bors was looking the other way, towards the little wood that bordered the meadow to the north. And as the swans passed on upriver it seemed that the throb of their wings was changed into a beat of another kind, the nearing beat of a horse's hooves.

And in the same instant that the heralds raised their long gilded trumpets to sound for the joust to begin, out from the wood rode a stranger knight on a white horse, and carrying the Virgescue, the plain white shield carried by a new-made knight until he had earned a device to bear upon it – or by a knight who wished to ride unknown.

All eyes were upon him as he headed for the end of the lists and reined in beside Sir Bors. And his voice rang hollow in his helmet, but clear through the wintry air. 'Sir Bors, pray you yield me this quarrel on the Queen's behalf, for I have a better right to it than you.'

'If the High King gives his leave,' said Sir Bors. 'Come,' and together the two knights rode down the lists to the canopied stand with the red dragon floating flame-like above it, where Arthur sat in the midst of his court. 'My Lord King,' said Bors, 'here is come another knight that would take upon him the defence of the Queen.'

Arthur looked at the figure in the plain dark armour carrying an unblazoned shield, and caught the light-flicker of unseen eyes looking back at him from behind the vizor, but nothing more. 'Your pardon, sir,' he said, 'you carry the Virgescue; how then may we judge your fitness for this combat?'

'He is a better knight than I am,' Sir Bors said quickly. 'Therefore I am freed of my promise.'

And the Queen leaned forward a little in her place among the Constable's men-at-arms, watching the newcomer with widened eyes, as she had watched him since the moment that he broke from the woodshore.

The King said slowly, staring straight into that faint eye-flicker behind the stranger's vizor, 'Is this true, that you wish to take the proof of the Queen's innocence upon yourself?'

'It is for that purpose that I am come,' said the knight. And Arthur was sure that he was speaking in a voice not his own, and a small sharp hope began to grow in him that he knew the true voice behind the disguised one. Also he was sure that Sir Bors knew, and would never have yielded up the quarrel to one who was not indeed a better knight than himself.

So he said, 'If Sir Mador agrees, then the quarrel is yours to take upon you as the Queen's champion in this Court of Honour – ' He checked. Almost, he had said, 'And may God give you the victory!' but justice was justice, and he was the King and must uphold it. So he ended, 'And may God give the victory to him whose cause is the true one.'

And when the thing was put to Sir Mador, who had come from his end of the lists to join them, he said, 'It was agreed between Sir Bors and me that we should settle this thing together unless a better knight than he came to take his place. If he swears that this is the better knight he spoke of, then I must accept his word and be content.'

So Sir Mador and the unknown knight saluted each other and rode apart to the opposite ends of the lists. Then the trumpets sang, and couching their lances they set their horses to a canter that quickened to a gallop as they swept in upon each other, the clods from their hooves flying up like startled birds behind them.

And as they came together, Sir Gawain said to Sir Ector of the Marsh beside him, 'Now I would wager a made falcon against a barley loaf that that is Lancelot. For all the bare shield he carries, I know him by his riding.'

For some knights had a way of losing speed in the last instant before the shock, but Sir Lancelot had a way of setting fire to his horse at that same instant, so that at the moment of impact he was travelling faster than the man he rode against; and oft-times that gave him the advantage. So now, as they came together in a pealing crash that echoed across the river meadows, Sir Mador's spear caught at the wrong angle and splintered into three pieces that flew up, turning over and over in the air above them, while the strange knight's spear, travelling like a lightning-shaft, took Sir Mador squarely on the shield and hurled him and his horse together back into a crashing fall.

Sir Mador rolled clear of the threshing hooves, and scrambled to his feet, flinging his battered shield before him and drawing his sword. And the stranger knight swung down from his saddle, tossing aside his spear, and, drawing sword also, charged in to meet him, while squires came running to take his horse and get Sir Mador's to its feet. So they came together, blade to blade, thrusting and traversing, tracing and foining, hurling together as it might be two great boars battling for the lordship of the herd.

The best part of an hour the struggle lasted, for Sir Mador was a skilled and valiant fighter, proved in many battles. But at last the strange knight caught him off-balance, and got in a blow that brought him half to the ground. But even as the stranger stood over him with blade upraised, Sir Mador was afoot again, and in the act of rising, drove his blade into the thick of the other's thigh, so that the blood ran down. The stranger staggered, then sprang in once more with such a buffet to the head that Sir Mador went down full length and all asprawl. The stranger bestrode his body and stooped to pull off his helmet. But Sir Mador cried quarter, in a voice thickened by the blow; and the stranger knight checked his hand.

'Quarter you shall have,' said he, 'so that you take back all accusation against the Queen.'

'That will I,' gasped Sir Mador. 'From henceforth I

will hold her blameless in this matter, and proved so by God's will in trial by combat.'

Then the squires came to lift him up and help him away to his pavilion; and the Constable's men-at-arms gladly fell back to give clear passage to Queen Guenever. And the Queen walked out from among them like one walking in her sleep, to where the High King stood under the royal canopy with hands held out to receive her.

And the stranger knight came as custom demanded, halting on his wounded leg, to make his reverence to the King. And King Arthur bent down to greet and thank him, the Queen also, her eyes suddenly very bright in her face that was beginning to wake back to life.

'Sir Knight,' said Arthur the High King, 'will you not unhelm, that I may see the face of the champion who has saved the life and the honour of my Queen?'

Then the knight pulled off his helmet, clumsy-fingered with the weariness of battle, and thrust back the mail coif beneath. And all men saw under the thick mane of badger-grey hair, the strange, crooked, ugly-beautiful face of Sir Lancelot of the Lake.

'So,' said Arthur, and he reached out his free hand to grip Sir Lancelot's mailed shoulder. 'Lancelot, my thanks to you, in God's name!'

'Nay,' said Sir Lancelot, 'no thanks are needed. Have I not been the Queen's champion since the day she belted on my sword?'

And the Queen gave him her hand, as was proper for a queen in thanks to her champion, so that for a long moment the three of them were linked together. And she let the tears that she could not hold back run free and in silence, rather than wipe them away before all those looking on.

Then the squires came to support Sir Lancelot away after Sir Mador, to receive the leech-craft of Morgan Tudd the King's physician.

And the knights came crowding round, voicing their joy at Lancelot's return; and Sir Gawain was shouting, 'Did I not say I knew him by his riding?' to anyone who would listen. And Mordred glanced round with a small east-wind smile for Sir Pinel, who had been beside him. But of Sir Pinel there was no sign. Nor was he ever to appear at court again. Mordred shrugged – the man might have made a useful tool. But Lancelot had been netted and fetched back to court; and the Queen's name had been smirched, and though she had been proclaimed innocent by trial of combat, people would never quite forget . . .

Enough harm had been done for that one day.

Sir Mordred strolled back to where the horses waited, smiling faintly, and playing with the peacock feather between his fingers as he went.

3

GUENEVER RIDES A'MAYING

Sir Lancelot's wound took long to heal. Winter and spring passed by before he could sit his horse or even walk without pain. And during all that time he must remain at court where he might have the leech-craft of Morgan Tudd. And though the Queen grieved for his hurt, taken on her account, she thought, 'Now at least he cannot be for ever riding away. Now surely he will turn, he will turn back to me as he used to do, before the Grail Quest came between us.'

But Lancelot, by putting out all the strength that was in him, did not turn to her again. Instead, he set himself to keep from being ever alone with her, and even to seek the company of other ladies and damosels, though never one above the rest. And as soon as his wound would stand it, he took to riding out by himself, to find sanctuary with the hermit at Windsor or in some other forest refuge.

And gradually the Queen's joy turned cold and angry within her. And when more than a year had gone by, one spring day when the court was at Camelot, she sent for Lancelot to her chamber, and when her maidens had left them alone, she said to him, 'Sir Lancelot, I see and feel daily that your love for me grows less. More and more as your wound heals you take to the forest; and even when you are here you turn your face from me and seek the company of other ladies as once you sought mine. Tell me now, and truly, have you taken back your love from me and given it to one younger and more fair?'

Standing before her, Sir Lancelot shook his big ugly head. 'My heart lies in your breast, Guenever, as it has done since the day that I was made knight. Surely you must know that. And every time I turn from you I tear at my own heart-strings. But you must know also that there is much whispered talk all about us here at court. And it is so that we must keep apart, lest harm come of it, to you, and to me, and above all to the King.' He was silent a moment, fidgeting with his sword-belt, and Guenever silent, watching him. Then he looked up and met her gaze, humbly but straightly. 'Also there is another thing, Guenever. Because of my love for you, God denied me what He gave to Percival and Bors when we followed the Grail Quest; and by that I know how deeply sinful is this love of ours, and how it cuts us off from His Grace.'

The Queen said, 'I wish that I could disbelieve you; for if it were another lady, another love, I could fight her – I could win you back from her as I won you back from Elaine the Lily. But you are hiding from me behind God.' She had spoken quietly at first, but her voice grew high and shrill until it cracked in her throat. 'And God I cannot fight. Go then, and be at peace with God! You say that you tear your own heart-strings when you turn from me, but do you not see that all this while you are tearing mine?' At the last, she was screaming at him. 'Go! Go! Be happy with your God, and never come near me again!'

And as Sir Lancelot turned without a word and blundered like a blind man from the room, she flung herself down sobbing upon the wolfskin rug before the hearth.

So yet again Sir Lancelot rode away; and this time more sorrowfully than ever before, for this was the first time that the Queen herself had bidden him go. But though he disappeared into the forest, not even Sir Bors now knowing where he rode, he was never far beyond a day's ride from Camelot, for in the changed and shadowed times since Mordred came to court he carried always with him an uneasiness lest some new harm should threaten the Queen when he was not by to guard her.

And so, even when she had sent him away, the Queen did not know how faithfully he kept near to her lest she have need of him.

And indeed it was well that he did so, for not many days went by before Guenever did indeed have need of her champion once again.

This was the way of it.

After he was gone, Queen Guenever did as she had done before, donning all her most brilliant gowns and making a great show of gaiety and laughter, that all might see how little it mattered to her whether he stayed or went. And within a little while, on the eve of May Day, she called to her ten young knights of the Round Table, and bade them to ride a'Maying with her on the morrow, into the meadows and woodlands round about to welcome summer in; to hear the cuckoo and bring home the white branches of the may.

'Come well horsed,' she said, 'and clad all in green as befits the day. And bring each of you a squire with you; and I will bring with me ten of my maidens, that each knight may have a maiden to ride with him, for May is the month of lovers, when no one should ride alone.'

So they made ready, and next morning while the dew was still on the grass, they set out, blithe as a charm of goldfinches, and all clad in springtime green, and their horses' harness chiming with little silver bells as they rode. Here and there they ambled and dallied, over the meadows and through the woodlands, singing and calling back to the cuckoo: the knights standing in their stirrups to reach up and break knots of creamy blossom from the hawthorn trees to stick in their caps or give to the damosels who rode with them.

And so, with song and laughter, they rode further and further into the forest.

Now there was a certain knight called Sir Meliagraunce, who at that time held one of Arthur's castles within seven miles of Camelot. And he had loved Queen Guenever in secret for many years. Often he had watched her when she rode abroad, dreaming of ways to carry her back to his own hearth. And on this day, when chance word reached him of how she rode close by, with no armed men about her but only a handful of knights and their squires, unweaponed and dressed in green for Maying, knowing that Lancelot was away from the court, it seemed to him that his chance was come. And all his sense forsook him, and thinking nothing of what must happen after, he called out his whole following of twenty armed men and a hundred archers, and led them down into the wooded valley where the Queen and her company rode, and silently ringed them round, keeping well back among the trees so that they suspected nothing until an arrow thrumming out of a nearby thicket pitched into the ground almost under the muzzle of the foremost palfrey.

The animal squealed and reared, startling those behind him, and for a moment all was confusion. And then as the Queen's knights fought to get their horses back under control, suddenly they found themselves surrounded by armed men on all sides; and out on to the track ahead of them rode Sir Meliagraunce, leather-clad but with his shield on his arm and his drawn sword in his hand.

'Sir Meliagraunce!' said the Queen, startled and not yet fully understanding. 'Is this some wild jest?'

'Jesting was never further from my heart!' cried Sir Meliagraunce, striving to thrust his way through the milling horses to her side.

'Then what meaning lies behind this strange and most discourteous behaviour?'

And now Sir Meliagraunce had reached her and grasped her bridle. 'No time for courtesy. Come with me now to my castle. I will answer all the questions that you choose to ask, so that you ride with me.'

'Traitor!' cried the Queen, trying to pull her bridle free as he wrenched her horse round. 'Remember that you are a knight of the Round Table! Will you shame yourself and dishonour all knighthood and the King who made you one of that brotherhood? Me you shall never shame, for I will kill myself before you touch me!'

'Fine valiant talk, madam!' said Sir Meliagraunce. 'But I am beyond caring for it. I have loved you these many years, and never before found the chance to gain what my heart desires!'

The Queen's knights had closed up around her and were seeking to drag him from her side, but they had no weapons, and from every side Sir Meliagraunce's armed men thrust in. And though they and the squires with them fought like the bravest of the brave to protect their lady, it was not long before all of them lay wounded upon the ground – though indeed a goodly company of Sir Meliagraunce's men lay sprawled around them.

Then seeing her knights lying so, and the men-at-arms standing over them with drawn swords, the Queen cried out in horror and pity, 'Sir Meliagraunce, bid your men to stay their hands! Do not slay my valiant knights who have been brought to this pass through their faith to me! Promise me that, and I will go with you. Promise it not, or fail in your promise, and I will indeed kill myself!'

'Madam,' said Sir Meliagraunce, 'for your sake I will spare them, and bring them with us into my castle, and see that their wounds are tended, if you will ride with me and smile upon me.'

So the wounded knights were heaved again on to horseback, some into the saddle, the more sorely wounded slung across their horses' withers. And with Sir Meliagraunce's hand upon the Queen's bridle, where the little silver bells still rang as though in mockery, they headed for his castle.

But as they rode, one of the squires, less sorely hurt than his fellows, seized his chance as they were fording a stream and, wheeling his horse, struck spurs to its flanks and galloped back the way they had come. Several of the archers loosed after him, but the arrows flew wide, and though some of the men-at-arms spurred in his wake, he soon shook them off among the trees.

'It will be not my questions, but my Lord the King's that you will be answering before long,' said Queen Guenever, 'and it is in my mind that they will be pressed home with the point of a sword! Better let me free now, and my knights with me, while you may!'

But Sir Meliagraunce was beyond listening; and he left thirty of his best archers posted at the head of the valley, with orders to shoot the horse of any knight who came after them, but on no account to harm the rider – just so much sense was left to him – and still clutching the Queen's bridle, and with the rest of his following close about him, he pressed on with desperate speed towards the castle that he held from the King.

Meanwhile, in the midst of the past night, Sir Lancelot, sleeping among the hounds beside the hearth in a forester's hut, dreamed that Guenever was threatened by some danger and calling for him. He was gifted or maybe cursed from time to time with the power of dreaming true. And he knew the true dreams from those which were but fancy. So when he woke, still in the wolf-dark of the night, he got up, quieting the hounds as best he could, told the drowsy forester that he must be away, and armed himself while the man, grumbling, saddled his horse. Then he mounted and rode away back towards Camelot.

All the rest of the night he rode, as though the Wild Hunt were after him. Dawn paled in the east, and he rode the morning sun up the sky, thundering on through the green and white and gold of May Day morning, until, some while still short of noon, he came up through the steep streets of Camelot town to the gates of the royal castle that crested the hill.

The first person he met was Sir Gawain, who shouted with gladness to see him.

But Lancelot had no time to spare for the joys of friendship. 'Where is the Queen?' he demanded.

'She rode a'Maying with ten of the younger knights and her bonniest maidens. They should be back soon enough now,' said Sir Gawain, looking into the other's haggard face.

And at that moment they heard more flying hooves coming up the street; and in through the gate, blood streaking his face from the great gash on his forehead, rode Hew, the young squire.

When he had gasped and stammered out his story, Sir Lancelot who had stood fretting with his mail gloves the while, shouted for a fresh horse, and when it was brought, flung himself into the saddle, calling to the King and his knights, who by then were gathering all about, 'Arm quickly, and follow me. At Sir Meliagraunce's castle you shall find me if I am still alive. And we may save the Queen!'

And he dashed out through the gate and down the steep narrow street, his horse's hooves striking fire from the cobbles, and on across the river by the three-arched bridge, the cloud of young-summer dust rising behind him, until the sunlit green of the forest gathered him into itself.

Presently he came to a place that showed signs of fighting; undergrowth broken down and bloodstains on the trampled grass; and a while further on suddenly his way was barred by thirty archers, each with an arrow nocked to his drawn bowstring. 'Turn back, Sir Knight,' said one, who seemed to be their captain, 'this way is closed to you.'

'By what right?' demanded Lancelot.

'Ne'er mind for that,' said the man, 'you shall not pass this way, or if you do, it shall be captive and on foot, for your horse we shall slay.'

'That shall be of small gain to you,' said Sir Lancelot, and striking spurs to his horse, charged them forthwith. Next instant came the twanging of released bowstrings, and a deep drone as of angry hornets, and the horse neighed shrilly and plunged to the ground, a score of arrows in its breast. But Sir Lancelot sprang clear as the poor brute rolled over, and sword in hand charged upon the archers. But they broke and fled, crashing away into the forest in all directions, so that he could come up with none of them.

Then Sir Lancelot went on his way on foot. But his armour and shield weighed heavy upon him, for full knightly harness was never meant for long walking in, and bore more painfully upon him with every spear's throw of distance that he covered. And beside this, the wound in his thigh, that he had got when he fought Sir Mador de la Porte for the Queen's innocence, though it was long-since healed, had left him with a leg that was not yet fully serviceable, and the weight and the chafe of his armour upon it began to irk him so that he could make less and less of speed, while all the while the dark taste of last night's dream was with him, Guenever in danger and calling to him – calling and calling. Yet with the kind of welcome he was like to meet at Sir

Meliagraunce's castle, he was loath to cast any of his harness aside.

But by and by he reached a track, and along the track towards him came a cart driven by one man, with another sitting on the side of it with his legs dangling.

A sudden flicker of hope woke in Lancelot. 'Hi, good fellows!' he shouted. 'What will you take to drive me in your cart to a castle not two miles from here?'

'Nay, you'll not come into my cart,' said the driver, 'for I'm heading the other way, to fetch wood for my lord, Sir Meliagraunce.'

'It is with Sir Meliagraunce that I have business,' said Sir Lancelot grimly.

'Then you can go and find him on your own two feet.' The driver would have whipped up his bony nag and driven over the knight in his path, but Sir Lancelot sprung on to the bow of the cart, and as the man turned his whip against him fetched him such a clout on the side of the head with his mailed fist that he tumbled down from his perch like a stoned bird, and lay still.

Then the other man cried out, 'Fair lord, spare my life, and I will drive you wheresoever you would go!'

'You know already where I would go – and that swiftly!' said Sir Lancelot, climbing into the cart. And the carter scrambled forward to take the reins.

'Sir Meliagraunce. Aye, you shall be at his gate before you can count to ten,' said the man, already heaving the horse and cart around. Then he set off up the track, rattling and lurching at such a speed as the old horse had not made for many a long year.

In the Great Chamber above the keep of Sir Meliagraunce's castle, Queen Guenever waited with all her maidens about her, and her wounded knights and squires upon the rush-strewn floor. For she had demanded to have all her people with her, that she and her maidens might tend their wounds, and also that Sir Meliagraunce might have no chance to come upon her alone.

And one of her maidens, watching from the window, called suddenly, 'Madam, come and see – there is a cart coming up the track, and a knight standing in it. Poor knight, he must be going to his hanging!' (For no man of armour-bearing rank would ride in a cart unless on his shameful way to the gallows.)

'Where?' said the Queen, and looking from the window she beheld the wood-cart, and the knight riding in it; and she knew with a knowledge of the heart, even before she could make out the device on his shield, that it was Sir Lancelot. 'Nay, that is no knight riding to a felon's death,' she said, 'though indeed he must be hard put to it, that he comes to my rescue in such a manner.' And to herself she said, 'Yet I knew that he would come – despite all things, I knew that he would come.'

And as she watched, the cart drew up before the castle gateway, and Sir Lancelot sprang down and shouted in a voice that set the hollow gate-arch ringing: 'Open the gates, Sir Meliagraunce, false knight of the Round Table and traitor to your liege lord Arthur. The High King and his company are not far behind me, but first stand I, Sir Lancelot of the Lake, ready to do battle with you and all your following!'

And he hurled himself at the little wicket within the great main gate, which in haste and panic had not been made properly secure, and burst it open and came charging through the knot of gate-guards inside, striking out right and left as he came, like a boar that breaks loose and charges with the hounds snapping about his flanks.

When Sir Meliagraunce knew that Sir Lancelot was within his gates, panic rose in him, and he bolted up to the Great Chamber and cast himself down at the Queen's feet, crying, 'Mercy, madam! Pray you have mercy on me, for I was driven to this madness by my love for you!'

'It is not for me to have mercy,' said the Queen, 'but for the knight who comes to rescue me, and for my lord the High King, who I doubt not follows hard after.'

'You can speak for me!' howled Sir Meliagraunce. 'Tell them I have done you no harm, but used you with all courtesy – ' And he tried to cling to the hem of her green skirts.

'Certainly you have used me with more courtesy than you have used my poor knights,' said the Queen, and drew back her skirts from his clinging hands.

'I was mad!' wailed Sir Meliagraunce. 'Only speak to Sir Lancelot and the High King for me, and I will serve you humbly in whatever way you choose!'

'Cease this outcry, and get up,' said the Queen at last, 'and I will speak to them for you, that they spare your life; for truly peace is better than war.'

And she went to meet Sir Lancelot as he came storming in search of her. And when they met they went for an instant straight into each other's arms. 'I knew that you would come,' said the Queen against his shoulder. 'Despite all, I knew that you would come to save me!'

And Sir Lancelot said, 'I dreamed you were in danger. I heard you calling me, and so I came.'

And then he pulled away from her, demanding, 'Where is Sir Meliagraunce?'

'In the Great Chamber,' said the Queen, suddenly mid-way between tears and laughter, 'and very sore afraid!'

'He has cause to be,' said Sir Lancelot, 'for now his death is upon him.'

'Nay! I have promised him that I will cry your mercy for him, since what he did, he did for love of me!'

And they moved further apart from each other, touching only with their eyes.

But after, Guenever took Sir Lancelot by the hand and led him up to the Great Chamber where were her maidens and the wounded knights and squires; and Sir Meliagraunce still kneeling, who looked at her with eyes like a beaten dog. So, slowly and with much labour and persuasion, she made a kind of peace between Sir Lancelot and Sir Meliagraunce, though even then it was agreed that they should fight the matter out in single combat that day week, before King Arthur in the jousting meadow below Camelot.

And hardly was that settled before the High King himself and his knights were in the castle courtyard.

And Guenever made peace also between them and Sir Meliagraunce on the same condition of single combat, for the King upheld Sir Lancelot, agreeing that no vengeance should be taken upon Sir Meliagraunce nor upon any of his people, but that day week should end the matter. 'But if either fails to keep his tryst,' said the King with a stern eye upon Sir Meliagraunce, 'then shall he be called craven ever after, and the shame of all Logres.'

That night they remained in the castle that Sir Meliagraunce held from the King; and next morning, with the Queen in their midst, and those of the wounded knights who were too sick to sit their horses borne in litters, they set out to return to Camelot. But when Sir Lancelot would have departed with the rest, Sir Meliagraunce came to him, smiling, and making great show of friendliness, and said, 'Gentle sir, the Queen has made peace between you and me, until the day comes that we settle this matter by weapon-skill for the honour of us both. But pray you tell me of your own accord that you feel no ill will towards me in the meantime.'

'None in the world,' said Sir Lancelot, shortly.

'Then do you prove it, by remaining here as my honoured guest until the day of combat comes.'

Sir Lancelot looked at the man's humbly smiling face, and scorn rose in him, and he felt sick. He would have liked to strike him; but Sir Meliagraunce was so small inside himself, and seemed now so contemptibly and pitifully eager to please, and Sir Lancelot was ashamed of his own contempt. So he said as warmly as he could manage, 'I thank you for your courtesy, and most gladly I will stay here with you until we ride for Camelot together.'

And so, after the rest had set out, he remained behind with Sir Meliagraunce.

Later that day his host asked Sir Lancelot would it please him to see the hawks in his mews, especially a very fine jerfalcon that he had lately had brought to him from the islands of the North. And Sir Lancelot, who loved falconry and always trained his own birds, said that it would pleasure him greatly. But as they went down to the inner courtyard which contained the mews, Sir Meliagraunce stood aside at a doorway for Sir Lancelot to pass through ahead of him. And Sir Lancelot, passing through, trod on the springboard of a trap cunningly concealed in the floor; and the trap opened beneath his feet and he fell twice the height of a man into a vault deeply floored with straw.

And Sir Meliagraunce made the trap secure again, and went on his way, heedless of the muffled shouting beneath his feet.

★

In Camelot time went by towards the appointed day
of combat. And on the last day of all, there came to
Arthur's court a certain young knight out of
Hungary, called Sir Urre. A most potent knight he
had been with his heart ever set on adventure; but
he came in sore need of help, lying weak and forespent in a horse litter, and his mother and sister
riding with him.

They were brought in and made welcome as honoured guests. But the King spoke to Sir Urre's
mother apart. 'Most welcome are you and your son
and the damosel your daughter to my court; but tell
me, lady, why you have brought him so far from his
own place to mine. Sick and weak as he is, so long a
journey must have been grievous hard for him to
bear.'

'Hard indeed; and long indeed the journey,' said
the lady, and he saw that she must have been fair to
look upon before sorrow came to her; but now she
was haggard and weary, and there was a wild and
seeking look in her eyes. 'Seven long years ago my
son, who sought adventure and high deeds even
more than most young men, was in Spain, and there
in a great tournament he fought with one, Sir
Alphegus, and slew him, but received from him first
seven wounds, three in the head and three in the
body and one in his sword-hand. It was a fair fight,
but the mother of Sir Alphegus cursed him for her
son's death; and she was one who had power from
the Devil in her. And by her black powers she so

wrought that my son's wounds should bleed and fester without healing and he should never be whole again until his wounds were searched by the best knight in the world. And so for seven long years we have travelled through all the lands of Christendom, seeking the best knight in all the world; but to no avail; and if we do not find him here, I fear me that my son will never be whole again.'

'Take heart, lady,' the King said kindly, 'for here in Britain – in Logres which is the brightness at the heart of Britain – your son must surely be healed of his wounds, for there are no better knights in Christendom than are gathered about my Round Table.'

But as he spoke, he wondered. Once, he would have known that that was true; he prayed that it was true still, but he could no longer be sure.

But now, with the wounded knight lying there in his pain and weakness, and the lady's anguished and beseeching gaze fixed upon his face, was no time to be listening to such doubts in his heart. 'I myself will be the first to lay hands upon your son,' he said. 'Well I know that I am not worthy to work this miracle; yet I am the High King, and if I go first, that shall give courage to my knights to follow me. For you must know well, madam, that this is no light thing that you ask of us.'

Then he knelt down beside Sir Urre, whose litter had been taken from its horse-shafts and laid upon the floor of the Great Hall. 'Sir Knight,' he said, 'I grieve for your suffering. Will you allow that I touch your wounds?'

'Do as you will with me, my Lord King,' said Sir Urre, his voice dry and weary in his throat; but it was clear that he had lost all hope of healing at any man's hands.

Then the linen bandages were laid back, and the King touched Sir Urre upon each of the seven sickening wounds. But though he was as gentle as might be, the sick knight clenched his teeth, and winced at every touch. And when he had touched them all, the seven wounds were just as they had been before.

'I knew that it would not be I,' said the King, 'but pray you be of good courage; there are better knights by far than I am, here in my court.'

Then one after another all the knights that were there at court came forward to lay their hands upon Sir Urre. Sir Gawain and his brothers, Sir Lional and Sir Bors and Sir Ector of the Marsh, Sir Bleoberis, Sir Kay the Seneschal and Sir Meliot de Logure, Sir Uwaine, Sir Gryflet le Fise de Dieu, Sir Lucan and Sir Bedivere, Sir Mador and Sir Persant of Inde – and Sir Mordred, at whose touch the wounded knight could not forbear a groan. And many others, a hundred or more. And when the last had tried in vain, Sir Urre was near to swooning with the pain and weariness of so many hands upon him. Yet his wounds were all unchanged, save that they bled the more from so much handling.

'Now we sorely need Sir Lancelot of the Lake,' said King Arthur.

'Aye, well, he will be here tomorrow,' said Gawain,

'when he comes with Sir Meliagraunce to keep their day of combat.'

Meanwhile Sir Lancelot had lain six days and six nights prisoned in the vault below Sir Meliagraunce's castle, and every day there came a maiden who opened the trap and let food and drink down to him on the end of a silken cord. And every day she whispered to him, sweet and tempting, 'Sir Lancelot, oh, sweet Sir Lancelot, I will bring you free out of this place if you will be my lord and my love.'

And every day he refused her, until on the last day her anger rose and she said, 'Sir Knight, you are not wise to spurn me, for without my help you will not win free of this captivity. And if you are still here at noon tomorrow, your honour will be gone for ever.'

'It would be greater dishonour for me to buy my freedom at your price,' said Sir Lancelot, 'and the High King and all men know me well enough, I hope, to know that it is not cowardice but some mischance or treachery against me that could hold me from keeping my tryst when the appointed day of combat comes.'

And the maiden secured the trap again and went her way.

Next morning, lying in the dark and listening to the sounds of the castle that filtered down to him from overhead, Sir Lancelot heard Sir Meliagraunce ride away, his horse's hooves ringing hollow on the courtyard cobbles and out through the gate arch to the lower court. And he beat his fists together in fury and despair. But soon after, the maiden came, and lifted the trap, and knelt weeping beside it, looking down at him, while he stood below her looking up. And she said, 'Alas! Sir Lancelot, I had hoped to win you, but you are too strong-set against me, and my love for you has been in vain. Yet I cannot see you dishonoured. Give me but one kiss in guerdon, and I will set you free, and you shall have back your armour, aye, and the best horse in Sir Meliagraunce's stable.'

'There is no harm in a kiss,' said Sir Lancelot. 'It is but courteous to thank a lady for her kindness.'

Then the maiden sent down a good stout rope with knots tied in it, in place of the silken cord. 'I have made the end fast to the bar-socket of the door,' she said. 'Trust me, it will bear your weight. Now climb.'

And Sir Lancelot swarmed up the rope, and standing beside her when she had made all secure again, he kissed her once. Only once, but long and tenderly, for he was a man to pay his debts. Then the lady brought him to the armoury, and served him as his squire, aiding him to put on his armour, and when he was armed, and his sword at his side and a spear in his hand, she took him to the stables, where twelve fine coursers stood in their stalls, and bade him choose whichever he would.

He chose one that was as white as milk, with an arched neck and a falcon's eye, and she aided him to saddle and bridle it, for the grooms, like everyone else in the castle, had gone streaming away after their lord to Camelot.

And in the lower court he mounted, and leaning down to her from the high saddle, said, 'Lady, my thanks are yours for all time; and all my life my service is yours if you should need it, for this day's work.'

And touching his spurs to the horse's flank, he clattered out under the gate arch, while the maiden stood looking after him with the taste of her own salt tears on her lips where his kiss had been, as other maidens had stood before her.

Sir Lancelot settled down into the high saddle, and set his horse's head towards Camelot. He had seven miles to cover before noon, and the time was short, with the sun already high in the sky.

Meanwhile in the meadow between the town and the river, all things had been made ready for the joust. The King and Queen and all the court had come down to watch; even Sir Urre had been borne down to the field on his litter and set in the shade of a clump of ancient alder trees. And Sir Meliagraunce had already arrived. And when the King, seeing that he rode alone, asked for Sir Lancelot, he showed great surprise. 'Sir Lancelot? Is he not here? He left me on the morning of the second day, to ride off on some business of his own; but I did not think that he would forget this day – unless . . .'

'Unless?' said the King.

'Unless, maybe, having been so long accounted the Queen's champion and the best of knights, and being no longer so young as once he was . . .' said Sir Meliagraunce, and grinned under the shadow of his open vizor.

'That sounds not like Sir Lancelot,' said the King.

And Sir Gawain standing close by growled into his rusty beard, 'And he that says so speaks foul slander! If Sir Lancelot comes not to keep this day, it is slain or wounded the man is – or lies captive somewhere!'

And if any had been looking at the Queen, they would have seen how her face faded to the whey-white of thorn blossoms.

But no one was looking at the Queen, for at that moment the sun flashed back from some point of swiftly moving light across the river, and upon the waiting quiet came the urgent beat of a horse's hooves, and craning that way they saw a knight on a white destrier come pricking out of the forest on to the river track. He headed for the three-arched bridge and came drumming over; and as he drew near, and they made out the device on his shield, the shout went up, 'It is Sir Lancelot! It is Sir Lancelot of the Lake!'

And if any had *then* been looking at the Queen, (but no one was, save maybe Sir Mordred) they would have seen her flush from her whey-whiteness to a painful fiery rose.

Sir Lancelot swung left-hand from the bridge on to the tilting ground, and reined to a trampling halt, his horse scattering foam from its muzzle.

Then the King sent squires to summon Sir Lancelot before him. And Sir Lancelot set his horse pacing forward up the field and reined in again, below the stand where the King sat with Guenever the Queen at his side.

'Sir Lancelot,' said the King, 'you come late to your tryst.'

And Sir Lancelot spoke up in a loud clear voice for all the company to hear, and told how Sir Meliagraunce had dealt with him in the past days. And Sir Meliagraunce would have turned his horse and been swiftly on his way; but the King checked him. And he sat by, with a frightened and sullen face, and could make no answer when King Arthur demanded of him whether he could deny the charge.

Then Lancelot said, 'My Lord King, this creature who calls himself a knight, and a knight of the Round Table, has sought by treachery to bring black dishonour upon my name; therefore, in place of the simple joust which was planned for today, I demand that he shall do battle with me to the uttermost.' Which was to say, to the death, neither man being free to yield himself to the other's mercy if he were defeated in the usual custom of a joust.

'The demand is granted,' said the King.

Then a fresh horse was brought for Sir Lancelot, and he and Sir Meliagraunce drew apart to the far ends of the lists, and turned, and at the trumpet's sounding, set their spears in rest, and came thundering down upon each other. And Sir Lancelot's spear took Sir Meliagraunce in midshield, and hove him backwards over his horse's crupper.

Then as Sir Meliagraunce scrambled to his feet, Sir

Lancelot swung down from his horse; and drawing their swords, they fell to hewing and smiting at each other, until at last Sir Lancelot got in such a blow to the side of his adversary's helm that he went down like a poled ox.

But Sir Meliagraunce scrambled towards Sir Lancelot and clung to his knees, crying, 'Spare my life! I yield me! I cry quarter and yield me to your mercy!'

Then Sir Lancelot did not know what to do, for this was a fight to the uttermost, and he was bound for his honour's sake neither to ask nor to give mercy, but to kill or be killed. Yet his gorge rose at the thought of killing a man grovelling at his feet.

'Get up!' he said. 'Get up and fight, if you would not shame your manhood more than you have done already!'

But the other went on grovelling and clinging and crying out, 'I yield! I yield! Spare my life!'

'*Get up!*' said Sir Lancelot in an agony. 'And I will lay aside my helmet and my shield and my left gauntlet and fight you with my left hand tied behind my back!'

Then Sir Meliagraunce ceased howling, and stumbled to his feet and cried out for all to hear, 'My Lord the King, take heed of this offer, for I will accept it!'

There was a sick silence, and then a murmur of distaste among the watching knights, and the King said to his friend, 'Sir Lancelot, are you set upon this?'

And Sir Lancelot said steadily, 'I never yet went back on my word.'

So the squires came and took his helm and shield, and bound his left arm behind his back; and the two knights stood once more face to face; and a murmur ran round the field at sight of Sir Lancelot standing there bareheaded and shieldless and one-handed, before his fully-armed opponent. Then Sir Meliagraunce swung up his sword, and Sir Lancelot stood as it were drawing him on with his bare head and shieldless left flank; then as the blade came whistling down, he side-slipped and twisted with a silver flash like a leaping salmon, swinging up his own sword Joyeux so that the two clashed and ground together and for a moment hung locked. And then the other blade was beaten aside, and Sir Lancelot's blade took his enemy on the helmet-crest with such force that both the helmet and the head within it were cloven in two, and Sir Meliagraunce fell dead upon the trampled ground.

Then the squires came and bore his body away, leading his horse after it. And while Sir Lancelot stood leaning on his sword and wiping the sweat out of his eyes with the back of his bare hand, the King himself went to him and led him to where Sir Urre lay upon his litter under the alder trees. And he told Sir Lancelot of the knight's wounds, and how they had all failed to heal him.

'And indeed,' said Arthur, 'we had small hope of success, seeing that his wounds may be healed only by the touch of the best knight in Christendom. But now that you are returned to us, the hope rises again within our hearts.'

'In mine also,' said Sir Urre; and his eyes clung to Sir Lancelot's face like the eyes of a sick dog. And his mother and sister were standing by.

'Not me,' said Sir Lancelot, 'this is for the best knight in Christendom. God forbid that I should think to achieve what so many good knights have failed to do!'

'It is for the best knight in Christendom,' the King said gently.

Sir Lancelot shook his head. 'I was, maybe, once.'

'Galahad is dead,' said the King, still more gently. And then, 'See now, you do this thing not out of any pride or presumption, but because your King commands you.'

'Then I must obey the King's command,' said Sir Lancelot. He was weary to the bone, and still rank with the sweat of battle. And he knew that if he tried to do this thing, and failed, he would be shamed before all his fellows of the Round Table. But he knelt down beside the litter, and set his hands together, one bare and the other still mailed, and prayed deep in his own heart where none might hear him save the One to whom he prayed, 'Oh God, make me your servant and your channel for the healing of this sick knight. By your virtue and grace, let him be made whole through me, but never *by* me.'

And then, seeing that he still wore his right-hand gauntlet, he stripped it off, and asked Sir Urre very humbly, 'Will you grant me now that I touch your wounds?'

'In God's name lay your hands upon me,' said Sir Urre.

And Sir Lancelot touched the wounds upon his head. And as he did so, it seemed that something flowed through him, like a wind or a fire or his own heart's blood. And the bleeding ceased beneath his hands, and the edges of the wounds drew together. And then he touched the wounds on Sir Urre's body and again the power and the love flowed through him and the wounds closed; and lastly he took Sir Urre's sword-hand in both of his, and felt it grow whole and strong again between his palms.

And he knew that at long last, with all his sins upon him, God had granted him the miracle he had prayed for all his life.

Sir Urre sat up, and looked about him in great wonder, then got slowly to his feet. And King Arthur and all his knights cried out in joy; and kneeling, bowed their heads and gave thanks to God for His mercy.

But kneeling still beside the empty litter, Sir Lancelot covered his face with his big swordsman's hands, and wept like a little child that has been beaten.

4

THE QUEEN'S CHAMBER

Time went by, and on the surface it seemed still that life stood at summer; but below the surface, the shadows were closing in on Britain. The shining light of Logres shone as high and clear as ever, but as a candle flares before it gutters out.

And more and more Sir Lancelot found himself remembering Sir Tristan, dead these nine years past. Sir Tristan sitting beside the fire in the Great Hall at Camelot, his little harp on his knee, turning the love between himself and Iseult of Cornwall into a harpsong of such piercing sorrow and sweetness that all his listeners wept to hear. For more and more Sir Lancelot's love for Guenever was becoming what Tristan's for Iseult had been, a power that dragged him where it would, as the moon drags the tides to follow it.

And always Sir Agravane and Sir Mordred watched him and the Queen, with hatred in their hearts for both of them and for the King also; the King above all, though they made pretence that all their concern was for his sake.

One evening when another May had come round, and again the cuckoo was calling in the wooded hills about Caerleon where the court was at that time, Sir Gawain and his brothers and their half-brother Mordred were talking together in the chamber high in the North Tower of the castle where Gawain had his quarters. It was a dark, austere room, with no beauty in it save for the flames upon the hearth and the yellowish-white skin of a great snow-bear with chunks of amber for eyes, that lay slung across the low bed-place. The four Orkney brothers were gathered about the hearth, while Mordred stood by the narrow window, a little removed – he never forgot, nor allowed them to forget, that he was no full brother of theirs – and played with a tiny jewelled dagger as though it were a flower between his fingers.

'We have all seen them together,' said Sir Agravane. 'We all know how often they are together, and more closely so when we do not see. The whole court knows of their love for each other; and it is foul shame that we should leave the King unwarned.'

'The King knows!' said Sir Gawain harshly. 'Do you think he is a blind fool?'

Gaheris said, puzzled, 'Then why does he do nothing?'

Sir Gareth said slowly, thinking the thing out as he went along, 'Do you not see? He knows, but he pretends even to himself that he does *not* know, because so long as he does that, he need do nothing to harm the two people he loves best in the world.'

'Well thought out, little brother,' said Gawain, 'but there's more to it than that.'

Sir Agravane said shrilly, 'And meanwhile they bring shame upon the King and our Round Table brotherhood, and upon the whole Kingdom of Logres!'

Sir Gawain kicked a smouldering log on the hearth and watched it burst into flame. 'There are others who do that,' he said, and glared at his brother. 'Leave it, Agravane.'

'You are the eldest of us, you should tell him.'

Rage and helplessness rose in Gawain and almost choked him. He could think of no way out, no way of thrusting back the evil. Even if he were indeed to tell the King – warn him – that would be to do Mordred's work for him, in the end. 'I will have no part in it,' he growled in his throat. His grey-streaked red hair seemed almost to rise like the hackles of an angry hound. 'If you do this, you will tear the Round Table asunder, for you must know that many of the knights will take sides with Sir Lancelot, while others will follow you and Mordred, thinking that in doing that, they stand true to the King – until in your own time you will stand forth against him yourselves. There will be red war, and the end of Logres and all that we have striven for so long. And who will be for the King then?'

'You will be for the King,' said Gareth, 'and I.'

'I also,' said Gaheris, 'and a few more. Most of us old hounds with grey muzzles.'

Sir Mordred spoke for the first time, playing with the dagger. 'Agravane, if you are afraid to come

with me to the King my father, I will go to him
alone.'

'Nay, I go with you,' said Sir Agravane. 'The time
has come when our liege lord must be forced to
know, and to *act!*'

And a sideways, lip-licking glance passed between
him and Mordred.

They turned together and left the room.

The three left by the fire looked after them. 'There
is no more that we can do,' Gawain said. 'God's teeth!
Even if we were to silence them this way – ' he
touched the dagger in his belt – 'their deaths would
force the thing upon Arthur's notice, and so bring
the splitting of the Round Table as surely as their
telling what they have to tell will do. But wae's me,
the darkness comes crowding in, my brothers.'

Mordred and Agravane found the King alone in
his council chamber, sitting in his High Seat with the
dragon-head foreposts and staring at nothing. And
kneeling before him as two just men who loved him
and could bear to see him wronged no longer, they
told him that Lancelot and his Queen were lovers.

The King heard them out in silence. Only his
hands clenched more and more fiercely on the
carved dragon-heads. The thing that he had always
prayed would not happen was happening. He was
being forced to know about his wife and his best
friend; and from that must come not only darkness
for the three of them, but darkness and ruin for the
Kingdom of Logres.

But he would not yield to the darkness without

fighting. When they had done, he rose slowly to his feet, unfurling all his great height like a banner. He had come, as the years went by, to stoop a little under the burden of his own height, as many tall men do; but he did not stoop now. He stood looking down at them as they knelt still at his feet; his nephew and his ill-begotten son.

'Have a care how you make that accusation,' he said. 'For once it is made, one or the other of you must prove it in the Court of Honour, against Sir Lancelot himself. It would not be the first time that he has fought for the Queen's innocence; and let you remember the end of that fight. And remember also the time that he fought Sir Meliagraunce with neither shield nor helmet and one hand bound behind his back, and yet Sir Meliagraunce was carried dead from the field.'

Agravane said with hurried eagerness, 'But if evil-doers are caught in their evildoing, seen by trustworthy witnesses so that the case is proved against them past all doubt, there is no need left for trial by combat.'

And Mordred, his voice smooth as silk of Damascus, put in 'That is the law, my lord father.'

And Arthur felt the trap closing in on him, for all his life he had striven for a world in which people obeyed the laws instead of relying always on the strength of their own sword-hands. He had striven also to make one law for all people, whether they be knight or swineherd or sewing-woman or the Queen herself.

'If you were to ride hunting tomorrow – a two days' hunt with a pitched camp for the night between . . .' Agravane went on.

And the King said quietly, but in a voice that grated in the back of his throat, 'You feel that I should turn my tail and slink away until the foul work is safely done?'

'No such thought was in our minds, my lord father,' said Mordred in the same silken tone. 'But it is only when you are away that Lancelot and the Queen come together. If you refuse, you will be standing of a purpose against the working of *your own law*!'

And Agravane thrust in, 'Do you ride hunting tomorrow and let it be known that you will not return until the day after.' His narrow face flickered with malice. 'So, the Queen will send for her peerless Lancelot, as she has done often enough before. Then we will gather witnesses, and for love of you, that you be no longer shamed, dear Uncle, we will take him in the Queen's chamber, and the thing will be proved.'

'And the Queen will be burned and Lancelot beheaded,' said the King.

Mordred said gently, 'It is the law.'

The King was silent, staring down at the two kneeling before him, while his thoughts raced in his head. They were right, as such rightness went; and there was nothing that he could do. But Gawain? The Orkney brothers were too close-bound in love and hate for their chief to have no awareness of the

565

game they hunted. Surely he would warn Lancelot. 'Dear God,' he prayed in the inmost places of his heart, 'there is nothing that I can do, but grant that Gawain warn Lancelot of the danger!'

Aloud, he said, 'So be it. Gather your trustworthy witnesses, and take Sir Lancelot of the Lake in the Queen's chamber if you find him there – and if you can. I hope, as I have hoped for few things in my life, that he will kill you both, and your witnesses with you! You have my leave to go from my presence.'

So next morning early the King sent for his hounds and horses, and rode hunting with a few companions, leaving word that he would be gone until the evening of the following day. And he bade neither Lancelot nor Gawain to ride with him.

But Sir Gawain could not have ridden on that day's hunting in any case. Ever since the wound that Sir Galahad had given him while they both rode upon the Quest of the Holy Grail, he had suffered at times from woeful pains in his head. At times of stress or sorrow the pain came upon him; and then he would drink to ease it. And so the pain came now, and he felt as though his head must fly in two, and he drank to ease the pain, more than usual because the pain was worse than usual, and fell into a dead sleep. And so he did not warn Sir Lancelot. And Gaheris and Gareth were both with the King's hunting party away in the greenwood chasing the lightfoot deer.

The first day of the King's hunting went by, and at Caerleon, as the warm dusk of early summer stole up from the river meadows, it seemed that shadows of another kind were closing in on the King's castle.

That night, Sir Lancelot sat late in his chamber talking with Sir Bors over a jug of wine. And as they sat, someone passed along the corridor outside the door, a page maybe, and whistling very softly an old tune from the hills of Wales.

Sir Lancelot raised his head to listen, and when the whistler had gone by he got to his feet and wrapped his long furred gown more closely round him, for the castle corridors even on a May night were chilly.

'Finish the wine, my cousin,' he said. 'I go to speak with the Queen.'

Sir Bors said, 'Take my counsel, and do not go tonight.'

'Why not?' demanded Sir Lancelot, his hand already on the latch.

'Because there is a dread on me,' said Bors. 'Because Sir Mordred and Sir Agravane watch you too closely, and it is not good to be watched by those two. Because the King is away this night, and I smell danger . . .'

'Have no fear,' said Sir Lancelot, 'I shall but go and speak with the Queen a little, and come back before you well know that I have gone.'

'Then God speed you,' said Sir Bors, 'and bring you safely and swiftly back indeed.'

And then as Sir Lancelot lifted the door latch, he called him back. And Sir Lancelot checked, half-smiling and half-impatient, 'What now?'

'Take your sword,' said Sir Bors.

Sir Lancelot hesitated a moment then, leaving the door ajar, turned back and took his great sword Joyeux from the carved chest on which it lay. And carrying it under his arm, muffled in the furred folds of his mantle, he went out and through the dark passageways of the castle to the Queen's chamber.

One of Guenever's ladies waited to let him in, then slipped out, closing the great door behind her. And he checked a moment to drop the bar into its wrought-iron socket, which was a thing he had seldom done.

Honey-wax candles burned in the Queen's chamber, and the moonlight slanted in through the high, deep-set windows. And in the mingled apricot-gold of the candles and buttermilk-white of the moon, the Queen stood humming softly and happily to herself, the same tune from her own hills that had sounded outside Sir Lancelot's door, while she poured wine from a silver flagon into the golden cup set with little dark river-pearls that she kept for her most joyous occasions and her best loved people. She looked up when Lancelot came in, and set the flagon down on the top of the beautifully painted chest below the window; and stood holding the cup and smiling at him as he came towards her.

The mingled light fell on her hair, which was unbraided and lying loosely on her shoulders. Guenever's hair was not like Lancelot's, that had turned grey at the time of his wild-wood sickness when he was but twenty-six years old; nor like Arthur's which looked as though he had raked ashy

568

fingers through the mouse-fairness of it. But single white threads shone here and there among the rest that was as black as ever it had been.

'Come and sit you, and drink,' she said.

He came, and they shared the cup between them; and sat, she in her great cushioned chair and he on the end of the painted chest, linking together their little fingers in the way of a young squire and his maiden, and talking quietly, content for a while just to be in each other's company, for they had been lovers so long that at times they were like an old wedded couple.

But they had been only a short while together when there came a jangling tramp of mailed feet outside, and a savage beating on the door, and the voices of Sir Mordred and Sir Agravane and of others behind them, shouting for all the court to hear, 'Sir Lancelot! Traitor knight! Now are you caught in your treachery!'

Lancelot and Guenever sprang to their feet. 'Alas,' whispered the Queen, 'now we are both betrayed!'

Lancelot looked hurriedly about him. 'Those are armed men outside. Is there any of the King's armour here in your chamber? If so, they shall have a fight to remember!'

The Queen shook her head. 'I have no armour here, nor any weapon. So now do I fear our long love is come to a bitter end.'

'Nay, for I have Joyeux,' said Lancelot. And with the uproar still going on like hounds baying for the kill beyond the door, he caught her into his arms and kissed her once, quick and hard. 'As I was ever your true knight, pray for my soul if I be slain.' Then flinging off his thick mantle he wound it round his left arm to serve for a shield, and drew his sword and turned to the door.

By now the men outside had brought a heavy bench from the Hall to serve as a ram, and the stout timbers were shuddering beneath its blows. 'Cease this tumult,' he shouted, 'and I will come out!' But to the Queen he whispered, 'When I have the door shut again, do you put up the bar, for I shall not be able to hold it long, and my hands will be full with other matters.'

Then, as for the moment the makeshift ram ceased its crashing, he took his stand just behind the door, setting his left foot behind it so that it might open no further than to let one man through; and sword in hand, he flung back the bar. The door flew back against his foot, and Sir Agravane shot through the opening; and Sir Lancelot forced the door shut and stood braced against it, while the Queen in frantic haste thrust home the bar in the face of the knights outside.

Agravane whirled about with a cry, and aimed a great blow at Lancelot; but Lancelot side-sprang, light without his armour, and took only the glance of it on his muffled left arm; and before his enemy could recover, dealt him a blow to the side of the neck that felled him on the instant, his head half off his shoulders.

'Now help me with all speed!' said Sir Lancelot;

and while the door leapt and juddered against its bar, and the baying from outside broke forth afresh, 'Traitor knight! Come out from the Queen's chamber!' the high voice of Sir Mordred rising over all, he and the Queen with frantic speed stripped off the dead knight's armour and Sir Lancelot dragged on such of it as was of most use and most quickly donned, the ringmail shirt and the helmet, and caught up Sir Agravane's shield.

'Come out and face us! Out, Sir Traitor!'

'Cease your uproar! I am coming!' shouted back Sir Lancelot. 'And as for you, Sir Mordred, my counsel is that you run far and fast before I come!'

And dragging back the bar, he flung open the door and strode out among them. Then, in the narrow passageway and at the stairhead across from the Queen's door, there was the clash and flash of weapons, half seen where the taperlight gleamed from the Queen's chamber into the dark; and man after man went down before the onslaught of Sir Lancelot of the Lake, tripping each other's trampling feet in the corridor, or pitching backward down the stair, until at last all twelve of those who had followed Sir Mordred and Sir Agravane lay dead as Sir Agravane lay within the Queen's chamber; and Sir Mordred with an arm dripping blood had fled away from the fighting into the night.

Then Sir Lancelot turned back into Guenever's chamber, where she stood like a queen carved in stone for laying on a tomb.

'Come with me,' he said.

But she answered, scarce moving even her white lips, 'No. I am the King's wife, I must stay and bear the Queen's part. Enough of evil has been done this night.'

Sir Lancelot stood for a moment more, breathing heavily and dabbing at a gash on his wrist, his gaze on Guenever's face. Then he said, 'It must be for you to choose. If danger comes to you out of this, remember that Bors and Lional and my brother Ector will stand your friends. And if I live, I shall be back.'

And he stumbled out into the dark, through the shambles beyond the door.

He managed to regain his own chamber unseen, and found Bors still waiting for him.

'Did I not warn you?' said Sir Bors, as soon as he realised who it was in Sir Agravane's harness.

It was in Sir Lancelot's heart to say, 'Yes. And you were right, always you are right; it is one of the least likeable things about you.' But there was no time. In as few words as might be, he told what had happened, while he snatched up his own helm and shield in place of those he bore. 'Do you and Lional and Ector stand friends to the Queen until I return,' he said, buckling on Joyeux. 'No harm can come to her under the law for seven clear days; and if I live, I will be back before then.'

'Where do you ride?' asked Bors.

'To Joyous Gard,' said Sir Lancelot, 'to gather my own men.'

They looked at each other, a long, bleak look, and so parted.

*

That night two men rode through the moonlit dark as though the Wild Hunt were after them. One was Sir Lancelot, taking the familiar tracks northward through the Welsh hills to Joyous Gard; and the other was Sir Mordred, with an arm swaddled in blood-stained linen, making for the King's hunting camp.

It was at the grey cock-light of dawning when Mordred reached the camp, and the King was already up and sitting on a tree-trunk with his head in his hands, his eyes red-rimmed in the haggard face of a man who had not slept all night.

When Sir Mordred half fell from his horse and came and stood before him, he looked up, and seeing the bloodstained linen and the grey face lit by pale eyes that blazed with malice, said wearily, 'So you found him, in the Queen's chamber.'

'There we found him,' said Sir Mordred. And he told the King from beginning to end of Sir Agravane's death and the fight outside the Queen's door.

'Did I not say that Sir Lancelot was a matchless knight?' said the King. 'Grief upon me that now he is my enemy, after the long years that he has been my dearest friend. Now the Round Table is broken apart for all time, for many of my best knights will hold to him in this matter. Now also, the Queen must die. I should be grateful to you, son Mordred, for the tender care that you have taken of my honour.'

And he bent his face again into his hands, and rocked himself as one in sorest pain; then sprang to his feet and shouted for his horse and his gear, and for the camp to be broken, for they were riding at once for Caerleon.

And so, at Caerleon, before the gathered council of his knights, in the presence of the Archbishop, and with clerks to write all down, it was ordained according to the law that Sir Lancelot should be beheaded if he were taken, and the Queen should be burned at the stake, for their unlawful love and for the deaths of Sir Agravane and the twelve knights.

Sir Gawain sought by all means in his power to gain mercy for them, but all to no avail.

'Do not you be over-hasty in this,' said Sir Gawain, with his head still ringing with the effects of the drink and the old wound. 'For though indeed Lancelot was found in the Queen's chamber, why should it not be as the Queen herself swears – that she bethought her suddenly that she had never thanked him truly for her rescue at his hands from Sir Meliagraunce, and so sent for him to make that matter good?'

'After a year?' said the King, looking straightly at his nephew. And it seemed that deep within him something was crying out, 'Why did you not warn them? In sweet Jesus's name could you not have warned them?' But aloud, he said only 'Nay, they must suffer as the law decrees.'

'Then at least leave the sentence a while before it is carried out.'

'Until the seventh morning after it was passed,' said

the King. 'And not a morning longer. That is for the Queen; and for Lancelot, whenever he be captured.'

But the truth was that he dared wait no longer, lest he weaken, and so bring to nothing the rule of law that he had fought all his life to establish in Britain.

'Then God grant that I be not by to see it,' said Sir Gawain.

'Why so?' said the King. 'What cause have you now to love Sir Lancelot or the Queen? For her sake he slew your brother Agravane.'

'Often enough I warned my brother Agravane,' said Sir Gawain, standing hunched and stubborn as an ox in the furrow. 'For well I knew what his ways would bring him to in the end. Moreover, they took Sir Lancelot fourteen against one, which is no fair fight. I will take up no blood feud for Agravane.'

But the King let the sentence stand.

And the days went by until it was the eve of the Queen's appointed death-day.

And then the King sent for Gawain to the Great Chamber high above the keep, where he was pacing up and down like a caged beast, and bade him make ready his finest armour, to take command next day of the escort that should bring Queen Guenever to the fire. 'For after Sir Lancelot, you are the Captain of the Round Table, and the thing is for you to do,' said he.

'Yet I will not do it, my uncle and my Lord King,' said Sir Gawain, 'for I will not stand to see her die, nor will I have it ever said that I was with you in your council for her death.'

And looking at him, the King knew that Sir Gawain would die himself before he changed from that. So he sent for Gaheris and Gareth and gave them the same commands. 'Do you both take command of the escort, and between you see the Queen securely guarded lest Sir Lancelot come to attempt her rescue.' For an innermost voice within him said, 'Surely Lancelot will save her, even now,' while another said, 'Yet that must not be, for if he rescue her and carry her away, and live, then indeed there will be civil war in Britain!' And between the two, it seemed to him that he was being torn asunder.

The two younger knights looked at him in horror; and Gareth said, 'Sir Lancelot knighted me!'

And Gaheris said, 'He saved me from Sir Tarquine, and always he has stood as a friend to me!'

'Nevertheless, you shall obey the orders of your king,' said Arthur, and his voice grated in his throat.

They stood rigid before him, and Gareth was greywhite, as though he himself were being ordered to the stake. But they had sworn fealty to the High King, and the habit of obedience and discipline was stronger in them than ever it had been in Gawain. And at last Gareth said, 'If that is your last word, then we must obey your orders, my liege lord, but we will not take up arms against Sir Lancelot, but go forth unarmed and in robes of mourning that the Queen may know to the end our love towards her.'

'I am with my brother in this,' said Sir Gaheris.

'In the name of God then, make you ready, and go forth in whatever guise you choose,' cried the King.

And Sir Gawain with the tears trickling into his red beard, said 'Grief upon me, that I was born to see this day!' And he turned and stumbled away to his chamber, his two brothers following.

And the King returned to his caged pacing up and down.

Next morning the Queen was led forth to the open space beyond the castle walls, where the stake waited for her with brushwood piled around its foot. And her queenly garments were stripped from her so that she stood up only in her white shift. And a priest was brought to confess her that she might be shriven of her sins. And then she was led towards the stake, and lifted up upon the pyre, and bound there above the heads of the people. And all the crowd who had gathered there in sorrow or in triumph fell back, so that only her escort remained near at hand; and the two figures in their darkly hooded cloaks of Sir Gaheris and Sir Gareth.

And the King stood watching from the high window in the keep, as rigid as though he too were bound to a stake. And he never saw the blink of light three times repeated from the tower of the old church opposite, in the instant that the Queen was brought out from the castle; for all his gaze was fixed upon the open space below.

A great quiet had fallen over the crowd, and the executioner's torch was already lit. And the King was listening for something, listening with an aching intensity that seemed to hold his very heart in check. And then he heard it – the drum of horses' hooves, far in the distance but sweeping nearer at full gallop.

Riding day and night, with many changes of horse along the way, Sir Lancelot was back from Joyous Gard, with his own fighting men behind him. Everybody knew that it was Sir Lancelot; the youngest weeping page and the executioner pausing, torch in hand, the High King in his window, and the Queen bound to her stake. They knew, even before the bright arrowhead of horsemen burst out from the narrow ways between the houses into the crowded square. He and his men had lain up in the woods overnight, while one of their number in an all-concealing cloak had entered the town and kept watch in the church tower, to signal with the sunlight on his shield the moment when the Queen was brought out clear of the castle walls.

The mailed arrowhead of horsemen drove into the crowd and through it, the early sunlight jinking on their weapons and harness; and the shouts and cries and weapon-clash and the trampling of horses' hooves came up in a surf-roar of sound to the King in his high window; and below him the fight swirled about the pyre, small with distance but terrible. The executioner's torch had gone down, to be trampled out beneath the horses' hooves. He saw Lancelot's blade rise and fall in desperate, slashing strokes, as he forced his tall destrier through to the pyre, and again the flash of Joyeaux's blade, this time slashing through the cords that bound Guenever to the stake. Far below, he saw the Queen hold out her white arms to her love, as Sir Lancelot reached from the saddle to fling a dark cloak around her. How like Lancelot, he thought, to remember that she would be stripped to her shift, and bring a woman's cloak with him. Next instant he had caught her from her footing among the piled brushwood and dragged her across his saddlebow. Then, holding her close, swung his horse round and with his own men closing all about him, was fighting his way out.

And then it was over, and the hoof-beats drumming away into the distance, no man following. And in the square below the castle walls the crowd were in a turmoil, and round the unlit pyre men lay dead on the stained and trampled ground. And still the High King stood as though captive in his window, torn between despair for what he knew must now come to Britain, even as Merlin had foretold, and a sick relief that Lancelot had saved the Queen.

A strange blackness came between him and the scene down in the square, between him and all the world, so that for a while he saw nothing more. But when the world came back to him again, he was still standing in the window, but holding to the deep stone transom, his forehead pressed down against his hand. And hurrying footsteps were blundering up the stair and into the chamber. He straightened himself from the window and turned, and found Sir Gawain standing before him, staring at him with blazing eyes in a terrible grey face.

Gawain said, choking on the words, 'He has killed Gareth and Gaheris!'

'Who?' said Arthur. His head felt numb and would not think.

'Sir Lancelot! He has killed Gareth and Gaheris! They are lying down there by the scaffold with their heads split open.'

The King shook his own head. He could not believe it; it must be that there was some mistake. 'Not Gareth. Not Gaheris either. He loved Gareth best of all the Round Table after you – and me.'

'They are lying down there with their heads split open,' Gawain repeated; and it was as though he must fight to get enough breath to speak the words. 'Lancelot killed them unarmed.'

'Unarmed,' the King said quickly, 'and in those grey-hooded cloaks. He would have had no means of knowing them.'

'Gareth was by half a head the tallest of your knights!' said Sir Gawain. 'By his height alone, no man could have failed to know him . . . I would not take up the blood feud for Agravane, but I take it up now for Gaheris and for Gareth. And I will not be laying it down again so long as the life is in me – or in Sir Lancelot of the Lake!'

And he flung himself down on a bench, his head in his arms, and wept gaspingly and agonisingly for the the death of his brothers; and for the old love between himself and Lancelot that was now turned to hate.

And standing unnoticed in a corner, gentling his

arm in its sling, Sir Mordred, who had come up behind Sir Gawain, smiled like one well content with the skilled work of his hands.

5

TWO CASTLES

Sir Lancelot carried the Queen away through the mountains to his own castle of Joyous Gard. And there he lodged her with all honour, as befitted Arthur's Queen.

And at Joyous Gard there gathered to him Sir Ector of the Marsh, his half-brother, and his kinsmen, Sir Bors and Sir Lional, and many more, upward half of of the Round Table, both for his sake and the Queen's.

And King Arthur would fain have let all things rest a while, that hot blood might have space to cool, and time might sort out the good from the evil. But those knights who were still of his following, Sir Gawain foremost among them, were at him night and day, that Sir Lancelot was his enemy and had carried off his Queen, and he should make war upon him as he would upon any other foe within his borders. And so at last the High King sent out the summons to all his warhost; and marched upon Joyous Gard.

Sir Lancelot had word of their coming, and knew that it was Sir Gawain more than the King who was against him; for Sir Bors and the rest had told him of how he had slain Sir Gaheris and Sir Gareth, and warned him of what must follow. That had made bitter hearing, for he would have hacked off his own right hand before he knowingly did harm to either of them. But the *mêlée* about the stake had been too fierce to leave time for singling out two unarmed men among the surging press of knights and men-at-arms, nor for choosing where his sword-strokes landed, nor for noticing that one dark-hooded figure was taller than all the rest about the stake. He had had no time or thought for anything but cutting his way through to save the Queen. But truly, after Gawain and the King, he loved Gareth best of all the Round Table brotherhood; and his heart seemed bleeding within him for their deaths at his hand. Now there was blood feud between him and Sir Gawain, and grief for that tore at him also. But there was no time for bewailing what had come to pass, with the King's war-host marching north against him.

So he gathered his fighting men and called in all the folk of the valley and the village beyond the gates, and their cattle with them, and penned all safe within the castle walls, and made ready in all ways that were possible. And the King came and pitched his war-camp below the walls of Joyous Gard, so that all the valley round about was fluttering with the pennants of his nobles and their knights. And he laid siege to Joyous Gard.

For fifteen weeks the siege dragged on, while the summer passed, and the fields along the valley floor were white with barley and golden with wheat, and the great ox-wagons should have been bringing in the sheaves that the horses of the King's war-host trampled down. But the castle was strong and well-garrisoned and still well-supplied, and at the end of that time it was no nearer to falling than it had been on the first day.

And then on a day towards the edge of autumn, Sir Lancelot spoke from the ramparts with the King and Sir Gawain sitting their great warhorses below him in the open stretch between the walls and the camp.

'My lords both,' said Sir Lancelot, 'you will gain no honour in this siege. You have sat here long and long, but you will not take Joyous Gard.'

'And you will gain no honour skulking behind castle walls,' flung back the King. 'Do you come out and meet me in single combat, that we may end this matter. I swear that no other shall be with me.'

This was the thing of all others that Sir Lancelot had dreaded, and the chief reason why he had held back so long. 'God forbid,' he said, 'that I should encounter with the most noble king in Christendom, and he my liege lord from whose hands I received my knighthood.'

'Out upon your fair language!' cried the King, beside himself with grief that he could only bear by turning it into anger. 'Know this, and believe it, that I am your enemy and always shall be; for you have slain my knights and borne away my Queen, and broken asunder the brotherhood of the Round Table and the Kingdom of Logres.'

'The slaying of your knights, alas, I cannot deny,' returned Sir Lancelot, 'and among them those that were dear friends to me, for which the grief will be upon me all my days. But it was done in the saving of the life of your Queen, whom you condemned to the fire. From that fire it was, and not from you, that I bore the Queen away, as I have saved her from other dangers before now, and received thanks from both of you.' And he leaned further out over the parapet and demanded, 'My Lord King, look in your heart – would you indeed have had her burn?'

'Shut your treacherous mouth!' shouted Sir Gawain, half-mad with fury, before the King could answer. 'Have done with this twisting of the truth; for all men know the shame of what lies between you and the Queen!'

Lancelot answered him in a lion's roar. 'Do you accuse the Queen, then?'

'Nay, I speak no word against the Queen. On you lies the guilt, the false treachery to your liege lord – '

'That is well for you,' Sir Lancelot flung back at him, 'for I will fight for the Queen's innocence as I have done before, against any man save the King. And if I come out against you, Sir Gawain, beware of my coming!'

And he turned and strode away down the rampart stair, with a parting insult from the man who had so long been his friend, ringing in his ears.

And the King, with Lancelot's question 'Would you indeed have had her burn?' sounding still in his own heart, wheeled his horse and rode back to the royal camp in silence, with Sir Gawain cursing and half-sobbing beside him.

*

Within the castle, Sir Bors and Sir Lional and Sir Ector and the rest came to Lancelot and said, 'It is time for fighting! We who love you know that it is for love of the King that you have remained so long behind these walls, hoping for peace between you. But the King will make no peace with you; not while Sir Gawain stands at his shoulder. And to bide longer within walls after the insults that have been flung at you this day will look like fear to men who do not know you as we do. Fight now, for your right and your honour, and we are your men!'

And Lancelot knew that they spoke truth; and knew also, that with the harvest lying wrecked and ungathered, the stores within the castle must soon be sinking low.

So next morning the gates and sally-ports of the castle were flung open, and with trumpets sounding and spear-head pennants fluttering many-coloured over all, Sir Lancelot led out his knights and squires and men-at-arms to the fight.

Then from the King's camp the trumpets crowed in reply, as fighting-cocks send their challenge one to another at dawn. And the King and his knights rode out to meet them; and the two companies rolled together like two great waves, and crashed upon each other; and all the open land below the castle was a'swirl and a'trample with battle, and the end-of-summer dust-cloud rising and billowing over all.

The whole day they fought. And in the thick of the fighting Sir Gawain, seeking Sir Lancelot, came up against Sir Lional across his way, and ran him through the body so that he dropped dead from the saddle. And Sir Bors, seeing what befell, and charging to avenge his brother, hacked down Sir Gawain, and then came shield to shield with Arthur himself. For a few straining and sweating moments they grappled together, their swords locked at the hilt, like the still centre at the heart of a whirlpool, among the surge of men and horses all about them; and then Sir Bors broke his blade free, and fetched the King a blow that pitched him down into the bloody dust under the trampling hooves of the battle. Sir Bors, plunging out of the saddle, stood over him with drawn sword, and a little gap opened as the fighting shifted, and Sir Lancelot was there.

Sir Bors shouted to him, 'Shall I make an end to this war?'

'Not in *that* way, unless you would lose your own head,' said Sir Lancelot grimly. 'For I will not see my liege lord either slain or shamed while I stand by!'

And he dismounted also, while Sir Bors, still sword in hand, stood back; and he helped the King to his feet again, and mounted him from his own knee back into the saddle of his snorting and trampling horse.

'My most dear lord,' he said, 'for Christ's sweet sake let us end this strife. Take back your Queen – so that you take her with love and honour, letting no more harm come to her. And I will cross the Narrow Seas to Benwick, and return no more, unless the time comes that you have need of me.'

'The law – ' said the King, drooping in his saddle.

'The Queen is not above the law – but must be as any poor woman – '

'And that you have proved. But mercy is above the law. Can you not give her your mercy, as you might give it to any poor woman?'

And the King looked down into the ugly, haggard face of the knight standing at his stirrup, and the love that he had had for him and for Guenever the Queen swelled within him until it seemed that his heart must burst through his rib-cage. And he said, 'Bring the Queen to me in tomorrow's morning, and she shall have all honour, and her place beside me again, and my love as she has had it all these years.'

And Sir Gawain had been carried from the field to have his wounds tended; so the truce was made, and the two armies drew apart.

A little later, straight from the battle and without waiting to disarm and wash off the sweat and the blood as at other times he would have done, Sir Lancelot went to the Queen in her chamber.

'Is the fighting over?' she asked; for she had not dared to climb the keep stair and watch, for dread of what she would see.

'The fighting is over. It *must* be over,' said Sir Lancelot heavily. 'Gawain has killed Lional – and many other good knights are slain. And for my sake Bors would have slain the King, if I had not stayed him.'

And the Queen looked into his face, and at what she saw there she gave a low cry and held out her arms to him.

But he drew away. 'Nay, I am still foul from the battle-field.'

'What have you really come to tell me?' she asked; and gestured her women from the room.

And Lancelot told her what had passed between himself and the High King.

She heard him through in silence; and when he had done, she said, 'The glove for me and the sword for you. Do you remember Tristan and Iseult?' And then she said, 'How if I will not go back?'

'You must go back,' said Sir Lancelot. 'Did I not tell you, Sir Bors would have slain the King for our sakes? If you return to him and take your old place, and if I go back to Benwick, then it may be that the wound that splits the Round Table apart and threatens all Logres will heal.'

'And we shall never see each other again,' said Guenever.

'And we shall never see each other again,' said Lancelot.

'God help us both,' said the Queen. 'For we shall surely need it.' And she pressed close to him, heedless of his battle-foulness and the harshness of his war-gear through the thin stuff of her gown. And she took his strange face between her hands and kissed him, once on the forehead and once on the mouth, and turned away to let him go.

Next morning early, the gates of Joyous Gard were opened wide, and Sir Lancelot, all unarmed and leading the Queen by the hand, came out. And behind him all his knights, unarmed likewise and bearing green truce-branches robbed from the castle garden. And so he led her to the King where he stood, his own nobles behind him, under an ancient hawthorn tree in the midst of the camp.

Then Sir Lancelot and the Queen knelt before the High King, and Sir Lancelot said in a loud clear voice for all to hear, 'My liege lord the High King, I bring here to you the Lady Guenever, your Queen. Mine alone is the blame if aught has been between us that should not have been; for she is as true to you as ever was lady to her lord; and if any knight dare to say otherwise, I stand ready to prove her innocence in single combat to the death!'

As he finished speaking, his gaze seemed drawn past the King, and for a moment it caught and locked with the pale gaze of Sir Mordred, who stood with a cluster of young knights a little to one side. And in that moment Sir Mordred smiled. His small silken smile made the gorge rise in Sir Lancelot's throat. But he spoke no word, and the King's son only went on playing with the late blood-red corn poppy between his fingers.

It was Sir Gawain who spoke first; grey-faced and red-eyed, with a bloody clout round his shoulder. 'I have said it before; I speak no word against the Queen. The King must do as he chooses in this. But between you and me, for my two brothers' sake, there is blood feud, and I am your enemy while the breath is in my body – or in yours.'

And the King stooped, still speaking no word, for

at that moment he could not, and lifted the Queen to her feet.

Lancelot rose, and stood before his king, his head up, and his hands clenched under the folds of his cloak. 'And now, my Lord the King, I take my leave of you, and of this land where I gained my knighthood and all that ever I have had of honour. I am for the south coast, and my own lands of Benwick across the Narrow Seas.'

'You have fifteen days,' said King Arthur.

And Lancelot said, 'The King is generous. It was only three that King Marc of Cornwall gave to Sir Tristan in like case.'

And in the minds of both of them was the old sorrowful story told by Sir Tristan himself beside the fire in the Great Hall at Camelot on that wild All Hallows' Eve so long ago. And they could have wept each on the other's neck.

Again it was Gawain who broke the silence. 'Wherever you go, see that your sword sits loose in its sheath, for I swear that I will come after you!'

'No,' Lancelot said, 'do not swear, do not come after me. For God's sake, do not hound the King into coming after me. Let the war end and its wounds heal over.'

Then he turned to Guenever, who stood white and watching at the King's side; and said clearly and proudly and again for all to hear, 'Madam, now I must leave you and my fellows of the Round Table for ever. Pray for me in the years to come, and if ever you have need of one to fight for you, send me word, and if I yet live, I will come.'

Gravely and distantly, he kissed her hand; then turned away, leaving her with the King.

He did not look back, nor did she follow him with her eyes, though it seemed that this was the last time that they should see each other in the world of men.

Indeed, there was to be one time more, but there would be little of joy in that meeting, for either of them.

So Sir Lancelot rode south through dust-dark forests beginning to flame with autumn, until he came to the coast. And there he took ship across the Narrow Seas, and so returned to Benwick and his own people. But he did not go quite alone. Most of the knights who had gathered to him at Joyous Gard returned to King Arthur's court and their old allegiance; but his half-brother Sir Ector of the Marsh, and his kinsman Sir Bors and a handful more, headed by old Sir Bleoberis who had been King Utha Pendragon's standard-bearer when he and the world were young, went with him or followed after. And in Benwick the knights and lords of his own following gladly welcomed him back.

The autumn and the winter passed, and for a while it seemed that there was peace in Britain. But Sir Gawain never for a breath of time forgot or forgave the death of his brothers; and day and night he urged the King to gather his forces and go after Sir Lancelot and finish the war indeed.

'For it was never truly ended,' said he, 'but only broken off midway. And so long as Lancelot sits lordly in his own domains, there will be knights to slip away to him whenever any ruling of yours displeases them.'

'Remember Sir Bors and Sir Ector, and others beside, are with him even now,' said Mordred gently and regretfully. 'And he has his own knights to gather to him also.' And he spoke of rumours that Sir Lancelot was gathering a war-host. And once it was gathered, what should it be used for, save for making war on his liege lord? And if ever Sir Gawain showed any sign that his wrath was cooling, Mordred would drip a little more poison into his heart to make the wound break out afresh. And the King was no more the man he had been. Something of his strength was gone, and of his faith in himself and his own judgement. Something seemed broken within him; maybe it was his heart. And so he listened to Sir Gawain whom he loved, and to Sir Mordred whom he tried not to hate, when he should have listened to the voice within himself. And when the year turned again to spring, he began gathering his war-host; and the land rang with the sound of armourers' hammers; and ships were made ready and lying in south coast harbours, waiting to ferry men and horses across the Narrow Seas.

And when the seafaring weather of early summer came, Arthur led his war-host across to Benwick, to carry forward the war against Sir Lancelot to its bitter end.

And behind him he left Sir Mordred to govern the kingdom during his absence, and to protect the Queen. His loyal knights were aghast at his decision, and full of dread. But the King had a sense of Fate upon him. He knew deep within himself that the pattern was almost finished; and the doom upon himself and all that he had fought for, which he had unleashed when he fathered Mordred on his own half-sister, was hard upon him; and maybe he would hold out his arms to it rather than seek to fend it off, seeing that there was no escape. No escape from the doom, no escape from the ordained end of the pattern . . .

'He is my son,' he said, 'he has something of my own gift for leading men. And there is no one else.'

So then, the High King left his son behind him and took his war-host across the Narrow Seas, and led them through the lands of Benwick until they reached its great castle. And they made their camp before the castle and laid siege to it, as they had done to Joyous Gard.

Then the knights who were with Sir Lancelot begged him to lead them out at once, to give battle. 'For we were bred and trained up for honourable fighting,' said they, 'not for cowering behind castle walls.'

'First I will send word to the King under the green branch,' said Sir Lancelot, 'for still I am bitter loath to fight my liege lord; and peace is always better than war.'

And he sent a maiden mounted on a white palfrey with a branch of green willow in her hands into the King's camp, to see whether peace might not be made once more between them.

But with Sir Gawain beside him, the King would not listen to her plea; and so the maiden returned weeping to Sir Lancelot.

And scarcely had she told of her failure, than Sir Gawain, mounted on his proudest warhorse and with a mighty spear in his hand, was before the main gate shouting, 'Sir Lancelot of the Lake! Is there none of your proud knights dares break spear with me?'

'I claim first spear in answer to that!' said Sir Bors. And he made ready and rode out to encounter Sir Gawain; and when they set their spears in rest and charged together, Sir Bors was unhorsed at the first shock and sorely hurt, and must have been lost, but that a band of knights charged out to his rescue and carried him back into the castle.

And next day Sir Gawain came again, and this time Sir Ector answered his challenge; and he also was felled, and borne back by his rescuers within the gates.

And the siege lasted many months, and again and again Sir Gawain came with his challenge. And it seemed that no champion could stand against him; for every knight who rode out in answer to his challenge he slew or wounded, and took no scathe himself. And then one day, sear and chill on the very edge of winter, Sir Gawain came yet again, and cried out, his great voice rough and echoing within his helmet, 'Are you listening, Sir Lancelot, traitor and coward? Or have you hidden your head beneath the pillows? Come out now and give me combat, or carry the shame for ever! For here I wait to take my vengeance for the death of my brothers!'

And Sir Lancelot could bear it no longer; and he bade his squires to harness and bring round his best horse, and he rode out to answer Sir Gawain's challenge. 'God knows it is with a heavy heart I join battle with you, Sir Gawain, both for the old friendship between us and because you are blood-kin to the High King, but you drive me to it, so now must I turn upon you as a boar turns at bay!'

'This is no more the time for words,' said Sir Gawain. 'Now you shall give me satisfaction for my brothers' slaying; and there shall be no breaking-off between us while the life remains in us both.'

Then they drew their horses far apart, and turning, couched their lances, struck in their spurs and came thundering down upon each other, while from the King's camp and the walls of Benwick Castle men looked on with the breath caught in their throats. They came together with such a rending crash that both horses and riders were brought down in a struggling tangle. The champions rolled clear of their horses and stumbled to their feet, drawing their swords, and fell to, thrusting and smiting and foining until their armour was hacked and dinted, and their blood ran down to spatter the trampled grass like the small crimson flowers that the people in eastern lands used to call the Tears of Tammuz.

And at last Sir Lancelot fetched Sir Gawain such a blow on the helmet that the blade bit through and made a great wound in his head beneath, in the place where the old wound had been, so that he might not rise again. And Sir Lancelot drew aside and stood gasping for breath and leaning on his sword.

And Sir Gawain cried out to him in an agony, 'Now slay on! For I swear that when I am whole I shall do battle with you again!'

'That must be as it will,' said Sir Lancelot, 'but I never yet slew a felled and wounded knight in cold blood; and sweet Jesu knows the blood is cold within me this day!'

And he turned and limped wearily away, while men from the royal camp came out and bore Sir Gawain, still raving, back to the King's pavilion, where the King's own physician Morgan Tudd waited to salve his wounds.

And the siege dragged on, and the wild geese came down from the North to winter in the marshes nearby and there was ice along the edges of the tracks. And so soon as Sir Gawain could sit firm upon his horse he was back at the gates of Benwick Castle, crying like a madman for Sir Lancelot to come out to him. 'For the last time we fought, by some mischance I had sore hurt at your hands, so now I come to take my revenge, and lay you as low as last time you laid me!'

'Now God forbid,' said Lancelot to his knights,

'for then I think that my time would be short indeed!'

But he called for his horse, and rode out. And again they fought, and again after long and desperate struggle, the battle ended as it had done before; and by evil chance the final blow of Sir Lancelot's sword fell yet again upon the selfsame place as the old wound. And Sir Lancelot, walking with a sick heart back towards his castle gates and his knights assembled there, heard behind him a terrible sobbing and gasping voice that cried after him, 'Traitor knight! Traitor knight! When I am whole again . . .' and then ceased as Sir Gawain sank into a deep swoon, and the men from the King's camp bore him away like one that is dead.

Sir Gawain lay for many days near to death and raving, while the siege dragged on through the chill and sodden winter, and the King's men endured as best they could under canvas or in the wrecked and empty town. And it was the edge of spring, with the days lengthening and the first catkins showing yellow on the hazel thickets, before Sir Gawain could sit on his horse once more. But as soon as he could bear spear and shield, his first thought was to ride out and challenge Sir Lancelot yet again; for now he seemed to have no room in his poor wounded head for any thought except this one.

But on the very eve of the day when he would have ridden out again, despite all that the King or his fellow knights could say to hold him back, news came from Britain that ended the siege.

6

THE USURPER

Left to govern Britain while the flower of the Round Table fellowship slew each other beyond the Narrow Seas, Sir Mordred was soon about the next part of his plans. His gift for setting fashions had become the gift for leading men, which his father the High King had known that he possessed. Already he had his following among the younger knights, and as the summer passed and turned to autumn, and then the winter went by, others who had never truly been Arthur's men gathered to him at Camelot; and the men of the North and beyond the Irish Sea began to creep back, sending in their leaders to speak with him behind closed doors, drawn by rumours of easier terms and a looser rule than ever they had had from Arthur Pendragon. Word began to go round too – no man knowing who started it – that if Mordred and not Arthur were King, the taxes that they had to pay for the safe-keeping of the realm would somehow be lighter, and the strong laws that he had made would be slackened. Men began to prick their ears, and those who were still true to the High King in their hearts were uneasy and bewildered, not knowing what they were supposed to do. And the whole realm began to grow unsure.

Guenever knew a little of what was going on, but she kept herself close in the women's quarters these days, rather than mingle with the new company at court; and she prayed with a heart full of dread for Arthur's return and for peace between the sundered halves of the Round Table, and that Arthur's return might not mean that Lancelot was slain.

The feast of Candlemas went by, and there were snowdrops in the castle's high-walled garden, and then the first short-stemmed primroses along the river banks below the town. And a day came; a grey shivering day that had none of the hope of spring in it, but a little moaning uneasy wind that made strange whisperings along the corridors and stirred the tapestries on the walls of the Queen's bower, where she sat at her embroidery with one of her favourite maidens.

When she was young she had worked fair and light-hearted things with her needle; a unicorn, milk-white on a background sprinkled thick with pinks and heartsease pansies, with birds and butter-flies among the leaves overhead. And later she had worked the proud red dragon of Britain upon golden damask, to make a shield-case for the High King. Now she was working angels with spread wings upon an altar hanging for the castle chapel. She had not the gift of prayer. Though she prayed long and often in these days, she knew that her prayers never truly took wing; so she embroidered the angels with their spread wings of gold and crimson and violet, with some half-hope that they might carry her prayers upward; or even that God might accept them as another kind of prayer. 'See, I am doing this for you. You who can do all things, pray you save Arthur – pray you save Lancelot – pray you save Britain from the dark.'

It was drawing in towards evening; soon it would be time for the pages to bring the honey-wax tapers. She could scarcely see to set the fine stitches any longer. She turned her embroidery frame to catch the last fading daylight from the western window. And as she did so, she was suddenly aware of distant sounds under the little uneasy wind; a flurry of startled voices; footsteps below in the courtyard. Somewhere a woman cried out, 'Now God save us!'

She set aside her frame and rose, spilling bright silks from her lap, and looked out of the window. Below in the inner courtyard people were gathering. She saw how they gathered in little knots, speaking together and yet seeming lost and unknowing of what to do with themselves; here and there one glanced up towards her window, and she saw their faces stunned-looking in the fading daylight, and suddenly she was cold afraid.

'Nesta,' she said, 'do you go down to the inner court and ask if word has come from Benwick. It is in my heart that something is amiss.'

And the maiden Nesta went out and down the winding stair.

Scarcely was she gone than the heavy door opened

again, and Mordred stood within the opening, Mordred clad in his usual midnight black that he wore as other men wore rose-scarlet, and playing gently with a peacock's feather, so that, meeting his gaze where she stood with the bright tangle of silks at her feet, the Queen felt as though she were being stared at by three bright unwinking eyes instead of two.

'What is it?' she said.

And he answered her with exquisite gentleness, 'Letters have come from Benwick. Arthur and Lancelot are both slain.'

For a moment the Queen's world swam and darkened, and all she saw clearly were the three eyes gazing at her, bright and mocking. But something in their gaze told her beyond all doubt that he was lying. And the world steadied again.

And she heard her own voice saying, cool and calm, 'I do not believe you.'

'Other people will,' he said, 'other people do. Do you not hear them?'

Somewhere in the castle a woman was weeping, and from St Stephen's church a bell began to tell.

'I can show you the letters,' Mordred said, smiling pleasantly; and she saw that he was so sure of himself that he did not care whether she believed him or not.

Still, she would not yield. 'Anyone can forge such letters and claim that they came from Benwick,' she said. 'A few bribes – '

Mordred's smile grew wider as he agreed. 'Anyone. Nevertheless, the people will believe. It will be true in a short while, in any case. And meanwhile, I go to make ready for my crowning.'

'Your *crowning*?' said the Queen.

'Of course. The High King is dead, Britain must have her new High King.'

And the Queen knew that it would serve no purpose to plead, nor to cry out upon him. Neither pleading nor wrath could touch him, for he breathed a higher and colder air than other men, and was beyond the reach of such things. So she said only, 'Go now. You have told me what you came to tell, and I would be alone.'

But the worst shock was still to come.

'I will go,' said Mordred. 'But presently I shall come again, from my crowning, and with the High King's circlet on my head, for there is another matter on which I would speak with you.'

'There is no other matter on which I have need to speak with you,' said the Queen.

'Ah, but there is: for it concerns you nearly. The matter of our marriage.'

Then the Queen did indeed cry out on him; a small, desperate cry, 'Our *marriage*? Mordred, you are mad!'

Mordred reached out the mocking peacock's feather and touched her cheek, and she jerked her head back as though from the touch of a hot coal. 'Nay, I speak good sense. With you to sit beside me, my claim to the High Kingship will be the more sure – and *you*, my sweet lady, will still be the Queen.'

'Mordred!' the Queen cried in horror. 'I am your father's wife!'

'Widow.'

'Widow or wife, it is all one in this matter. I am your stepmother!'

'A fat purse of gold to the Church, and the Church shall cut that tangle swift enough,' Mordred said. And then, 'Seeing that after all there is no shared blood between us as there was between my father and *my* mother.'

And looking into his eyes, the Queen understood for the first time the full depth of his hatred for the High King.

Somehow she wrenched her gaze from his, and made a great show of stooping to gather up her embroidery silks. She knew that she must play for time. 'When the High King hears of this, he will come back – ' she began.

And Mordred said, 'When the High King hears – *if* the High King hears – it will be too late.'

'You must give me time,' she whispered, 'time to think – to pray . . .'

And Mordred said, 'Surely I will give you time; all that lies between now and tomorrow's morning. Think and pray as much as you wish, madam; in the end you must yield yourself to do as I will.'

And he turned and left the chamber.

The Queen stood where he had left her, alone and unmoving, until in a little while Nesta returned, white-faced, with the grievous news as she had heard it in the inner courtyard. Then the Queen opened her clenched hand; and the brilliant silks for the angels' wings fell to the ground again, stained with blood where she had closed her hand upon the needle hidden within them without ever knowing it.

'It is all lies,' she said, 'all lies.' And she told the maiden of Mordred's visit and what had passed between them; and when Nesta began to shiver and cry out what should they do, she said, 'Peace, my maiden; I am thinking what we shall do. I am thinking now!'

She knew that she must get away from Camelot, where she was surrounded by men of Mordred's following. At London, the royal castle was still held by Sir Galagars, an old and faithful knight of the Round Table, who she was sure would still be true to Arthur. If she could get there and put herself under his protection; under the protection also of Dubricius, the aged Archbishop, she might be safe. But before all else, she must get word to Arthur of his son's treachery.

So she bade Nesta to bring her pen, ink and parchment, and set herself to write a letter, bidding the girl meanwhile to find a certain one among her household squires, and bring him to her with all speed, telling him nothing on the way lest they be overheard. She feared that already her own household might have been taken from her and replaced by Mordred's men. But she had not yet finished her desperate letter when her maiden returned, and the squire Hew with her.

The young man knelt at her feet. 'Oh, my lady – the King – '

'The King is not dead,' she said quickly, still writing. 'It is all an evil plot of Mordred's to seize the Crown and force me to wed with him.' And while the squire gasped and stammered between astonishment and relief and fury, she finished the letter, warning her lord of what was going forward, and telling him also of what she herself planned to do. Then she folded it, and sealed the packet with a little engraved stone that hung among the jewels at her neck.

'Hew,' she said, 'will you ride for me again, as you rode for me when Sir Meliagraunce had me captive in his power?'

'To the world's end, my lady!' said the squire.

'Nay, not so far. But to Benwick. Get out of Camelot this night and make for the south coast. Take the first ship you can find. I will give you journey-gold for the passage; also for a horse – it may be that you will have to escape from here on foot – and carry this to the High King with all speed!'

Even as she spoke, giving the packet into his eager hand, she heard a distant roar of voices from the Great Hall, and the bright neigh of trumpets, and knew that Mordred was already proclaiming himself High King.

That night, under cover of the first dark, the squire got out from Camelot as from an enemy camp, and headed for the south coast, bearing the Queen's letter.

And in the morning Guenever, who had lain wakeful all night, bade her maidens to dress her in her finest blue-violet gown, and painted her eyes and her lips and put on her finest jewels. And when Mordred came again to her chamber, she received him sitting stately in her great cushioned chair beside the hearth. And she looked on him more kindly than ever she had done before, even though the golden circlet of the Pendragon was upon his head.

Mordred noticed the blue-violet gown and the jewels and the kinder aspect, and smiled within himself, thinking that he knew what they meant. 'Madam, I had forgotten in the time since Lancelot went overseas how beautiful you are,' he said. 'You have been thinking of the matter of our marriage that we spoke of last night?'

'I have been thinking,' said the Queen. 'Yesterday I was startled and angry and spoke in haste; but the more I thought, the more I came to see that since I am in your power and you can force me to do what you will, it would be but foolishness to struggle against you. Therefore – ' she smiled ruefully, speaking to him as though half in jest, in the words of a knight beaten in the joust to the victor who stands over him with a drawn sword – 'I yield me, and cry your mercy . . . If Archbishop Dubricius gives us the Church's leave, I will marry you – and as you yourself said, I shall still be the Queen.'

'Madam, you are wise as well as beautiful!' said Sir

Mordred. 'I will send word to the Archbishop within this hour. And a gift of gold.'

The Queen shook her head. 'Sending word will not be enough. Nor will a gift of gold. I must speak with him myself.'

'As you will,' said Mordred. 'I will have him sent for.'

'Nay,' said the Queen, 'he is very old: too old to travel lightly, and of too high estate to be whistled for like a dog. If we are to gain his leave, I must go to him as a suppliant – ' And then, as she saw refusal in his face, 'Give me until tomorrow's morning to make ready for the journey; and if you fear that I plan some escape, send a strong escort of your own knights with me, so that you allow me also to have certain of my own maidens for my company. Indeed you have no more choice than I; for if I come to the Archbishop in supplication, and show myself willing for this marriage, it is in my mind that I shall win from him the Church's leave. Then I will marry you, as I have said; but without the Church's leave I cannot be your wife; and indeed our marriage would weaken, not strengthen, your claim to the High Kingship.'

So Sir Mordred yielded to the Queen's demands; and next morning, with her favourite maidens about her, and a strong escort of Sir Mordred's men, she set out for London.

Five days they were upon the journey, lodging in royal manors or in abbey guest-houses along the way. For the heavy ox-drawn cart with its cushions and tented tapestry hangings made slow travelling along the rutted roads that were still more like watercourses after the winter rains. And every lurching, jolting wheel-turn of the way, the Queen's heart was out before her, straining towards the grey-walled castle that was her only hope of safety from the terrible fair-haired man behind her, and where she and Sir Galagars might make a strong point to hold for the rightful king. And always she wondered how it was with her young squire; how far he had got on the way to Benwick; if he was on the way to Benwick at all, or lying dead in a ditch somewhere, and her letter already in Mordred's hands.

When they reached London at last, she found that they were not to lodge in the King's castle as she had always done, but in the royal manor, just outside the city. Her maidens looked at her with anxious eyes; but after she had had a little time to think, it seemed to the Queen that this was a difficulty easily overcome, and without the fighting in the outer courtyard that must have followed, had she ridden in through the castle gates to claim Sir Galagars's protection with a score of Mordred's men around her. She had been beyond caring that she was leading her escort into a trap, but the life of every man still loyal to her lord the King was precious to her, and some of them also would have died in the fighting.

The next day very early in the morning, the Queen bade horses to be brought round; for she and her maidens would go to pray at a certain shrine and holy well to Our Lady in the fields near Westminster, where she sometimes went when the

King held his court in London. All her life, save in the fighting times, she had been used to ride abroad whenever she would, with no escort save a few of her ladies with her. And the knights of Sir Mordred's following had no good reason to say her nay, especially with the steward and the manor people all around to hear. So the palfreys were brought round; and muffled close in thick-furred mantles against the chill March wind that blew upriver, the Queen and her maidens set out towards Our Lady's shrine.

But as soon as they were beyond sight of the manor, they changed direction, turning into a narrow lane that led towards London and, setting their palfreys to a swifter pace, rode hard for the city and the royal stronghold, through the wind and the scurrying spring rain.

And so a while later those within the castle heard a great beating upon the main gate, and when it was opened, in rode a little company of wet and storm-blown women. And as the foremost of them flung back her hood, the men of the gate-guard knew her for the Queen.

'Make the gates fast!' she cried to them. 'Enemies of my Lord the King will be here before long!'

They made haste to do her bidding, while pages and squires came to aid her and her maidens to dismount, and hard behind them Sir Galagars came swiftly to receive her. And when he heard what she had to tell, he was greatly wrath, and the castle was made secure to withstand all that Sir Mordred, now calling himself the High King, might bring against it.

★

And when the escort found how the Queen had escaped from them, they sent hurried word to Mordred, the usurper, and he gathered all the fighting men who were of his following and near at hand and sent out his summons to those who were further off to gather to him in London. And in a frenzy at seeing his smooth plans beginning to go awry, he rode for London with all speed, leaving the foot soldiers to follow after. And when he reached London, he sat down all about the castle to lay siege to it.

And he sent in heralds under the green branch with rich gifts for the Queen, bidding her leave this foolishness and come out to her wedding.

But the Queen sent back his gifts, the jewels and the rare perfumes and the pair of milk-white hounds, and with them her message, short and to the point, 'Nay, I come not out from these walls, false traitor, for rather than wed with you, I will die by my own hand!'

Then came Dubricius the Archbishop, small and wizened with age, but with eyes like hot coals in his sunken face, and he entered Mordred's camp, his clergy about him, and cried out upon the usurper, 'Sir, what will you do? Will you first anger God and then shame yourself and all knighthood? The Queen is your father's wife, and how may you wed with her without mortal sin?'

'My father is dead,' said Mordred, biting the words off one by one.

'Even if that were true, still would she be your

611

stepmother; still would a marriage between you be mortal sin!'

'*My father is dead,*' repeated Mordred. 'And I am the new High King, with the High King's powers. Therefore cease your prating, for I will silence you by having your head struck from your shoulders, if there is no other way!'

'I do not believe that Arthur is slain,' said the old man. 'And I am not the only man in Britain to believe that this tale of his death is but a foul lie set about by yourself that you may seize his power in the land, and his Queen with all! I too can threaten, and I bid you to leave off from this evil, or I will curse you with bell and with book and with candle!'

'Curse and be cursed to you!' cried Mordred, and his silken smile had become a snarl; but he dared make no attempt against the old man, for there was a cold doubt in his heart whether even his own men would obey him if he ordered them to seize the Archbishop.

So the Archbishop withdrew to the great abbey church, and gathered the monks under their abbot and his own clergy about him. And there before the high altar where he had set the High King's circlet upon Arthur's head more than thirty years ago, he cursed Arthur's son by bell and by book and by candle, cutting him off from all the rights and blessings of the Christian Church.

With all the forms and ceremonies of the Church, and with all the strength that was within himself, he cursed him; and when the cursing was finished, he was empty and spent, and knew that he was old; old beyond his Archbishophood, and the last of his strength for the battles of good and evil upon this earth was gone from him.

Then he thought of Merlin, who had stood with him on the day that Arthur was crowned: Merlin with his own strength spent, since then, long ago gone to his enchanted sleep. Not for him, Dubricius, that long quiet darkness under the magic hawthorn tree; but in his last years the quiet of loneliness and poverty and prayer. So he took his leave of those about him, and wearing the rusty habit of a poor monk, and mounted on a mule, he rode out from London city, none guessing as the threadbare and hooded figure passed them by that the great Archbishop rode that way.

And so he went, day by day, until he came to Avalon of the Apple Trees. And there he found the little wattle-built abbey church and its beehive cells surrounding it, that Joseph of Arimathea and his companions had built when first he came to Britain carrying the Holy Grail. Through all the years between, men had dwelt there, living a life of prayer and of help to the poor. But slowly their numbers had dwindled. The living-huts were empty now, and freshly turned earth lay over the grave of the last of the brotherhood.

And in London, Mordred sent again to the Queen, with gifts and fair speeches, begging her to come out to him; but she sent back the same answer as before, that she would die by her own hand before she became his wife. And then in wrath and growing fear, he set to lay siege to the castle in good earnest; and every day his war-host grew, as more and more of his following from up and down the land came in answer to his summons.

But still the royal castle held against them, and they could not come at the Queen.

And meanwhile, the squire Hew had reached Arthur's camp before Benwick Castle, and brought the Queen's letter to the King's pavilion, where he sat late with Sir Gawain, whom he had summoned to share a cup of wine with him in the hope that he might yet be able to persuade him not to ride out again next morning against Sir Lancelot.

He took the letter from the mired and weary squire, and broke the seal, and read it through without a word. And without a word he gave it to Sir Gawain.

And while Sir Gawain read it also, there was silence within the tent; a core of silence amid the sounds of the camp and the bluster of the spring gale blowing outside. But when he reached the end of the letter, Gawain let out a great roar, baffled and grief-stricken like some wild thing in a trap, and flung the closely written parchment on the bed-place beside him and buried his battered head in his arms.

The King picked up the letter again, and gentled it in his hand because the Queen had written it and found means to send it to him, while at the same time grief and anger at the news it brought tore each other within him. And he sent his tent squires to beg this one and that among his war-leaders to come to him; and then began to ask the squire Hew for more details than were in the letter. And while he was doing so, Sir Gawain lurched to his feet and caught up his sword-belt that he had slackened off and laid beside him earlier, and began to buckle it on again, with furious haste, as though the enemy were in the windy dark outside the tent-flap.

And the King looked at him and said, 'Sir Gawain, you are excused this warfare.'

But Sir Gawain raised bloodshot eyes to his face, and said, 'Sir, of all the warfares and quarrels of my life, this is the one that I would least hold back from.'

'It will be to fight your own brother; your last remaining brother.'

'I have no brothers now!' Gawain roared. 'Mordred is more dead to me than all the rest. I am all that is left of the Orkney brood, and I am your man as I always have been.'

So next day the King's camp was struck, and the war-host marched away towards the coast, Sir Gawain with the rest of them. And watching from the ramparts of Benwick Castle, with a puzzled frown between his brows, Sir Bors said to Sir Lancelot beside him, 'Now what could draw them away so suddenly – unless it be ill news from Britain?'

'Ill news or not,' said Sir Lancelot, 'it can be no matter that concerns us any more.' But his eyes followed the last moving flicker of the distant rear-guard until it disappeared into the forest, and he would have given all that he had in life if it could have been his concern again.

The King and his army came to the coast, and when the hastily summoned fleet had gathered, they took ship again for Britain. But Mordred had got word of their coming; and when, after a stormy crossing, they drew at last to land at Dover, they found the usurper and all his rebel war-host waiting for them.

Then the King's trumpets and the rebel trumpets crowed against each other in the wild spring dawn; and there began a great and terrible struggle that lasted all day, as the King's men ran their ships ashore and sprang overboard into the shallows, and the rebels came charging out to meet them. A battle fought out in the grey swinging shallows of the Narrow Seas, and on the sloping shingle that was soon running red, and along the cliff paths and among the chalky hummocks and the coarse wind-shivered grass. Until at evening the cold spitting rain died out, and the skies broke up and let through a sodden yellow gleam and the King's men gained the cliff-tops and swept them clear, as Mordred and his men gave back and broke, and streamed away into the eye of the wild sunset.

But the victory had been sorely paid for, and the bodies of knights and men-at-arms lay dark like sea-wrack along the tide-line and up the cliff paths and clotted thick about the stranded ships. And the King, having given orders for the succouring of his wounded and the burying of his dead, knelt beside

Sir Gawain in the small rough chamber high in
Dover Castle where he had been carried by the men
who had found him lying among the dead with the
old wound in his head burst open again by a fresh
blow.

Gawain opened his eyes and looked at him by the
light of the kelp fire burning on the hearth. 'I am for
death, this time,' he said.

And bending over the narrow cot, Arthur put his
arms round him and raised him a little, and said, 'Ah
Gawain, Gawain, my most dear nephew, you and
Lancelot I loved best of all my knights; and now I
have lost you both, and all my earthly joy is gone.'

'And it is all my doing,' said Sir Gawain, stumbling
over the words with a tongue that seemed made of
wood. 'For if Sir Lancelot had been with you as once
he was, this grievous war would never have come
about . . . And now you have need of Lancelot more
than ever you had before, and it is through my
hunger for revenge that you have lost him, when he
had no ill-will towards either you or me . . . And I – I
would be at peace with him now, but it is too late.'
And lying against the King's shoulder, he closed his
eyes so that it seemed as though he swooned or slept.
But when the King would have laid him down, he
opened them again and asked, 'Is there pen and
parchment to be found in this castle?'

'Lie still, and never trouble for pen and parchment
now,' said the King.

'It is the last thing that I shall do in the world,'

mumbled Sir Gawain. 'But I must write to Sir Lancelot, who was once my friend . . .'

And when pen and parchment and a taper were brought to him by one of the clerks who moved always with the war-host, he wrote with great difficulty, the King propping and steadying him the while.

'Unto Sir Lancelot, flower of all noble knights that ever I saw or heard of, I, Gawain, send you greetings, and beg your forgiveness in the name of the old friendship that was between us. In the name of that same friendship, come with all speed and with every knight and fighting-man that you can muster, for the traitor Mordred has raised rebellion against our Lord the King, who is in sore need of your sword. Mordred has made the people to believe him slain, and sought to take the Queen for his wife, who has shut herself away from him in the royal castle in London. This day we landed at Dover and put the traitor to flight, but there must be much more fighting ere all be done. In this day's battle I received a sore dunt upon my head, in the very place where you wounded me before Benwick Castle, and I write this to you in the hour of my death. Come swiftly, before Mordred can gather more rebel troops. Pray for my soul when you come beside my grave; but Arthur lives and has great need of you, and without your coming the Kingdom of Logres is lost. I write to you as with my heart's blood. Farewell.'

Towards the end of the letter the writing began to wander and stray across the page; and when the last word was written, the quill dropped from Sir Gawain's hand, and his head fell back. 'Pray you send this,' he said.

'I will send it,' the King promised, and kissed him on his battered forehead. His eyes closed, and when the King laid him down this time he did not open them again.

7

THE LAST BATTLE

Mordred had fled away westward, and as he went, he harried the lands of those who would not join him. But there were many, in the days that followed, who did join him; for fear because the thing had gone too far for them to expect mercy from Arthur now, or because they chose the usurper's lawless rule, or simply because they had loved Lancelot, and for his sake would draw sword for any leader who was against Arthur, which was the saddest reason of all. Yet there were as many who took up their arms and came in to fight for their rightful king; and so when the High King also hurried westward in pursuit of his traitor son, there was little to choose for size and strength between the two war-hosts.

They swept past London, along the great ridge that reared its back above the forest country; and the King longed to check and ride for the city for one last sight of Guenever the Queen. But it was not the time, and he contented himself as best he might by sending three messengers on fast horses to make enquiry and bring him back word that all was well with her, while he pushed on westward without slackening the pace and purpose of his march.

Twice the war-hosts met in battle, and twice the High King thrust the usurper back. And so at last, far over into the western marsh-country, the two armies faced each other for the greatest battle of all, encamped upon opposite sides of a level plain bleak and open among the wet woods in their first spring-time green and the winding waterways of those parts. And when Arthur asked of an old woman who came in to sell eggs and cheese in the royal camp, 'Old mother, is there a name to this place?' she said, 'Aye, this is the plain of Camlann.'

That night, when all things had been made ready for the battle that must come next day, Arthur lay in his pavilion and could not sleep. Beyond the looped-back entrance where his squires lay, the open plain stretched away like a dark sea, with the hushing of the wind through the long grass and the furze scrub for the sounding of the waves, to where the enemy watch-fires marked its further shore. His mind seemed full of whirling memories, and the sea-sound sank and changed into the whisper of reeds round the margin of still water . . . Still water . . . Lake water lapping . . . And Merlin standing beside him on the day that he received Excalibur. Merlin's voice in his ears again across all the years between, saying, 'Over there is Camlann, the place of the Last Battle . . . But that is another story; and for another day as yet far off.'

Now the day was here, waiting beyond the dark-ness of this one spring night. A night that was dark indeed. The doom that he had unwittingly loosed so long ago when all unknowing, he fathered Mordred upon his own half-sister, was upon him, and upon all that he had fought for. And tomorrow he and Mordred must be the death of each other. And what of Britain after that? Torn in two, and with the Sea Wolves and the men of the North waiting to come swarming in again?

In the chill dark hour before dawn, he fell into a state between sleeping and waking. And in that state he dreamed a dream – if it was a dream.

It seemed to him that Sir Gawain came in through the entrance to the tent, armed and looking just as he used to, though it was maybe strange that he came pacing in as though no tent squires lay across the threshold, and none of them seemed to see him come. And Arthur sat up and stretched his arms to him in joyful greeting. 'Welcome! Gawain, my most dear nephew! Now thanks be to God that I see you hale and living, for I thought you dead and grave-laid in Dover town!' And then he saw that behind Gawain thronged the bright-eyed misty shapes of women, foremost among them the Lady Ragnell, Gawain's seven-years' wife; and he was glad that Gawain had found his own lady again, for the years that he had shared with her had been his best as a knight and as a man. And Arthur asked, 'But what of these ladies who come with you?'

'Sir,' said Gawain, 'these be all of them ladies whom I fought for or served in some way when I was man alive. God has listened to their prayers and for their sakes has been merciful to me and granted that I come to you.'

'It is for some urgent cause that you come,' said the King.

'It is to forewarn you of your death. For if you join battle with Sir Mordred this day, as you and he are both set to do, you must both die, and the greater part of your followings with you, and the Kingdom of Logres shall indeed go down into the dark. Therefore God, of his special grace, has sent me to bid you not to fight this day, but to find means to make a treaty with Sir Mordred, promising whatever he asks of you as the price of this delay. A truce that shall gain you one month of time; for within that month shall come Sir Lancelot and all his following, and together you shall overcome Sir Mordred and his war-host, and so shall the kingdom be saved from the dark.'

And suddenly, with his last word scarcely spoken, he was gone from the place where he had been and the bright-eyed shadows with him.

And in a little, Arthur saw the green light of dawn growing pale beyond the tent flaps. Then he arose and summoned his squires to fetch Sir Lucan and Sir Bedivere and two of his churchmen. And when they came and stood before him, he told them of the vision he had had, and the thing that Sir Gawain had told him. And he charged them to go to Sir Mordred under the green branch, and make truce with him that should last a month. 'Offer him lands and goods,' said the King, 'as much as seem reasonable – anything that seems reasonable. Only do you win for me and for all our people this month's delay.'

So Sir Bedivere and Sir Lucan and the two churchmen went forth under the green branch, and came to the enemy camp. And there they spoke long with Sir Mordred among his grim war-host of fifty thousand men. And at last Mordred agreed to these terms: that he should have the lands of Kent and the old Kingdom of Cornwall from that day forward, and the whole of Britain after the King's death.

It was agreed between them that Arthur and Mordred should meet an hour from noon, midway between the two war-camps, and each accompanied by only fourteen knights and their squires, for the signing of the treaty.

And Sir Bedivere and Sir Lucan returned to the royal camp and told Arthur what had been arranged; and when he heard them, a great relief arose in him, for he thought that maybe after all God was showing him a way to turn back the dark and to save Britain. But still, he did not trust his son, and he had the men of his war-host drawn up clear of the camp and facing the enemy, and when the horses were brought, and he mounted, his chosen fourteen knights around him, and he was ready to ride out to the meeting, he said to the captains, 'If you see any sword drawn, wait for no orders, but come on fiercely, and slay all that you may, for there is a black shadow on my heart, and I do not trust Sir Mordred.'

And on the other side of the plain, Mordred gave orders to his own war-host: 'If you see any sword drawn, come on with all speed and slay all that stand against you, for I do not trust this treaty, and I know well that my father will seek to be revenged on me.'

And so they rode forward, and met at the appointed place midway between the battle-hosts, and dismounted, leaving their horses in the care of their squires, to discuss and sign the treaty, which the clerks had made out twice over upon fine sheets of vellum. Then the treaty was agreed, and first Arthur and then Mordred signed it, using the King's saddle for a writing slope; and when that was done, wine was brought and first Arthur and then Mordred drank together, both from the same cup. And it seemed that there must be peace between them, at least for this one month, and the doom and the darkness turned aside.

But scarcely had they drunk and their copies of the treaty been fairly exchanged, when an adder, rousing in the warmth of the spring day, and disturbed by the trampling of men and horses too near her sleeping place, slithered out from among the dry grass roots, coil upon liquid coil, and bit one of Mordred's knights through some loose lacing of the chain-mail at his heel.

And when the knight felt the fiery smart, he looked down and saw the adder, and unthinkingly he drew his sword and slashed the small wicked thing in half.

And when both war-hosts saw the stormy sunlight flash on the naked blade, they remembered their orders, and the harm was done. From both sides there rose a great shouting and a blowing of horns and trumpets, and the two war-hosts burst forward and rolled towards each other, dark as doom under their coloured standards and fluttering pennants, jinking with points of light like the flicker of summer lightning in the heart of a thunder-cloud, where the sour yellow sunshine struck on sword-blade and spear-point; and giving out a swelling storm roar of hooves and war cries and weapon-jar as they came.

Then Arthur cried out in a terrible voice, 'Alas! This most accursed day!' And hurling himself into the saddle, drove spurs into his horse's flanks, and swung him round with frantic haste to join the forefront of his own on-coming war-host. Sir Mordred did likewise in the same instant; and the battle closed around them both.

The sorest and most savage battle that ever was fought in any land of Christendom.

It was scarcely past noon when the fighting joined, but soon the clouds that gathered overhead made it seem like evening; and as the dark battle masses swept and swirled this way and that, lit by bladeflash and torn by the screams of smitten horses and the war-shouts and the death-cries of men, so the black cloud mass that arched above them seemed to boil as though at the heart of some mighty tempest, echoing the spear tempest upon Camlann Plain beneath. And many a terrible blow was given and many mighty champions fell; and old enemies fought each other in the reeling press, and friend fought friend and brother fought brother. And as the time went by the ranks of both war-hosts grew thinner, and more and more the feet of the living were clogged by the bodies of the dead; and one by one the banners and pennants that were tattered as the ragged sky went down into the mire; and all the mire of Camlann's trampled plain oozed red.

And all day long Mordred and the High King rode through the thick of the battle and came by no hurt, so that it seemed as though they held charmed lives; and ever in the reeling thick of the fighting they sought for each other, but might never come together all the black day long.

And so day drew to the edge of night; and a great and terrible stillness settled over the plain; and Arthur, who had had three horses killed under him since noon, stood to draw breath and look about him. And all was red; the blade of his own sword crimsoned to the hilt, and the sodden mire into which the grass was trampled down; even the under-bellies of the clouds that had been dark all day were stained red by the light of the setting sun. And nothing moved over all Camlann Plain but the ravens circling black-winged against that smouldering sky; and nothing sounded save the howl of a wolf far off, and near at hand the cry of a dying man.

And Arthur saw that two men stood close behind him; and one was old Sir Lucan and the other Sir Bedivere, and both sore wounded. And of all the men who had followed him back from Benwick or gathered to his standard on the march from Dover, and of all those men, also, who had been his before they were drawn from their loyalty by Mordred's treachery or by their love for Lancelot, these two, leaning wearily on their swords beside him, were all who remained alive.

And the black bitterness of death rose in Arthur the King, and a mighty groan burst from him.

'Grief of God! That I should see this day! Grief upon me for all my noble knights that lie here slain! Now indeed I know that the end is come. But before all things go down into the dark – where is Sir Mordred who has brought about this desolation?'

Then as he looked about him, he became aware of one more figure still upon its feet; Sir Mordred in hacked and battered armour, standing at a little distance, alone in the midst of a sprawling tangle of dead men.

And Arthur would not use Excalibur upon his own son; and so, to Sir Lucan who stood nearest to him, he said, 'Give me a spear; for yonder stands the man who brought this day into being, and the thing is not yet ended between us two.'

'Sir, let him be!' said Sir Lucan. 'He is accursed! And if you let this day of ill destiny go by, you shall be most fully avenged upon him at another time. My liege lord, pray you remember your last night's dream, and what the spirit of Gawain told you. Even though by God's grace and mercy you still live at the day's end, yet leave off the fighting now; for there are three of us, while Sir Mordred stands alone, and therefore we have won the field; and once the doom day be passed, it will be passed indeed, and new days to come.'

But, 'Give me life or give me death,' said Arthur, 'the thing is not finished until I have slain my son who has brought destruction upon Logres and upon all Britain, and for whom so many good men lie slain.'

'Then God speed you well,' said Sir Bedivere.

And Sir Lucan gave the King his spear, and he grasped it in both hands and made at a stumbling run for the solitary figure. The terrible red drunkenness of battle was upon him, and he cried out as he ran, 'Traitor! Now is your death-time upon you!'

And hearing him, Sir Mordred lifted his head, and recognised death, and with drawn sword came to meet him. And so they ran, stumbling over the dead, and came together in the midst of that dreadful reddened field, under that dreadful bleeding sky. And the High King smote his son under the shield with a great thrust of his spear, that pierced him clean through the body. And when Sir Mordred felt his death wound within him, he gave a great yell, savage and despairing, and thrust himself forward upon the spear-shaft, as a boar carried forward by its own rush up the shaft of the hunter, until he was stayed by the hand-guard; and with all the last of his strength he swung up his sword two-handed, and dealt the High King his father such a blow on the side of the dragon-crested helmet that the blade sliced through helm and mail-coif and deep into the skull beneath. And at the end of the blow Sir Mordred fell stark dead upon the spear, dragging it with him to the ground. And in the same instant Arthur the King dropped also, not dead but in a black swoon, upon the stained and trampled earth.

Then Sir Lucan and Sir Bedivere came and lifted him between them, and by slow stages, for their wounds were sore upon them, they bore him from the battlefield, and to a little ruined chapel not far off, and laid him there in the shelter and quiet that the place offered, upon a bed of piled fern that looked as though it had been made ready for him, before the altar.

And there, when they laid him down, Sir Lucan gave a deep groan and crumpled to the earth at his feet; for the effort of getting his king to shelter had been too great for him, with the gaping wound that was in his belly.

And when Arthur, coming back to himself, saw Sir Lucan's body sprawled there, the grief rose in him, and he cried out 'Alas, this is a sore sight! He would have aided me, and he had more need of aid himself!'

And Sir Bedivere knelt weeping beside the dead knight, for they had loved each other as brothers since the days when the Round Table was young.

It had been dark when they reached the chapel, but now the skies had cleared, and presently the moon arose, sailing high and uncaring above the dreadful stillness of Camlann Plain. And looking with shadowed sight out through the gap in the far wall where the stones had fallen, Arthur saw not far off the whispering reed-fringed shores of a lake. White mists scarfed the water, shimmering in the white fire of the moon; and the far shores were lost in mist and moonshine, so that there might have been no far shore at all. And Arthur knew that lake. He knew it to his heart's core.

And gathering all that was left of his strength, he said to Sir Bedivere, 'To this lake . . . To another part of this lake, Merlin brought me, long ago . . .' And it seemed to him that he was forcing the words out so hard that they must come forth as a shout, but they came only as a ragged whisper that Sir Bedivere must bend close to hear. 'Now leave your weeping; there will be time for mourning later on for you – but for me, my time with you grows short, and there is yet one thing more that I must have you do for me.'

'Anything,' said Sir Bedivere, 'anything, my liege lord . . .'

'Take you Excalibur, my good sword, and carry it down to yonder lakeshore, and throw it far out into the water. Then come again and tell me what you see.'

'My lord,' said Bedivere, 'I will do as you command, and bring you word.'

And he took the great sword from where it lay beside the King and, reeling with weakness from his own wounds, made his way down to the water's brink.

In that place, alder trees grew here and there along the bank, and he passed through them, stooping under the low branches, and paused, looking down at the great sword in his hands; and the white fire of the moon showed him the jewels in the hilt and played like running water between the clotted stains on the faery-forged blade. And he thought, 'This is not only a High King's weapon, this is the sword of Arthur, and once thrown into the lake it will be lost for ever, and an ill thing that would be.'

And the more he looked, the more he weakened in his purpose. And at last he turned from the water and hid Excalibur among the roots of the alder trees.

Then he went back to Arthur.

'Have you done as I bade you?' said Arthur.

'Sir, it is done,' said Bevidere.

'And what did you see?'

'Sir,' said Bedivere, 'what should I see under the moon, but the bright ripples spreading in the waters of the lake?'

'That is not truly spoken,' said the King, 'therefore go back to the lake, and as you are dear to me, carry out my command.'

So Sir Bedivere went back to the lakeshore, and took the sword from its hiding place, fully meaning this time to do as the King had bidden him. But again the white fire of the moon blazed upon the jewelled hilt and the sheeny blade, and he felt the power of it in his hands as though it had been a live thing. And he thought, 'If ever men gather again to thrust back the dark, as we thrust it back when the Table and the world were young, this is the only true sword for whoever leads them.' And he returned the sword to its hiding place, and went back to the chapel where the King lay waiting for him.

'Have you done my bidding, this second time?' asked the King.

'I cast Excalibur far out into the lake,' said Sir Bedivere.

'And what did you see?'

'Only the reeds stirring in the night wind.'

And the King said in a harsh and anguished whisper, 'I had thought Mordred the only traitor among the brotherhood; but now you have betrayed me twice. I have loved you; counted you among the noblest of my knights of the Round Table, and you would break faith with me for the richness of a sword.'

Bedivere knelt beside him with hanging head. 'Not for the richness, my liege lord,' he said at last. 'I am ashamed; but it was not for the richness, not for the jewels in the hilt nor the temper of the blade.'

'That I know,' the King said, more gently. 'Yet now, go again swiftly; and this time do not fail me, if you value still my love.'

And Sir Bedivere got stiffly to his feet, and went a third time down to the water's edge, and took the great sword from its hiding place; and a third time he felt the power of it in his hand and saw the white moon-fire on the blade; but without pause he swung it up above his head, and flung it with the last strength of arm and breast and shoulder, far out into the lake.

He waited for the splash, but there was none, for

out of the misty surface of the lake rose a hand and arm clad in white samite, that met and caught it by the hilt. Three times it flourished Excalibur in slow wide circles of farewell, and then vanished back into the water, taking the great sword with it from the eyes of this world. And no widening ring of ripples told where it was gone.

Sir Bedivere, blind with tears, turned and stumbled back to the chapel and his waiting lord.

'It is done as you commanded,' he said.

'And what did you see?' said the King.

'I saw a hand that came out of the lake, and an arm clothed in white samite; and the hand caught Excalibur and brandished it three times as though in leave-taking – and so withdrew, bearing the sword with it, beneath the water.'

'That was truly spoken and well done,' said the King; and he raised himself on his elbow. 'Now I must go hence. Aid me down to the water side.'

And Sir Bedivere aided him to his feet and took his weight upon his own shoulder, and half-supported, half-carried him down to the lakeshore.

And there, where before had seemed to be only the lapping water and the reeds whispering in the moonlight, a narrow barge draped all in black lay as though it waited for them, within the shadows of the alder trees. And in it were three ladies, black-robed, and their hair veiled in black beneath the queenly crowns they wore. And their faces alone, and their outstretched hands, showed white as they sat looking up at the two on the bank and weeping. And one of

them was the Queen of Northgalis, and one was
Nimue, the Lady of all the Ladies of the Lake; and
the third was Queen Morgan La Fay, freed at last
from her own evil now that the dark fate-pattern was
woven to its end.

'Now lay me in the barge, for it has been waiting
for me long,' said Arthur, and Sir Bedivere aided him
down the bank, and gently lowered him to the hands
of the three black-robed queens, who made soft
mourning as they received him and laid him down.
And the Lady of the Lake took his battered head into
her lap; and kneeling beside him, Queen Morgan la
Fay said, 'Alas, dear brother, you have tarried
overlong from us and your wound has grown chilled.'

And the barge drifted out from the shadows under
the alder trees, leaving Sir Bedivere standing alone
upon the bank.

And Sir Bedivere cried out like a child left in the
dark, 'Oh, my Lord Arthur, what shall become of
me, now that you go hence and leave me here alone?'

And the King opened his eyes and looked at him
for the last time. 'Comfort yourself, and do the best
that you may, for I must be gone into the Vale of
Avalon, for the healing of my grievous wound. One
day I will return, in time of Britain's sorest need, but
not even I know when that day may be, save that it is
afar off . . . But if you hear no more of me in the
world of men, pray for my soul.'

And the barge drifted on, into the white mist
between the water and the moon. And the mist
received it, and it was gone. Only for a little, Sir

Bedivere, straining after it, seemed to catch a low desolate wailing as of women keening for their dead.

And then that too was gone, and only the reeds whispered on the desolate lakeshore.

And Sir Bedivere turned and stumbled away, making for the dark woodshore that was not far off and seemed to offer shelter from the terrible white moonlight and the loneliness that the barge had left behind.

All night long, blind with grief and stumbling with the weakness of his wounds, he wandered among alder woods and sour willow scrub, until at dawn he came upon a wattle-built chapel with the ruins of living-cells clustered about it. From one cell, less ruined than the rest, came the faint gleam of a rushlight, and sounds of movement within; and making towards it, he fell across the threshold; and the ancient and ragged hermit, who had once been the Archbishop Dubricius, took him in and cared for him.

8

AVALON OF THE APPLE TREES

As soon as he received Sir Gawain's letter, Sir Lancelot set to gathering all the fighting men of Benwick, and when they were gathered, and arms and stores made ready with all haste, and the needful ships and galleys brought together, he sailed with them across the Narrow Seas, and landed in Dover.

From the Dover men he demanded what was the news of the High King. And they told him of the battle that had been fought out there on the shore, close on a month before, and how the High King had beaten Mordred back and come at last to land; and they told how Sir Mordred had fled away westward with Arthur close upon his heels; and they told him of the shadowy tidings that had come back to them of a last terrible battle fought somewhere in the West, and how in that battle both armies were brought to naught, and Sir Mordred slain, and the King slain also, or, as some said, not slain but borne away into Avalon to be healed of his wounds. But of that, no man knew for sure, and all seemed wrapped in mist and shadows.

But when Sir Lancelot asked as to the fate of Sir Gawain, that they knew full well; and they led him within the castle, to the chapel, and showed him before the altar the new-laid slab of grey stone beneath which the last of the Orkney breed lay buried.

And Sir Lancelot kneeled down, smelling the sea wind through the high unglazed windows, and hearing the crying of the gulls, and wondered if Sir Gawain was in any way aware of them too; and if they seemed to him one with the sea wind and the gulls of his northern home. And there he remained all night, his great ugly head bowed and the tears falling on his joined hands, praying for the soul of Sir Gawain, and weeping for the wild, fiery-haired and fiery-hearted knight who had been for so many years his friend, and then his enemy, and who he now felt to be his friend again.

And in the morning he called all his knights and nobles together and said to them, 'My brothers, I thank you all for coming with me into this country, but it seems we come too late; and for that, the grief will be upon me through every day of my life that yet remains to me. Nevertheless, do you wait here under the command of my cousin Sir Bors for one month, and obey and follow him as you would me. But if at the end of that month I have neither returned to you nor sent you any word, then do you return to your own land, and God's grace go with you.'

'And you?' said Sir Bors. 'What is it that you do, during this month?'

'I go westward,' said Sir Lancelot, 'first to London, that I may be sure that all is well with the Queen, and

thence westward still, towards Avalon; and after that
– I do not know.'

'Sir,' said Sir Bors, 'to ride alone through Britain in
the present state of the realm is surely madness; for
you shall find few enough friends in the wilderness,
and may have sore need of trusted men at your back.'

'I have ridden the length and breadth of this land
with no man at my back before now,' said Sir Lancelot, 'and found few friends indeed. One man alone
may pass easier than a score, if enemies are around;
and be that as it may, this is a quest on which I must
ride alone. So fare you well.'

And next day at the first paling of the morning, he
rode away over the downs and through the Wealden
forest towards London.

But when he reached London city and came to
the royal castle, Sir Galagars the castellan told him
that Queen Guenever was no longer there. For close
on a month ago word had come to them from Sir
Bedivere of the great battle in the West, and of
Arthur's passing; and in the night after the word
came, she disappeared, and five of her maidens with
her.

'Pray you tell me if there is any thought in your
mind as to where she can have gone,' said Sir Lancelot, swaying with weariness and caked with the
mire of hard riding, and fighting down the desire to
howl like a dog and strike out at the troubled old
knight before him.

And Sir Galagars shook his head and said, 'Maybe
she has gone westward, towards Avalon.'

'And none has sought her?'

'She left word that she knew the place she went to, and none were to seek her,' said the old castellan. 'And she is still the Queen, her orders to be obeyed. Nevertheless, we have sought her, and found no sign.'

Sir Lancelot spent one night in London, and next morning he heard Mass, and then, with a fresh horse under him, set out once more. But now, before all else, he rode westward to find the Queen.

Hither and yon he rode the forest ways while their green flame of springtime darkened towards summer, praying in his heart that he might find her before she came to any harm, and passing often through stretches of burned woodland made hideous by wrecked homesteads and the bones of men and cattle picked bare by gore-crows that marked the path of Mordred's westward march. And wherever he came upon living man or woman, he asked for news of a lady riding with five maidens, who might have passed that way. But no one had seen them go by.

And at last, on the evening of the fifteenth day after leaving London, he came to Almesbury and sought shelter for the night in the great nunnery there. For in those days it was the custom that abbeys both of monks and nuns would have guest-houses within their gates, giving shelter and welcome to all comers, both men and women, be they queens or nobles on fine horses or poor folk who travelled on foot.

So the Lady Abbess made Sir Lancelot welcome,

and sent for servants to stable and tend his weary horse, and herself led him towards the guest-chambers.

And as they passed along the cloister, Sir Lancelot saw a nun coming towards them, calm and remote in her habit of black and white. Her head was bent, and he could not see her face in the shadow of her veil. But as they drew nearer to each other, she gave a small breathless cry, and her hands that had been hidden in her wide sleeves flew up to her breast. He would have known her hands anywhere. And she swayed, and crumpled to the ground in a swoon. And Sir Lancelot found himself looking down into the face of Queen Guenever.

He would have stooped to lift her, but the Lady Abbess stayed him with a gesture of one hand, whose calm authority he knew he must not disobey. And other black-and-white sisters came like a gentle flock of birds, and gathered her up and supported her away.

Next morning early, by special consent of the Abbess, Sir Lancelot and the Lady Guenever spoke together in the north cloister walk. It was a most fair morning of early summer, and in the topmost branch of the medlar tree in the midst of the green and peaceful cloister garth a whitethroat was singing. Lancelot gazed long into the face of Guenever who had once been the Queen; and her black hair with the silver strands in it was hidden by her veil, but her eyes were the same willow-grey eyes that he had always known, only that the shadows in them were deeper now.

'So you are come back from Benwick,' she said at last. 'Was that to help Arthur?'

He bowed his head. 'Gawain wrote to me – in the hour of his death – and told me of all that had passed, and the fight at Dover; and that Mordred was fled away westwards and Arthur after him. He told me how that you had taken refuge from Mordred in the royal castle at London. He bade me come, for our leige lord the King had sore need of me. And I gathered my fighting men and came with all speed. But when I reached Dover, the last battle was fought and over, and I was too late. And when I came to London, seeking to know if all was well with you before I went on westward after the King, they told me of Sir Bedivere's message, and how on the night after its coming, you slipped away, and five of your ladies with you, and they could come by no word of you since.'

'And so you came seeking me,' said Guenever. 'And find me as you see me now.'

'Was that for Arthur's sake?' said Lancelot.

And Guenever told him, 'It was through my love for you and yours for me that all these ills have come about, and my Lord Arthur is slain or gone from us, and the realm of Logres is no more. Therefore, when Sir Bedivere's letter reached me, I came here secretly, and with those of my maidens who love me best. And in this quiet place I took upon me my vows, to dwell here, a nun, all the days of my life that may be left to me, praying for my soul's-heal, and that God may forgive me my sinning and you yours. Praying also for the souls of my Lord the King and those, the very flowers of knighthood, who died on Camlann Plain.'

'The King's death is not sure,' said Lancelot, not seeking to change her resolve, but only to speak some comfort to her.

But she shook her head. 'Not in my lifetime will he come back; not in yours . . .' And then she said, 'In this world, you and I must meet no more. Therefore I set you free, as never I was strong enough to do before. Get back to your own land, and take a wife and live with her in joy. But let you remember always, love, to pray for me, that God may forgive me my sins and grant me my soul's-heal.'

'Nay, sweet madam,' said Sir Lancelot, 'I have loved you since the day that I was made knight, and I grow too old to be changing my ways. Well you know that for your sake I will wed with no lady, though you give me my freedom a hundred times. Never will I be false to you, but I will keep sweet company with you in another way; for the vows that you have taken upon you, I will take also; and change my knightly harness for a hermit's garb, and pass the rest of my days in prayer and fasting.' He smiled with great gentleness, the old twisted smile. 'But always my chief prayers shall be for you, that you shall find peace and your soul's-heal.'

'Pray for your own,' said Guenever. 'Pray for your own.'

'That will I. But you know well that I was never one gifted with prayer, though that was not for lack of trying. Therefore if my praying will suffice for but one of us, I shall do well enough, thinking that your soul is maybe the lighter for my prayers. I believe that God will not begrudge me that.'

And he put out his hand to touch her. But she drew back. 'Nay,' she said, 'never again.'

His hand fell to his side, and they looked at each other, the one long moment. And the whitethroat in the medlar tree was singing, singing as though the heart would burst within his breast.

Then Guenever turned and walked away. And Lancelot stood watching her go, until the shadows of the cloister had gathered her into themselves. And then he turned and made for the outer courtyard where his horse was waiting for him, blundering as he went, like a man who has lost his sight.

So Sir Lancelot rode on westward, making for the marshlands close about Avalon, and seeking always for further news of King Arthur. And so he came one evening up from a country of reeds and winding waterways and damp alder woods on to higher ground, and saw before him a wattle-built chapel with a cluster of patched-up bothies around it, all set between two hills, and heard a little bell that rang to Mass.

And Sir Lancelot dismounted and led his horse up the last slope, and hitched its bridle to the low-hanging branch of an ancient apple tree, beside the chapel; and he went in to hear Mass.

It was dim and shadowy within the chapel, after the westering sunlight that had filled his eyes outside, and at first he did not know the aged and withered holy man with scarcely any voice left to him who celebrated the Mass for the great Archbishop Dubricius; but little by little, as though his eyes and his heart cleared together, the recognition came to him, and he knew also that the brown-robed brother who aided him was Sir Bedivere. He was not surprised, but accepted them as right and fitting; and he saw that they knew him and accepted his coming as right and fitting also, the most natural thing in all the world.

And when the Mass was over, they welcomed him and bade him come with them to their living quarters, and there they supped on black rye bread and spring water, and spoke together of the things nearest to their hearts.

'What of the King?' Lancelot asked.

But they could tell him no more than Bedivere had already told in his letter to the Queen. And Lancelot was puzzled. 'But this place is Avalon,' he said, half in question. 'Bedivere, you said – the King said he was for Avalon, to be healed of his wound.'

'Also that if I heard of him never more in this life, I was to pray for his soul,' said Bedivere in his brown hermit's habit.

Lancelot shook his head. He was too spent and

weary to think, but he had looked to find Arthur here, or to be shown his grave.

'But this is Avalon,' he said again.

And the old Archbishop saw his bewilderment, and answered him kindly, never knowing that he did so almost in the words that Merlin had spoken to the young Arthur on the day that he received Excalibur. 'Avalon of the Apple Trees is not like to other places. It is a threshold place between the world of men and the Land of the Living. Here we are in the Avalon of mortal men. But there is another Avalon. The King is here but he is gone beyond the mist.'

Merlin would have understood what he meant; but Merlin was thirty years and more asleep beneath his magic hawthorn tree, and Sir Lancelot was too weary to understand.

But he knew that he had come to the end of his journeyings.

'Will you receive me into your fellowship?' he said at last. 'And give shelter and grazing to my horse, for he has served me well.'

'That will we, and gladly,' said Sir Bedivere.

And the old Archbishop said, 'Welcome, my son.'

So Sir Lancelot laid by his knightly harness, he who had been the best of all the knights of Christendom, and took upon him the brown habit that the others wore.

When the full month had gone by, and there was no word from Sir Lancelot, the war-host waiting at Dover made ready to depart, as he had bidden them.

But Sir Bors himself, and Sir Ector of the Marsh, Sir Blamore and Sir Bleoberis and certain others of Sir Lancelot's kin and closest friends chose to remain in Britain and seek until they found him if he lived, or gained sure word of his fate if he were dead. And so they parted and, singly, they rode Britain from end to end, seeking their lost leader.

And so one day Sir Bors happened on the chapel and its little gathering of huts between two hills, and the ancient apple trees snowy with blossom, for it was spring; and a warhorse grazing quietly below the chapel, among the lesser apple trees that grew there. And he heard a little bell ringing to Mass.

And when he hitched his horse to the lower branch of the tree beside the chapel, and went to answer the call of the bell, there within were three brown-clad brethren; and one of them, so old that only the life in his brilliant eyes seemed still to bind him to the world of men, was the Archbishop, and one was Sir Bedivere, and one was Sir Lancelot of the Lake. Sir Bors knew that his search was finished. And after they had shared Mass together, he begged the Archbishop that he might join them.

So Sir Bors also changed his knightly gear for a rough brown habit, and loosed his horse to graze beside Lancelot's, and turned him to a life of prayer and fasting for what remained of his days.

And within half a year, came Sir Blamore and Sir Bleoberis, and by little and little, certain others of the old lost brotherhood of the Round Table. And when in due time the ancient Archbishop died, Sir Lancelot, whom he had made a priest while he yet lived, stepped into his place, and celebrated the Mass for the rest as he had done, and for all who chanced to pass that way.

So they continued for seven years, living in prayer and poverty and giving their help and comfort to all who sought it; and keeping the last light of Logres alive as they kept the honey-wax candles burning on the rough altar, while the darkness flowed in over the rest of the land. For though Constantine, Duke of Cornwall and a young and distant kinsman of Arthur, had taken the High Kingship and led his troops to battle under the dragon banner, he was not Arthur, and there was little that he could do against the Sea Wolves, and the Old People from the mountains and the North.

And the seven years went by; and then one night, and three times in the same night, Lancelot dreamed that Guenever lay dying, and that she called to him, not to come to her while she lived, but to come none the less, with seven of the brethren, and a horse-bier, to fetch her body away to Avalon for burial.

So he arose, and woke the others, and they made a horse-litter of willow saplings, and chose out the two of their warhorses that were oldest and wisest and most gentled with age; and then they set out for Almesbury, the eight of them walking barefoot all the way.

And though from Avalon to Almesbury is but thirty miles, yet the journey took them three days, for they were growing old, and no longer strong to walk long distances as they had used to be. And when they reached Almesbury and came to the nunnery, Guenever had died quietly in the night before their coming.

And when Sir Lancelot was brought to the chamber where she lay, still in her habit, with her hands folded on her breast, those who stood about them saw how he looked long into her face, and did not weep, but gave one great heavy sigh that sounded as though it might have been the going out of his own soul.

Next morning the body of Lady Guenever was laid upon the horse-litter, and with Lancelot and the brethren walking four on either side, they set out to bear her back to Avalon.

And when they reached the little abbey church, they made her a grave before the altar, and wrapped her close in softest silk that the sisters of the nunnery had made ready for her, and Sir Lancelot himself sang her funeral Mass. And they laid her in her quiet grave and strewed the flowers of late summer over her, and made an end.

But from that day, Sir Lancelot began to sicken like an old, tired hound. He scarcely ate or drank, and grew gaunt as a shadow, pining and dwining away. And within six weeks from the time that he laid the Lady Guenever in her grave, he too was dead.

And while he lay awaiting burial, before the altar, Sir Ector of the Marsh his half-brother, who had for seven years been seeking him, came to Avalon, and saw torches burning in the church, through the windy autumn dusk, and heard the sound of slow and stately chanting. And he dismounted, and hitched his horse to the lowest fruit-laden branch of the ancient apple tree that grew beside the place, and drawn by something, he scarcely knew what, went in through the open door.

Inside he saw brown-clad brethren kneeling in the wind-fretted torchlight, and one who lay before the altar with his big bony hands folded on his breast. And he knelt down just within the door, and waited. And in a while, when the chanting ended, and the brethren rose and turned to see who the newcomer might be, then he knew them in the same instant that they knew him. And the old man who had been Sir Bors came to him gently, holding out his hands.

And Sir Ector looked among them, from Sir Bedivere to Sir Bleoberis and the rest, and asked, 'Have you any word of Sir Lancelot? I have sought him these seven years and more.'

'Your search is over,' said Sir Bors, and led him towards the altar, the others standing back to let him through as though he had some special right. Then he was standing beside the body that lay there, looking down at it. And for three full heart-beats of time even then, he did not know whose it was, for Lancelot had so wasted away over the past weeks that scarce might any man know him for Sir Lancelot of the Lake, foremost among all the knights of Christendom.

Then as he stood wondering, while the autumn wind swooped round the chapel and the torchlight flared and guttered, he saw that the hands folded on the dead man's breast were a swordsman's hands and a horseman's hands, and the gaunt face with its two sides that did not match with each other was the face of Lancelot his brother.

Sir Ector gave a choking cry and flung aside his sword and shield so that they fell with a clash and clangour upon the rough paved floor. And the great sorrowing words rushed from his heart into his throat and seemed to choke there, and then broke free.

'There, Sir Lancelot, there thou liest, thou that were never matched of earthly knight's hand. And thou were the courtliest knight that ever bore shield. And thou were the truest friend to thy lover that ever bestrode horse. And thou were the truest lover of a sinful man that ever loved woman. And thou were the kindest man that ever struck with sword. And thou were the goodliest person that ever came among press of knights. And thou wast the the meekest man and the gentlest that ever sat in hall among ladies. And thou were the sternest knight to thy mortal foe that ever set spear in rest.'

And he knelt, and kissed his brother upon the forehead, and with grief and weariness fell half-swooning beside him.

So Sir Lancelot also was grave-laid, and his great tortured heart found peace at last.

Sir Bedivere and several of the brotherhood remained at the little church and its hermitage all the rest of their days, gathering others to them, so that at last the place became an abbey again; and later still, mighty and beautiful stone buildings arose where the little wattle church and its surrounding bothies had been. And men began to call it Glastonbury.

But Sir Bors and Sir Ector, Sir Bleoberis and Sir Blamore went afar off, into the Holy Land, and there died upon a Good Friday for God's sake.

And save for a valiant glimmer here and there, the darkness flooded in over Britain.

But Sir Lancelot had once said to the King his friend, while they walked at sunset in the narrow orchard below the walls of Camelot, 'We shall have made such a blaze that men will remember us on the other side of the dark.'

And indeed he had spoken truth, for the stories of Arthur and his knights are told and re-told even to this day.